# One Step at a Time

BERYL MATTHEWS

MICHAEL JOSEPH
*an imprint of*
PENGUIN BOOKS

MICHAEL JOSEPH
Published by the Penguin Group
Penguin Books Ltd, 80 Strand, London WC2R 0RL, England
Penguin Group (USA) Inc., 375 Hudson Street, New York, New York 10014, USA
Penguin Group (Canada), 90 Eglinton Avenue East, Suite 700, Toronto, Ontario, Canada M4P 2Y3
(a division of Pearson Penguin Canada Inc.)
Penguin Ireland, 25 St Stephen's Green, Dublin 2, Ireland
(a division of Penguin Books Ltd)
Penguin Group (Australia), 250 Camberwell Road,
Camberwell, Victoria 3124, Australia (a division of Pearson Australia Group Pty Ltd)
Penguin Books India Pvt Ltd, 11 Community Centre,
Panchsheel Park, New Delhi – 110 017, India
Penguin Group (NZ), cnr Airborne and Rosedale Roads, Albany,
Auckland 1310, New Zealand (a division of Pearson New Zealand Ltd)
Penguin Books (South Africa) (Pty) Ltd, 24 Sturdee Avenue,
Rosebank, Johannesburg 2196, South Africa

Penguin Books Ltd, Registered Offices: 80 Strand, London WC2R 0RL, England

www.penguin.com

First published 2005
1

Set in Monotype Garamond
Typeset by Rowland Phototypesetting Ltd, Bury St Edmunds, Suffolk
Printed in Great Britain by Clays Ltd, St Ives plc

A CIP catalogue record for this book is available from the British Library

ISBN-13: 978-0-718-14864-5
ISBN-10: 0-718-14864-9

# One Step at a Time

The moving finger writes; and, having writ,
Moves on: nor all thy piety nor wit
Shall lure it back to cancel half a line,
Nor all thy tears wash out a word of it.

Edward Fitzgerald,
*The Rubáiyát of Omar Khayyám*

| WORCESTERSHIRE COUNTY COUNCIL | |
|---|---|
| 268 | |
| Bertrams | 09.12.05 |
| | £18.99 |
| AL | |

# I

*Wapping, London, June 1934*

'No, Dad!' Amy Carter dug her heels in and skidded on the path as her father dragged her along, the defiance earning her a sharp clip around the ear, which made her head ring.

'I ain't got time for your nonsense,' he growled, giving her another tug. 'My ship sails in three hours and your mum needs you.'

Tears of frustration filled her eyes as she stumbled. 'But, Dad, we was going to have reading and writing. I'm the only one who can't read well. I want to read and write like all the others.'

'You'll be fifteen in December. You'll never do that now.' He continued to pull her along, his grip biting into her thin arm. 'You're too bloody stupid.'

'I'm not stupid,' she muttered under her breath and stopped struggling as the familiar pain ran through her. 'Everyone calls me that, but I'm not! I just can't read or write proper.'

'Course you are. I found you in a class with the eight-year-olds.' Her father glared down at her in disgust. 'Where's your shame?'

'I don't care what they think of me.' That was a lie, of course. She did care so very much, but she'd do anything to read and write properly, even suffer being put in the little class for this lesson. 'I'm not stupid,' she whispered again, close to tears.

She walked along now, a picture of dejection, clutching the piece of paper from class. Why couldn't she read? Everyone else did it easily enough, but the letters all looked funny to her and when she tried to write them they came out muddled up – or so they told her. She tried so hard until sheer frustration made her beat her hands on the desk and cry out in fury. That always got her a caning, but she couldn't help it. She wasn't stupid! She *wasn't*, but it didn't matter how many times she told herself this, the hurt and humiliation were still there. But when the others called her names she didn't let them see how their taunts wounded her. They weren't going to get that satisfaction.

'What's the matter with Mum now?' They'd reached their house in Farthing Street. It was a modest place near the docks, and four families shared the three floors. Amy and her mum had three rooms on the ground floor. There was one toilet out at the back and that was for everyone. It was enough for them because her dad was hardly ever home.

'She's sick again.' He pushed her through the door, slung his kit bag over his shoulder and stared down at her for a moment. 'I didn't mean to call you names, Amy. You have enough of that from everyone else, but you mustn't get so upset about not being able to read. You'll get through life fine without it.'

'I can write, Dad, look.' She held out the scrap of paper for him to see. 'I was doing better today.'

Her father took a quick glance and shook his head sadly. 'Your spelling's worse than your granddad's was.' Then he turned and strode off.

Kicking the door shut, she fumed as she stared down at the writing she had been so proud of a while ago. Tears welled up in her eyes and threatened to spill over. It was all right him saying she'd get along without it; he didn't know how it upset her. She had this awful hollow place inside her, and what with looking after her mum a lot of the time, she didn't have much of a life. She had missed so much school it was no wonder she couldn't blasted well read! Dad was never here long enough to see how bad it was for her. Being a merchant seaman he just sailed away, calm as you please, leaving her to ride the storm at home.

She wandered into her mother's room, knowing full well what she would see. Her mother was propped up in bed looking pale and exhausted. Amy hadn't been able to find out what was the matter with her. She would be all right for a while, and then take to her bed again, coughing and not being able to eat.

'Your dad gone?' Dolly Carter asked as soon as her daughter came in.

'Yes, he came and took me out of school and then left.' Amy looked carefully at the woman in the bed. Her left eye was swollen. 'What you done to your face?'

'I had a fainting fit and hit my head as I fell.' Her mother touched her sore face. 'I told him not to fetch you from school. I could've managed until you finished your lessons.'

Amy wasn't too sure she believed this story, because her dad had a short temper, but she'd never seen him hit her mum. 'You ought to see the doc if you're that bad.'

'They can't do nothing for me.' Her mother sat up straight. 'Now, get me a nice cup of tea, there's a good girl.'

Apart from the two bedrooms, the only other room they had was a scullery. It was large enough to have a table and chairs in there, and by the old black-leaded stove there was a shabby but comfortable armchair. Amy filled the kettle with water and put it on to boil, then gazed in the larder, grunting with satisfaction. When her father had been home there was always plenty of grub in the place. She made some cheese sandwiches while she was at it.

Loading it all on a tin tray she took it to her mother. What she saw made her stop in fury. Her mother was dressed and peering in the mirror as she tried to hide the bruise with heavy make-up. 'What you doing?'

'Trying to make myself look presentable.' She eyed the tray Amy had plonked on the dressing table. 'Good girl, you've made me a bite to eat. Don't want to drink on an empty stomach.'

'You're not going out?' Amy spluttered. 'Dad got me because he said you were too sick to be on your own.'

'He shouldn't have done that. I know how much school means to you. But I feel better now, and a night out will do me good.'

Amy could have screamed in frustration, but there was no point getting in a rage about it. Her dad had been worried, that's all. 'That a new frock you're wearing?'

'Do you like it?' Her mother preened. 'Got it off the tallyman. Not bad, is it?'

'Nice.' Amy might not be able to read, but she was no slouch when it came to money, and she knew her mother would have some to spare. Dolly always did when Dad came home flush from a long trip at sea. 'I need a new one myself, and shoes; these let in the wet. Don't know what the neighbours must think when they see me walking around looking like a rag bag.'

That made Dolly stare at her daughter, eyeing her up and down critically. 'You're quite right. You could do with some new things. The tallyman'll be here soon, so you'd better choose something then. Can't have everyone saying you're scruffy as well as . . .'

Clenching her hands behind her back, Amy forced out a smile. 'I know what everyone says about me, Mum.'

'I'm sorry, Amy.' Her mother looked upset. 'I know you can't help what's wrong with you. People say such nasty things, but I know you're not daft.'

Amy knew that's what everyone thought and it distressed her so much. She had seen people who weren't right in the head, and she wasn't like them. She wasn't! Her mum and dad got impatient when she couldn't get things right, and they said things they were sorry about after. But she wasn't lazy like the teachers thought; she tried so hard.

She plonked herself in the old armchair and buried her head in her hands. She wouldn't cry. She wouldn't!

When the tallyman arrived ten minutes later she looked through his book and picked out a pretty summer dress in green with tiny flowers around the neck and short sleeves, and a pair of shoes with a bar across the instep. She didn't have any trouble making out pictures, and although she couldn't read how much they cost, they looked good.

'Right, I'll bring them the day after tomorrow. That will be an extra one and six a week, Mrs Carter.'

Amy watched carefully as the tallyman wrote the order in his book, fascinated to see him do it with such ease. Her heart ached to be able to do that.

When he'd gone, her mum shut the front door. Business was always done on the doorstep. The tallyman was never asked in.

'Why don't you forget about school?' Her mother spoke gently. 'Most kids are working by fourteen.'

'But, Mum, I can't get a job if I can't read or write my name.'

'Course you can, factories don't care about that sort of thing. All you got to do is put a cross for your name. If you haven't learnt to read by now you'll never do it, and I see how upset you are sometimes when you come home. Think about it, Amy.' With that Dolly left the house, heading for the Lord Nelson just down the road.

Amy knew her mother wouldn't be back until chucking-out time. Her dad had dragged her out of school for nothing this time. It wasn't always so, because at times her mum was terribly sick and Amy couldn't leave her side, but she'd recovered quickly today.

Wandering back to the scullery she set about making herself a huge doorstep of bread and cheese, and it went down well with a glass of milk. Nicely full, she sat at the table, cupped her chin in her hands and stared moodily at nothing. Perhaps it would be better if she went out to work. She was desperate to learn to read, but the teachers didn't seem to have time for her. All they kept doing was putting her in younger and younger classes. The other children all sniggered at her, calling her beastly names, but she kept her head up defiantly, and if they ganged up and punched her, she walked away as if she didn't care. Well, her mum was right, she wouldn't go back again, because tomorrow she'd get herself a job. But there was no way she was going to put a cross for her name.

She went to her bedroom and brought back the sheets of paper her gran had done for her about five years ago. They were dog-eared from constant use, but she treasured them. Her gran had died three years ago and that had been a terrible blow, because she had been the only one who had had any patience with Amy, and tried to help.

Smoothing out the first page she gazed at it. Granny had drawn pictures and written underneath what they were. There were animals, fruit and all sorts of things. The pictures were really good, but the cat was her favourite. It had a cheeky face and looked as if it was smiling. Her granny had been so clever. Why hadn't she taken after her?

She traced her finger over the letters, trying to fix the shapes in her mind, but when she copied them, they didn't look the same, no matter how hard she tried.

Half an hour later she gave up and decided it would be better if she concentrated on her signature. Her initials were AC, so she sorted through the sheets until she found a large A for apple, and C for cat. She had seen lots of people sign things, because she always watched very carefully, and they just scribbled. The tallyman's name just looked like a wiggly line. With tongue sticking out in determination, she began to practise.

After quite a while she gave a satisfied grunt. She had managed to make the same marks over and over again. Whether it was anything like her name, she didn't know, but it was better than a cross!

Now she was hungry again, and stood up to rifle through the larder to see what she could find. There was a tin almost full of biscuits, so she made tea and dunked them until nearly half of them had disappeared. Then she practised her signature again, just to be sure she could still do it. It took a great deal of concentration, but it looked something like those she had done earlier – at least she thought so. She would just act as if she knew what she was doing if there was something to sign.

It was only eight o'clock and the sun was still shining. Amy knew her mother wouldn't be back for ages yet, so, slipping the spare key into her pocket, she left the house. She would wander down to the docks and see if her dad had sailed yet. But she'd been so upset about being taken out of class that she hadn't asked him the name of his ship. It was always in big letters, and if she already knew the name she could sometimes pick out the right one when she got close enough. Some days she *could* make out words, but other days were hopeless and she couldn't read at all. That usually happened if she panicked or was feeling miserable. Then everything was just jumbled up.

Her heart missed a beat when she saw a gang of boys at the end of the road, and they jeered as she got near them.

'Barmy Amy can't read. She can't read,' they chanted. 'She ain't got no brains.'

Her step didn't falter. Walking through the middle of them and ignoring their grinning faces, she moved unhurriedly until she was past them.

Once round the corner and out of their sight, her bottom lip trembled, but she refused to let the tears of self-pity flow. She was always being picked on, both in and out of school. Why did they have to be rotten to her? She'd never done anything to hurt them. No one wanted to be her friend. Why? She was always on her own, and very lonely.

There were three girls she knew across the road, laughing and walking arm-in-arm. Amy watched, longing to be with them, but they ignored her, just like always. Her mouth set in a determined line. They were too soppy and giggly for her, anyway. She didn't need them.

Running the rest of the way to reach her vantage spot, she saw a ship setting out, its horn blasting. Oh, it was lovely. Was her dad on that one? If only she were a boy, she'd be able to go to sea like him and visit all the lovely places he told them about. It had crossed her mind to cut her hair short and try to pass herself off as a boy, but it wouldn't work: she was already sprouting breasts. Looking down at her chest she grimaced; they were quite big and she wouldn't be able to hide them for long. Her dad said she was going to be pretty like her mum, but she couldn't see it. Her hair was long, dark and much too curly, her eyes were green with a strange upward tilt at the corners, and her mouth was too big. No, she didn't think she was going to be attractive, but she certainly wouldn't pass for a boy. She giggled when she thought what fun it would be to try, but with her dad away so much she couldn't leave her mum. When Dolly was bad she could hardly lift her head off the pillow. That's when there was no time for school as Amy's days were taken up with cooking, shopping and cleaning.

How she wished her life was different. How she longed to be like the other children. But she wasn't. It was no good trying to kid herself about that. Her eyes filled with tears and she brushed them away before they could spill over. Her granny had told her she was special, but she couldn't believe that. She just didn't fit. If only she could sail away like her dad.

Amy watched the ship until it was out of sight, sighing wistfully. It was nice to dream though.

On her way back to the house she was relieved to see the boys were no longer there. The older she got the more the vicious comments hurt. She wanted to cry and bash their grinning faces, but the boys were always in a crowd and they were a rough lot. The girls weren't much better. None of them would hesitate to beat her up, she knew, because a few times she hadn't been able to stop herself from lashing out at the boys and girls after school. She always got the worst of it as they ganged up on her, and others would rush over to join in the fun. Then she would have to hide somewhere out of sight and sob in misery and pain, not understanding why they wanted to be horrible to her. She had tried to be friends – she really had – but just because she was different, they tormented her.

Letting herself into the house, she went straight to the

scullery and picked up her papers, gazing at her granny's careful letters and drawings. These were Amy's most precious possessions and she took them carefully back to her bedroom, tucking them in the chest of drawers under her knickers, wishing Gran were still alive. She was sure Gran would have found out why she couldn't read. Her granny had said she wasn't daft in the head; she just didn't see things the same as everyone else.

Amy sat on the edge of her bed, head bowed now she was alone and didn't need to keep up the pretence, and raged inside. Why didn't she see the words properly? There wasn't anything wrong with her eyes; she could see clearly for miles, and close to as well.

Her mum came back then, so Amy quickly undressed and slipped into bed. Dolly had others with her, and Amy heard the clink of bottles as they put them on the table. Their laughter was loud and she knew they wouldn't leave until all the booze was gone.

'Let's have a cuppa, Dolly,' someone shouted.

Amy stuck her fingers in her ears to shut out their racket. Her mum would be in a sorry state in the morning.

She hoped that lot didn't eat all the biscuits.

# 2

Before Amy could have some breakfast she had to clear up the mess from last night. There were bottles in the sink, on the floor and tipped over on the table, spilling out the dregs. That would have to be scrubbed before it was fit for use again. The smell of stale beer was disgusting. With a resigned sigh she filled a bucket with soapy water and set about cleaning up, not caring how much noise she made. Her mum wouldn't stagger out of bed until about lunchtime after the night she'd had.

When the place was spick and span again she put the kettle on and went to her mother's room, pulling back the curtains to let in the light.

A groan came from the bed. 'Shut those bloody curtains. My head's splitting.'

Amy ignored the order and ground her teeth. 'Why'd you drink so much, Mum? You know it makes you feel bad the next day.'

Her mother shielded her eyes from the sunlight streaming into the room. She looked a mess. She was still wearing her make-up and it was all smudged, leaving the sheets covered in orange powder. As soon as Amy could get her mother up those sheets would have to be washed. This was not her favourite job, but the weather was good so they could be hung across the back yard. In the winter it was a nightmare trying to get things dry. Her mother didn't seem to care if things weren't too clean, and was quite happy to leave everything to her daughter, who couldn't stand living in dirt.

A bucket of soapy water and a scrubbing brush worked wonders.

'You want a cup of tea, Mum, and something to eat?'

'Just tea.' Dolly opened one eye. 'Did we leave the place in a pickle?'

Amy nodded. 'I've cleaned it up.'

The eye closed and her mother groaned. 'You're a good girl. Don't know what I'd do without you. Get me that tea. My mouth feels like the inside of a bird cage.'

Grimacing, Amy returned to the scullery and found the kettle boiling away nicely. She was never going to drink like that. They were all happy while they were doing it, but the next day was awful. It was hard to understand why they did it. Her dad was the same; he liked his booze, and when he was home her mother got into the habit of spending hours in the pub. Once he'd gone back to sea her mum usually settled down to a quieter life.

She made the tea and took a cup in to her mother. Dolly gulped it down, although it was boiling hot.

'Ah, that's better.' After a coughing fit, her mother wiped her eyes. 'You going to school today?'

'No, you told me to get a job, and that's what I'm gonna do.'

'Oh yes, I forgot that. It'd be a big help if you could. Your dad won't be back for ages. He's gone to the other side of the world to a place called Australia.'

Lucky devil, Amy thought, but didn't say it out loud. 'We won't see him for months then.'

Her mother shook her head – carefully. 'But he'll turn up loaded with money, so we'll have a good time. One thing about him, he don't gamble away his earnings like some of them. But in the meantime, anything you can earn will help. Where you going to try?'

'Don't know.' Amy hunched her shoulders. She didn't want to do this, but what choice did she have? School wasn't doing her any good, and she was fed up with the others jeering at her all the time. She wouldn't tell anyone she couldn't read. She'd had enough of people making fun of her.

'There's all those buildings by the river where they make clothes and things. You might get something there.'

'I'll try. Will you be all right for a while?'

'Yes, I'm just going to have a little sleep, then I'll get up.' Dolly closed her eyes. 'Don't slam the door when you go out.'

Amy pulled the curtains across again to cut out the light, and went back to the scullery. Her stomach was churning about finding a job, so she poured herself a cup of tea and had a slice of bread. That was all she could manage. Then she dragged a brush through her hair, trying to make it look tidy, but it just shot back to its usual springy mass. There was so much of it: perhaps she should cut some off, but her dad said she mustn't do that because it was pretty hair.

Slipping a key into her pocket, she left the house quietly and headed for the river.

The buildings here were drab, run down and probably damp inside from the river lapping at their doors. The first thing she noticed was some women standing outside one place, talking and waving their arms about. Amy hurried up to see what they were doing.

The women were reading a notice stuck on the door. She stood behind them, unable to decipher the writing. This was going to be harder than she'd thought if she couldn't even make out what the notice said.

'You don't wanna work here, Flossy,' one woman said. 'Heard bad things about the place. Marshall's work you like a slave.'

13

The woman who'd been addressed as Flossy stared at the notice. 'But it says here they need workers, pay and conditions good.'

Another woman snorted in disgust. 'Don't believe that. My girl tried it last year and didn't stay more than two weeks. Said the work was terrible hard.'

'Ah, well, your girl's no weakling.' Flossy turned away from the notice. 'Let's try somewhere else. I got to get something cos my Sid's been laid off again. He's never been able to hold down a job.'

Another woman looked gloomy. 'It's getting bloody hard to find work. We've all got to try and get jobs today.'

As they walked away, Amy hesitated for only a second before opening the door and slipping inside.

The place was huge, like a warehouse, and that was probably what it had been at one time, Amy figured. There were long benches where girls sat sewing by hand or by machine; other girls were running around with arms full of clothing. Along the entire length of one wall were racks loaded with finished garments. Amy had never seen so many clothes in her life.

'What do you want?' a short, balding man asked, looking rather harassed.

'Um, the notice on the door said you need workers. Good pay and conditions,' she added.

The man sighed. 'You don't want to believe everything you read. But come with me and I'll take you to the boss.'

Amy was pleased with that bit of deception. The man believed she could read the notice. Bit of luck those women being there. She followed him, hoping her luck was going to hold.

'Young girl to see you about the notice you put outside.'

The man behind the desk continued to frown and mutter

over something he was reading. He was a gaunt man, quite old, Amy thought. He must be at least forty. His black hair was peppered with grey and he was wearing thick glasses. He didn't look too friendly and she clenched her hands in front of her to stop them shaking.

'Boss.'

He looked up then, his dark brown eyes unfocused for a moment. 'Sorry, Jim. The price of material's going up again. How the hell are we supposed to make a profit?'

Jim shrugged. 'Perhaps you don't want to take on more workers after all.'

At those words Amy's hopes were dashed. 'Your notice outside said you do,' she blurted out.

The boss turned his gaze to her for the first time. 'You're a bit young, aren't you?'

'I look younger than I am because I'm short. I'm fifteen.' Squaring her shoulders she held his gaze. It wasn't much of a lie. She'd be fifteen in December.

He didn't seem to believe her, but he nodded to Jim. 'We've got to have workers or we'll never meet our targets. I'll see to this.'

When Jim had gone back to work, the boss said, 'Sit down. What's your name?'

'Amy Carter, sir.' She perched on the edge of the seat while he sorted through a drawer in his desk until he found what he was looking for.

'That's your hours and pay. Read it and if you want the job sign your name at the bottom and write down your address.' He pushed the paper and a pen towards her.

Panic surged through her. What was she going to do? She pretended to read it while trying to stop her heart from thumping erratically. After what she thought was a reasonable amount of time for anyone to read the form, she picked up the pen and signed her name, just as she had practised last night. She gripped the pen hard, trying not to stick her tongue out between her teeth with the effort. He wasn't watching so she pushed it back and stood up.

'Be here by seven-thirty on Monday. I don't tolerate lateness.'

'I won't be late, sir.' She made it to the door before he called her back.

'You haven't put your address down.'

'Oh, sorry.' She smiled apologetically, still holding on to the door handle. 'It's twenty-three Farthing Street, Wapping.'

To her immense relief he picked up the pen and wrote it down for her.

She shot out of the building as fast as her legs would carry her, elated that she had got away with it. The only trouble was she didn't know what she had to do when she started there in the morning, or what the pay was, or how long her hours were. Still, she had got the job, and all she would have to do was watch the others. She would soon get the hang of it.

Eager to tell her mum the news, she ran home and tumbled into the scullery, out of breath. Her smile was even wider when she saw her mum up, dressed, and drinking tea, looking much better.

'I've got a job at Marshall's, Mum. I start on Monday and they don't know I can't read. I fooled them easy.' She then explained what had happened.

'That was smart of you, Amy.' Her mother poured her a cup of tea. 'How much you going to get?'

'It was all on the bit of paper, but I couldn't make it out.'

'Well, from what I've heard of that place, it won't be much, but it'll be a help.'

Amy toyed with her cup, her excitement melting away when she noticed her mother's drawn face. 'Are you going to be all right? It's not like school. I won't be able to stay home or they'll throw me out.'

'I know that.' Dolly gave a determined nod. 'I'll manage. I'm glad you'll be earning because you need to be able to look after yourself. I might not be with you for too long.'

There was something in her mother's voice that made Amy glance up sharply. 'Aw, Mum, don't talk like that. You'll be fine if you look after yourself and don't drink quite so much.'

'I won't from now on. Your dad's going to be away for months and I've got to look after you. He worries about you.'

'Does he?' That was news to Amy. She really didn't know him all that well. He was just the man who turned up for a while occasionally and then disappeared again. And when he came home he was a stranger to her; he certainly never showed his feelings.

'Oh, yes. He wasn't going to take this ship, but I made him, because he can't go turning down work. I told him I'm not going to die for a year or two.'

Amy was alarmed by this talk of dying. Her mother had said things like this before, but only in a joking way. She was serious this time. 'Why don't you see a doctor and find out why you cough so much at times?'

Dolly shook her head. 'I know what's wrong with me and there's nothing they can do. If they get their hands on me they'll send me away, and what would happen to you then? Of course, living by the docks don't help much.'

'We could move.'

Her mother patted her hand. 'It's too late. Nothing will help now.'

Amy chewed her lip anxiously. 'What's wrong with you?'

'It's to do with the lungs. It's got some funny name but I can't remember it now.' Dolly smiled brightly. 'Anyway, there's nothing to worry about yet. You start your new job and try to save a few pennies each week, just so you've got a little put aside for a rainy day.'

'I'll do that.' Apart from looking tired and rather thin, her mother was quite cheerful today, so Amy put the worrying conversation behind her.

'I know I haven't always been patient with you, Amy. Watching you struggle to read has been painful, and we can't help wondering if it's our fault somehow. But we do love you, and you mustn't worry so much about it, lots of people can't read or write.' Her mother stood up. 'I'll go shopping and see if I can get something tasty for our dinner.'

When Dolly had left, Amy slumped into the old armchair by the fireplace; it was cold now because it was summer, but in the winter it was a lovely warm spot. She thought back over the talk she'd had with her mother and couldn't help worrying about the future. It would be a stormy passage if what her mother feared was true. But it couldn't be. She shook her head in denial. Her mother was just being gloomy cos Dad had gone back to sea. She was always a bit down then, and she had a hangover from last night's binge. Yes, that's all it was.

She jumped up and hunted through the larder for the biscuits. There was one left, so she sat down again and munched thoughtfully. It was no good her mum telling her not to worry that she couldn't read or write, because she did. It made her feel ashamed and worthless. She had struggled, fretted and lashed out in frustration and disappointment. But nothing did any good.

\*

The 'something tasty' her mother brought back was a couple of meaty lamb chops, and with mashed spuds and greens they made a filling meal.

After Amy had cleared up and made them a pot of tea, it was still only two o'clock.

Her mother drank her tea and sighed. 'I'll just go and have a little rest this afternoon. What are you going to do this afternoon?'

'Amy grinned. 'The weather's nice so I thought I'd go for a walk.'

'You ought to have friends to go out with.' Dolly frowned at her daughter. 'You're always on your own.'

'They don't want nothing to do with me.' When her mother's frown deepened, she said airily, 'Anyway, I don't need them. They think they're so good, but they're not. Gran always said I was special, and I'm going to do something special in my life, then I'll be able to laugh at them!'

'That's the way. Don't let them upset you.' Her mother hauled herself to her feet, holding on to the table for a moment, then turned and headed for the bedroom.

'Mum, are you going out tonight?'

'No, Amy.' She glanced over her shoulder. 'I'll stay in and read to you, shall I?'

'Oh, please.' Amy's smile was as wide as it could get. 'I'd like that.'

Once her mother was asleep, she slipped out of the house, still smiling. She loved her mum reading to her. She had this wonderful book called *Pride and Prejudice* all about the upper classes, and Amy never got tired of hearing it. How she would love to be able to read it for herself.

There was a bounce in her step as she headed for the river. If the jeering boys had been on the corner of the street, she wouldn't have cared. She'd got herself a job, and that was more than they'd done. Her mother had promised not to drink so much, and Amy was sure she'd be strong again if she did that. Dad had a good ship this time and would come home with loads of money after such a long trip.

The sun was warm on her face and arms, and she sang to herself as she walked along.

For once she didn't make for the docks, but instead found a quieter stretch of the Thames. It had been a long walk to get there, but worth it.

Sitting down on a tuft of grass she tucked her knees up and pulled her frock over to cover them. The sun was brilliant and it looked as if little diamonds were glistening on the water. She gazed into the river and laughed out loud when she saw ducks upending to feed.

'Lovely, aren't they?'

Amy jumped at the sound of a man's voice, shading her eyes to look up at him.

'Mind if I sit here as well?'

She shrugged. 'The river don't belong to me.'

'I'll take that as a yes, shall I?' He eased himself down beside her, stretched out his long legs, opened a large book and began to make pencil marks on the paper.

She watched in fascination as a picture began to take shape, not daring to speak because he seemed lost in what he was doing. He was a young man, about twenty she guessed. He had brown hair and light brown eyes. Studying him carefully she noted the highly polished shoes, good clothes, and hands that looked as if they hadn't done a day's work in their life. He spoke real proper, too.

Finished with her detailed inspection of him, she turned her attention back to the drawing, gasping in delight. 'That's here! That's the swan over there. It looks just like it.' She swivelled round until she was kneeling; she'd never seen anyone do that before.

He turned his head and smiled at her. 'I hope it does.' Tearing the page out he proffered it. 'Would you like it?'

Her fingers itched to take it, but hesitated. 'I couldn't. It's yours.'

'I can do more. Tell you what, I'll sign it and when I'm famous you can sell it for a lot of money.'

His eyes were full of mischief, making her laugh. 'You sure you're gonna be famous?'

'Of course. You've got to have belief in yourself or you'll never succeed in life.' He signed the drawing at the bottom and held it out for her. 'There you are, that's my name.'

She peered at it. 'What's it say?'

'I didn't think my signature was that bad!' He laughed. 'My name's Benjamin Scott. What's yours?'

She sat back again, rather bashful, but not before she had taken the precious drawing and placed it carefully beside her on the grass. 'Amy Carter.'

'Nice to meet you, Amy Carter, and where do you live?'

'Near the docks, Farthing Street. My dad's in the merchant navy. He's gone to Australia.'

'Ah, an adventurous life, eh?'

She nodded, and hugged her knees again.

'Do you mind if I draw you?'

'What you want to do that for?' She couldn't help giggling at the idea.

'Because you look pretty sitting like this beside the river.'

'Go on – don't be daft. I'm not pretty.'

'I mean it, Amy.' His pencil began to move over the page. 'Sit still and look across the river.'

There was silence for a while as he sketched away, then he said, 'Turn and face me now, Amy.'

What a laugh, she thought, having someone draw her picture. Bet those children who taunted her had never had their face in a picture. The customary hurt flooded back as she remembered all the nasty things they said to her, but then she banished it. She refused to think about them. This was fun.

It seemed no time at all before he was standing up.

'Thank you, that was perfect.'

She scrambled to her feet. 'Can I see it?'

Tucking the pad under his arm he smiled down at her. 'I'll let you see it one day.'

Amy watched him stride away, disappointed. He'd had kind eyes, and she didn't think she had ever seen anyone as tall as that. Still, she had one of his pictures. She picked it up, careful not to crease it, then started back for home.

Mum was just getting the tea ready when Amy arrived, and while she buttered a slice of bread, Amy told Dolly all about the nice man who had drawn her picture.

'He wouldn't let me see it,' Amy explained, 'but he gave me this.' She spread the picture out for her mother to see.

'That's really good.' Her mother looked concerned. 'But you shouldn't talk to strange men when you're out on your own.'

'He was all right, Mum. A proper gent.' Amy went into her bedroom and put the lovely picture in her drawer where it would be safe, and then went back to the scullery. Once they'd had their tea her mother would read to her.

This was one of the best days she'd ever had!

# 3

Benjamin couldn't get home quickly enough, breaking into a trot to reach his car parked further along the river. He had come to Wapping looking for something different to sketch, and he had certainly found it!

Excitement raced through him as he swung the starting handle on his Austin, a present from his father after he had left university. When the engine burst into life, he jumped in and headed for Chelsea. His parents had been disappointed when he had left Oxford, but once they had realized that he really wasn't the academic type and the only thing he wanted to do was paint, they had accepted his decision.

The feeling of guilt rose, as it always did when he thought of the sacrifices they had made to give him a good education. They were by no means poor, but helping a son through university had been a financial drain on the three draper's shops they owned. They were getting back on their feet again now he insisted on paying his own way.

One day he would make it up to them, to thank them for their faith in him. His painting was improving all the time and he was even beginning to sell a few canvases. All he needed was something exceptional to catch the critics' and gallery owners' eyes. And today he was sure he had found it. What a face that young girl had, and her eyes were like nothing he had ever seen. He would have to get them right, for they said so much about her.

Pulling up outside the house where he was renting the top floor, he leapt out of the car and loped up the stairs, taking them two at a time.

Once in the attic studio he shrugged out of his coat, tossing it over a chair in the corner of the room. Without bothering to change into the old clothes he used for painting, he put a new canvas on the easel, opened his sketchbook and set to work.

Time no longer existed for Benjamin. The picture of Amy sitting by the river was roughed out, and that canvas replaced with another. This was for the full-face picture of her, and the one he was the most excited about. He had to get it down while he could still see her clearly in his mind's eye. God, he wished he had her here!

'Ben!'

His only comment was a muttered curse as he heard his friend running up the stairs.

'What the devil are you doing? We're supposed to be going to Sheila Watkins' birthday party and you're covered in paint, as usual.'

'Go away, Howard!'

There was silence as his friend studied the two pictures, perching on the edge of a tall stool to watch the portrait take shape. He spoke softly, never taking his eyes off the canvas. 'I hate to disturb you, Ben, but we did promise to go tonight.'

'Damn!' Ben tossed down his brush, his concentration gone. Wiping his hands, he said, 'I'll have to leave it until tomorrow now.'

His friend's smile was wry and full of sympathy. 'Where did you find her?'

'Sitting by the river.' Ben stepped back to study his work.

He had always considered himself a landscape painter, but not any more.

'Phew, Ben, I knew you were good, but . . .' Howard waved his hand at both paintings. '. . . these are fabulous.'

'They will be when they're finished.' Ben gazed at the portrait critically, pleased with his friend's reaction. He trusted Howard, who had a marvellous eye for what was right. 'I haven't captured the eyes yet. There was so much in them. Youth, innocence and a deep, deep hurt that went to her very soul. Even when she smiled it was still there.'

Howard shot his friend a speculative look. 'You're getting poetic. Did you ask the girl about her life?'

'No, if I'd tried that she would have run away, and I didn't want to lose her until I'd finished the sketches. I knew that sitting beside me was something special. Someone special.'

Continuing to study the paintings, Howard pursed his lips in concentration. 'Got a bit of a gypsy look about her, but she isn't conventionally beautiful.'

'I agree.' Ben didn't look up from cleaning his hands with white spirit. 'But what a fascinating face.'

'I know this is only the first laying down of paint, but are the eyes really that colour?'

Ben squinted, visualizing the young girl when she had looked at him. 'Slightly darker, but I haven't finished yet.'

Excitement lighting his face, Howard shoved his hands in his pockets and began pacing. 'I think you've really got something here. I'll ask Thomas from the Summerfield Gallery to come and have a look.'

'No.' Ben spoke sharply, making Howard frown. 'That's kind of you, but I don't want anyone to see these until they're finished.'

'All right, if that's how you feel.'

'I do.' Ben smiled. 'I'll let you know when I'm happy with them. Now I suppose I'd better get ready for this damned party. How the hell did we get invited, anyway?'

'They know our respective parents.' Howard's face broke into a grin. 'You're an unsociable devil when your mind's on painting, which is nearly all the time. I hope you've remembered to get a present for Sheila?'

'I did this for her.' Ben picked up a small painting of a single yellow rose, holding it out for Howard to see.

'Oh, very pretty.' His friend's tone was sarcastic. 'Not your best work.'

'Agreed, but it's how I pay my rent. For some strange reason this kind of thing sells.' Ben shoved the painting in a bag. 'I look forward to the day when I can just paint what I like, but that isn't possible when we're short of money.'

Howard nodded, perched back on the stool again and stared at the portrait. 'Does rather stifle the artistic talent, doesn't it? I'm making awful things like jam pots and biscuit barrels. God, how I hate it, but we've got to eat — sometimes.'

'Can't argue with that.' Ben knew what a tough time Howard was having. He rented the basement of this house and it was often a struggle to find enough money to pay his rent. Ben helped when he could, but it wasn't easy. The two of them never turned down an invitation, in the hope of getting a free meal. That showed just how bad things were at times.

Like Ben, Howard Palmer came from a middle-class family, but because he had chosen to become a sculptor, they had refused to give him any financial help — until he had come to his senses, as they put it. Howard was a brilliant sculptor and had been a good friend of Ben since childhood. They had both dropped out of university at the same time to pursue their dream of having a gallery of their own one day.

Ben realized they had both fallen silent, lost in thought as they stared at the portrait, dreaming of a successful future. 'And what are you giving Sheila?'

Howard started. When he looked up his eyes were unfocused for a moment, then they gleamed in amusement. 'I've made her a vase.'

'I'm sure it's very pretty.'

They burst into hoots of laughter, their introspective mood disappearing.

Howard stood up and slapped Ben on the back. 'She's going to get two unusual and unique presents. Get cleaned up. Hope there's plenty of food, because I haven't had a decent meal all week.'

Sheila Winslow lived in a charming house in Richmond, right by the river. The place was already crowded when Ben and Howard arrived, and as it was a lovely evening the guests had spilt out into the garden. They had been at university with quite a few of them, so they said hello before going to find Sheila.

She saw them and came over, arms open wide, to kiss them on the cheek, gushing enough to make everyone turn and watch her. 'Oh, good, you made it. I couldn't have a party without my two favourite artists.'

Ben groaned deep in his throat. For some peculiar reason Sheila seemed to think it was clever to be friends with two struggling artists. Not that he had ever considered her a friend, more of an acquaintance really.

Howard had managed to keep his smile in place as they gave her their presents.

Ripping open the packages she held each one up for

everyone to see. 'How quaint. You are such clever boys,' she simpered. 'Do go and get yourselves a glass of champagne.'

Without a moment's hesitation they headed for the dining room and the food.

'I'd rather have a pint,' Howard said, still grinning. 'She's gone overboard with her dress tonight.'

Ben eyed her critically as she laughed with a group of her friends. 'Hmm.'

'It's the latest fashion. You don't approve?'

'A bit too glittery and revealing for my taste. I like a touch of mystery about a girl.'

'Like the girl you met today?'

'Yes.' Ben gazed into space, remembering, and wishing he were back in his studio. Then his stomach growled and reminded him why they were here. 'Let's get at the food.'

The large dining-room table was loaded with all kinds of tempting things, so they grabbed plates and piled them high. For several minutes they just munched away, not speaking.

When Howard's plate was nearly empty, he rolled his eyes in appreciation. 'Mrs Winslow certainly knows how to cater for a party.'

'Well, it is her daughter's twenty-first.' Ben eyed the table, trying to decide what to sample next.

'Is it?' Howard helped himself to another two slices of ham. 'This is wonderful.'

They were about to fill their plates again when Mrs Winslow sailed up to them, a tight smile on her face.

'You boys look as if you haven't had a decent meal for a week.'

'Longer than that, Mrs Winslow.' Ben smiled with good humour as the woman made a disapproving sound. The way they lived was a fact of life to them, and as long as they could practise their art, then every sacrifice was worthwhile.

'I don't know what your parents were doing, allowing you to throw away your education and become starving artists.'

'They'll be proud of us when we're famous and making lots of money.' Ben studied his empty plate and thought a large slice of strawberry cake would look good on there.

'You are both living in a dream.' She almost snorted, but she was far too well brought up to do any such thing. 'It will never happen. Howard, you come from an affluent family and yet you have cast it all away. And what for? So you can make pots and statues.'

'But they are very good pots and statues.' Howard was not at all put out by the criticism; he'd heard it all before.

'And you, Benjamin.' Mrs Winslow turned on him now. 'What is your poor father going to do? You should be training to take over the family business, not wasting your time painting pictures no one will ever want. You are the only child, so what will happen when your father can no longer work?'

'He said he would sell the shops.'

She tossed her head in disgust. 'Neither of you has any sense of responsibility. Well, do carry on eating. I'll get Cook to make you up a parcel of food to take away with you.'

As soon as she walked away Howard made a dive for the food again. 'That's her act of charity for the day. Feeding two disobedient sons.'

A huge slice of strawberry cake slid on to Ben's plate. 'I'm not too proud to take it.'

'Nor me.'

They grinned at each other, knowing full well that many people considered them mad. It didn't bother them one tiny bit.

When they couldn't eat another mouthful they went back to the party. Sheila made a great show of dancing with them, but she soon lost interest when she found they didn't know all the latest dances.

As soon as it was polite to do so, they left, carrying a large parcel from the cook.

Ben didn't give a damn what anyone thought or said about him. He was a good artist and one day his talent would be recognized. And one day, too, he and Howard would have their own gallery as a showcase for their work.

Curled up in the armchair like a contented kitten, Amy listened to her mother reading. Dolly often stumbled or hesitated over words, but Amy didn't mind as she always lost herself in the story. One day she was going to be able to sit and read to herself. She was determined. Her mum was doing well this evening; she'd been reading for a long time.

'That's enough for tonight.' Her mother closed the book. 'I'm tired now and think I'll go to bed.'

Amy stretched and stood up. It was only half past eight, but her mum was pale, her hands shaking slightly. 'Thanks for reading to me, Mum. Would you like a cup of cocoa or something? I'll bring it in to you if you like?'

'That would be nice. I'll have tea please, Amy.' Dolly stood up and began to cough, holding on to the table for support.

Filling a glass with water, Amy gave it to her, watching her sip it until the coughing stopped.

'Shall I help you to bed, Mum?'

'I'm all right now.' She gave a tight smile. 'Read for too long, I expect.'

'Oh, that was my fault. I'm sorry.' Amy felt guilty about asking her mother to read so much.

'No it isn't.' She straightened up and faced her daughter.

'Nothing's your fault, Amy. You've been dealt some rotten cards in life and you're not to blame for that. You did well today finding work when there's so much unemployment around.'

Amy watched her mother go to the bedroom and glowed with pride over the rare compliment. She was glad now that she wasn't going back to school and having to face the other children's cruelty. Where she was going no one knew she couldn't read properly, and they never would. It was going to be her carefully guarded secret from now on.

She made her mother the tea, pouring one for herself before she went to bed. She mustn't be late on her first day.

After taking the tea in to her mother, she went back to the scullery to drink her own, feeling happier than she had ever done. Her mum said she was going to look after herself now Amy wouldn't be able to spend so much time at home. If she ate properly and rested when she was tired, she would soon get better. And when her dad came home her mum would be happy again.

# 4

It was twenty minutes past seven when Amy arrived at the factory for her first day, but there was already a crowd of women and girls waiting for the boss to come and open the doors. Amy was nervous about starting work and hadn't been able to eat any breakfast. She had put extra in her lunch box though, knowing she would be starving by the time they had a break.

Hanging back shyly, not daring to speak to anyone, she waited, hoping she wasn't going to be sick with worry. If they wanted her to read something perhaps she could say her eyes were bad? That might work.

'You starting here today?'

The girl in front of her had turned and smiled. She was slightly older than Amy, had dark brown hair and hazel eyes. She was also about three inches taller than Amy, who was no more than five feet one. Her smile was bright though, making Amy smile back at her.

'Yes.' It had come as a shock to be spoken to in that friendly way, and she blushed uncomfortably.

'My name's Gladys.' The girl pointed to the lunch box Amy was clutching. 'Brought your own grub, I see. We can eat together. I know a nice spot.'

'Thank you.' Amy could hardly believe her ears. This stranger was offering to spend time with her. Such a thing had never happened before. 'My name's Amy.'

All chance to talk stopped then, as the boss arrived and opened the door to let everyone in.

Gladys winked as they streamed in. 'See you at one o'clock, Amy.'

Amy watched in amazement as the women rushed to their benches and began work immediately, heads bent and fingers flying as if their very life depended upon it.

'Don't just stand there, girl.' The man who had taken her to see the boss yesterday glowered at her. 'Come with me.'

Remembering his name was Jim, she followed, trotting to keep up with him as he made for a long bench in the middle, which was piled high with cut-out garments. Next to it was another table and standing around it were two men and three women with scissors in their hands, cutting around patterns at great speed. She couldn't help wondering what all the rush was?

'Right, now your job will be to keep all the workers supplied. They must not run out of sewing and have to wait while you bring them more.'

Her gaze swept around the room. The women appeared to be working in groups, and there were lots of them. Some were on machines and others sewing by hand. With eyes wide, she asked, 'How will I know when they need more?'

'I'll tell you.' He picked up a pile of cut-out items from the table and thrust it into her hands. 'Take this to blouses.'

'Er . . . where are they?'

His irritated mutter showed that he had little patience. 'They've all got big notices on poles by the benches.' Spinning her round to the left he gave her a push. 'Move yourself!'

Her heart was thudding as she walked forward, scanning the signs above the benches. She was in a panic now, and when that happened words became meaningless squiggles. She continued walking, hoping she was going in the right direction. What was she going to do? They would see she couldn't read and throw her out.

'Amy,' Gladys whispered. 'They're for me.'

She stopped and nearly cried in relief, handing over the material with shaking hands. 'Sorry.'

'Don't look so worried. You'll soon get the hang of it.' Gladys carried on with her sewing.

*I can't do it.* Amy wanted to cry out in despair as she struggled to calm herself down. It was then she noticed that every bench was working on different material. On Gladys's they were all sewing identical white blouses; next to them the women had navy blue skirts. She let out a huge huff of relief. That's how she would be able to tell where to deliver the next lot of work.

Feeling a little calmer now she hurried back to the cutting table.

'You'll have to move quicker than this.' The foreman gave her a harassed glare as he thrust another armful of material at her. 'Take this to the petticoats.'

The material this time was silky and pink, so Amy cast a wild look around. Pink, pink, she chanted to herself, running from bench to bench until she found the right one.

When she got back the foreman had disappeared so she fished in her pocket for a piece of paper and stub of pencil. She always carried these with her in case she needed them. And she certainly did now!

The sketch she made was rough, but the different work-benches were clear enough. Gladys's bench was right in the middle and she worked her way from there, drawing a picture of a blouse, then the petticoats and skirts on the other two she knew. By the end of the day she hoped to have a little picture over every bench to guide her.

By the time the dinner bell sounded she had over half the

benches marked, and knew the system was working. It was a tricky business because she didn't want anyone to see what she was doing, but luckily they were all too busy to take notice of her. As long as they were kept supplied with work no one even bothered to look at her.

'Come on, Amy.' Gladys caught hold of her arm. 'We've only got three-quarters of an hour.'

Picking up her sandwiches, Amy left the factory with Gladys. Outside most of the workers were sitting on boxes or the ground, eating and talking.

'I like to get right away for a while if the weather's all right.' Gladys slipped her hand through Amy's arm as they walked along, chatting away about how she wished she lived somewhere with green fields and hills.

Amy was content to listen, enjoying the novelty of being with someone who wasn't calling her rude names. It was nice, and she hoped Gladys was going to be a friend. She'd never had one before.

'This'll do.' Gladys stopped under a large oak tree. 'I sit here and look up at the branches. It's so beautiful, even in the winter.'

After settling down they began munching on their food. Amy was hungry now and very relieved to have survived the morning. She'd finish working out who was doing what by the end of the day, and tomorrow wouldn't be so frightening.

She cast Gladys a shy glance and noticed she had her head tipped back looking up at the tree. Amy did the same, watching the slight breeze rustle the leaves, making shimmering fingers of sunlight pierce the dense canopy. It was lovely, and very peaceful, if you ignored the noise from the docks not far away. Of course the spot she'd gone to yesterday was much better, but this was all right for today. Her mind drifted back to that place by the Thames, and she couldn't help wondering what that man would do with her picture. It would be lovely to see it one day, but she doubted she ever would. Still, she had one of his drawings. How she wished her gran were still alive. Gran would have loved it. Perhaps she'd be able to buy a frame for it sometime and put it on her bedroom wall. She smiled to herself at that thought.

'Lovely, ain't it?'

'Yes.' Amy finished her food, wishing she'd brought a bit more with her. She must put in another sandwich for tomorrow. Feeling quite relaxed now, she asked, 'Why do you all work so fast?'

'Because we get paid for how much work we do. It's bloody hard labour, but if you can't keep up with what they want, they chuck you out. My dad was killed in an accident at the docks two years ago and my mum needs the money.'

'Oh, I'm sorry.'

Gladys's usually smiling mouth set in a straight line for a moment. 'He was a good man and my mum's never got over losing him.' Then she smiled again. 'You still got your dad?'

Amy nodded.

'What's he like?'

'He's all right, but we don't see much of him. He's in the merchant navy and he's gone to the other side of the world this time. He won't be back for ages.'

'I'll bet he has lots of tales to tell when he does come back.' Gladys stood up and dusted down her skirt. 'We'd better get back now.'

Amy did the same and fell into step beside Gladys, merely nodding. She changed the subject. 'Perhaps your mum will marry again one day.'

'I doubt that.' Gladys grimaced. 'Thought the world of him, she did, and hasn't got eyes for anyone else. She's still not bad-looking and ought to find someone to look after her. She's had plenty sniffing round her. Bloody stupid, if you ask me.'

'Oh.' Amy had never heard a woman swear so freely; her mum never did, and she found it a bit embarrassing. 'Er . . . do you mean your mum has men after her?'

'Amy, you are a funny one. Are you really as innocent as you look? You've gone all pink.'

The usual hurt was back. It hadn't taken long for the insults to come. 'I'm not daft!'

'I didn't mean that . . .' Gladys stopped, concerned. 'I wasn't being rude, Amy. You seem to live in a little world of your own, not taking much notice of what's going on around you, and I think it's nice.'

'Do you?' That was hard to believe.

'Yes.' Gladys smiled. 'I like you. Can we be friends? We could go to the pictures on Saturday evening. They've got *King Kong* showing.' This was announced with a wiggle of delight.

'Is it good?' Amy didn't know what to say, as she'd never heard of the film. In fact she'd never even been to the pictures. It was at that moment she realized just how lonely she had been since her gran died.

Gladys laughed. 'Just you wait and see. Will you come?'

'Yes please.'

They reached the factory with only two minutes to spare, and Amy walked in almost bursting with happiness. She had a friend and was going to the pictures with her at the end of the week. She'd have her new dress and shoes by then.

*

Although the hours were long and the days hectic, Amy was happy. Her sketch of the worktables was a big help for the first couple of days, and as the week went on she had to refer to it less and less. It was easier to remember who was working on what by the feel and colour of the materials. No one was shouting at her, nor calling her beastly names and saying she was stupid, and her mum was getting better. Dolly was even talking about finding a job in a shop if she could.

Picking up the next batch of cut-out blouses, she hurried to the bench where Gladys was working.

'Pictures soon,' Gladys whispered. 'I'm looking forward to seeing *King Kong* again.'

'Have you seen it before?' Amy was surprised.

'Yes, twice. It's a real scary picture.'

Amy giggled at her friend's expression, but didn't linger; she hurried on to the next job. The tallyman had brought her dress and shoes round and she was looking forward to wearing them.

'Amy!'

She spun round to face the foreman as he strode towards her, praying she hadn't done anything wrong. 'Yes, sir?'

'Can you sew?'

'Yes, my gran showed me.'

He gave her the material he was holding. 'Do the hem on this and let me see what you can do. Careful though. This is special and we don't want to have to unpick it.'

Amy took the garment and ran her fingers gently over the cream-coloured material. It was so soft and fine. She'd never seen anything like it.

'Er . . . I can't work quick like the others.'

'I don't want you to. Take your time and do tiny stitches. Sit over there by the window.'

For the next hour Amy concentrated on doing her best stitching. Her gran had always done such beautiful work, and she was determined to show the boss how well she had been taught.

'Let's have a look.' The foreman took the garment from her, frowning as he examined what she had done. After giving her a startled look he headed for the office without saying a word.

The confidence drained out of her. It wasn't good enough. She sat on the high stool for a few moments, swinging her legs, then sighed and stood up. It had been nice sitting here sewing, but she had better get on with keeping the women supplied with work.

She set off, not looking where she was going, and nearly cannoned into the boss. With a neat bit of footwork she just managed to avoid him. 'Sorry, sir,' she gasped. She was desperate not to lose this job. It was a different world to her but she had found her place in it; she didn't want to go back to being alone again.

He put out a hand to stop her tearing away. 'Where did you learn to sew like this?'

'My gran taught me, sir.'

'Can you embroider?'

Amy nodded. 'My gran was really good and she showed me all the stitches.'

'That's a good find, Jim,' the boss said to the foreman. 'Give her the Richardson trousseau and I'll arrange for her to have an extra shilling a week while she's working on it. We haven't got anyone else who can do such fine work.'

Amy's mouth dropped open. An extra shilling a week. She'd be able to save that like her mum told her, she decided, hoping the special job would take a long time.

*

By the end of the week, Amy was humming to herself as she sewed. The boss was pleased with her work and his praise had made her blush with surprise. She was good at something!

On Saturdays they only worked until one o'clock and she was very excited as she queued up for her wages. When her time came she managed her much-practised signature with comparative ease. Again she reflected how it was strange that her mood affected her ability to read and write. If she was in a panic nothing made sense, but if calm and relaxed she could usually make out some words.

Gladys was waiting for her at the door. 'Still coming to the pictures tonight?'

'Yes.' Amy nodded eagerly. 'What time?'

'Seven at the Regal. I'll wait outside for you.'

'All right, I'll see you then.'

Amy ran home. She couldn't remember feeling this happy before. She had her first week's money in her pocket and, best of all, she had a friend!

'Mum!' She dashed indoors waving her wage packet. 'I got paid and I'm going to the pictures tonight. Gladys asked me.' Out of breath, her wide mouth turned up in a smile, she plonked herself down at the table and pushed the packet towards her mother. 'How much have I got?'

'My goodness, you are excited.' Her mother poured her a cup of tea, smiled, and then emptied the money on to the table.

'How much?' Amy rested her elbows on the table, beaming with pleasure as her mother counted the money. 'I couldn't read what it said in the book, but I signed my name all right.'

'There, I told you you'd manage, didn't I? You've got thirteen shillings.'

Amy's eyes opened wide and she bounced in her chair. 'They said I was to have an extra shilling because my sewing was good. Have I got that?'

'Yes, look, sixpence for half a week.' Her mother pointed to the figures on the front of the envelope. 'It says here: wage twelve shillings and sixpence, plus the bonus.'

Although she could often make out figures better than words, she was much too excited to do it now. It sounded like a fortune to her though. 'Can I have some to go out tonight?'

'Of course you can.' Dolly began to separate the coins. 'The extra money you must save. Put it in the brown teapot. We never use that.'

Amy scrambled to get the old chipped pot off the shelf, put it on the table and dropped the sixpence in, listening to it make a satisfying tinkle as it settled in the bottom. Then she waited expectantly.

'Any money you put in there will be yours and I won't touch it for anything.'

Amy nodded.

'Now, one and six is for the tallyman, two shillings for yourself, and that leaves the rest for your keep.' Her mother sighed and studied her daughter seriously. 'You must save something each week, Amy. It's most important that you have a little money behind you if it's needed.'

'I'm only getting extra while I do this special sewing, Mum.' Amy stared at the two bob she'd been given to spend on herself. 'I don't mind if I only have a shilling a week for myself when the extra stops coming.'

'No, that won't be necessary. You're working hard and deserve to have a little money in your pocket. When you don't get it any more I'll take less for your keep.'

'Thanks, Mum.'

'Good, now that's all settled. What time are you going out tonight?'

'I'm meeting Gladys at seven. I'm going to wear my new frock and shoes.'

'And very smart you'll look too. That green dress suits you a real treat. It's almost the same colour as your eyes.'

'Oh, is it?' She hadn't noticed that. It had been the shade that had attracted her. She loved nice colours, like the blue of the sky, the green of trees, and she would gaze for ages at the golden autumn leaves as they fell and made a carpet on the ground. Not that there was much chance of seeing the full beauty round here, but she would take herself off to a park and walk along crunching the dry leaves under her feet. It was lovely.

'Let's have a bite to eat and then I'll have a rest before I go out as well.'

'You going down the pub?' At once Amy was worried. She didn't like her mother mixing with the crowd from the Lord Nelson. She'd seen them at chucking-out time, shouting and weaving about all over the place. When her dad was home it didn't concern her so much: he was a big strong man and her mother was safe with him; but she didn't like Dolly going there on her own.

'I'm only going for a quick drink at the Crown with Mrs Preston.'

'Oh.' Amy smiled in relief. Mrs Preston lived two doors down and was always friendly. That didn't seem too bad. 'You said you were going to look for a job. Have you had any luck?'

'There isn't much about, but the newspaper shop on the corner needs help on two days a week. Thursday and Friday. I start next week.'

'Oh, Mum, that's wonderful. That'll be just right for you.' Amy went to hug her, but was pushed away.

'You mustn't do that, Amy. You'll catch my cough if you get too close.'

'No I won't, Mum.' But Amy sat down again. 'You're not so bad now. It's almost gone.'

'It comes and goes.' Her mother tried to smile. 'Now, what picture are you going to see?'

'*King Kong.*' Amy's excitement was back.

Her mother pulled a face. 'Is that all that's on?'

'Dunno.' Amy shrugged. 'Gladys is crazy about it, and I haven't seen it. I haven't seen anything.'

'No, you haven't.' Dolly looked sad. 'Your dad and me was never one for the pictures. We should have taken you though.'

'Don't matter, Mum. I'll be able to see lots now I'm earning some money.'

'And you've got a friend at last.'

When her mother put bread, butter and cheese on the table, Amy ate hungrily, looking forward to the pictures. She hugged the word 'friend' to herself in awe. She'd always envied the other girls with their friends; now she had one.

When she arrived at the Regal, Gladys was already there standing in the queue, waiting for her.

'Over here, Amy, I've saved you a place.'

There were one or two disgruntled mutters as Amy pushed in, but neither girl took any notice of that. It wasn't long before the early show turned out and they began to file in slowly.

Once inside Amy gasped in wonder. It looked like a palace, with red velvet seats and a patterned carpet, also in red. There were little lights around the walls, and the ceiling was carved and painted gold in parts. It was the most beautiful place she had ever seen. A girl with a torch showed them to their seats at the back of the stalls.

'This'll do.' Gladys grinned. 'I like to be nearer the screen really, but those seats cost more.'

Amy was too excited to do more than smile as she gazed around. Then the lights dimmed and the show began. There was a short B film before the main feature, and when *King Kong* came on she could hear Gladys sigh in excitement, but Amy was more interested in the scenery. However, she was soon drawn into the make-believe world and was sorry when it was over. It had been frightening to see the big ape catch the girl.

After saying goodbye to Gladys, she hurried home and was pleased to see her mum already there, on her own and sober.

She got ready for bed that night in a glow of happiness she hoped was going to last for ever.

5

A gust of cold wind swirled around Amy as she sat by the river, making her pull her coat around her chin for warmth. It was October now and the summer was over, but what fun it had been.

Licking her ice cream she gazed across the water, watching two elegant swans glide along. Although it was cloudy with a hint of drizzle in the air, it was still a lovely spot. She wondered if the man she'd met four months ago ever came back here to draw. It wasn't likely, she thought, catching a dribble of ice cream as it ran down her finger; he would probably need sunshine for his drawing. His picture was safely in her drawer until she could have it framed.

The last of the ice cream was popped in her mouth and she wiped her sticky fingers on her hanky. Her sigh was one of contentment as she rested her chin on her knees. She'd been saving something every week, like her mum had told her, and if she didn't spend all of her two shillings pocket money, the last pennies were put in the pot as well. She'd be able to put an extra shilling in this week because Gladys couldn't come to the pictures today. Amy was sorry about that: they'd gone every Saturday since she'd started at the factory. Amy had considered going on her own, but it wouldn't be so much fun without Gladys. She'd give it a miss and go next week when her friend could make it.

She could still taste the ice cream and licked her lips with pleasure. She hadn't been able to resist it when she'd seen the 'Stop me and buy one' tricycle. They wouldn't be coming round much longer now the weather was getting cold. She still had a little money left over, and as her mother had been looking rather tired and drawn this last week, she would buy them both a lovely orange on the way home. Dolly would like that.

With her mouth watering in anticipation, Amy stood up and headed for the greengrocer's and then home.

Amy's warm glow of contentment vanished when she found her mother sitting at the table in the scullery with her head in her hands.

'What's the matter, Mum? Are you feeling bad again?'

There were dark smudges under her eyes when she looked up at her daughter: she had been crying.

'Oh, Mum.' Amy sat beside her. 'Don't you feel well again? You've been fine since you've been working at the paper shop.'

'They sacked me yesterday,' her mother muttered, concentrating on folding up the newspaper she had been reading.

'Why'd they do that?' Amy gasped. Her mother had liked the job, and talking to all the people who came into the shop. It had given her a real lift and made her happy over the last few months.

'Said they didn't want me no more.'

'Never mind, Mum.' Amy smiled encouragingly. 'You'll find something else, and Dad will be home soon, won't he?'

When her mother didn't answer, Amy showed her the two oranges. She had picked the two biggest she could find. 'Look, I've bought us a treat. Have that and when you go out for your drink with Mrs Preston you'll soon feel better.'

'I'm not going out tonight. I'll just go and have a rest.' She stood up. 'I don't want any tea, Amy, I'm not hungry.'

'But, Mum' – Amy was alarmed now – 'don't you want your orange? I'll peel it for you.'

'That would be nice.' Dolly gazed at her daughter, then gathered her into her arms, holding on tightly and murmuring, 'I'm so sorry.'

Amy watched in astonishment as her mother walked towards the bedroom. She couldn't remember Dolly ever showing her that much affection before. Her mother was not a demonstrative person. She must be feeling very bad, so it was a good job Gladys couldn't come out tonight.

After peeling the orange and putting it on a saucer, she took it into the bedroom. Her mother was fast asleep, so Amy left it on the bedside table for her to eat when she woke up.

Returning to the scullery, she made a pot of tea and settled down to practise her reading and writing. Her mum would get over her disappointment and be better in the morning.

The door of his studio opened quietly and, out of the corner of his eye, Ben saw Howard come in, but he didn't stop painting. His friend perched on the high stool in his usual position and watched, not speaking.

After about fifteen minutes, Ben shot him a sideways glance. 'You're very quiet. Haven't you got anything to do?'

Howard stood up and stepped towards him, a newspaper rolled up in his hand. 'Where are the paintings of the girl?'

'They're on the bench covered by a sheet. Have a look if you want to.'

The sheet was quickly removed and Howard studied the paintings intently.

'What do you think?' Ben stood beside his friend, head on one side and lips pursed in critical concentration.

47

'They're beautiful, especially the full-face portrait.'

'Hmm. I like that too. What do you think I could get for them?'

'What did you say her name was?' Howard tapped the newspaper against his leg.

'Amy Carter.' Ben shot his friend a curious look. 'Why so interested in who she is?'

'There might be a good reason for that. Do you know where she lives?'

'Farthing Street, Wapping. Don't know the number though.'

Howard let out a slow whistle. 'In that case don't sell these yet. They could be worth a fortune in a little while.'

'What on earth are you talking about?' Ben laughed. 'I know they're some of my best work, but—'

'Read this.' Howard unrolled the newspaper and thrust it at him, pointing to a section at the top of the page. 'They mention that the man has a daughter called Amy.'

Leaning against the bench, Ben began to read an account of a trial taking place at the Old Bailey. When he'd finished he bowed his head, remembering the young, innocent girl sitting by the river and smiling at him. Pity swamped him.

'Oh, hell!'

Howard shook his arm to gain his attention. 'Do you think it's her father?'

'She told me her father was in the merchant navy and had gone to Australia this time.'

'That's it then.' Howard was now pacing the room. 'Hang on to those paintings.'

Ben erupted in fury. 'Of course I'm hanging on to them! I can't sell them now. Probably not ever.'

'Yes you can. When the trial's over.'

'I never thought you were a callous sod, Howard.' Ben

had rounded on his friend. 'What do I show them as, huh? Buy a painting of a murderer's daughter?'

'Sorry.' Howard held up a placating hand. 'I didn't mean it to sound like that. He might not be found guilty, and even if he is, you'll be able to sell them after a year or so. They're too good to stay under the sheet, Ben.'

'No, I can't sell them.' Ben shook his head sadly. 'She was such an intriguing girl. Poor little devil. Things could get tough for her.'

'We might be jumping to conclusions.' Seeing his friend had calmed down, Howard slapped him on the back. 'Come on; let's go for a drink. All we can do now is wait and see what happens.'

'You're right.' Ben ran a hand through his untidy hair. 'I could use a pint or two.'

Still in their old working clothes, they got in the car and Ben headed up the road.

'Hey!' Howard exclaimed. 'We've just passed the Hare and Hounds. Where are we going?'

'Wapping. There's a pub there called the Lord Nelson. It's a bit rough, but the regulars are bound to know the man on trial.'

'How do you know this place?'

'Saw it on one of my sketching trips.'

Howard shrugged. 'You do go to the oddest places.'

'You know I like to draw things with character.' Ben grinned at his friend. 'Don't worry. You'll be quite safe, especially if we buy a few drinks.'

'At least at six feet four you're big enough for me to hide behind.'

'Coward.'

'You bet.'

*

49

The pub was crowded but strangely subdued when they arrived.

'Two pints of your best bitter, landlord.' Ben leant on the bar and gazed around, then back at the man pulling the pint. 'Have one for yourself.'

'Thanks, mate.' The landlord put the overflowing glasses on the counter and pulled another for himself. 'Haven't seen you here before.'

'We're just passing through and felt thirsty.' Ben drank down half of the pint in one go and rolled his eyes. 'You serve a good beer.'

'Best in the area,' the man said proudly.

Ben nodded. 'No wonder you're so busy.'

'It's usually livelier than this, but when they've got a few pints down them they'll forget about the murder.'

'Oh?' Ben looked interested. 'What murder is that?'

The landlord was called to serve someone else at that moment, and when he went to the other end of the bar, Howard muttered, 'You should have been a bloody actor. And where did that cockney accent come from?'

'Not bad, eh?' Ben grinned. 'Drink up.'

'Hope you've got enough money for this, Ben, because I'm broke.'

'I've got enough. I sold a painting today.' Ben took a pound note out of his pocket and put it on the counter.

Howard's eyebrows shot up. 'Does that mean we get to eat this week?'

'Might even stretch to a bottle of cheap wine.'

'That good, eh?' Howard looked considerably more cheerful now.

'Yep, and I've got a commission for another one. My luck's changing.'

'Wish mine would.' Howard gave a ragged sigh. 'You're propping me up, you know that, don't you?'

'Don't get so disheartened. You're a damned good sculptor, and you'll make it one day.'

They stopped talking when the landlord came back to them.

'Two more, landlord.' Ben handed him the money and watched while he pulled the pints and put the money in the till, returning with his change.

'What's this about a murder?' Ben prompted.

'One of our regulars when he's ashore, a merchant seaman, Greg Carter, killed a man. Just got off his ship and had a barney with a bloke on the dock. He pulled out a knife and stabbed him.'

'That's terrible.' Ben sipped his beer. 'Lives nearby, does he?'

'Farthing Street. Folks around here aren't happy cos the man who died was well liked. Had a nice missus and three kids.'

'What about the man who killed him? Did he have a family?'

'Wife and daughter. They won't be able to show their faces again.'

'That's right.' A man tottered up to the bar for a refill. 'Andy was my mate. He might have had a quick temper, but there was no cause to kill him.'

Ben paid for the man's beer. 'What was the row about?'

'Said Andy picked his pocket and stole his money.' The man downed his beer in one gulp and looked hopefully at Ben. 'But if you ask me it was the other way round. Carter probably gambled away his pay and didn't want to go home with nothing in his pocket.'

A nod to the barman and the glass was refilled.

'Andy would never have done that. He wasn't a thief even if he did have some extra money in his pocket. Probably had a win at the dogs the night before. He was always right lucky.' The pint went the way of the other one.

Howard tugged at Ben's sleeve. 'Time to go.'

'Right.' Ben gave the two men a bright smile. 'You said the man on trial had a daughter. Do you know her name?'

'Amy,' the landlord told him. 'She ain't quite right in the head.'

'Thanks.' Ben frowned and tossed some more coins on the counter. 'Have yourselves another drink on me.'

'Thanks, mate. Right good of you.'

They left the pub and walked round the corner to where they'd left the car.

'Well, that settles it.' Howard slid into the passenger seat. 'It sounds like her father.'

'Maybe, but I don't understand his last remark about her not being right in the head. She seemed perfectly normal to me. In fact I'd have said she was a bright kid.'

'Well, it must be her. There can't be two Amy Carters living in Farthing Street.'

Ben nodded in agreement, his expression grim.

# 6

At lunchtime on Monday, Amy picked up her sandwiches and walked towards Gladys, a smile on her face, eager to find out what her friend had been doing over the weekend. The smile died as Gladys looked away, took the arm of another girl and left the building with her.

The snub was unmistakable and Amy was completely bewildered as the old pain of rejection rushed back. She hadn't felt like this since she had started working here. Over the last four months she had grown in confidence, and whereas she would have once accepted this kind of attitude, things were different now. She wanted to know why her friend had ignored her.

Running hard, she caught up with them. 'Gladys, what's the matter? What have I done?'

'Nothing.' Gladys looked embarrassed. 'It's not your fault, but my mum said I mustn't have nothing more to do with you.'

'Why?' Amy was stunned by this sudden turnaround. Was it all going to start again: the taunts and nasty comments, the rejection? Her mouth thinned into a firm line. Well, she wasn't going to put up with it any more. 'Tell me why?'

The girl with Gladys snorted. 'You know why. Go away. We don't want the likes of you with us.'

'I wasn't talking to you,' Amy snapped. She'd never liked this one – Janet was her name, and she worked on the cutting table.

'Look, Amy.' Gladys shuffled uncomfortably. 'Things

have changed and I can't see you no more. You must know that.'

Amy watched them walk away, completely mystified. What was she talking about?

Something had gone terribly wrong and by Friday Amy was seriously worried. Her brief period of happiness had come to a sudden end. No one at the factory spoke to her unless they had to. Her mother was refusing to step outside their door, and she was sure all the neighbours were watching her as she walked up the street. She had asked her mum what was going on, but Dolly wouldn't talk to her.

Amy no longer looked forward to her day or the pleasure of going to the pictures every Saturday with Gladys. Last week she had been so happy, but in a short few days everything had changed. And the upsetting thing was, she didn't know why.

She was barely inside Marshall's door when the foreman came up to her.

'The boss wants to see you, at once.'

She left her coat on a chair and hurried to the office. Perhaps he had another special job for her? The door was open so she knocked and waited for him to look up.

'You wanted to see me, sir?'

'Come in and shut the door.'

She did as ordered, not liking his sharp tone, and stood in front of his desk, trying to think if she had done something wrong. Nothing came to mind. She was very careful to work hard and do as she was told.

'I'm afraid we are going to have to let you go – as of now.'

'Pardon?' What was he talking about? Let her go where?

He muttered under his breath, clearly not liking this. 'I've had orders from the owner to sack you.'

She swayed with the shock, struggling to take in what he'd just told her. 'What have I done? I've been working hard and doing the special jobs for you. You said my sewing was good . . .' She stopped babbling when he lifted his hand to stop her.

'It hasn't got anything to do with your work. It's because of this.' He waved a newspaper at her. 'The man who was killed was a distant relative of the owner.'

'Killed?' The room seemed to be moving and she gripped the front of the desk to stop herself from falling over. 'What are you talking about? What has that got to do with me?'

'Oh, come on, you know what this is all about. Everyone does.'

'I don't. I don't!' Her frantic cry echoed around the small office.

He opened the newspaper and laid it in front of her. 'Look at the headline. "Convicted of murder and to hang".'

'Who? Who?' She was so confused by now that the words were just a muddle and tears began to trickle down her face. She moaned, 'I don't understand. I can't read it.'

When he swore under his breath she looked up, utterly bereft. She had lost her job and was now being accused of something – but she didn't know what it was.

The breath hissed through his teeth. 'My God, and no one's had the decency to tell you?'

She shook her head; not caring that she had blurted out that she couldn't read. Something terrible must have happened, but what could it have to do with her?

'I'm sorry.' His voice softened. 'If it was up to me I'd keep you, but I have to follow orders. Your father has been convicted of murder and sentenced to hang.'

Her legs gave way and she dropped to her knees, resting her chin on the desk. Her father was in Australia, wasn't he?

'Jim!' The boss called the foreman in. 'Give us a hand here.'

She was incapable of moving as the two men helped her to a chair.

'Bloody hell, Jim,' the boss exploded. 'She didn't know. She hasn't been able to read the news placards about the trial. I've just had to tell her we don't want her because her father's going to hang for killing someone the owner's related to. Where the hell is there any justice in that! How can this child be to blame and have to suffer?'

'She can't read?'

'No.'

'Hell, boss, she hid that well.'

'Yes, she's a bright kid, but what chance is she going to get round here with everyone knowing the victim?'

This conversation all sounded very far away to Amy as she sat hunched up, dry-eyed with shock. Now she understood why everyone had been giving her strange looks, and why her mother was refusing to go out. But she should have been told. It was cruel to leave her to find out like this. It was impossible to believe that her dad had done this terrible thing. And her mother wasn't strong . . .

Hauling herself up, she stood on shaking legs. She must get back to her mother.

'Easy now.' The boss steadied her, but she shook him off and reached out for the newspaper on his desk. This was only managed by holding on to the back of the chair. Once it was in her hand she let go of the chair and turned slowly to face the door, willing her legs to move.

The boss placed an envelope in her other hand. 'I've paid you up to the end of the week.'

Holding tightly to the newspaper and her wage packet she forced herself to take a step forward. Somehow, she managed to walk out of the office and across the factory floor to the front door. She was vaguely aware that work had stopped in the factory and everyone was watching her, but she kept her head up and concentrated on taking one step at a time.

'Well, don't just stand there gawping,' the boss thundered. 'Get back to bloody work or I'll sack the lot of you. I'm just in the mood to do it as well.'

Amy had just reached the door when someone put her coat around her shoulders.

'Don't forget this, it's cold outside. I'm sorry, Amy.'

Through the haze of pain she recognized Gladys's voice, but she didn't look at her or stop moving. If a friend couldn't stick by you in times of trouble, then they weren't worth bothering with.

After closing the door in the face of her so-called friend, she shuffled round until she was going in the right direction. One foot in front of the other, she told herself through gritted teeth. Just one foot in front of the other, that's all there was to walking.

It must have worked because the next thing she knew she was in the scullery, and had dropped like a stone into one of the chairs at the table.

Her mother was there and watched her daughter, hollow-eyed. 'You know and they've sacked you.'

Amy nodded and slapped the wage packet and newspaper on the table. 'You should have told me, Mum. It wasn't right to let me find out like this. It wasn't right.'

'I know, but I'm a coward, Amy, and was hoping they wouldn't find him guilty. Then it would have all blown over in no time.'

'But that didn't happen, and now we have to face this horror.' Amy refused to cry after seeing the state her mother was in. She looked absolutely terrible. 'Have you seen him?'

Her mother sobbed as if her heart would break. 'Yes, he's in Pentonville.'

'Did he do it?' Amy had to know.

'Yes, but he said the man was a thief and a bully. He was only defending himself. He wasn't going to lose all that money he'd made on this long trip. It would have bought a little house of our own.'

'Why's he going to hang then?'

'Because the judge and jury didn't believe him. No one came forward to speak up for your dad.' Dolly gripped her hands together tightly until the knuckles were white. 'We won't get any of the money. They said there was no proof that it belonged to your dad. It's being given to his wife and kids.'

A long sea trip all for nothing. Amy shook her head in disbelief. No wonder her father fought so hard. 'I'll go and see him.'

'No, no.' Her mother lifted a tear-stained face. 'He said he doesn't want to see either of us, because it will make the last week of his life even harder. He feels real bad, Amy. Says he's let us both down by losing his temper. It was a lot of money, but it wasn't worth hanging for.'

The following week dragged by for Amy and her mother. No neighbours came round to give them support or help. It appeared that they had all known the murdered man, and so had taken the killing personally; they were determined to ostracize the murderer's wife and daughter, even though they were innocent victims in this tragedy.

When Amy went out shopping for food she kept her head up and looked everyone straight in the eyes, defying them to say anything unpleasant to her. But it was only a façade, and once in the safety of her home the barrier crumbled.

The hanging was to take place early on the morning of 22 October. Amy and Dolly had hardly slept during the last week, and were sitting at the table by six o'clock that morning, watching the minutes pass. Amy felt as if her heart was being gripped tightly and she could hardly breathe. How desperately frightened her father must be feeling. She had never been close to him, but she felt deeply for him now. He shouldn't have to be facing this. Hanging was an abomination, in her opinion. She had always believed it was a terrible thing to do to someone, but she had never dreamt it would happen to anyone she knew, least of all her father. Supposing the truth came out about this other man later on? It would be too late then. Her father shouldn't have killed him, of course, but he didn't deserve to die by hanging.

They watched the clock, every second an agony. Amy held on to her mother as Dolly looked near to collapse. When the minute hand reached five past the appointed hour, her mother buried her head in her hands and rested them on the table. 'It's all over now.'

'That quick?' Amy whispered.

'It's done in a few seconds, so I'm told.'

Amy lifted her mother out of the chair and managed to get her into bed, then she returned to the scullery and curled up in the armchair and allowed her grief to surface.

After that her mother's health deteriorated quickly. It was as if she had given up; four days after the hanging, she died. Amy was on her own, and through the fear and grief she knew she was going to have to grow up fast.

Not being able to read properly was now a huge handicap as she struggled with arrangements for the funeral. She had to bury her pride and ask strangers to read things for her. Her mother had had a small insurance policy, which would cover the cost of a simple funeral. Then the tallyman called and wanted the outstanding balance paid in full. Amy was glad she had the money in her old teapot, and was grateful her mother had insisted she saved a little each week. Luckily she had put more than a shilling a week away when she could afford it, but after paying off the debt of eight shillings, she only had sixteen shillings left. That wasn't going to last her long, as the rent was six shillings a week. She was going to have to find another job, and fast.

For two days running she went to the Labour Exchange and stood patiently in line until her turn came, but they had nothing for her. So many people were looking for work, and she couldn't take anything that needed reading or writing, which severely restricted the jobs she could do. If she'd been a boy she could have done manual labour, like being a dustman or digging roads, but as a girl that was out of the question.

Returning home after another fruitless search, Amy found the rent collector waiting for her. She was surprised. 'But I've paid for this week.'

'I know, miss.' He cleared his throat. 'The thing is you're too young to stay here on your own. I'm to tell you that you have to leave by the end of next week.'

'Leave?' She gasped in horror. 'But where will I go? This is my home.'

'Sorry, but it isn't up to me.' He tipped his cap. 'I'll come by for the keys when your time's up.'

As he walked away cold fear gripped Amy. She hadn't believed things could get any worse, but they just had. Her mother's funeral was tomorrow. After that she had one more week. What was she going to do? She didn't have any relatives she knew of that she could go to, and no one round here would help. She and her mother had found that out as soon as her father had been arrested.

'Oh dear God,' she prayed desperately. 'Someone help me, please!'

# 7

He was being shaken roughly. Ben opened one eye and saw Howard standing beside the bed with a steaming bowl of something in his hand. 'Go away!'

'Can't do that.' Howard smirked. 'Your mother's been again.'

'Oh God, not more chicken soup?'

'Don't know what you've got against it.' His friend sat on the edge of the bed and began to eat with obvious enjoyment. 'Can't waste good food.'

Ben groaned and pulled the pillow over his face. This was the worst bout of influenza he'd ever had. It had laid him out for two weeks, and that was unheard of. It was unusual for him even to catch a cold.

'Your mother looked at you this morning, declared you were better and it was time you got up.' Howard scraped out the bowl and put it on the bedside table.

'She would.' Ben tossed the pillow aside and squinted at his tormentor. 'Even when I was a child she used to say that she couldn't feel whatever was wrong with me, so I was to stop making a fuss.'

'That's exactly what she said today.' Howard grinned in amusement, stood up and whipped off the blue knitted socks his friend was wearing. His feet were sticking out of the end of the bed as usual.

'Hey, my feet will get cold.'

'Why don't you get a bigger bed?'

'Can't afford it.' Ben tucked his feet up and stretched his arms above his head. 'I feel as weak as a kitten.'

'Some kitten!' A look of mischief crossed Howard's face as his hand shot out and dragged the covers off the bed. 'Have a bath and a shave. You'll feel better then.'

'That sounds like another of my mother's homilies.'

'Good guess. She was about to come up and drag you out of bed herself, but I managed to stall her.'

'Well, thanks for that anyway.' Ben opened both eyes just to test that the blinding headache had finally disappeared. It had, and he sighed with relief. Hauling himself upright he sat on the edge of the bed and waited for a moment, wondering if he should risk standing up. 'What time is it?'

'Ten in the morning. I'll get you some breakfast. What do you want?'

'Not chicken soup,' Ben said with feeling. 'What else have we got in the place?'

'Your mother brought along a basket of goodies this morning, saying you would be ravenous when you finally came to. There's sausages, eggs, bacon, things like that.'

'Did she?' Ben sat up straight. 'That was thoughtful of her. You can cook us both a huge fry-up. She's absolutely right; I am starving.'

'Your mother's a treasure, Ben. I don't think you appreciate her enough.'

'Oh, I do.' He gave a wry smile. 'I just don't show it, and she'd be horrified if I gushed all over her. And talking of appreciation, Howard, thanks for looking after me. I don't know what I'd have done without you.'

'Think nothing of it.' Howard slapped him on the back, nearly knocking him off the bed. 'That's what friends are for, and I've had plenty of help from your mother and our landlady. But we're all damned relieved to see you without that fever. Worried us half to death, I can tell you.'

Ben watched his friend wander out, humming happily to himself, then he gritted his teeth and set about cleaning himself up. It was an effort, but he had to admit that he did feel better after a bath and shave. His stomach growled in anticipation as he walked into the kitchen they shared and saw Howard busy with the frying pan.

'How many eggs do you want?' Howard asked, not taking his eyes off the sizzling bacon.

'How many have we got?'

'A dozen.'

'I'll have three then.' He eased himself into a chair, reminding himself to thank his mother as soon as he could. There was a pile of newspapers on the chair next to him, so he reached for them.

'Leave those until you've eaten.' Howard picked them up and tossed them on to the windowsill. 'I've kept all the back numbers for you, but if you read them now you won't enjoy your breakfast.'

'Why?' Ben frowned, then forgot about everything as Howard put a plate piled high in front of him.

'You'll feel stronger once you get that inside you.'

He nodded in agreement and began to eat, savouring every mouthful. It was wonderful. He had thought at one time that he would never want to eat again. Howard was no cook, but a simple fry-up was not beyond his capabilities.

There was silence while they cleared their plates, mopping up the grease with slices of bread.

Ben sat back and sighed. 'Lord, but I was hungry. How long is it since I've had solid food?'

'All you've had is hot lemon, gallons of water and soup for the last fortnight.'

'No wonder I was hungry.' Tipping his chair back on two legs he reached out for the papers. 'Now I've got to catch up on what's been going on in the outside world. Is that trial over yet?'

Howard nodded. 'Over, found guilty, and hanged.'

'What?' Ben's chair thumped back on all four legs again. 'That was bloody fast! Why didn't you tell me?'

'Ben, you had a fever and were delirious for a while. When you began to come out of that your mother threatened me with instant destruction if I so much as breathed a word about it to you.'

'Bad as that, was I?'

'Worse.' Howard eyed his friend and grimaced. 'It frightened the life out of me. Don't do it again.'

'No fear.' Ben glanced around. 'I see my mother has had a tidy-up as well. Where's my coat?'

'What do you want that for?'

Ben struggled to his feet. 'I'm going to see if I can find Amy. She might need help.'

'Oh, come on, Ben, you can hardly stand up, let alone go traipsing around in the rain.' Howard looked alarmed. 'Give yourself a couple of days to get your strength back.'

The room began to go out of focus, and Ben grabbed hold of the chair to steady himself.

'For heaven's sake, sit down!' Howard pushed him back into a sitting position. 'I can't drive, and you certainly won't be able to in that state.'

'Perhaps you're right.' Ben reluctantly took his friend's advice. 'I'll go and find her tomorrow.'

The next morning Ben did feel stronger, so after they'd finished off the rest of the eggs and a couple of slices of bread, he considered he was fit enough to go out.

His friend wasn't so sure as he watched Ben lace up his shoes. 'Why don't you leave it another day? And what are you going to do if you do find her? You've only met her once, Ben.'

He stood up and shrugged into his coat. 'I just want to make sure she's all right. And you're right, I have only met her once, but I've painted her twice, and feel as if I know her. I'm worried, Howard. Humour me, eh?'

Muttering under his breath, Howard grabbed his own coat.

'You don't have to come if you've got things to do.'

'You've only just got out of your sick bed, and if you think I'm letting you wander around on your own so soon, then you're very much mistaken.' Howard followed him to the door.

Their landlady was in the hall and glared at them. 'You're never going out, are you? You've hardly got over that terrible fever.'

Ben playfully gave her a quick peck on the cheek. 'I'm perfectly fit again, Mrs Dalton, but it's sweet of you to worry about me.'

She wasn't able to hide the smile. 'I see the old charm is back. All right then, but I hope you're well wrapped up. There's a nasty wind out there and it's drizzling.'

'I've got my vest on,' he teased, 'and two pullovers.'

The landlady turned to Howard. 'You're the sensible one here; don't let him stay out too long. He might look like a big strong boy, but that was a nasty bout of influenza he had.'

'We'll be back within the hour.' Howard crossed his heart, knowing he was probably lying. Once Ben set his mind to something it was near impossible to stop him.

'You be sure you are.' She walked away, shaking her head

and muttering, 'They haven't got the sense they were born with.'

'Sometimes,' Ben said as he started the car, 'I feel as if I've gained another mother.'

'Don't complain.' Howard grimaced as they shot round a corner and had to brake suddenly because a van was coming the other way on the wrong side of the road.

Completely unruffled, Ben lowered his window, said something uncomplimentary, and continued as if nothing had happened. He gave Howard a sideways glance. 'You were saying?'

'I said don't complain if our landlady treats us like sons because she always lets us off when we can't pay the rent on time.'

'Oh, I'm not. I was just stating a fact.'

'Like you did to that van driver?' Howard snorted. 'One day someone's going to punch you on the nose.'

'You think so?' Ben's grin showed he was amused at the thought.

'Not everyone's going to run when you stand up and tower over them, Ben. You should have been a boxer, not an artist.'

'Not likely! A mild-tempered man like me standing in a ring and letting someone try to knock him senseless?'

Howard roared with laughter. 'I don't know how you can delude yourself like that. Anyone upsets you at their peril.'

All that produced was a deep chuckle.

'Anyway, providing we get to Wapping in one piece, what are you going to do if you find the girl?'

'You've already asked me that. I'm just going to check that she's all right.'

*

67

They parked the car at the bottom of Farthing Street and walked up the road. The houses were all the same: two floors, a basement and no front gardens. Ben hunched his broad shoulders as the cold wind hit him. He wasn't sure he was up to this, but for some reason he couldn't fathom, he just had to see her again. He was probably wasting his time, but at least he would feel easier after seeing her.

A woman was just coming out of a door and he stopped her. 'Excuse me, but could you tell us where Amy Carter lives?'

'Number twenty-three, but you won't find her in.' She didn't seem too pleased about being stopped. 'It's her mother's funeral today. She'll be up at St Joseph's.'

'Where is that?' Ben was shocked at the news. The poor little devil had lost her mother as well!

'Turn right at the top of the road, then keep straight on. It's about a ten-minute walk from here.' With a look that said he'd wasted enough of her time, she stalked off.

'Not very friendly.' Howard ran a hand through his wind-blown hair. 'Wonder if the kid's got any other family?'

'That's what we're going to find out.' Ben's long legs began to eat up the ground as he headed for the church.

Howard caught him up. 'Hold on, Ben, we've got no business going to the church. Let's wait in the car until she comes back.'

His suggestion was ignored, so he said no more. He could tell from his friend's grim expression that he was very concerned. By now Howard was more than a little curious to find out what was so special about this young girl.

It took them less than ten minutes, and a quick glance in the church showed it to be empty. They walked round the side and met the vicar. Howard stopped him when he looked as if he was going to hurry past them. 'We're looking for the Carter funeral.'

'You're too late; it's all over. The daughter is just saying her last private goodbye.' The vicar sighed deeply. 'I don't suppose she'll mind if you go to the graveside though. No one else bothered to turn up. It makes you wonder what happened to Christian compassion.'

'Where is the grave?' Ben was looking around the church-yard as he spoke.

'It's round the back. Did you know Mrs Carter then?'

'No.' Ben shook his head. 'I know her daughter.'

'Ah, well, young man' – the vicar looked up at Ben, sympathy showing on his lined face – 'see what you can do for her. She won't talk to me, but I think she's in real difficulty.'

Ben practically ran round the side of the church, then stopped suddenly, looking at the small figure of Amy stand-ing by the open grave, her head bowed. There was only one simple bunch of flowers on the ground.

'Oh, Ben.' Howard spoke softly, not bothering to hide the emotion in his voice. 'This isn't right.'

'No, it isn't.'

They walked quickly to the graveside and Ben's heart ached when he saw Amy's face. She didn't look at all like the smiling girl he had sketched with such enthusiasm. Her eyes were red and swollen, and with the acute perception of an artist he read her expression. There were myriad emotions showing on her expressive face: sorrow, anger, and the thing that took his breath away – hopelessness.

'Amy.' He touched her arm. 'I'm so sorry.'

She started in surprise, glancing up at him without recognition.

'Don't you remember me? We met by the river and I gave you a drawing.'

'What are you doing here?'

'We heard the news and have come to see if you are all right.' Howard gave her his clean handkerchief, as the one she had in her hand was a sodden ball. 'My name's Howard and I'm Ben's friend. Let's take you home. It's cold and we need to get you out of this rain.'

'Home?' Her face crumpled and she suddenly began to sob in great wrenching cries that shook her body. She was ashamed of herself, but it had all been too much for her and the dam burst. 'I haven't got a home. They're turning me out at the end of next week. How could they do that?'

Ben tried to hold her, to give her some comfort, but she pushed him away, her swimming eyes now blazing.

'Go away! You don't know me. What do you care what happens to me?'

'We do care. That's why we're here.' Ben didn't try to touch her again; instead he took a step back, giving her space. This poor girl was at the end of her tether. 'Have you got somewhere to go?'

She gestured to the empty graveside in derision. 'Does it look like it? No one came. What happened to all those *friends* who were only too happy to join her in the pub? Where are they? Can you tell me that?'

'Ben.' Howard stood beside him, speaking softly. 'We can't leave her like this. Mrs Dalton's got a spare room.'

'I was thinking the same thing.' Ben was blazing angry now. 'How could something like this happen? She's only a kid.'

Amy heard and turned on them. 'Stop whispering about me. I've had to put up with that all my life. And I'm not a kid. I'm fifteen soon.'

'Sorry.' Ben held up his hand in apology. 'Will you let us help you?'

'Why should you?' She frowned, puzzled.

70

'Because you need help and it's obvious that we're the only people around. We might be able to get you a room in the house we live in. We know our landlady's got a spare room.'

'You must be joking!' The tears had dried now and she was bristling with defiance. 'No one's going to take me in. I'm the daughter of a murderer – or didn't you know that?'

'Yes, we do.' Howard's tone was coaxing. 'But what your father did doesn't change who you are.'

'How do you know?'

'Because I've seen the paintings Ben's done of you. My friend has a way of seeing into the character and even soul of a person. They are beautiful, Amy.'

She sniffed and blew her nose. 'Your landlady won't give me a room. When my dad was condemned, we were sentenced with him. All our so-called friends disappeared as fast as they could. My mother couldn't take it. She wasn't strong and she just gave up.' Her voice broke.

'But you're going to be strong, aren't you?'

Ben watched with relief as her shoulders straightened slightly and her head lifted. 'I haven't got any money.'

'Neither have we.' Ben gave her an encouraging smile. 'Our landlady's very understanding. Why don't you come back with us and meet her?'

She shrugged, gave one last sad look at her mother's grave and turned away. 'All right.'

# 8

This was hopeless, but what other choice did she have? She just had to make it on her own. If she didn't then the welfare would get hold of her and she'd end up in a home or something worse. They had already been round asking her lots of questions. She'd lied and told them she had a job and could look after herself. She could just picture what her life would be like in an institution once they found out she couldn't read or write properly. Everyone would gang up on her, tell her she was thick, and she wasn't going through that again. Not that she really knew anything about such places, of course, but they were bound to be awful. If these two were daft enough to believe their landlady would give her a room, then let them try.

'This way, Amy. My car's at the bottom of your road.'

She looked up at the tall man she had met by the river. Car? She thought they didn't have any money?

As if he'd read her mind, he said, 'It was a present from my parents.'

Now his family had money! The little spark of hope his offer had kindled began to go out. It would be sensible to be careful, since it looked as if they were telling her a pack of lies. Well, she'd see this place they lived in, and if the 'kindly' landlady didn't exist she'd run like hell. Her mother had often warned her about the sort of men who liked young girls, but she was desperate enough to take a risk. She'd be daft not to find out if this was a genuine offer of help. Goodness knows she needed it.

She eyed them cautiously as they walked towards the car. They were both big and strong-looking. The one she'd met at the river was the tallest, but not by much, only about four inches, she thought. They both seemed kind, and she hoped her summing-up was correct, or she could find herself in a lot of trouble. She nearly laughed out loud at that thought. She had nothing but trouble!

When they reached the car, Ben opened the door. 'Here, sit in the front with me. Howard can get in the back.'

Her courage suddenly disappeared and, frightened, she hesitated. 'I'll walk. Tell me where this place is.'

'Amy, you can't walk there. We live in Chelsea.'

Oh dear, that was a long way, and much too far to go on foot.

Howard gave her an understanding smile. 'We only want to help. We wouldn't harm you in any way.'

She studied the expression in his brown eyes and felt he was telling the truth. There was a gentleness about him that made her feel ashamed of not trusting him. Taking a deep, steadying breath, she slid into the car. She had a shilling in her pocket, so if this didn't turn out well, she could get back here all right.

While they drove along she sat tense and silent. This was a stupid thing to do, she kept telling herself, and her mum would be furious if she knew. She looked down at her clasped hands as the tears gathered once again. But her mum wasn't here any more, and somehow she was going to have to look after herself. And she was terrified of being put in a home – the mere thought of it made her shudder in horror.

Soon the docks were behind them and they were driving along an elegant street. It was a new world to Amy, and despite her anxiety about being with these men, she couldn't help admiring the houses. They looked so big, with steps leading up to the front doors, and brass letterboxes gleaming on beautifully painted wood. They were all different colours. She liked nice colours. On some steps there were stone tubs holding plants. She thought that was lovely. Absorbed in the scene she forgot her fear, but only for a moment. It came rushing back when they stopped outside an even larger house. She gasped. It was a palace!

'Here we are.' Ben got out of the car and came round to open her door.

She stood on the pavement and stared in wonder. She would never be able to afford rent in a place as grand as this.

Howard joined them. 'Come in and meet our landlady.'

She shook her head as the tears of disappointment threatened to spill over. Somewhere deep inside she had still been hoping this would be the answer to her prayers, but it wasn't. It was hopeless. Her shoulders slumped. 'You shouldn't have brought me here. I haven't got a job or enough money for a place like this. Tell me where the bus stop is, please.'

'Don't go.' Ben blocked her way as she appeared ready to run. 'Let's talk to our landlady, Mrs Dalton. If she can't take you in then I promise we'll find you somewhere else.'

'Give it a try.' Howard's voice was quiet and coaxing. 'Where are you going to stay if you don't let us help?'

When she looked up at him her eyes were full of terror and the words tumbled out. 'If I can't look after myself they'll put me in a home. A woman came to see me when Mum died, and they've sent me a letter.'

'What did it say?' Ben asked.

'I haven't opened it, but they're going to put me in a home. I just know it!' She was shaking with a mixture of cold and fear.

Howard was frowning fiercely. 'You'd better read it.'

'I don't want to.' She fished in her pocket and held out the letter to him. Her intention had been to ask the vicar to read it for her, but she had forgotten all about it. 'You read it if you want to.'

He looked puzzled that she should let him read a private letter, but he slit open the envelope and pulled it out.

Ben looked over Howard's shoulder. 'It's just to say that someone will be coming to talk to you in a few days to assess your situation. Nothing has been decided, Amy. Come inside and we'll talk this over with Mrs Dalton.'

They were still standing on the pavement, but fortunately the rain had stopped and the sun had come out, making it feel a little warmer.

Howard took her arm. 'Come on, Amy, we'll get this sorted out.'

Thoroughly bemused by now, she allowed them to lead her into the house. The inside was every bit as lovely as the outside. There were coloured glass windows either side of the front door, casting pretty patterns on the tiled floor as the sun glanced through them. All around the edge of the ceiling were carved flowers – roses – and they were picked out in gold. A staircase ran up from the middle of the hall where the wood had been polished so highly you could almost see your face in it. But for all its grandeur, there was a homely feel to the place. Amy had always been sensitive to atmosphere.

'Ah, there you are at last. You've been out for two hours.' Mrs Dalton studied Ben carefully and tutted in disapproval before turning her attention to Amy. 'And who is this?'

'Erm . . . I'm Amy.' She edged closer to Ben, just to be on the safe side. At first impression the landlady was a stern-looking woman and didn't look too pleased about something. In her early fifties, she had light-brown hair without a trace of grey yet, and piercing light-blue eyes. She was well built, but not fat.

'Amy needs help.' Howard eased Amy forward. 'She's had a rough time, so we've brought her to you.'

'I see.' She looked thoughtful, and then smiled, transforming her face and demeanour from stern to kindly. 'You'd better all come into the kitchen. I'll make us a pot of tea and you can tell me about it.'

The kitchen was enormous. Amy turned in a circle, taking everything in. There were shelves everywhere, holding plates, pots and all manner of cooking implements. A most delicious smell filled the room and she spied a large cake cooling on a rack, along with two pies. She gave a delicate sniff – apples. They were apple pies.

'Sit down.' Mrs Dalton put a kettle on the stove and laid out cups and plates. 'I think the cake will be cool enough to cut now.'

Sitting down as ordered, Amy folded her hands in her lap, quite speechless. At the start of the day she'd had to face the sorrow of her mother's funeral, alone and frightened. And now she was here, in this beautiful house, being given tea and cake. It was unbelievable.

The tea was soon made. Mrs Dalton poured them all a cup and cut large slices from the cake, handing one to each of them. Amy's mouth fairly watered. Her piece was as big as the slices the others had. She didn't attempt to eat until she saw Howard wink at her and take a big bite.

'Now, Benjamin.' Mrs Dalton stirred her tea. 'Tell me why Amy needs our help?'

Amy chewed as she listened to Ben telling the story. He didn't leave anything out, and when he told the landlady about her father, she swallowed hard. Now she would be sent away.

By the time Ben had finished talking, Mrs Dalton was shaking her head. 'That's a sad story. We had better see what we can do for you, my dear. Now show me this letter you've received.'

Hope flared in Amy at those words. She handed over the envelope. She had prayed for help. Were her prayers about to be answered?

Mrs Dalton stood up. 'I've got a room on this floor I think will do you very nicely, Amy. There is a bathroom next door and a kitchen down the end of the hall which you will share with Mr Ted Andrews, but he won't be much trouble because he eats out a lot of the time.'

Amy couldn't wait to see the room, ignoring for the moment the fact that she knew she couldn't afford it.

They all trooped along behind Mrs Dalton until she stopped halfway down a long passage and opened a door.

'This is the room. It's pleasant and I think you'll like it.' The landlady smiled and stepped aside to let the eager girl go in.

It was wonderful. There was a single bed with a dark red eiderdown on it, and curtains of the same shade with small cream flowers along the bottom. It also held a wardrobe, dressing table and an armchair over by the window. It was all so lovely Amy couldn't help rushing to look out of the window.

'Oh, Mrs Dalton,' she cried in delight, 'you've got a garden with trees and flowers.' Craning her neck to get a better view, she pointed in excitement. 'There's a tabby cat in the garden. Is he yours?'

'That's Oscar.' The landlady's smile was full of amusement. 'He thinks he owns me, not the other way around. Cats are funny creatures like that.'

Amy giggled, and the sound surprised her. She hadn't laughed for what seemed a very long time.

'Do you like the room?'

'Yes, Mrs Dalton, it's beautiful.' She nodded, giving Ben and Howard a sad glance, serious once again. 'Er . . . how much is the rent? Only I haven't got a job or much money.'

'We'll discuss the rent when you've found work. Let's take one step at a time, my dear. The room is yours if you want it.'

Amy was flabbergasted. 'But . . . but you must tell me how much, please.'

'Very well. The rent will be two and six a week. When you can afford it.'

'Two and six?' Amy had to sit down in shock. Even she knew that was ridiculously cheap. The armchair was very comfortable.

While she was struggling to find her voice, the cat sauntered in, tail in the air, took one look at her and leapt on to her lap. His paws kneaded her skirt until he was satisfied, then he sat down looking smug.

Ben laughed. 'Oh, you've made a conquest there, Amy. Oscar's very choosy about whom he sits on.'

Her hand came out and began to stroke the soft fur until a loud purr vibrated through his warm body. This couldn't be real. She must be dreaming and would wake up soon to find herself alone and homeless again. But if it was a dream she hoped she never woke up. She looked at the three people in the room and could almost see wings on them. They were turning out to be guardian angels.

'Why don't you move in right away?' Howard tickled the cat behind the ear, making the animal squirm in ecstasy. 'We'll take you back to collect your things.'

She looked up and saw them all smiling in encouragement. This wasn't a dream. It was really happening!

'That's a capital idea,' Mrs Dalton agreed. 'If you've got

any small pieces of furniture you'd like to bring, there will be room for them. Your china and things like that can go in the kitchen. I shall expect you to look after yourself like the boys do.'

'I will. I won't be any trouble, Mrs Dalton. You won't know I'm here.'

'Oh, I don't need you to be that quiet.' The landlady patted her shoulder. 'I like to hear people around. That's why I let out most of this great rambling house. I couldn't bear to live here alone after my husband died four years ago.'

'I'm sorry.' Amy knew all about the heartache of losing someone: she'd lost two parents in such a short space of time.

'It's all in the past now.' Mrs Dalton spoke briskly. 'Now, there's just one more thing to deal with. The Council must be informed of your new address. Would you like me to deal with them for you?'

'Oh, yes please, Mrs Dalton.' Panic raced through Amy. 'They won't stop me living here, will they?'

'I doubt that very much. You leave everything with me.'

'Now that's settled, let's go and collect your things, Amy.' Ben pushed himself away from the wall he had been leaning on.

'Oh no you don't, young man.' Mrs Dalton glared at him. 'You've done enough today. Your mother will never forgive me if you have a relapse. You're going back to bed.'

'Are you ill?' Amy was alarmed, but now she looked at him carefully she could see he was very pale and had deep shadows under his eyes.

'I'm fine.'

'No you're not, Benjamin. Do as you're told or I shall be very cross.'

A look of mock horror crossed his face. 'I can't risk that, Mrs Dalton.'

'And you'd better not. Now.' She turned her attention back to Amy. 'Ted Andrews closes his shop at lunchtime on Wednesdays. He's got a van and I'm sure he'll help move your things.'

'That's a good idea. We'll get more in the van than Ben's small car.' Howard smirked at his friend. 'We'll get Ben safely tucked up in bed, then I'll give Ted a hand.'

Amy was still concerned about Ben being ill. 'What's been wrong with you?'

'A nasty bout of influenza, but I'm over it now.'

'Don't you believe it, Amy.' Howard made a show of testing his friend's temperature by placing his hand on Ben's forehead, only to have it pushed irritably away. 'He got out of a sick bed to find you.'

'Oh, don't exaggerate, Howard. I got out of bed because I was tired of doing nothing.'

'And now you're going back for a couple of hours. You can't rush these things. One step at a time, remember.' Mrs Dalton smiled at Amy. 'You look comfortable there, so why don't you rest until Ted comes home?'

Amy nodded, completely exhausted. As she watched them leave her room, the words ran through her mind in awe. *Her room!*

The cat on her lap sighed and tucked his head under his paws and, comforted by the warm animal sleeping contentedly, Amy drifted into the first real sleep she'd had since her father had been convicted of murder.

'I'm glad you brought her here.' Mrs Dalton ushered the boys back into her kitchen. 'That poor little girl has had a lot of bad things to deal with in her young life.'

Ben's expression was grim. 'To have her father tried and hanged for murder must have been like living a nightmare.'

The letter Amy had received was still on the table and Howard picked it up. 'What can we do about this?'

'You can leave that with me.' Mrs Dalton took it out of his hand. 'They'll have to be told she's moved, and they'll probably be only too pleased to know she has a home and someone to look out for her. I'll go and see them tomorrow.'

'Thanks, Mrs Dalton, that's very kind of you. We knew you'd be the right person to bring her to for help.' Ben leant on the table and sighed deeply.

'You go and rest, Benjamin, before you collapse again. We'll look after Amy.'

He didn't argue. The events of the morning had taken more out of him than he'd realized.

# 9

The cat jumping off her lap woke Amy up. She looked around, startled by her strange surroundings, and as every-thing came tumbling back she gave a little sob of relief. At the funeral she had been in utter despair, then someone she had only met once came to her and took charge. Now, unbelievably, she was with people who seemed to care what happened to her. Who would have thought a chance meeting by the river would have led to this? But how glad she was that it had.

There was a knock on the door and Mrs Dalton came in with a man. He was probably in his sixties; slightly crumpled in appearance, with grey thinning hair and a slight stoop.

'Amy, this is Ted Andrews and he's offered to help you move your things.'

She scrambled to her feet. 'Thank you, Mr Andrews.'

He smiled then, making deep crinkles at the corners of his pale blue eyes. She liked him instantly.

'Shall we go then? Howard's already in the van.' He moved aside to allow Oscar to scurry from the room and chuckled. 'That cat doesn't like men, so he'll be delighted to have another woman living here.'

'He's been asleep on my lap.' Amy brushed down her skirt, feeling shy. These were all strangers; she couldn't believe how kind they were being to her.

'Off you go then.' Mrs Dalton hustled them out. 'We want to see Amy nicely settled by teatime. Bring everything you need, and any food you have. Don't want it to go bad, because you won't be going back there.'

Howard was leaning on a dilapidated black van when they got outside. The three of them managed to squeeze in the front, and after a bit of coughing and shuddering it started and they were on their way.

'Er . . . is Ben all right?' She was still concerned that he had been ill and had not yet completely recovered.

'He'll be fine in a couple of days.' Howard grinned. 'He's sprawled out on his bed fast asleep at the moment.'

A rumble of amusement came from Ted. 'And there's plenty of him to sprawl, but he's a tough boy and it won't take him long to get his strength back.'

'You're right, Ted, but he gave us all a scare. How's business?' Howard changed the subject. 'Has it picked up at all?'

'Not much, but with so many out of work I've been able to pick up some good books. I give them a fair price, which is more than the pawnbrokers do.'

Books? Amy listened with great interest; she couldn't contain her curiosity. 'Do you sell books?'

'That's right. I've got a small shop in Chelsea selling second-hand books.' He cast her a quick smile. 'It's just a hobby really, but it keeps me active. I'm retired, but I like to have something to do.'

'Ted used to be an English teacher,' Howard explained.

'Oh.' Her eyes opened wide and she looked at the man driving with renewed interest. He must be really brainy.

'Do you like books, Amy?' Ted changed gear after a lot of resistance from the engine.

She nodded and looked down at her hands. She loved books, the feel of them and the special smell of bindings and printed paper, and she yearned to know what was inside them. As ever, the humiliation of *not* knowing washed over her.

Ted seemed to know where he was going and they stopped right outside the house she had lived in all her life. Now she knew she was leaving it, she wasn't the slightest bit sorry. The place didn't hold many happy memories.

Once inside, Howard looked in the rooms. 'What do you want to take, Amy?'

She pursed her lips in thought. 'There's a small table in my mother's room, and I'll have one of the kitchen chairs. They can go by the window in my room, but apart from a few personal items and crockery, I don't need anything else.'

'What are you going to do with the rest?' Howard began taking things out of the larder and putting them in a basket.

'I don't know.' Everything had happened so fast Amy hadn't thought that far ahead.

'Well, I'll buy that chest of drawers off you.' Ted ran his hands over it. 'That's a nice piece of oak. It'll do fine in the shop to keep my papers in. How much do you want for it?'

She stared at him, not having the faintest idea what such a thing would cost. 'I don't know. You have it if you want it.'

'No, I must pay you for it, Amy, you can't afford to give things away.' He pulled out his wallet. 'How about a pound?'

'A pound . . . ?' She was lost for words. It was hard to believe that anyone would want her old furniture. She nodded quickly. That money would pay for her room for a while, giving her time to find a job. 'That's plenty.'

He handed her a pound note and she put it in the old brown teapot, clutching it to her.

'You've got a few quite nice pieces here.' Ted continued to prowl the room. 'Tell you what, I've got a friend who runs a second-hand furniture shop near mine. Would you like me to bring him here tomorrow? I'll make sure he gives you a fair price for the stuff.'

'Oh, yes please. I've paid the rent until the end of this week. Then I've got another week to get out.'

'Right, let's get this loaded up.' Ted paused as he pulled out one of the drawers of the unit he'd just bought. 'My goodness, these are very good.'

He was holding her grandmother's drawings and Amy stood beside him as he looked through the sheets.

'My gran did those. She was very clever.'

'I'll say she was. Did your grandmother do them for you when you were a little girl?'

'She was trying to teach me to read.' Amy avoided giving her age, not wanting to admit that she had been about ten, by which time it had become obvious that she wasn't able to read.

'You've looked after them well.' Ted took something else from the drawer. 'Ah, Ben's work.'

Amy nodded, relieved the subject had been changed. 'He gave me that.'

Ted slapped his forehead with the palm of his hand. 'Of course, that's where I've seen you before. Ben's painted you sitting beside the river in the same spot as this.'

'I met him there one day when he was drawing.'

'Now I understand. All Mrs Dalton told me was that she had taken in a young girl who needed our help. I didn't immediately connect you with the girl Ben told me about.' His look was one of compassion. 'That turned out to be a lucky day for you, didn't it?'

'Yes.' Amy whispered as the horror of what might have happened to her if she hadn't met Ben swamped her for a moment. 'I don't know what I would have done if Ben and Howard hadn't come looking for me.'

'You'll be all right now.' Ted patted her arm in a fatherly fashion. 'Mrs Dalton's a kind woman, and she'll look after you.'

It was a comforting thought and made Amy's eyes mist over.

'Have you got everything you need, Amy?' Howard had come back after loading things into the van.

'I think so.' Wandering through each room she checked that she had collected together all the small personal things like brushes, mirrors and little jars from her mother's dressing table. There were family photographs in a biscuit tin, so she took those as well. She wouldn't be able to bring herself to look at them now, after what had happened to her father, but perhaps one day she would, when the loss of both parents didn't hurt so much.

Closing the front door she put the key in her pocket and turned to walk to the van.

She stopped in mid-stride as she saw the neighbours had come out to see what was going on.

It was Mrs Preston who came up to her. 'Where are you going, Amy?'

How dare they! All the hurt and fury came to the surface as she faced these callous people. 'It's none of your business! And what do you care – what do any of you care?' She glared at them, shaking with anger. 'You abandoned us when we needed you the most. My mother died a broken woman and not one of you had the decency to help us or show kindness.'

'We all knew Andy,' one woman muttered.

Amy spun to face her. 'Yes, you all knew him, but you've made him into a saint in your minds. You've all forgotten what a nasty, vicious piece of work he was. What my father did was wrong and he's paid for it, but you had no right to condemn us as well. We did nothing wrong!'

Howard and Ted were standing either side of her, but they didn't interfere. There was just a quiet mutter of encouragement from Howard. 'Atta girl! You tell them, Amy.'

Her legs were shaking so much that it was hard to walk, but Ted placed a hand under her arm as support. She had never in her life exploded like that but, heavens, she felt a whole lot better. Never again was she going to allow people to put her down. She was as good as anyone else, and better than these narrow-minded people.

Howard helped her into the van, holding her shaking hands as they drove away. She grimaced. 'Sorry about that, but it made me so mad when they pretended to be concerned where I was going.'

'It needed to be said.' Ted nodded. 'I was proud to stand beside you.'

'Me too.' Howard squeezed her hand. 'You shamed them.'

Amy fell silent, absorbing their comments. Someone was proud of her. It was a new experience for her.

Ben was waiting for them when they arrived back, and Amy had recovered her composure by the time they pulled up outside the house – her home from now on.

'You can leave the chest of drawers in the van. That's going to the shop tomorrow.' Ted hauled the kitchen chair out and carried it up the steps.

'You go and make us all a nice cup of tea.' Howard winked at her. 'And leave us to unload everything for you.'

Amy made a large pot of tea and then trotted back and forwards from her room to the kitchen, putting everything neatly away. The men drank their tea as they worked. The table and chair fitted perfectly by the window, a clock and a couple of vases went on the mantelpiece, along with the old brown teapot holding her money. She smiled at the scene. It was a lovely room and looked ever more like home now it had some familiar pieces around. Oscar watched the activity with a disapproving air from the comfort of the armchair.

'That looks a treat.' Mrs Dalton nodded her approval. 'Have you got any food, my dear?'

'Yes, Mrs Dalton.' Amy dived into the old pot and pulled out five shillings. 'I can pay you two weeks rent in advance. Will that be enough? I can manage more because Mr Andrews bought a piece of furniture off me.'

The landlady waved it away. 'Pay me at the end of each week, just as everyone else does. I'll make you out a proper rent book.'

She put the money back, comforted to know that she would be able to pay her way. And if she sold the rest of the furniture tomorrow, that would keep her going for a while.

Seeing that she was settled, everyone went back to their own part of the house, and Amy made for the kitchen she was to use. She was starving now after that burst of rage. Her stock of food was meagre but it was enough for tonight and breakfast. She'd go shopping tomorrow.

After heating up the contents of a tin of soup, she made some cheese sandwiches and a pot of tea. Loading it all on her tray she took it back to her room and sat at the table where she could see the garden. She must ask Mrs Dalton if she could go out there and look at the plants sometime.

Oscar had been following her around and kept rubbing against her legs, looking up with imploring eyes. She laughed, poured some milk in her saucer and gave it to him. It was lapped up with gusto, and then, having got what he wanted, he trotted to the door and demanded to be let out.

She enjoyed every mouthful of her tea and, after washing

her dishes and putting them away, she returned to her room to practise her reading and writing before going to bed. This was her nightly routine and she was even more determined to get the hang of it somehow or other.

This wasn't right. Ben studied the portrait of Amy through narrowed eyes. Now he'd seen her again he knew why he hadn't been completely happy with it. He jumped slightly as Howard came and stood beside him. 'I didn't hear you come in.'

'From the look on your face I'd say you don't like what you see.'

Ben positioned Howard right in front of the painting. 'Take a good close look. The eyes are too small and they are more of a smoky green, aren't they?'

'I don't agree, Ben. She was upset and has been crying a lot. That would have made them seem a slightly different colour, but they do need to be larger, I think.'

'You could be right.' Ben rubbed his chin thoughtfully. 'I'll give her a couple of days to settle down and then ask her to sit for me. I knew there was something wrong with it, but I just couldn't pin it down.'

'There's also something else you've missed.' Howard perched on the stool and gave a wry smile. 'She looks too timid in this.'

Ben frowned. 'Well, she is.'

'From what I saw today there's a determined girl with an inner core of fire.' Howard then told Ben about her confrontation with the neighbours.

'Good Lord, I wish I'd seen that.' Ben began to study his painting with fresh eyes. 'Yes, fire, that's what's missing.'

'You'll be able to study her carefully now she's living here. I'm glad you insisted on finding her today, and I'm beginning to see what intrigued you so much about her. Once seen, never forgotten, eh?'

'That's right.' Ben threw a sheet over the picture. 'Mrs Dalton will look after her now.'

'She will, and we're all damned lucky to be living here. I reckon Mrs Dalton only lets out rooms so she can have people in the house. She doesn't seem to be interested in the money side of it.'

'I suspect that her husband left her quite well off.' Ben raised his eyebrows. 'She just wants to mother us, except for Ted, of course.'

Howard chuckled. 'She wants a mature man around in case we get out of hand.'

'No doubt, but did you notice how Ted was treating Amy with so much kindness? I would say she's going to find a replacement mother and father here.'

'She needs something like that.' Howard nudged his friend's arm. 'And we could be her brothers.'

Ben nodded, still serious. 'She's going to need looking out for as she's still only a child really. I don't know what kind of a life she had before this double tragedy overtook her, but she doesn't seem to have anyone, not even friends she could have gone to.'

'You're right, and I'm glad we were able to help.' Howard shook his head sadly. 'Poor little devil.'

'We'll keep an eye on her. Coming out for a pint?' Ben stood up straight and stretched.

'Do you feel well enough?' Howard eyed his friend doubt-fully. 'And have you got any money?'

'Yes, to both questions.'

# 10

The bed was lovely and comfortable, and Amy so exhausted after the trauma and grief of the last couple of weeks that she slept soundly right through the night. The chirping of the birds woke her up at seven-thirty, and she listened with a smile on her face. That was pretty. Her gaze swept around the room, and even in the half-light it was charming. She still couldn't believe this was real.

But it was! Yesterday morning she had lost everything: mother, father and home. She had been drowning. Then by an incredible stroke of good luck she had been thrown a lifeline, which she had grabbed in desperation. It was now up to her to show how grateful she was by making a new life for herself and not giving these kind people any cause to worry about her.

Jumping out of bed she collected her soap and towel, then headed for the bathroom. It all looked very grand to her, with gleaming white porcelain and wallpaper covered with little forget-me-nots.

After washing and dressing she cleaned everything until it was once again as spotless as she had found it. Then she went to the kitchen to toast the last of her bread and make a pot of tea.

She was just wiping the sink and draining board down when Mr Andrews came in.

'My goodness, Amy, you're about early. The two boys never drag themselves out of bed until around ten o'clock.'

'Good morning, Mr Andrews.' She smiled shyly. 'I'm usually up earlier than this, but I slept on.'

'I expect you were tired out.' He smiled when she nodded. 'What are you going to do today?'

'Er . . . well, I must get some shopping and then see if I can find a job.'

'Would you come to my shop around lunchtime? It's in the King's Road. We'll take my friend to see if he wants your furniture.'

'Of course. Do you think he will?' She didn't think it would be worth much, as they hadn't had anything of value, but it would be nice to get the rooms cleared out, and a few extra shillings would be welcome.

'Bound to.' He grinned. 'Jake can sell anything.'

'Thank you ever so much, Mr Andrews.'

'It's no trouble, and call me Ted, everyone does.' He took a frying pan out of a cupboard and put some sausages in it when the fat was hot. 'Have you had your breakfast?'

'Yes, I had some toast.'

He gave her a horrified glance. 'That's no good for a growing girl. Sit yourself down and I'll cook you something.'

She watched him put bacon and eggs with the sausages and her mouth fairly watered. It smelt delicious.

When he put the plate in front of her, she said, 'I'll buy the eggs and things today and you can use them tomorrow.'

'You don't have to do that.' His eyes crinkled at the corners as he gave a smile. 'I'm delighted to be sharing my breakfast with you.'

She swallowed a piece of sausage and shook her head. 'You must let me repay you. You've all been so kind and I don't want to be a burden to you. I can look after myself.'

'I'm sure you can, and I can't imagine you being a burden to anyone.'

That remark made her dip her head and concentrate on her plate, not wanting him to see the sadness in her eyes as she remembered. As soon as it had become obvious that she wasn't going to be able to read or write, she had seen what a burden that was for her parents. They had been disappointed in her; not able to understand why their only child was so dumb. Well, she wasn't going to let that happen here. Determination filled her, making her lift her head.

When the plates were empty, Amy stood up and began clearing the table. 'I'll wash up. You get off to your shop.'

'That's a fair swap for breakfast.' Ted grinned and got to his feet. 'I'll see you around lunchtime then, Amy.'

'I'll be there, and thank you, I really enjoyed the food.'

He left with a wave and she set about washing up. Then she went back to her room, made the bed and tidied up. She must buy some polish and dusters while she was out. Putting money in her purse, she was ready to start her day.

'Morning, my dear.' Mrs Dalton met her in the hall. 'Did you sleep well?'

'Oh yes, the bed was lovely and comfortable.'

'Good, now here's your front-door key.'

'Thank you. Could you tell me where the nearest shops are?'

'Go out of the door, turn left and you'll find a corner shop at the end of the road. They sell just about everything.'

Amy was about to walk to the door when she stopped and turned. 'Mrs Dalton, I was wondering if it would be all right if I went into the garden now and again, just to look at the plants. I won't touch anything.'

'Of course you can, Amy, we all use it. You'll find a clothes line out there and a basket of pegs so you can dry your washing when you do it.'

'Oh, that's lovely. I was wondering what to do about my washing.'

'There's also a small sitting room on the next floor for all my tenants to use. There's a wireless and gramophone there for you as well. You are not restricted to your room.' She smiled. 'Anything else?'

When Amy shook her head, the landlady went up the stairs. She was going to love it here, Amy thought as she hurried out of the door.

It was only fifteen minutes' walk to the shops, and Amy bought everything she needed. She'd been quite extravagant, just this once, because she had to return the food Ted had given her, and she had bought a few tins as a standby as well.

Returning to the house she put everything away in the larder. As if by magic Oscar appeared and began his act of asking her to take pity on him, which she did, of course, by giving him a saucer of milk.

After licking the dish clean, he flicked his tail and stalked off.

'I'm not going to make a habit of this,' she called after him.

He didn't bother to look round. The only indication he gave that he'd heard her was another flick of his tail as he disappeared, no doubt heading for the garden.

As she still had plenty of time before meeting Ted, she decided to see where the washing line was. She found it halfway down tied between two trees. There were all sorts of plants she had never seen before. Not many flowers, of course, they were all finished, but she could just imagine how beautiful it would be in the summer.

To her surprise the garden was much bigger than it looked from her window. There was a high hedge at what she had thought was the end of the garden, but there was a wooden gate and a large area behind it. In it was a very peculiar brick structure, all blackened as if it had been burnt. She touched it cautiously, but it was cold.

'I wouldn't advise you to do that when I've fired it up.'

She jumped and spun round, hand over her heart. 'Oh, Howard, you frightened the life out of me. What's it for?'

'It's a kiln. I make vases and dishes to earn a bit of money, and I need to fire – that means bake – them in there before I decorate them. There's some in there now and I've come to get them out.'

'Could I see?' There was eagerness in her voice.

'Sure.' He began to remove bricks from the front to reveal an opening. 'This is a bit crude, but it works all right.'

Peering over his shoulder to see what he was doing, she gasped in delight when he pulled out a tray with six vases on it. Crouching down beside him she took the one he was holding out to her. 'What do you do with this now?'

'I paint them different colours.'

'Do you put flowers and patterns on them?' She was completely fascinated.

He shook his head, laughing. 'I'm a sculptor, not a painter.'

She turned the pot round and round in her hands. 'This would look lovely in dark blue with yellow and orange flowers round the middle.'

'That sounds too ambitious for me, but why don't you have a go?'

'Could I?' Her eyes opened wide in excitement. 'Oh, but I might spoil it.'

'That's all right. Look at this.' He showed her a crack at the base. 'That happens sometimes in the firing, so I'll have to scrap it. You could practise on this one.'

95

'I'd love to, but I can't do it now because I've got to meet Ted at his shop soon.'

'Come to my workshop any time, Amy. I'm in the basement.'

'Thank you, I'd love to. Now, can you tell me how to get to the King's Road?'

'I'll take you, Amy, I'm going that way.'

They both jumped at the sound of Ben's voice.

'I don't know how anyone with feet as big as yours can move so quietly,' Howard muttered, after nearly dropping the pot he was holding.

Standing with hands in pockets and grinning, Ben looked as if he'd never had a day's illness in his life. 'That's the result of my mother yelling at me for years to be quiet. What time are you meeting Ted?'

'He said about lunchtime.'

He glanced at his watch. 'It's nearly twelve now, so we'd better get going.'

Amy handed the pot back to Howard and stood up. 'Thank you for showing me this.'

'My pleasure, and don't forget you're going to paint one for me.'

'I won't.' She had to trot to catch up with Ben, and they were soon on their way.

'Are you feeling better today?' She studied his face. He looked more like the person she'd met at the river, but she was still concerned about him.

'I'm fine. Don't take any notice of Howard and Mrs Dalton. They fuss too much.' He shrugged his shoulders, dismissing their concerns.

Ah, Amy thought, a smile tugging at the corners of her wide mouth. He wasn't an easy patient, and she could just imagine the trouble they must have had with him. 'They only fuss because they care.'

'I know.' He grimaced. 'I'm not used to being ill.'

She changed the subject. 'What are you going to the King's Road for?'

'More paints.' He pulled up outside the bookshop and turned to face her. 'Amy, would you come and sit for me sometime? I've painted you from my sketches, but the portrait isn't right.'

'Well, yes, you tell me when you want to do it.' She got out of the car, waving as he drove away. She felt a surge of wonder. Howard wanted her to paint one of his pots and Ben had asked her to his studio. It was all very exciting!

Ted was busy with a customer when she went in, so she wandered around looking at the shelves packed with books of every shape and size. The usual empty feeling inside her was there again. So many books, so many words, and all denied her. If only—

'You're early, Amy.' Ted had finished serving.

'Ben gave me a lift.' She hoped she'd wiped the pain from her face as she turned.

'I don't close until one o'clock for lunch. Let's go in the back and have a cup of tea.'

She went behind the counter and followed him into a room with a rickety table, two chairs, and a small gas stove and sink. The rest of the space was crowded with books, piled up in every available space.

'My goodness,' she exclaimed, 'you've got nearly as many books in here as out in the shop.'

'I've just bought those and haven't had time to sort them yet.' He cleared a chair so she could sit down. 'Do you take sugar?'

'One please.'

He made the tea, gave her a mug and sat in the other chair. 'Jake will be here soon and then we'll see what he'll offer for your things.' Ted rummaged under a pile of papers and found a small tin. 'Want a biscuit?'

'Please.' As she spoke someone came into the shop and Ted went to see what they wanted.

Amy finished her tea, but only took one biscuit from the tin because she thought it would be rude to take more.

'Jake's here, Amy.' Ted looked into the room. 'We're going in his van. It's larger than mine.'

The van was big enough to take all her furniture, including the beds. Jake was about Ted's age, but whereas Ted was fairly tall and slim, Jake was short and rotund, with a cheery smile.

'Let's go and see what you've got, young lady.'

It wasn't easy to get up the high step into the van, so Jake lifted her in, and from the ease with which he did it, it was obvious he was very strong.

'That's Jimmy, by the way.' Jake pointed to someone in the back.

Amy swivelled round and saw a young boy, not much older than herself. He was sitting on a pile of old carpets and grinned shyly at her.

Ted directed him to Farthing Street, and once inside number twenty-three, it didn't take Jake long to examine everything, with Jimmy trailing after him.

'Hmm, tell you what, I'll clear the place out for you and give you . . .' He was muttering and doing calculations in his head. 'Seeing as you're a friend of Ted's I'll give you three quid.'

'Five. It's worth that, Jake. There's a couple of good pieces here.' Ted spoke sternly to his friend.

'I've got to make a profit.' He looked scandalized. 'But seeing as it's you, I'll make it four, and not a penny more.'

Amy watched the two men haggling and pulled a face at Jimmy, making him giggle.

'What do you think, Amy?' Ted gave her a sly wink. 'Will you take four pounds?'

She nodded dumbly. That was a fortune to her.

'Done!' Jake peeled the notes from a bunch he had wrapped in an elastic band, and gave them to her. 'Right, Jimmy, let's get this lot shifted.'

The boy leapt into action and Ted grinned, pulling her out of the way of the men intent on their work. 'That money will tide you over until you find a job.'

'It will last me for ages.' She smiled gratefully. 'Thank you very much. I would never have managed this on my own.'

'It was a pleasure. Now tell me what kind of a job you're looking for?'

'Anything.'

'That should make it easier to find something then.' Ted ushered her back outside and up into the van.

When they started off the van was crammed to the roof and there was no sign of Jimmy. Amy guessed he must be wedged in with all the furniture.

On their way Jake stopped so Amy could give the keys to the rent collector and tell him the place was empty.

It was with a great sense of relief that she got back in the van. She wouldn't have to go back there again. That part of her life was over.

## 11

Although she now had plenty of money in the old teapot, Amy was still determined to get a job as quickly as possible. She had to show she could look after herself, not only to reassure Mrs Dalton and everyone else, but to prove to herself that she could make her own way in life, despite the handicap of not being able to read properly.

She was up early and insisted on cooking Ted his breakfast with the food she had bought the day before. He told her where she could find the Labour Exchange, and, after washing the dishes and making sure everything was clean and tidy, she headed for the bus stop.

The Labour Exchange was in a street just off the King's Road, and the place was crowded. Her chances of getting a job didn't look too hopeful and she decided that whatever they offered, she would take, and worry later how she was going to cope.

When her turn came the man behind the desk looked her up and down. Before he had a chance to speak, she said, 'I'll take anything. I'm not fussy.'

He shuffled through some cards and picked one of them. 'This has just come in. Hammond's shoe shop along the road needs a junior to train as sales assistant. Go along right away and you might be lucky.'

'Thanks.' She was immediately on her feet, took the slip of paper from him and shot out of the door, anxious to get there before anyone else. How hard could it be to sell shoes?

The shop was only five minutes' walk away and the sign

clear enough for her to decipher. The manager saw her at once.

'Have you had any experience of shop work?' He examined her carefully, but she knew she was clean and tidy.

'No, sir, but I'll soon learn. And I'm a hard worker.'

'Very well, come into my office. I'll take your details and you can start next week.'

She followed him in trepidation, praying that this wouldn't involve any writing. But she needn't have worried because he just asked questions about her age, where she lived and things like that. He wrote them down himself. There was an anxious moment when she said her name was Carter and he stopped writing, looking up at her questioningly. Holding her breath she kept a smile on her face. Her father's trial and hanging were still fresh in people's minds, but if he said anything she would deny it. Carter was quite a common name.

But much to her relief he just returned to writing it down without saying a word. Her address was a good one in Chelsea so there was no reason for anyone to connect her with Wapping.

'Your hours will be nine to six, an hour for lunch and a half-day on Wednesdays. The pay will be ten and sixpence to start with, rising to twelve shillings if you are suitable. You can start on Monday and will be on a month's trial.'

'Thank you, sir.'

Amy left the shop almost skipping with happiness. She was sure she could smile at the customers and sell shoes. That wouldn't need any writing!

She was so proud of getting a job that quickly; she was bursting to tell someone her good news. A quick glance in Ted's shop showed him busy and laughing with a group of customers. She didn't like to interrupt him so she caught the bus home. It was amazing how quickly she had accepted the new house as home, but she had.

When she arrived there didn't appear to be anyone around. Howard had told her she could go to his workroom to paint that pot, and she made her way down to the basement. She hesitated outside a door and listened. She could hear tapping coming from the room, so she knocked gently and waited.

'If that's Oscar scratching at the door, go away. If it's anyone else, come in.'

Turning the handle she pushed the door half open and looked in. 'It's only me, Howard, are you busy?'

'Hi, Amy.' He was holding a hammer and chisel in his hands and was covered in dust from the large piece of stone he was working on.

In fact the whole room was a mess and Amy's tidy mind wanted to sort it out at once. There was dust and clay everywhere. The floor was littered with stone chippings and pots in various stages of creation.

'Make some tea, Amy, would you?' He ran a hand over his head, leaving streaks of dust like grey hairs. 'I'm gasping.'

There was a sink in the corner of the room and a gas ring. It didn't take her long, but the cups had to be rinsed out thoroughly to remove the dust before she poured tea for them both.

'Ah, bless you, you're a lifesaver.' He gulped the tea and held the cup out for a refill before she had even taken a sip of her own. She poured him another one and stared at the thing he was working on.

'What do you think?' He swept over the figure with a soft brush, then stood back to study it critically. 'It's not quite finished yet.'

'I can see that.' Amy thought it was the most beautiful

thing she had ever seen, but . . . She wasn't too sure what to say. 'Er . . . it's lovely, but she hasn't got any clothes on.'

Howard grinned at her. 'Are you shocked?'

'No, no, of course not.' She wasn't going to admit that, and although she knew she had led a sheltered life, she had seen statues of naked women before. She had never thought that a man had carved them, that was all. Silly of her. 'How do you decide how to make them stand, the length of legs, and things like that?'

'That's easy, I work from photographs.' Howard showed her a photograph of a young girl standing just like his statue. 'Models pose for us when we need them.'

Her mouth dropped open as she studied the picture. 'Do you mean girls do this for you?'

'Yes, and they make a decent living out of modelling.'

Now she *was* shocked. 'They get paid for taking off their clothes?'

Howard began to laugh at her scandalized expression. 'Amy, it's quite normal for artists to employ models like this.'

'Does Ben paint them as well?' This was taking a bit of believing.

'Of course.'

'Well, I never!' There was a lot more to this art business than she had imagined. She had to clamp down on a giggle of amusement as she pictured Ben and Howard working with naked models.

'We don't think anything of it.' His lips twitched. 'It's just like the life classes we had at university.'

'You drew naked girls at school?'

'Oh, Amy.' Howard doubled over with laughter. 'You ought to see your face. We had naked male models as well.'

'*Never!*'

That was too much for Howard and he roared. His laughter was so infectious that she couldn't help doing the same. This was a very different world from the one she had grown up in. She couldn't wait to find out more.

The door opened and Ben strode in. 'What are you two up to? I could hear your shrieks all the way up the stairs.'

Amy mopped her eyes and tried to compose herself while Howard explained, making Ben chuckle. It was a deep throaty sound she found appealing.

'It's quite true,' Ben told her, his eyes glinting with amusement. 'I'll show you some of my sketches sometime. There's nothing offensive in them. Just look at Howard's sculpture. Don't you think that's good?'

'It's beautiful. I just didn't realize girls earned money by taking off their clothes and posing naked.' She didn't miss the amused look that passed between the friends. They must think her very innocent – which she was, of course – but they were opening up a completely new world for her, and she felt she could talk to them. 'I knew there were women who did . . . er . . . other things. I saw them round the docks.'

'You mean prostitutes.' Ben seemed totally unperturbed by the subject, examining the teapot to see if there was anything in it. 'This is quite different, Amy, we only deal with professional models, when we can afford them, which isn't often. It's just the same as me painting you.'

She stared at him in alarm, remembering that he'd asked her to come up to his studio and *sit* for him. 'I'm not taking my clothes off!'

'I'm only painting your face, Amy. I don't want to be distracted from that by the rest of you.' He winked at Howard. 'Though when you're a couple of years older we might ask.'

From their expressions it was obvious that they were joking, so she smiled and picked up the kettle to make more tea. 'I'll still say no!'

'There's a challenge, Ben.'

'And one I won't forget.' Ben emptied the dregs from the teapot in the sink. 'Are you making more tea?'

'Looks like it.' She waved the kettle at him. It was delightful, laughing and joking together like this. It brought home to her just how lonely her life had been up to now. The two men were so different. Ben was the more serious; there was an air of strength and reliability about him. He was such a powerful-looking man that in truth she felt a little shy around him. The impression she had gained from the moment she'd met Howard was one of gentleness and she felt she could say anything to him without worrying about it. There was one thing they had in common though; they cared about other people. Witness how they had looked after her and brought her to this lovely house and safety, although Ben had only met her once, and Howard not at all. She would always be grateful to them for rescuing her. The fact that her father had been hanged for murder didn't seem to matter at all to them.

After making the tea, she poured them all a cup and sat on a stool, her eyes shining. Now she could tell them both her good news. 'I got a job today and I start next week.'

'Well done, Amy.' Ben leant down and kissed her cheek. 'That was quick. What are you going to do?'

'Junior assistant in a shoe shop.' She sipped her tea and smiled over the rim of her cup.

'That's wonderful!' Howard smirked at his friend. 'Hey, Ben, at least one of us will be earning some money. Mrs Dalton will be pleased!'

It was only then Amy spotted the vase Howard had said

she could paint some flowers on. 'Can I have a go at this?' she asked eagerly.

'Of course, I've left everything there for you. Sit at the bench and I'll show you how to use the paints.'

For the next hour Amy was lost in the new interest of painting. She didn't worry about being too careful, because she knew the pot was only going to be thrown away. Ben and Howard were talking quietly in the background, but she ignored them, tongue between her teeth as she concentrated.

Gradually she became aware of silence and looked up to find both of them watching her intently. 'This is terrible.'

Before she had a chance to pick up the pot and throw it into the bin holding broken pieces, Howard caught her hand.

'Whoa, don't touch. What do you think, Ben?'

'Primitive but striking. A touch of Clarice Cliff about it.'

'Exactly!' Howard lined up more vases in front of her. 'When you've got time, Amy, come down here and do more just like that.'

'Why?' She frowned, glancing from one to the other. 'And who's this Clarice something?'

'She's a ceramic designer, growing in popularity.' Ben studied the vase, lips pursed. 'This is good. Have you done any painting before?'

'No, but I do love nice colours.'

'Ah, there you all are.' The landlady came into the work-room. 'Amy, there's someone here to see you.'

'Me?' Her heart did an uncomfortable jump. Who would come to see her here?

'Now, don't you worry.' Mrs Dalton smiled. 'I went and told the Council that you were now living with me, as we'd agreed, and they've sent a man to talk to you, that's all. They're just checking that everything is respectable and in order.'

That wasn't a bit reassuring and Amy leapt to her feet. 'I'm not going in a home! I'm not. I can look after myself. Don't let them take me away from here, please.'

'Shush.' Ben and Howard were by her side at once. 'No one's going to do that.' Ben's mouth was set in a determined line. 'We won't let them.'

She was shaking in panic by now and Howard was holding her hands, talking quietly, in his soothing way.

'You're not a child. They can't make you do anything you don't want to, and you have a good home here. They won't take you away.'

'Now, my dear, don't take on so. I've told them that I will look after you until you are eighteen. They just want to check that you are happy with the arrangement.'

'I am. I am.'

Mrs Dalton took her arm. 'Let's go and talk to the man and get this over with then, shall we?'

Amy followed her into the sitting room where a severe-looking man was waiting for them.

'Ah, there you are at last.' He glanced at the papers in his hand. 'I see you have agreed to be Miss Carter's guardian, Mrs Dalton.'

'That is correct.'

He turned his attention to Amy. 'Are you happy to live here?'

'Yes, sir.' She nodded vigorously. 'I've got a lovely room and a job.'

'And what is this job?'

'Junior assistant in a shoe shop in the King's Road.' Amy was so relieved she had this piece of information to give him.

'That's respectable enough. Now show me your room.'

She hurried along the corridor and opened her door,

allowing him to enter first. It was hard to breathe as she watched him examine the room, even to checking that the bed linen was clean.

'Do you share with anyone?'

'No, sir, it's all mine.'

'Do you like Mrs Dalton?'

'Yes, she's very kind.' When he concentrated on making notes, Amy couldn't stand the uncertainty any longer. 'Please don't make me leave here, sir. I want to stay. I start my job next week and everyone's very kind to me. They don't care that my dad was hanged.' She was close to tears and hated pleading, but it filled her with horror to think she might have to leave here. 'I want to stay.' Those few words came out in a whisper.

He looked at her then and smiled. 'I can see that, Miss Carter. You've had a difficult time just lately and I see no reason to move you. Mrs Dalton is a respectable woman of some means, and is prepared to take responsibility for you. But if you have any problems in the future you are to come and tell us. Is that understood?'

'Yes, sir.' She sagged against the door in relief.

He nodded and walked out of the room and back to Mrs Dalton, who had remained in the sitting room, allowing Amy to be interviewed on her own.

How she made her legs move was a mystery to Amy. She had been so frightened: she had heard such tales about children being taken into care.

'That all seems to be in order, Mrs Dalton. If you'll just sign these papers, I'll be on my way.'

It was soon done, and Amy waited while Mrs Dalton saw the man out. When she returned she couldn't keep the tears of gratitude at bay and they ran down her cheeks like a flood. She hadn't come from a demonstrative family, so she stifled her desire to throw her arms around Mrs Dalton and sob out her thanks.

Wiping her hand over her wet cheeks, she said, 'I don't know how to thank you. I'll never be any trouble to you, I promise.'

'I know that, my dear.' Then Mrs Dalton put her arms around Amy and kissed her cheek. 'There, it's all over now, you're safe here, and I always did want a daughter. I was never blessed with children.'

This outward show of affection was strange to Amy, but it was so comforting.

There was a sharp knock at the door, and it opened slowly as Ben and Howard looked in.

'We heard him leave.' Ben stepped inside the room, quickly followed by Howard. 'What happened?'

'Amy can stay with us.' Mrs Dalton gave the boys a stern look. 'This is now my new daughter, so you'll mind your manners and treat her with respect.'

'Mrs Dalton, you're a gem.' Ben lifted his landlady off her feet and spun her round.

'Put me down, you fool.' But she was laughing as her feet touched the floor again and Howard hugged her as well.

Amy then received the same treatment from them.

'This is wonderful! Now we've got a sister, Howard.'

And as Amy looked at the smiling faces around her, she felt as if she was in heaven.

# I 2

After a quiet weekend settling in, and still hugging her happiness to her, Amy set off for her first day in the shoe shop.

As soon as she arrived the manager, Mr Broad, introduced her to the two senior assistants, Mrs Green and Mrs Jones. Her first job was to make them all tea, and this was something she did cheerfully, speaking only when spoken to.

They had no sooner finished their tea when the customers began to arrive.

It was a busy shop and Amy enjoyed the bustle of people coming and going. For the first two hours she just watched the assistants, listening to what they said to customers, but it soon became obvious that it wasn't going to be as easy as she had first thought. When a customer asked for a certain shoe they had to go into the back of the shop where there were shelves lined with boxes. The style and size were written on the outside of the box and you had to find the right one. There was worse to come though. Once the customer had bought the shoe, the assistant had to write out the sales slip showing the type of shoe and the price.

During the morning her happiness dissolved and the usual frustration took its place as she tried to hide her disability. As she was new it was easy to claim that she didn't know where everything was kept when another assistant asked her to get a shoe from the back. But she wouldn't be able to get away with this for very long.

The manager, who had been watching her carefully, came

up to her at the midday break. 'You can serve customers this afternoon, but I'll work with you for a while just to see that you do the job properly. You must make the customer feel that they are the only person you are interested in, be helpful and smile. Now take your break.'

'Yes, sir.'

She left the shop, walking blindly, not bothering to notice where she was going. What was she going to do? The two other women assistants hadn't had time to say much to her, and anyway, she was too young for them to want to bother with. She'd been told their names, but as with so many things, it had slipped right out of her mind. And with the manager looking over her shoulder all the time she would never get away with it. The words and numbers would be a jumble once she was nervous. He would spot her trouble at once!

Without realizing she had walked in that direction, she found herself outside Ted's shop. A quick glance inside showed it to be empty of customers.

When the bell tinged over the door, Ted came out from behind a high bookshelf. 'Hello, Amy, on your lunch break, are you?'

All she could manage was a nod. She shouldn't have come in here. What did she think she was doing? There was only one thing she could do, and that was not go back to the shop. It would be too humiliating if they discovered she couldn't read properly. And they would! But that would be a coward's way out and she would only have to face the same problems in another job – even if she could get one. Jobs were hard to come by, and she'd been incredibly lucky to get this with so much unemployment around. It was absolutely essential that she be able to look after herself. She mustn't give in at the first sign of difficulty, for this was something she was always going to have to face. As much as it pained her, she just didn't see how she was ever going to be able to read much better than she could now. Somehow she had to find a way around the problem, but coming in here had been a mistake. She couldn't ask Ted to help her – she just couldn't. She would be so ashamed.

Turning to walk out again, Ted caught her arm. 'Wait! You look upset. What's the matter?'

'Nothing.' She shrugged. 'Working in the shop is not as easy as I thought it was going to be, but I like it.'

'Good. I'll close the shop and we can have a cup of tea together.' Ted didn't give her a chance to refuse as he put the 'closed' sign on the door. 'Have you got your sandwiches with you, or have you already had something to eat?'

'They're in my bag.' She wasn't sure she could manage to eat anything, but allowed Ted to lead her into the back of the shop. It would be rude to walk away when he was being so kind.

He set about making a pot of tea, and then sat at the small table with her. 'I know you're pretending to be all right, but you have a very expressive face and I can see something is bothering you.'

She dipped her head, feeling helpless. 'No one can help. I've tried so hard, but it's no good. Everyone says I'm stupid.' Her mouth thinned in frustration. 'I'm not. Why can't I do it?'

'Do what, Amy?' Ted spoke gently, seeing how upset she was.

Realizing what she had nearly done, she sat up straight and smiled brightly. 'Oh, it's nothing. I found the work a bit confusing, but I'll soon get used to it. I didn't know there were so many different styles of shoes. And out the back they've got a big room absolutely packed with boxes.'

She was babbling, but she didn't care. She had nearly told him she couldn't read. The only place she hadn't been able to hide the fact had been at school, but she wasn't ever going to let anyone know again. She would work out some way to manage at the shop, just as she had at the factory. 'Everything's fine.'

'All right, Amy.' His smile was wry. 'If you don't want to talk about it, let's have tea and eat our sandwiches.'

Relieved she hadn't blurted out her secret, she took the sandwiches out of her bag, opened the packet and held them out to him. 'I've only got bread and jam, but would you like one?'

'I would, thank you.' He took one and they began to talk about all sorts of things.

Gradually she found herself relaxing in his company, enjoying the stories about some of his more eccentric customers, which made her laugh.

When it was time to go back to the shop, she didn't feel so agitated. If she kept calm everything would be all right. She hurried up the road, determined to do well in the afternoon.

But when she saw the manager waiting for her, her confidence seeped away and she knew she was going to have to be very clever to stop them finding out.

As she was the junior assistant she couldn't serve a customer until the other two senior assistants were busy. She watched every move they made, following them when they went round the back to get shoes from stock. Every bill was scrutinized with great care as it was made out, and she was pleased to see that there wasn't much to put on the slip; as long as she got the price right, they might not notice her spelling mistakes.

It was the middle of the afternoon before they were busy

enough for her to have a customer of her own. It was an elderly woman who reminded her of her gran, and she went up to her all smiles, copying what the other assistants did.

'Can I help you, madam?'

'I'd like a pair of black lace-ups.' She sat down heavily and sighed. 'My bunion's killing me in these. They're too tight.'

'Let me have a look.' Amy felt completely at ease with this customer, even though she knew the manager was watching her closely.

Removing the right shoe she ran her fingers over the woman's foot, feeling the distortion near the big toe, exactly the same as her granny had had. She had always worn a slightly larger shoe to give her more room. 'You need something in very soft leather so it doesn't press too much.'

'That sounds good.' The woman smiled at her. 'Can you find me something?'

'I'm sure I can. What size do you take?'

'A five.'

'Why not try a half-size larger just to see if that feels better?'

'Worth a go, I suppose.'

With another smile, Amy went to the stockroom. She had seen something this morning. Now where was it?

The manager was right behind her and she struggled to keep calm. If she didn't then she would never get through this. She looked up at him. 'What do you think would suit the customer, sir?'

'What size did she want?'

'Five, sir.'

'And you suggested a half-size larger, didn't you?' He pulled out a box. 'This is a five and a half.'

'Thank you, sir.' Now she had the shoes she needed to

find out the price. She deliberately turned the box label away from her as if searching for the price. 'I hope these aren't too expensive.'

'They are eight and sixpence.' The manager turned the box round for her to see.

After pretending to read it, she smiled confidently. 'Ah, that's right. Madam might be able to afford these.'

He nodded. 'Let's see if you can sell those to her.'

Amy went back into the shop. 'I'm sorry to have kept you waiting, madam. Try these and see if they are more comfortable, and if not we'll find you something else.' She had been listening to the other two assistants' sales patter and copied them with ease.

The shoes fitted perfectly and when the woman walked up and down, she smiled in relief. 'Oh, these feel wonderful. That extra half-size was a good idea of yours.'

'My grandmother had the same problem and she used to wear a slightly larger size.'

'Ah, well, you know what you're talking about.' The woman sat down again. 'I'm glad you served me. Now, how much are they?'

'Eight and sixpence, madam.' She had been saying the amount over and over in her head so she didn't forget it. 'They are of the softest leather and will last you a long time if you keep them polished.'

'Quite right. You are a sensible girl.' The customer looked at the manager who was still hovering in case Amy made a mistake and lost the sale. 'Good girl you've got here, and such a lovely smile.'

He bowed slightly. 'I am pleased you are satisfied with the service, madam.'

'Indeed I am.' She handed Amy her old shoes. 'Wrap these up for me, dear. I'll wear the new ones.'

Amy put them in the box, her heart pounding. Now all she had to do was write out the sales slip. All!

She wrote very carefully, knowing it would be fatal to rush. It looked all right when she'd finished but she was careful not to let the manager see, then she took a pound note from the customer and went to the pay desk.

Much to her relief the cashier didn't question the bill and Amy hurried back with the customer's change.

She was shaking by the time the woman left the shop. Had she got away with it?

'That was a good sale, Miss Carter, and you had a pleasant way with the customer. Keep that up and you will do well here.'

'Thank you, sir.'

He left then, and when she had another customer an hour later, he was nowhere to be seen. Luckily, one of the other assistants was in the back and Amy pleaded ignorance of the system and the shoes were found for her. She made another sale and was relieved to have survived so far.

There was a tap on the studio door and Ted walked in. 'Am I disturbing you, Ben?'

'No, I've just finished for the day.' He wiped his hands with a cloth dipped in turps.

'That's good.' Ted studied the landscape and grinned when Ben pulled a face. 'Are you ever satisfied with your work?'

'If I ever get to that point I'll stop trying to improve.'

'Hmm, Howard's the same, I think. I swear he throws those pots across the room sometimes.'

'He does.' Ben began cleaning his brushes. 'How's business?'

'Ticking over.' Ted sat on the stool. 'Amy came to see me today in her break, and she was in a terrible state.'

'Oh?' Ben stopped what he was doing. 'Wasn't the job at the shop going well?'

'I don't know. She seemed on the point of telling me something, and then changed her mind. The smile she gave me as she offered me one of her jam sandwiches was very forced.' Ted shook his head. 'Something was worrying her, I'd bet my shop on it.'

Ben opened his pad at the sketches of Amy he had done by the river. 'I felt there was worry and frustration in her eyes when I met her.'

Ted examined the pictures. 'A secret, that's what you've captured. I had the strong feeling today that she's hiding something she doesn't want anyone to know about.'

Ben whistled through his teeth. 'That's very observant of you. I felt there was something, but I haven't been able to pin it down, and that's why I haven't finished the portrait. It just isn't right.'

'She's a strange little thing, with so much going on behind her eyes,' Ted mused. 'I wish I'd been able to get her to talk to me.'

'Perhaps someone at the shop knew about her father.'

'Maybe, and perhaps I'm just imagining things.' Ted rubbed his chin. 'That business with her father can't be easy for her. I'm sure she doesn't want anyone to find out about that.'

'I agree, but we can't force her to confide in us. When she knows us better she might talk more freely.'

'You're right, Ben. When she went back to work she was bright enough, so I expect I was making something out of nothing.' Ted pulled a face and changed the subject. 'Have you seen those drawings her grandmother did for her when she was teaching her to read?'

'No, are they good?'

'Yes, there was real talent there. She's drawn the alphabet with a picture underneath for each letter. It would make a terrific children's book.'

'Are you thinking of doing something along those lines?' Ben knew that the love of Ted's life was books.

'That's a tempting idea, but much too expensive to produce with all those pictures. Pity though, because they are excellent.'

'I'll ask her to let me have a look at them. Perhaps Amy has inherited some of the talent?' Ben leant against the bench. 'She's an intriguing girl, isn't she? I'm just dying to get her to sit for me, so I can study her properly.'

Nodding, Ted walked over to the portrait, standing in front of it with his head on one side. 'I think you've captured her very well.'

'Do you think so?' Ben joined him and shook his head. 'No, it isn't right. I've a feeling there's a lot more to her than I've shown.'

Ted laughed. 'You're a perfectionist, Ben. The picture is beautiful.'

'Perhaps, but it can be better. Now she's living here I think I'll start all over again.'

'I think you just like painting her, Ben.'

'I do, it's a real challenge. I was captivated by her unusual face as soon as I saw her.' Ben's smile was wry. 'Perhaps one day I'll do a painting worthy of her. I can't wait to see what she looks like in three or four years' time.'

'I don't think she'll ever be what is classed a beauty.' Ted looked up at Ben, a question in his eyes. 'What do you think?'

'You're right, but she has something much more enduring than beauty.'

'Ah, the artist's eye. I'm going to get myself something to eat now.' Ted lifted his hand in a wave and left the studio.

Ben stayed where he was, studying the sketches through narrowed eyes. Yes, he'd start all over again as soon as he could get her up here. And if she stayed in the house he would do a sketch for every year of her life and see how much she changed as the years went by. That thought filled him with the kind of enthusiasm he'd felt when he had first met her sitting alone by the river with a dreamy expression on her face. He had wondered then what she had been thinking, and he was even more intrigued by her now. He was looking forward to delving below the surface and finding out what she was really like. And there was a great deal to find out, he was absolutely sure of that fact.

## 13

The buses were crowded and Amy had to let two go before she managed to squeeze on one. It was nearly seven when she reached home, where she made straight for the kitchen.

Ted was there. 'Hello Amy, how did you get on this afternoon?'

'I sold two pairs of shoes,' she told him proudly, 'and the manager told me I was good with the customers.'

He gave a quiet smile. 'That's good. Would you like a cup of tea?'

She nodded. 'I'm gasping and I must get something to eat as well. All I've had were those jam sandwiches.'

'That will never do. You must eat because you're already too thin.'

'Oh, I've always been skinny.' She dismissed Ted's concerns and opened the larder. 'I'll cook us both something for tea. Now, what have we got? Hmm, what about scrambled eggs on toast?'

'That'll do nicely.'

Amy spun round just as Ben and Howard sat at the table with expectant expressions on their faces.

'Are you boys cadging again?' Mrs Dalton swept in carrying a bowl full of eggs and holding them out for Amy. 'Here, it looks as if you're going to need these, but don't let them take advantage of you, Amy, they're quite capable of getting their own food.'

There were at least a dozen eggs in the bowl and Amy

took them gratefully. If she was going to feed the four of them, then they would be needed.

Ted took money out of his pocket. 'How much do we owe you, Mrs Dalton?'

'Nothing, Ted, I don't mind giving you and my children a few eggs.' Her smile was affectionate as she looked at Amy. 'How did your first day at the shop go?'

'Quite well. The manager was pleased with me.'

'Good girl, I knew you'd do well.'

Praise was something Amy had had very little of in the past and she felt herself colour with pleasure. It made her all the more determined to make a success of the new job. 'Would you like some tea as well, Mrs Dalton?'

'No thank you, my dear. I'm visiting friends this evening so I'll leave you to it.' Giving everyone another broad smile, she left the kitchen.

'Well!' Ben's eyebrows shot up. 'I know she likes to mother us, but that's the first time she's ever called us her children.'

Howard sat back, balancing his chair on the back legs. 'In that case, do you think she'll let us off the rent this week?'

'Why don't you two make more effort to sell your work?' Ted was shaking his head as he looked at the boys. 'You're both very talented.'

Ben shrugged his shoulders. 'There's a depression on, Ted. People aren't spending money on luxuries, and that's what we produce.'

'I'm well aware of the economic situation, but those with money are still buying.'

'If they are then they're not coming our way.' Howard ran his fingers over the contours of the cruet set in the middle of the table, his expression gloomy.

'What about that gallery or shop you're always talking about? You could probably rent premises quite reasonably at the moment.'

'We still need money to do it though, Ted.' Howard stood up and pulled out the linings of his pockets. 'Look, I haven't got a penny to my name.'

All the time the discussion was going on, Amy busied herself cooking their tea. When she served it up the boys attacked it as if they hadn't eaten for a week, uttering moans of appreciation and making her smile.

'You're a lifesaver!' Howard's gloom had disappeared. 'Will you paint me some more vases and I'll see if I can sell them?'

'All right.'

'Amy, Ben would like to see the drawings your grandmother did for you.' Ted said, pouring them all another cup of tea.

Ben cleared his plate and smiled. 'Ted told me they're very good.'

Seeing they had almost finished eating, she cleared a space on the table. 'I'll get them now.'

She was soon back with the precious sheets and spread them out so Ben could see them.

'You're right, Ted, they are good.'

Kneeling on a chair, elbows on the table, Amy beamed proudly. 'My gran was ever so clever. She could draw, sew, and she knew lots about all sorts of things.'

'Everyone's clever at something or other, but we all have different talents.' Ben winked at her. 'You're an excellent cook, and I'm sure you have many more talents.'

That made her giggle. 'Scrambled eggs isn't cooking. Anyone can do that.'

'I can't, and neither can Howard. Our eggs end up like rubber.'

'They certainly do.' Howard, frowning fiercely, picked up the drawing of the cat.

'That's my favourite.' Amy ran her finger over the cat's face. 'It looks as if he's laughing.'

'Hmm.' The frown disappeared. 'If I make some of these, will you paint them for me, Amy? They might sell in that little odds and ends shop in the King's Road.'

Ben lifted his hands in horror. 'I know we're desperate, Howard, but cats . . . ?'

'It's worth a try.' Howard picked up the sheet. 'Can I borrow this? I'll take good care of it.'

She hesitated, remembering the chaotic mess of his work-room. 'All right, but don't get it dirty, will you?'

'Promise.' He grabbed a biscuit from the plate Amy had put on the table, and left the kitchen to start right away.

Ben also stood up then. 'Don't forget you promised to sit for me, Amy. When do you think you can come up to my studio? I'd like to finish your portrait. It must be in daylight though.'

'I have Wednesday afternoons off, will that be all right?'

'That will be perfect.' He stopped at the door and turned his head. 'Thanks for the food.'

Ted also disappeared quickly, and she knew why the kitchen had emptied so rapidly. There was a pile of washing-up to do. But she didn't mind and it was soon all clean and packed neatly away.

It was such a pleasure each time she walked into her lovely room knowing it was all hers and she was safe here. It was early November now, the nights were drawing in, and there was a real nip in the air. Switching on the small electric fire she pulled up the armchair and was about to settle herself in front of the warmth when there was a plaintive meow at the door. When she opened it, Oscar slid in, sat by the fire and began to wash, paying special attention to his whiskers.

'You've had your tea then, have you?' He looked up when she spoke, rumbled nicely, then returned to his cleaning.

Amy sat down, wondering how Howard was getting on with the model of the cat, for she couldn't help thinking that Oscar was rather like that cat in the picture. Her musing brought her dear gran much closer and was comforting, but how she wished she were here now to talk to. Her first day at the shop had turned out all right, but she couldn't keep pretending to lose her pen, or any of the other inventive ways she'd used to hide the fact that she couldn't read or write very well. Still, what was it Mrs Dalton had said? Ah yes, one step at a time. That's all she could do, get through one day at a time. She hadn't done too badly so far. She gazed around the room, still not being able to believe her luck. She had a home, friends and a job. Everything was going to be all right.

As if in agreement with her, the cat jumped on to her lap, turned round a couple of times to find the most comfortable spot, then sat down, purring contentedly. Amy laid her head back and closed her eyes, letting the tension of the day drain away. She was too tired to practise her reading tonight, but she would try extra hard from now on. Perhaps on her way to work one day she could buy a magazine and try to read some of that. And if she went to the shop carrying that, they would believe she could read perfectly. She smiled to herself. That was a good idea; she hadn't thought of that one before . . .

Oscar's meow woke her up. He was standing by the door demanding to be let out. The room was lovely and warm now so she turned off the fire and opened the door for the cat, following him along the passage to the kitchen.

After giving him a saucer of milk, she made herself a cup of cocoa.

Mrs Dalton came in. 'Ah, that's a good idea. It's cold out tonight and getting foggy. How I hate that stuff. No matter how well you know the road, it's so easy to lose your way.'

'Would you like some cocoa?' Amy asked, admiring her coat. Fancy owning a real fur coat.

'Yes please, dear. I'll bring you some milk in the morning so you and Ted have enough for your breakfast.' She sat down and removed her gloves.

'Did you have a nice evening?' Amy poured milk into the saucepan to heat for the drink.

'It was very pleasant. Now, tell me how you're getting on at the shop and if you think you'll like it?'

'Once I get used to it.' Amy poured the hot milk into a cup and stirred the cocoa. 'I worked in a factory before, and it's quite different, but I enjoy talking to the customers.'

'Give it a week and you'll soon get used to it.' She took the cup from Amy, smiling. 'I know you've had a tough time losing both your parents when you're so young, and I want you to come to me if you have any worries or problems, no matter what they are. Will you promise to do that?'

'Yes, Mrs Dalton, and I'm ever so grateful to you for letting me live here. You've all been very kind.'

'We've got a nice little family here and you make it complete.' Mrs Dalton drank her cocoa. 'You just consider yourself one of us now. We live our own lives, but help each other out when needed. Benjamin and Howard threw away a good education to follow their desire to become artists. They are both very talented, but I can't say I approve of what they've done. They are fine boys though.'

Amy nodded in agreement.

'Ted is a steady dependable man and will go out of his

way to help anyone in need. He came to live here when he lost his wife three years ago. It suits him; he has his independence but doesn't have to live in a house on his own. I know how hard that is when you've had a long and happy marriage.' She stood up. 'You can come to any of us, Amy. You're part of our family now.'

Amy smiled, her eyes misting slightly with emotion as she watched Mrs Dalton leave the kitchen. She hadn't been close to her father, but it hurt her to know he ended up in such a terrible way, and she still missed her mother dreadfully. To be told she was now one of this made-up family was very comforting. She felt guilty about keeping a secret from them, but she couldn't tell them about her difficulty with reading and writing. She just couldn't. They would think she was stupid and that would hurt. It was very important to her that they liked her. So important that she knew she would do anything she could to stop them finding out.

She stayed through Tuesday without too many problems, and Wednesday was half-day, so Amy knew she only had to get through a few hours. Before going to the shop she stopped at a newsagent's and gazed at the array of magazines, wondering what to buy, when one with a film star on the cover caught her attention. Picking it up she traced the name with her finger, spelling the letters out in her head. Then she remembered: Claudette Colbert; she'd seen her when she used to go to the pictures with Gladys. Oh, how she had enjoyed their Saturday evenings. Gladys had been the first friend she'd ever had, but in the end she had deserted her, just like everyone else. She felt cold right through. That mustn't happen where she was living now. It would be more than she could bear!

'You going to buy that *Picturegoer*?' the shopkeeper called to her from behind his counter.

'Yes please.' She hurried over to him, holding out the magazine. 'I was just making sure I hadn't read it.'

'That'll be a shilling then.'

She handed over the money thinking that it was rather a lot, but worth it if she could make the boss believe she could read all right.

The others were already in the back of the shop when she arrived and she smiled brightly. 'Good morning.'

'Ah, you've bought the new *Picturegoer*.' Mrs Green picked it up from the table where Amy had left it while she took off her coat. 'Mind if I have a look? We've got ten minutes before the shop opens.'

'Go ahead.' Amy was quite pleased with this idea. 'I haven't had a chance to look at it yet, but thought I'd read it on the bus going home.'

Then there followed a discussion about films, which Amy was able to join in without any trouble at all.

Once the shop opened on the dot of nine there wasn't time for talk as the customers began to arrive. They were busy, but not so busy that Amy had a customer of her own, so she helped by wrapping the shoes for the other assistants and generally being useful in any way she could.

She was happy until they had a delivery of new stock. The boxes were dumped in the stockroom in teetering, random piles by the delivery men.

The manager arrived then, the first time she had seen him that morning, and he shook his head when he saw the chaos.

'Start sorting that lot out, Miss Carter, by putting them in style and size.'

'Yes, sir.'

When he'd left she sat on the floor and gazed at the mountain of boxes, her mind working furiously to think of a way to carry out this task.

She would have to open each box and see what the shoe was like, and then they could be separated into various piles. That would be a start. It was a good thing that everyone else was busy and had left her alone.

For the next hour she worked as quickly as she could, but it took time to look in every box. Then she was left with the job of sorting them into sizes. This was a bit easier because she could make out figures better than letters and could recognize the sign for a half size. Care had to be taken though because she could confuse the numbers 5 and 6. She'd just have to do the best she could.

Progress was slow and she was dismayed when the manager came back.

'Haven't you finished yet?'

'Nearly, sir, I've got them all into style, and am now putting them in size order.'

'Humph.' He looked in the shop and said quietly, 'Mrs Green, could you come and give a hand here? I want these all on the shelves before we close at one o'clock today.'

He left as soon as the assistant came in, and Amy breathed a sigh of relief. He hadn't been too pleased with the time it had taken her, but she thought she had done rather well.

'Right, we'll start with one style at a time.' Mrs Green was eyeing the boxes with determination. 'You hand them to me and I'll pack them away.'

Amy thought this was a great idea and it only took them another half an hour to clear the floor.

By this time the morning was nearly over and Amy's confidence was growing. All right, she had been slow, but she had managed. In time she would work out how to do everything. She could only pray they gave her that time.

The kitchen was empty when she arrived home, so she made herself some cheese on toast and opened the magazine, determined to read some of it. It was a painstaking task, but she persevered, dwelling on each word until she could grasp it, and only then moving on to the next.

'Ah, good, you're home.' Ben had looked in. 'Don't forget you're coming up to my studio this afternoon.'

'I haven't forgotten.' But in truth she had. With the strain of trying to sort out the shoes, it had gone clean out of her head.

'Come up when you've finished eating.' Then he was gone.

Howard burst in when she was washing up her dishes. 'Amy, I've sold that vase you decorated and the shop wants six more like it.'

'But you were going to throw it away because it wasn't perfect.' She couldn't believe he'd sold her puny effort.

'After it came out of the kiln again it looked fine, so I took it to the little shop that sells some of my things. The man liked it and said it sold within the first hour.' Howard grinned. 'He wants more, so can you do some today?'

'I've promised to go up to Ben this afternoon, but I'll come as soon as he's finished painting.'

'Wonderful! I'll show you the cat then.'

As he hurried away she sat down with a thump. Well I never, what a laugh. An artist was painting her, and now she had been asked to paint more pots! There was a busy afternoon ahead of her and she'd better get a move on.

The door to Ben's studio was open when she got there

and she peered in cautiously. This was the first time she had ever been up here and, by the look of things, it wasn't much tidier than Howard's workshop, except that in place of a layer of dust, there was paint all over the floor. It wasn't very large and had a sloping roof, but there was a big window making it light and bright. Ben was standing in front of a canvas on an easel and covering it with a layer of dark cream paint.

He glanced round when she tapped on the door. 'Come in, Amy, and sit on that chair in front of me.'

She did as instructed.

Ben changed his brush. 'Look straight at me.'

It was fascinating to watch him. He worked silently, a deep furrow in his brow as he studied her, painted, then stared at her again and again. She couldn't help feeling shy at the intense scrutiny, not being able to understand why he wanted to paint her funny face.

'Don't blush, Amy.'

The unexpected sound of his voice made her jump and she felt even more uncomfortable when he came over, tipped her head up with his fingers under her chin, and stared deep into her eyes. Without saying a word he returned to his painting.

What was he seeing? she couldn't help wondering as she watched his total concentration; it was as if he were in another world. Certainly not the face she saw in the mirror every morning, because if that were the case he wouldn't want to paint her.

It was hard to guess how long she had been sitting in the same position, and she longed to stand up and stretch, but she didn't like to move until he told her she could.

'All right, Amy, that'll do for today.' He smiled. 'You've been very patient.'

Standing up she stretched and rolled her head from side to side to ease the ache in her neck. 'Can I see what you've done?'

'Not yet. I'll need you to sit for me a few more times, then I'll let you see it when it's finished.'

'All right.' She was dying to see what he'd done but knew she would have to wait. 'I'm going to Howard now to paint more pots.' Her generous mouth turned up in amusement. 'Did you know he had the nerve to sell that pot I painted?'

'Did he?' Ben leant against the bench, the air of distraction and concentration gone now. 'I'm not surprised. It was really quite good.'

'Do you think so?' She was as doubtful about that as she was about her face.

'I wouldn't say it if I didn't mean it. Your grandmother could draw, and it looks as if you've inherited her talent.'

Glowing with his praise, she made her way downstairs to Howard's workroom. He was in the same kind of mess as before, but covered with clay this time instead of white dust.

'Hi, Amy, he's let you off at last, has he?' Howard gestured with a hand caked in clay. 'I've lined the pots up with the paints ready for you. Do as many as you can.'

Nodding, she sat down and gasped in delight when she saw the figure of the cat in front of the vases. 'Oh, this is beautiful.' She beamed at Howard.

'Not bad.' He pursed his lips, not looking too sure. 'It will look better when you've painted it. Do anything you like with it. I've got more in the kiln.'

Amy couldn't wait to get started; this was something she had discovered she really liked doing. She'd do the vases first and save the cat for last. It was the image of the drawing, and she wished her grandmother could see it.

For the next hour she experimented with most of the

paints, and the six vases were soon finished. She felt so free; there was none of the tension and frustration she suffered from when she tried to read and write. The colours seemed to glow and everything was so clear. Now what should she do with the cat? The picture she saw in her mind's eye made her giggle softly to herself. Why not? He'd said she could do anything she liked!

The finishing touches were just being put to it when she became aware that Howard was watching her.

When Ben walked in Howard said, 'Come and look at this. Have you ever seen a blue cat covered with white daisies?'

They roared with laughter and Amy joined in.

'You're not going to try and sell this are you?' She couldn't help laughing as they looked at the grinning cat with a daisy draped over its ear.

'I most certainly am!'

At that moment Mrs Dalton and Ted arrived.

'Look at the mess you're all in!' Mrs Dalton tutted in disapproval. 'Get yourselves cleaned up and come to my dining room in thirty minutes. Everyone's eating with me tonight.'

Ted winked at Amy when there was a stampede from the boys as they rushed to wash and change.

Mrs Dalton's lips twitched. 'It's surprising how fast they can move when there's the offer of a decent meal.'

# 14

By Saturday Amy was really worried. It was becoming more and more difficult to hide her trouble with reading and she had used up every excuse she could think of: the light in the stockroom was bad; her eyesight wasn't too good. She knew the manager was not happy with the amount of time it took her to find the correct shoes, and was now watching her every move. For the first few days he had been giving her time and help because she was new to the job, but she could sense that his patience was running out.

They were very busy and Amy was getting more customers than she could handle. The more agitated she became the harder it was to read the labels on the boxes. The woman she was trying to serve at the moment was annoyed because she had brought her the wrong shoes – twice!

'This is not what I asked for,' she declared in a loud voice when she was given the wrong style again.

Amy hurried back to the stockroom, now desperate to find the right shoe. This woman was going to cause her trouble if she didn't stop shouting so that everyone in the shop could hear.

The manager stormed into the room after her. 'Why are you taking so long? You're going to lose this sale if you don't hurry up. And why do you keep bringing her the wrong shoes?'

'I'm sorry, sir.' Amy bit her lip to stop it trembling. 'I can't seem to find what she's asking for.'

'What does she want?'

'A black suede with a bar across the instep, size four.'

He muttered under his breath, took a box off the shelf and thrust it into her hands. 'It's right in front of you. Now get back to her quickly, and for heaven's sake smile!'

That was easier said than done, but she tried hard to be pleasant, and could have screamed in frustration when the customer declared that she didn't like the style after all. When she left without buying anything, Amy knew that was another mark against her and prayed for the terrible day to end, hoping she was still going to have a job when they closed at six o'clock.

Closing time arrived, and when the last customer had gone, the manager locked the door, then turned to Amy. 'I want to see you in my office, now, Miss Carter.'

She followed him, hoping she was only in for a telling-off.

He didn't waste time. 'I'm disappointed in you. I thought at first you were going to be suitable, for you have a pleasant way with customers, but you appear to be incapable of working under pressure. And you are far too slow finding what the customer requires. You mustn't keep them waiting or they will go elsewhere.'

'I'm sorry, sir, but—'

He stopped her with a shake of his head. 'You have been making excuses all week and I have made allowances because you are new to the job, but you've had enough time to find your way around the stock. Everything is clearly labelled, but you stand in front of the shelves as if you don't know what you're looking for.'

Another excuse sprang to her lips, but she held it back. She was in enough trouble without making things worse by saying the wrong thing.

The manager sat on the edge of the desk and folded his

arms. 'You seem bright enough so will you tell me why you can't do the job?'

Her head came up in alarm. He didn't know, did he? He couldn't; she had been very careful. 'I can do the job, sir. It's just taking me a while to get used to it. I'll be quicker next week.'

Don't sack me, she pleaded silently, watching his expression carefully.

His sigh echoed in the tiny room and she watched in horror as he picked up a shoe box from his desk and held it out to her.

'What style does that say on the label?'

She was in such a state of agitation by now that the words were a meaningless jumble. Slipping her finger under the lid she began to lift it . . .

'Don't look inside. I've seen you doing that a lot this week. Read the label out to me.'

All she could do was guess. 'Ladies' black leather.'

'And the size of the heel?'

'Two-inch, sir.' She was afraid to breathe.

He took the box from her and tossed it on to the table. 'It says: brown leather lace-up with a one-inch heel.'

Amy felt herself crumple inside as she realized that this was the end for her, but she stood up straight, although it was a tremendous effort. This job had been so important to her, but now she was going to lose it.

'Why the blazes didn't you tell me?' He was furious. 'You can't read, can you?'

'Yes I can.' She defended stoutly. 'It takes me a while to make out the words, that's all. I can manage if you'll give me a chance. I'll learn all the styles off by heart and where they are.'

'I can't employ you.' His voice had softened. 'You must see that?'

When she looked back at him her mouth was set in a firm line, determined not to show how unhappy and embarrassed she was.

He handed her a wage packet. 'Sign for this in the book. You can write your name, I suppose?'

'Yes I can!' Now she was angry. 'I've been writing sales slips all week.'

'So you have.' He watched as she carefully signed her name.

Then without a word she turned and left the shop by the back door. She didn't immediately go to the bus stop, as she needed time to compose herself and decide what was the best thing to do. But one thing she was sure about, she couldn't tell Mrs Dalton and the others she had been sacked after only a week. They would want to know why.

Walking along the King's Road, her head down, she was oblivious to the cold wind blowing her hair around her face. She had been sure she could do the job, and she would have if they hadn't found out so soon. All she had needed was a bit more time and she would have worked out a way, but the manager hadn't been prepared to give her that chance.

Her jaw clenched in frustration as she stood in line at the bus stop, refusing to let the tears of shame fall. She had until Monday to decide what to do.

Monday morning and Amy was up and dressed for work at her usual time. She'd really enjoyed yesterday, painting for Howard, then sitting for Ben in the afternoon. Ted had brought home a large joint of beef, given to him by a butcher friend, and she had cooked lunch for all of them, except

Mrs Dalton, who was out for the day. She seemed to have lots of friends.

At the end of the day, comfortably tucked up in bed with Oscar curled up next to her, she had decided what to do. The first thing was to find another job, and if she went out and returned home at her usual time each day, they wouldn't know she had been sacked. She was going to tell them, of course, but it wouldn't seem so bad if she had another job to go to.

'One step at a time, eh, Oscar?'

The cat looked up and blinked in agreement.

Although very worried, she couldn't help laughing at the way she had begun to talk to the animal. Her mother would never have a pet around, and Amy found him good company and comforting.

The thought of her mother brought the sadness back. Dolly had never been overly affectionate, but that was because she had been ill, and the horror of the trial and hanging had been too much for her. She was sure her mother had loved her, though, and she missed her.

Finishing her breakfast, she stood up with a determined air. That part of her life was over and she had been given a chance to start again. Amy already adored each member of her adopted family, and she was *not* going to let them down.

She left the house, her steps sure as she walked to the bus stop. There wasn't anything to worry about. She had enough money in her old teapot to last her for a while. When she had asked Mrs Dalton for a rent book, she'd said that as Amy was in her care, she wouldn't have to pay rent until she was eighteen. Such kindness was overwhelming, and she'd buy her a nice present when she had enough saved. It would be a way of showing how grateful she was.

A bus came as soon as she reached the stop and she

jumped on. With a bit of luck she might get to the Labour Exchange before the crowd.

One week passed, then two, and three. There just weren't any jobs around that she could do, and dozens of applicants for each job as it became available. The endless search was taking its toll on Amy, and making it harder and harder to keep up the pretence that she was still working.

After being turned down again, she returned home. It had been yet another tiring, frustrating week.

Before even taking off her coat, Amy went to the kitchen. She was gasping for a cup of tea. Lost in her own world of misery, she wasn't immediately aware that the little room was crowded.

'Happy birthday, Amy!'

She gasped in surprise as Mrs Dalton, Ted, Ben and Howard began to sing the birthday song – not very tunefully. In the centre of the table was an iced cake with a lighted candle on the top, plates piled high with sandwiches, and little dishes of jelly.

'What's the date?' Amy was stunned. So much had been happening in her life just lately that she hadn't given her birthday a thought.

'My dear girl.' Mrs Dalton came and kissed her cheek. 'Don't tell me you had forgotten such an important day. It's the eighth of December and, according to the information given to me when I took over your care, this is your fifteenth birthday.'

'Oh, I had forgotten.'

Each one came forward in turn and gave her a parcel until her arms were full. She could feel the tears fighting to escape and she blinked rapidly to keep them at bay. Her father had never been around on her birthday, and her mother hadn't made much of them, so this celebration was quite outside her experience. She just stood there hugging the presents, her throat tight with emotion, unable to speak.

'Open them, Amy,' Howard urged.

She opened them one at a time. There was a lovely warm dress from Mrs Dalton in cherry red. 'Oh, Mrs Dalton, this is the loveliest dress I've ever had.' Amy held it up in front of her to let everyone admire it.

'That's a stunning colour.' Ben nodded approval. 'I'll have to paint you wearing that; it looks lovely with your dark hair.'

'That's what I thought when I saw it.' Mrs Dalton checked the size. 'That should fit you all right, but we can change it if it doesn't.'

'I'm sure it will be fine.' Amy wasn't going to let such a lovely creation be returned to the shop in case they didn't have another one the same colour.

The next parcel was from Howard, and she cried in delight when she held up the cat she had painted. 'Thank you, that will look lovely in my room.'

'The shopkeeper said it was lovely as well, and has ordered a dozen, but I told him he couldn't have that one.' Howard gave her an impish grin. 'You've got a lot of painting to do.'

'I'll spend all day tomorrow doing them.' The misery she had felt was pushed to the back of her mind. She wasn't going to spoil this moment.

The next present was from Ben. It was a framed sketch of her sitting by the river.

'That's to remind you when we first met.'

'I love it. Thank you, Ben, and can I have it on my wall?' she asked.

'Of course. I'll do it this evening for you. Have you still got the drawing I gave you?'

She nodded.

'I'll frame that for you as well, if you like?'

'Oh, please!'

There was only one more present left and that was from Ted. Amy's heart nearly stopped beating when she held a lovely leather-bound book in her hands. The misery and shame were back in full force as she clutched the book to her. The tears would not be denied any longer.

'It's beautiful, thank you, Ted.' She wiped the back of her hand over her wet cheeks.

He smiled gently. 'When we were moving your things I noticed you had a book by Jane Austen and thought you might like another one.'

'I would; she writes such lovely stories.' When she was quiet tonight she would try to see what the book was called. As she looked at their smiling faces and the presents littering the table, she knew she couldn't tell them her secret. She just couldn't.

'Come and cut your cake, Amy.' Ben held out a knife. 'We're all starving.'

'Are you ever anything else?' Mrs Dalton declared, making them all laugh.

Amy took the knife from Ben before blowing out the candle and sending up a silent wish that she would find another job soon, then she cut the cake.

The food disappeared with great speed, as it always did with the two boys around. Mrs Dalton made them all laugh by saying that it wasn't surprising as there was a lot of them to fill up.

Listening to the laughter and chatter around the table,

Amy thought that she had never had such a lovely birthday. If she hadn't lost her job she would have been completely happy, but although she refused to dwell on it, the memory lingered, waiting to pounce and bring the worry back.

When they'd finished eating, Amy began to clear the table, but Mrs Dalton stopped her.

'I'll clear up for you tonight, my dear. You show Benjamin where you want your picture.'

Leaving Mrs Dalton to it, they all trooped into Amy's room. The first thing she did was hang the dress in the wardrobe. It was so lovely and she couldn't wait to wear it. Then she put the smiling cat on the mantelpiece while Ben disappeared to get a hammer. The book she placed on the table by the window and ran her finger over the title. It was a single word beginning with 'E'; she could see it quite clearly.

'I hope you haven't read *Emma*?' Ted was standing beside her.

'No, I haven't.' Her smile was bright. That was the truth, anyway.

'Let me know what you think of it.'

'I will.' It would take her a long time, but she was determined to read some of it.

'Right, where do you want this, Amy?' Ben was back.

'On the wall opposite my bed so I can see it when I wake in the mornings.'

The job was soon done and she sat on her bed to make sure it was in the right position. 'That's perfect, thank you.'

'If you've got the other one I'll take it with me and frame it for you.'

She scrambled to her feet and took it out of the bedside table drawer.

'I'll let you have it back sometime tomorrow.' Ben took it from her and looked around the room. 'I think it will go on the same wall as the other one, don't you?'

'Yes please.'

'Let's give Amy some peace and quiet.' Ted began to usher the boys out. 'She looks tired.'

'Come down in the morning as soon as you like, Amy.' Howard had stopped in the doorway and looked back. 'I'll leave everything ready for you. Paint as many pots and cats as you can.'

'You can't have her all day,' Ben protested. 'I'll need her for a couple of hours in the afternoon.'

'All right, but I'll time you.' Howard grinned. 'My need is greater than yours.'

Ted raised his eyebrows. 'I can see you're not going to have a moment to yourself with these two. Don't let them monopolize all your time.'

Ben gave Ted a wry smile. 'That's what brothers are for, aren't they?'

'That's as maybe.' Mrs Dalton had looked in. 'But you can let your sister get some rest before you run her ragged tomorrow.'

That made everyone laugh as they filed out and left her alone.

Amy was staring at the closed door when she felt Oscar rub round her legs. She swept him up and felt his body vibrating with a deep purr, resting his head on her shoulder.

'What do you think of that?' she asked the cat, running her hand along his sleek back. 'I've got two brothers! I've got a proper family and they gave me a birthday party and presents. Isn't that wonderful?'

A wet tongue rasped up her neck, making her squirm.

'Yuck! And I've got you.' He dug his claws into her shoulder, just to emphasize the point.

She sat on the chair by the table and gazed at the book. 'They're all so kind,' she whispered, 'and I'm keeping things from them. But how can I tell them?'

The cat didn't answer. He was fast asleep.

# 15

Yet more cold, frustrating days had passed and Amy still hadn't found a job. There was just nothing around that didn't need reading and writing. All the factory jobs were snapped up as soon as they were advertised because there were still a lot of people out of work. She was beginning to despair of ever finding anything she could do. And her conscience was really bothering her. She still hadn't told anyone at home that she was out of work, and it got harder as each fruitless week passed. The decision not to tell them until she had another job was now bitterly regretted, but every time she steeled herself to say something, the words just wouldn't come.

There was a cold wind blowing as she walked along Fulham High Road, head down, trying to decide what to do for the rest of the day. This trip had been another waste of time and bus fares, but she went after any job, anywhere. She was that desperate.

Spotting a café she went in for a cup of tea. It would be warm in there and she could spend an hour or so over her tea.

After buying her drink she sat down, sighing wearily. It seemed hopeless.

'Hello, Ben.' Ted frowned. 'You look worried. What's up?'

'I'm not sure.' Ben ran his hand through his thick hair to push it away from his eyes. 'You got a couple of minutes?'

'Sure.' Ted put the 'closed' sign on the door. 'I'll make us some tea.'

The small room at the back of the shop was piled high with books as usual, and Ben had to clear two chairs before they could sit down.

Once the tea was made, Ted sat opposite him. 'What's troubling you?'

'There's a small gallery just opened in Fulham and I've been to see if they would be interested in my work.'

'And were they?'

'Yes, they've taken three landscapes to see if they sell.'

'That's good, isn't it?' Ted was puzzled. Ben didn't look very pleased about it.

'Oh yes, very good.' Ben sipped his tea.

'But . . . ?' Ted prompted.

'After I left the gallery I was sure I saw Amy walking along by some shops.'

'In Fulham?'

Ben nodded. 'By the time I'd found somewhere to stop she had disappeared.'

Ted frowned. 'You sure it was Amy?'

'Certain, but what was she doing there, Ted?'

'No idea, but I've sensed something was bothering her for some time. I've tried to get her to talk to me, but she won't. Whatever problems she's got she's keeping to herself.'

'But we'd all help her, she must know that by now?' Ben sat back, his eyes narrowed in concern. 'Do you ever see her during the day?'

Ted shook his head. 'She came in the first day she started at the shop, but I haven't seen her since.'

'That's strange. You're only a couple of minutes away. I'm worried, Ted.'

'Me too.' He stood up and pulled Ben to his feet. 'Come on, let's see if we can find out what's happening. I've met the manager a couple of times, and I need a new pair of shoes.'

The shop wasn't busy, and the manager came over to them as soon as they walked in the shop.

'Hello, Mr Andrews, it's nice to see you again. What can I do for you?'

'I'd like a pair of black shoes please. Something sturdy, size nine and a half.'

'Of course.' He smiled at Ben. 'And anything for you, sir?'

'Nothing, thanks.'

After instructing one of the women assistants to get the shoes, the manager stayed to talk, asking Ted how business was.

Ben scanned the shop looking for Amy, but there was no sign of her. 'Haven't you got a junior assistant called Amy Carter?

'Not now, I'm afraid I had to sack her. Such a shame, she was pleasant and good with the elderly customers. But I couldn't keep her.'

Ted took the shoes from the assistant when she came back, put them on and walked up and down to see if they were comfortable.

Ben could hardly contain himself, but Ted was talking to the manager again and he couldn't interrupt. She had lost her job. Why the hell hadn't she told them?

'Hmm, these feel fine. I'll take them.' Ted sat down, removed the shoes and put his own back on, returning to the subject of Amy. 'If she was good with the customers why couldn't you have kept her?'

'She hadn't been honest with me when I interviewed her. She was clever and fooled us for a week, but it didn't take me long to realize there was something wrong with her.'

Ben couldn't leave it to Ted's casual approach any longer. What did he mean, there was something wrong with her?

146

'Amy's a friend of ours and there isn't anything wrong with her.'

The man looked perplexed. 'But you must know she can't read or write properly.'

'*What?*' Both of them spoke at once, immediately on their feet in shock.

Ben felt as if he had been punched in the stomach. 'You must be mistaken.'

The manager grimaced. 'I'm sorry you didn't know. I missed it myself at first. She was very inventive with her excuses.'

When Ted had paid for his shoes, they made their way back to the bookshop in stunned silence. Ted didn't bother to put the 'open' sign back on the door as they both marched into the back room.

Ben paced the small space. 'She was only there a week, so what on earth has she been doing since then? And why hasn't she told us she can't read? Why, Ted?'

'She's ashamed to tell us?'

'Oh, but she needn't feel like that.' Ben ran his fingers through his hair, concern etched on his strong features. 'We're her friends.'

'Will you stop walking up and down, Ben, you're disturbing the dust.' Ted took hold of his arm and pushed him into a chair. 'I expect she's had to suffer a lot of unkind remarks while she's been growing up, and she might think we'll do the same if we know.'

'But we wouldn't!'

'No, but she doesn't know that.'

Ben picked up a book from the table, flicked through it and tossed it back. 'I wonder why she can't read? She's a bright girl.'

'I can't answer that, but while I was teaching I did come

across a boy who had a problem reading. Like Amy, he wasn't lacking in intelligence.' Ted found a bottle of whisky in the cupboard and a couple of glasses. 'Let's have a drink and decide what to do. Amy needs help, but we're going to have to be very careful because she's guarding her secret well.'

'What do you suggest?' Ben was on his feet again. 'We can't just let her wander around day after day in the cold. And I believe that's what she's doing.'

'She's probably trying to find work, Ben. We can't interfere, and until she tells us herself, there isn't much we can do.'

Ben slumped back in his chair. 'Mrs Dalton and Howard must be told.'

'No!' Ted's expression was grim. 'By all means tell Howard, but we must never let her know we have found out. Amy must go to Mrs Dalton herself.'

'But will she?'

'I believe she will, and let's hope it's soon.' Ted held up the bottle. 'I could do with a stiff drink. Do you want one?'

Ben held out one of the glasses. 'Why not?'


After sitting in the dingy café in Fulham for an hour, Amy had made up her mind. She couldn't go on like this. She was cold, hungry and very miserable. It was time to go to her 'family', confess all, and ask for their help. Her stomach heaved when she remembered the names she had been called at school. They echoed in her head: Barmy, stupid Amy, she can't read! It would be impossible to bear it if Ben, Howard, Ted and Mrs Dalton thought that about her. But if they did she would have to face it even if it tore her apart. Which she knew it would, for she loved each one of them and cared so much what they thought of her. They were going to be *so* angry with her.

She left the café and found the bus stop she needed, eager now to get the unpleasant task over with. Many things in her life had been hard to face, but she'd managed to get through them. This was just one more.

It was four o'clock when she reached home. Gritting her teeth she marched towards Mrs Dalton's sitting room. She had been so kind; she must be told first. Amy choked back a sob, fighting for control. Mrs Dalton was going to be so disappointed to learn she had lost her job weeks ago.

The house was quiet. Grasping every bit of courage she could muster, she tapped on the door.

'Come in.'

Turning the handle slowly she stepped inside.

'Amy.' Mrs Dalton put down the book she had been reading. 'You're early, dear.'

'I need to talk to you, please.' Her voice wavered.

'Come and sit down. You look upset. Tell me what's happened.'

Amy perched on the edge of an armchair and, taking a deep breath, told her about losing her job after only a week. 'I should have told you before but I was hoping to find another job quickly. Only I haven't been able to. I'm so sorry . . .'

'You haven't told me why they sacked you.' Mrs Dalton's voice was gentle.

Amy looked at her with tortured eyes, and she still hedged. 'They said I was too slow.'

'That's hard to believe. Why were you slow?'

The truth couldn't be avoided any longer, and Amy gazed down at her clasped hands. 'I can't read or write properly.'

'I know that, my dear, but I've been waiting for you to tell me.'

'You know?' Amy's head came up sharply.

'Of course. When I agreed to take over your care I was told everything about you.' She reached across and took hold of Amy's hands. 'You are a very brave girl and I'm proud of you.'

'Proud?' Amy stared in disbelief. 'Do the others know?'

'I haven't told anyone, but' – she gave Amy's hands an encouraging squeeze – 'I think it's time you told them as well.'

'Oh, no!' She shuddered. 'They'll think I'm stupid. I'm not, Mrs Dalton. I'm not! I try very hard and practise almost every evening. I'm getting better; I can write some, and sign my name. Only I got flustered at the shop and when I do that everything gets muddled.'

'No one in this house is going to think badly of you, Amy.' Mrs Dalton stood up. 'Let's go to my kitchen, have tea, and then when the boys and Ted come home you can tell them. Don't worry, my dear. All any of us want to do is help you through this difficult time.'

Amy stood up carefully, not sure her legs would support her. Mrs Dalton had known all along and didn't think she was stupid. The relief was enormous and she saw how silly she had been to hide the fact that she had lost her job. She would have told her mother, and Mrs Dalton had taken on that role. She wouldn't hesitate to go to her in the future.

There were lovely fat scones, jam and a sponge cake, but until she had told the others, Amy didn't think her insides would hold anything as substantial as this.

'Just tea, please.'

'I understand.' Mrs Dalton smiled and poured them both a cup of tea. 'We can eat these later.'

They talked quietly and Mrs Dalton listened as Amy told her about her search for work, her difficulties at school and how she longed to be able to read properly. For the first time since her father's trial, Amy unburdened herself, and – also for the first time – she felt secure.

'Right, I expect they're all home now, so let's go and tell them, shall we?'

Amy gulped hard, nodded, and followed Mrs Dalton along the passage to the kitchen she shared with Ted, and the boys haunted for food. She wasn't looking forward to this one little bit, but it had to be done.

When they walked in, Ben, Howard and Ted were all there, cups of tea in front of them and looking serious.

'Ah, good, you're all here.' Mrs Dalton put her arm around Amy's shoulder. 'We have something to tell you, haven't we, dear?'

'Umm, yes.' She gazed down at her feet until Mrs Dalton squeezed her shoulder, making her lift her head and meet the eyes of the three men watching her. The words came out in a rush. 'I lost my job weeks ago because I can't read properly.'

Why were they smiling? Were they going to laugh at her? Oh no! She turned to run from the room but had only taken a couple of steps before she was swept off her feet by Ben and swung round.

'You were too good for that job.'

Howard rubbed his hands together. 'Good, I need lots more pots painted, and now you'll have the time. They've sold all the others.' He held out a pound note. 'That's your share.'

'But, but . . . I can't take your money.'

'Yes you can, Amy. I'll give you a quarter of everything we sell that you've painted. The cats are causing a lot of interest.'

Her fingers closed over the pound note just as Ted spoke. 'And you can help me in the shop on Saturdays.'

Glancing in disbelief from one smiling face to the next, she struggled for words. Didn't they understand? 'But I can't read.'

'You don't need to when you paint my pots, or sit for Ben, and all you've got to do is smile at Ted's customers.'

'And take their money,' Ted pointed out.

'Well I never!'

Howard roared. 'I love the way you say that.'

'I was so afraid to tell you in case you thought I was daft in the head.' Amy was bubbling with relief. 'I could hug you all for being so nice to me.'

'What are you waiting for then?' Ben held his arms wide.

When she ran into them he swung her round, whispering in her ear, 'Don't worry, Amy, everything's going to be all right.'

When everyone in the room had received her thanks, Amy was quite flustered. The response was the opposite to what she had expected, but how wonderful it was, and she wanted to do something for them.

She rushed to look in the larder and saw that Mrs Dalton had put another bowl of eggs in there for them. 'I'll make you all scrambled eggs on toast, shall I?'

Every seat around the table was immediately filled, and even Mrs Dalton joined them. Amy was bursting with happiness as she set to work. They didn't mind! They didn't think she was stupid.

'I've got some fresh-baked scones and jam we can have after.'

'I love your scones, Mrs Dalton.' Ben winked at Amy. 'They're almost as good as Amy's scrambled eggs.'

While they were eating she was asked about her difficulty with words, and for the first time in her life she talked freely about it.

Ted was nodding as he listened, then pushed a piece of paper and a pen in front of her. 'Would you write something for me, Amy? Don't worry about spelling, just a few sentences about Oscar, your room or how you like living here. Anything that comes into your head.'

She chewed her lip in concentration as she wrote slowly, crossing out a word every so often.

Looking very doubtful she pushed it across to Ted and watched anxiously as he read it.

'This is very interesting. I've seen something like this before. I had a boy in my class who wrote in a similar way. He confused the B and D as well, often putting them in the wrong order, just like Amy.'

Was there someone else like her? Amy leant towards Ted to see what he was pointing out to the others, her embarrassment disappearing fast as she saw there was only interest on their faces: no ridicule.

'She's spelt some words phonetically,' Howard said.

'Yes.' Ted nodded. 'Clever, isn't it?'

Clever? Amy was now kneeling on the chair. What were they talking about? She couldn't contain herself any longer and the words tumbled out. 'But it isn't right, is it? And who's this other person who wrote like me? I thought I was the only one. What was he like?'

'He was a ten-year-old boy in my class and I noticed he was reluctant to hand in his homework. When he finally did, I saw something like this. The spelling was bad, but the work was brilliant. He was very intelligent.'

'What happened to him?' Amy couldn't wait to hear about this.

'He became a lawyer, and a very successful one.'

'A lawyer?' She almost fell off her chair. 'But how could he do that?'

'With a lot of hard work and determination. As he got older his reading and writing skills improved, and I worked with him until he was old enough to go to university.'

Amy's mouth dropped open as she stared at Ted in amazement. 'Could . . . could you help me?'

'I'd like to see what we could do.' He smiled with understanding in his gentle eyes.

'I'm going to read!' Her chair wobbled alarmingly as she wriggled with joy. 'I want to read lots of books; write long, long letters . . .'

'Whoa.' Ted caught her chair to steady it. 'Don't get too excited. I'm sure we can improve your ability, but you should have had help a long time ago.'

Her spirits plummeted. 'My gran helped me, and I try hard all the time. I practise every night.'

'Well, that must be why you've made as much progress as you have, but it's going to be hard for you.'

'Do you mean it's too late for me to learn?'

'Don't look so disappointed, Amy.' Ted patted her hand. 'I'll set you some exercises, and we'll work together for about an hour each day. You will be able to improve, but we must face the fact that you might never be able to read and write fluently.'

Her generous mouth thinned. 'What's wrong with me, then?'

'I don't know, my dear; I wish I did. One thing I'm sure about though is that it has nothing to do with your intelligence. Apart from that one problem you are a normal, bright girl.'

That piece of news helped and she managed a smile. 'If I can learn a bit, I don't mind. I'll never stop trying.'

'Good for you.' Mrs Dalton, who had been listening intently, spoke for the first time. 'The moment I met you I knew you had courage. The problems and tragedies you had would have knocked out anyone else, but you haven't let them grind you down. I'm proud of you, dear.'

'We all are.' Ben leant across the table and ruffled her unruly hair playfully. 'When I saw you by the river I just knew you were special. There was something about you I couldn't forget.'

'I'm ever so glad you didn't.' Amy sighed. 'I wouldn't have found such a nice home with all of you.'

'And we wouldn't have found such a talented sister.' Howard was serious, then he chuckled. 'I've got loads of pots for you to paint.'

There were howls of protest from the others. 'You and your pots!'

'And I think it's time we had those scones, don't you?' Mrs Dalton stood up as everyone round the table nodded in eager anticipation.

## 16

The next few days flew by. Howard was now making small dogs as well as cats and, with the decorated vases, they were selling well in the run-up to Christmas. Amy had shelved any thoughts of getting another job in order to help Ben and Howard. She was painting and delivering new stock to the couple of shops taking Howard's work, and it was giving her enormous pleasure to see him earning some money at last. Ben's paintings at the Fulham gallery were also selling quite well. Both boys were earning a good reputation for their excellent work. They insisted on paying her for the painting and running around she did on their behalf, and she was earning almost as much as the shoe shop had paid her. Added to this was the payment for the Saturday working for Ted. She loved watching the customers as they browsed the shelves for something special. They would often sit on one of the chairs Ted provided for his customers, absorbed in the book in their hands. How her heart ached to be able to do that. With Ted's help and encouragement she hoped she would improve.

Ted had just found her another book, for an older age group this time, and as it was quiet in the shop for a moment, Amy was leaning on the counter reading it. As she struggled the usual frustration raced through her.

'Don't do that, Amy.' Ted had come up behind her and spoke firmly.

She glanced round at him. 'Do what?'

'Look at your hands.'

They were in tight fists. She uncurled them, laying them flat on the counter, bowing her head and muttering under her breath.

'Take deep breaths,' he ordered more gently this time. 'I know it's hard, Amy, and I know how much you want to be able to read like the rest of us, but you must try to control your frustration. You are really doing well.'

Her sigh was deep. 'Am I ever going to be able to pick up a book and read it easily?'

'I can't answer that question because I don't know what's stopping you. I have asked friends in the teaching profession, and although some of them have come across a child with similar difficulties, no one knows what causes it.' Ted closed the book in front of her. 'One day they will discover what the condition is, and something will be done about it.'

'It will be too late for me though, won't it?'

He took hold of her hands as they began to clench into fists again. 'I know you're going to think this is a daft thing to say, but try not to let it mean so much to you. I believe it's holding you back. If you could be pleased with every step forward you make, even if very small, I think that would make you relax and give you more freedom.'

'I'll try.' She smiled then, the tension easing away as it always did when he talked to her like this. He had gone to a lot of trouble to convince her that she wasn't daft in the head and she knew he was right. Yet the taunts of her school days were still a vivid memory. What a miserable time that had been.

But it was behind her now. She was with people who accepted her for what she was and never belittled her, in fact they continually praised her for the things she could do well, especially her cooking!

'That's better.' Ted gave a slow smile and let go of her

hands. 'You have such expressive eyes and I saw the tension leave you. What are you amused about?'

'I was just thinking how much Ben and Howard like my cooking.'

He tipped his head back and laughed out loud. 'Those two are always hungry. They spend more time in our kitchen than their own.'

'I know, and I swear they're getting bigger every day. Ben is a giant, and Howard isn't far behind him.'

'That's because they're eating regular meals now.' He leant on the counter beside her. 'Do you know, Amy, I believe they are going to make their mark in life; they are so talented. One day Ben will be able to paint what he likes without worrying about earning money, and Howard will not have to produce so many vases in order to eat. He is a sculptor of exceptional ability.'

Amy nodded, agreeing with every word. How she adored these wonderful artists.

'They're only twenty and have got a good future ahead of them.' Ted lifted her chin, making her look directly at him. 'And so have you. Don't you ever forget that.'

'I'll try not to.'

That was the end of their talk because the shop became busy again, and the rest of the day was hectic. Amy was once again happy, her frustration gone as she talked and joked with the customers. Many of them knew Ted personally and often asked him to find a certain kind of book for them, which he was always happy to do. She didn't know what the future held for her, but if Ted said it was good, then she'd believe him. The more she got to know him, the more her respect for him grew. If it weren't for her trouble with words her happiness would be complete. She couldn't ask for more than she already had.

*

Mrs Dalton was waiting for her when she arrived home with Ted that evening.

'Ah, there you are, my dear. It's not long till Christmas and I wondered if you'd like to come shopping with me next Saturday. That's if Ted will let you have the day off?'

Ben strode along the passage, smiling broadly. 'Don't forget I want to do another picture of you, and Howard's lined up dozens of pieces to be painted.'

'You never want to paint me again, surely?' Amy gasped. 'Why don't you find a pretty girl?'

'I don't want a pretty girl.' He bent and whispered in her ear: 'I want a beautiful one, and that's you.'

'Oh, you do tease.' She laughed, pushing him away.

'Why doesn't she believe me, Howard?' He turned to his friend who had just come up from the basement.

'About what?'

'I told her she's beautiful.'

Howard walked over to Amy, put his face close to hers, studying the curves and structure of her face. 'Hmm, you're right, absolutely stunning. I think I'll have to do a bust of her.'

'What?'

Ben and Howard roared with delight at her expression of horror.

'That means just your face and shoulders.' Howard leant on Ben, doubled over with laughter. 'Ever since Amy saw me doing a sculpture of a naked girl she's afraid we're going to ask her to take her clothes off.'

Mrs Dalton glared at them. 'You had better not.'

'Don't worry.' Ben composed himself with difficulty. 'She's already said she won't, and anyway, we're only interested in our little sister's face. It's fascinating.'

Amy placed her hands on her hips. 'I think you both need glasses!'

'Or something tasty for tea?' Ben suggested hopefully.

'Ah, I see what all the flattery is about. Come on then, let's find out what we have in the larder.'

She was nearly tripped up in the rush.

The following Saturday morning Amy tipped out the old teapot to see how much money she could afford to spend. She wanted to buy a nice present for all of them and Mrs Dalton would be able to advise her. The only money she had spent over the last few weeks had been for food, and with the money now coming from Howard and Ted, she had been able to save quite a bit. Slipping four pounds into her purse she put on her coat, looking forward to the day.

'Amy,' Mrs Dalton called. 'Are you ready?'

Amy met her by the front door. 'Where are we going?'

'I thought we'd try Oxford Street.'

'Lovely.' Amy held open the door for her. 'I've never been there.'

'You'll like it; there are lots of shops.'

Mrs Dalton was right, and there were also crowds of people Christmas shopping.

'You need a winter coat,' Mrs Dalton declared, ushering her into a shop. 'Let's see what they've got in here.'

'Oh, I don't think—'

'It's no good you protesting. I'm buying you a coat for Christmas.'

Knowing it was useless to argue when Mrs Dalton was in this determined mood, Amy patiently tried on coat after coat, until they finally decided on a lovely dark brown wool, as it wouldn't clash with the red dress Mrs Dalton had bought her for her birthday. When she tried to look at the price tag it was taken out of her hands.

'Don't you worry about the cost.' Mrs Dalton handed it to the smiling assistant. 'We'll have that.'

After that the day was a blur of activity as they searched each shop for suitable presents. While they were in one large store and Mrs Dalton was busy, Amy took the opportunity discreetly to visit another counter. There she sniffed loads of scents until she found one that smelt something like the one her landlady always wore, and after paying for it wandered back to rejoin Mrs Dalton.

'What shall I buy the men?' she asked. 'I've got about three pounds to spend on them.'

'I think Ted would like a pullover. It gets a bit chilly in that shop of his, and the boys could do with a decent pair of gloves each. I know their sizes.'

Much to Amy's delight she found a lovely pullover and two pairs of leather gloves with a warm lining. The presents took every penny of the money she had, and Mrs Dalton tried to persuade her to buy cheaper gifts, but Amy wouldn't hear of it. They were all special to her, and she wanted to give them something special.

They had lunch in a proper restaurant. Amy could hardly eat for excitement and her generous mouth was tipped up in a permanent smile, and she was glad she'd put on her red dress. Everyone looked so smart.

It was gone four when they arrived home, loaded with parcels, tired, but pleased with what they had bought. Even Oscar hadn't been forgotten. Amy had found him a small brightly coloured ball, soft enough for him to pounce on and chew.

Amy was disappointed when she heard that Ben and Howard would be going to stay with their parents over the holiday. But of course they would, and it had been selfish of her to think they would all be together. Ted would be staying though, as he didn't have any family to go and see: he and his wife had never had children. Mrs Dalton had bought a splendid Christmas tree and would be cooking lunch for the three of them, with Amy's help.

Early on Christmas Eve they gave out the presents, and Amy was relieved to see that she had managed to buy Mrs Dalton's favourite perfume, and the pullover and gloves fitted perfectly. She already had the coat, but Mrs Dalton had bought her a scarf to go with it as a surprise. Ted gave her a cream-coloured cardigan, Ben had bought her a box of three tablets of lavender soap, and Howard's gift was a set of delicate handkerchiefs with a different coloured flower in each corner. They were all such luxuries and she was thrilled with every gift, but more importantly to Amy, they were given with obvious affection.

'Right.' Ben stood up. 'Get your coat, Amy.'

'Er . . . Why?'

'Because I'm taking you to meet my family. I'll bring you back this evening.'

'And you're going to meet mine on the way to Ben's.' Howard began to collect up the torn wrapping paper.

She looked from one to the other of the two she loved as brothers. 'But your families won't want to meet me.'

'Amy,' Ben tutted, 'you have such a low opinion of yourself. They've been hounding us for weeks to bring you to meet them.'

'That's right,' Howard agreed. 'My parents can't wait to meet the girl who has finally helped me to make some money.'

'Go on,' Mrs Dalton urged. 'Wear your new things.'

\*

Amy sat in the car not at all sure about this, but she had been pushed into getting ready. Mrs Dalton had even dabbed a bit of perfume behind her ears and fussed with Amy's unruly mass of hair until it was in some kind of order.

Howard's family lived in Kensington, but she was too nervous to take much notice of the road or the house. She hung back as everyone greeted the boys, wishing she were back home.

'You must be Amy. I'm Howard's father.' The man standing in front of her was quite youthful-looking without a sign of grey in his brown hair. There was a smile on his face, but she wasn't sure if she could like him. From what she had heard, he had refused to help his son when he must have known he was struggling.

'And I'm Howard's mother. It's lovely to meet you at last.'

Ah, she could see whom the son took after; his mother had the same gentle eyes. All she could manage though was a 'How do you do?'

Once in the sitting room she gazed round in admiration at the decorations strung across the room, and the most enormous tree: it nearly touched the ceiling. Then she nearly giggled when she saw one of her and Howard's cats sitting on the mantelpiece looking completely out of place in the elegant surroundings.

Howard's mother smiled when she noticed Amy looking at it. His father hadn't missed her interest either.

'Howard tells us they are selling well.'

'Er . . . yes they are.' When she glanced at Howard he gave her a sly wink.

'My father's relieved I'm no longer starving.'

'Of course I am, my boy. I had hoped you would give up this crazy idea, but it's obvious that isn't going to happen, and nothing would please me more than to see you make a success of things.'

'Ted says they are both very talented and have a good future ahead of them.' Amy felt she should pass on that piece of information.

'Ted Andrews,' Howard explained.

'Let's hope he's right.'

They stayed for only an hour and were then on their way to Ben's family in East Sheen. She was feeling a little more relaxed by now and took notice of the area as they arrived. The house was modest compared to Mrs Dalton's, but Amy felt immediately at ease when she walked in. It was furnished for comfort, although elegant in a homely way.

'Amy' – Ben placed a hand on her shoulder – 'meet my parents. And the lady sitting in state by the fire is my grandmother.'

Before she had a chance to say anything, the elderly woman beckoned her over.

'Come here, girl, let me have a look at you.'

The appraisal was thorough and Amy felt the corners of her mouth turn up in amusement. This was just the sort of thing her own grandmother used to do when she met some-one for the first time.

'Humph.' The grandmother spoke at last. 'You'll do. You can kiss my cheek.'

Amy did so and her smile spread. 'I'm pleased to meet Ben's grandmother.'

'If you've quite finished, Mother?' Ben's father raised his eyebrows. 'We'd like to greet our guest as well.'

The father was as tall as his son. They were both big men, but the aura of strength was tempered by the amusement showing in their eyes. The mother was also quite tall and towered over Amy, but then just about everyone did, she thought wryly. Mrs Scott had a determined air about her, but when she smiled Amy was instantly reassured. She had been worried about meeting Ben and Howard's parents but, much to her relief, they were all nice people and made her feel welcome.

It turned out to be the happiest Christmas she could remember. After spending Christmas Eve with Ben's family, he brought her back and she had a lovely time with Ted and Mrs Dalton.

The boys didn't return until the New Year, and then the three of them set about the business of selling paintings, pots and sculptures. They were all determined to make 1935 a more profitable year.

# 17

'Happy birthday for tomorrow, Amy.'

She glanced up as Ben and Howard came into the workshop, and the pot she was attempting to throw collapsed in a wet mess as she shook with laughter. They were standing in the doorway each holding out a chrysanthemum, one of her favourite flowers for painting, but even more amazing was the fact that they were wearing suits and ties!

'Why thank you, kind sirs.' She stood up as they came towards her, reaching out for the flowers with hands caked in clay. They had been speeding through the year of 1935 and she hadn't even noticed December arriving. 'What are you all dressed up for?'

'We've decided it's time for us to open our own shop.' Howard's eyes were gleaming in anticipation.

'Oh, that's wonderful!' When it looked as if she was going to come near them with her muddy hands they stepped back in alarm.

'Get cleaned up, Amy,' Ben instructed, making sure she didn't touch his one and only good suit. 'The shop next to Ted's is empty and we're going to have a look at it.'

'That should be perfect.' She knew it well, and it was bigger than Ted's bookshop.

'Don't just stand there.' Howard turned her towards the sink. 'Wash the mess off and change.'

'You want me to come with you?'

The friends looked at each other and sighed dramatically, then turned their attention back to Amy.

It was Ben who spoke. 'We're going into business – the *three* of us: Scott, Palmer and Carter. And you and Howard have got to learn to drive.'

Amy's headlong flight towards the sink came to a sudden halt and she turned her head. 'I can't learn to drive, can I?'

'Not legally until next year when you're seventeen, but I'll start showing you how to drive now, and then you will be ready to take your test when you're old enough.'

'I'd like to be able to drive.' The idea excited Amy. 'So you're going to teach us?'

'I am.'

Howard held his hands up in horror. 'No fear, Ben. Ted will teach us.'

'Coward.' Ben didn't seem at all put out by the refusal. 'You can ask Ted, but I'm teaching Amy, and it's not the slightest bit of good you arguing about it.'

'I wouldn't dare.' Amy grinned. 'Perhaps I'll end up as a racing driver.'

Howard pulled a face. 'That's a possibility if Ben teaches you.'

Continuing over to the sink she washed her hands. 'I think it will be fun.'

'That's my girl.' Ben shot Howard a smug glance. 'Amy's not so easily frightened.'

After a quick wash and change of clothes they were on their way to see if the shop would be suitable. They had all been working very hard over the last few months and sales of everything they produced had increased markedly. Ben's paintings were becoming quite popular. The word going round was that this was an artist who was going places, and his work would increase in value. Some people were buying as investments. Amy didn't know how the talk had started, but she had her suspicions that Ben and Howard might have started the rumour themselves. They were a couple of very enterprising young men. It was the same with Howard's beautiful sculptures, and the pots painted by Amy were selling as fast as she could produce them. This was the right time for them to branch out, and she was thrilled to be a part of their success.

As soon as they arrived, Ted joined them. 'The keys have been left with me so you can take your time looking around.'

In fact it didn't take them long to decide. There was good window space, and a large room upstairs just perfect for a gallery. The downstairs would be ideal for Howard and Amy's work. The whole place would need a good clean, walls painted and shelves fitted downstairs.

They were fired up with enthusiasm when they went to the letting agency to sign the agreement. After Ben and Howard had signed, Ben handed Amy the pen, pointing to the place where she should put her signature as well, his expression telling her plainly that they were in this together.

She signed, very pleased that she had practised how to do this all that time ago. She wouldn't have to embarrass herself, or them, by putting a cross for her name. Her life was very happy and full now and it was hard to remember when it had been different.

Ben pocketed the keys, they shook hands with the agent and made their way back to Ted's. They were surprised to see Mrs Dalton there wearing her best hat.

'All settled?'

Ben rattled the keys. 'The shop is ours.'

'Good, it's about time you did this.' She ushered a customer out as soon as he'd paid for his purchase and locked the door. 'You're closing early today, Ted, because I'm taking you all out for a double celebration: Amy's birthday tomorrow and the new business.'

'Marvellous!' Howard rubbed his hands together. 'Where are we going?'

'To the Lyons Corner House in Marble Arch. It's a wonderful place to have afternoon tea.'

They couldn't all get in Ben's car, so Mrs Dalton went with Ted in his van.

Amy was speechless when they arrived. The place was huge, with sparkling chandeliers, tall plants and music playing in the background. It was also crowded.

They had a table where they could see everything clearly and Amy watched, turning this way and that way, not wanting to miss anything. There was a big plant behind her, and after examining it carefully she swivelled back to the table and caught a glint of amusement in Ben's eyes.

'What is it?' she whispered.

'A palm tree.'

'Never!'

He nodded.

Satisfied with that bit of information she focused on the waitresses. They were really smart in their white aprons and funny little hats. Leaning towards Ben, she whispered again, 'Don't they move fast?'

'That's why they're called "Nippies".' He spoke quietly close to her ear. 'Why are we whispering?'

She hit his arm. 'Stop teasing. I've never been anywhere like this before.'

And she had never seen so many cakes. They tried them all until they couldn't eat another crumb. Amy sighed, eyeing the one remaining iced cake on the stand. It was a shame to leave it but she would burst if she tried to eat anything else.

'That was lovely; thank you so much, Mrs Dalton. This has been a wonderful birthday celebration.'

When she looked back to the centre of the table, the cake had disappeared. 'Who had the cake?'

Ben and Howard looked innocent, but it was a sure bet that one of them had eaten it. There wasn't much of her to fill up, but it seemed impossible to satisfy either of the two of them. Growing boys, Mrs Dalton always declared. Amy studied them under lowered lashes, her mouth twitching at the corners. She hoped they didn't grow any more!

Ted stood up. 'The celebration isn't over yet. Come back to the shop.'

They piled back into the cars and headed for Chelsea again, only to find that Ted had gone mad and bought a bottle of champagne.

It was sacrilege but they drank it out of mugs, laughing and making plans for the future. Amy had never tried champagne before, but thought it was a bit like lemonade. 'Ben said we've got to learn to drive,' she told Ted, grinning as the bubbles tickled her nose.

'Yes, it would be a good idea.' Ted emptied the bottle by refilling everyone's mugs.

'I hope you'll teach me, Ted.' Howard smirked. 'Ben's a good driver, but he's too fast for my liking.'

'I don't mind doing that.' Ted glanced at Amy. 'And what about you?'

'I'm teaching her. She's not afraid of me, are you?'

'No, Ben,' she said meekly, and then burst into laughter as if it was the funniest joke she'd ever heard.

'Oh dear.' Ben rested his arm on Ted's shoulder. 'I think the drink has gone to her head.'

Mrs Dalton peered at Amy, looking quite flushed herself. 'Perhaps we shouldn't have let her have strong drink.'

'It's only like lemonade.' Amy thought that was a huge joke as well.

'I think you'd better take her home, boys.' Ted shook his head. 'And don't let her behind a wheel in that state.'

'I'm not drunk!' She looked in her mug and tipped it upside down. 'Oh dear, it's all gone.'

In one swift movement, Ben whipped the mug out of her hands, lifted her off the floor and tossed her over his shoulder, making her squeal. Beating on his back with her small fists, she cried through her giggles, 'Put me down, you fool!'

Ignoring her remonstrations, he marched out to the car with her in this undignified position.

She couldn't think what all the fuss was about. She felt fine!

The next week flew by as they scrubbed, painted walls and made the shop ready for the Christmas trade. Ben and Howard's fathers came along to try out their carpentry skills by building shelves to display the pottery, and they were delighted with the upstairs when paintings were lining the walls. The mothers were often there to make tea and offer encouragement; in fact it was turning out to be quite a family affair. Even Grandmother came to see if she approved, and when she did, Ben declared that nothing could stop them now. Amy knew them all quite well now, and her respect for them grew. They must have been very worried when their sons dropped out of university, but they had given them the freedom to pursue their dream. She had judged Howard's family as uncaring, but that quite clearly wasn't true. They had believed that his desire to make it as a sculptor had merely been a whim and had expected him to give up quickly. As soon as they'd realized that wasn't the case they had rallied round to help. But Amy knew that neither Howard nor Ben would take money from their parents. They wanted to make it on their own and everyone respected that desire.

One week before Christmas they opened the shop, hoping they hadn't made a terrible mistake. All the time they had been working to get it ready they had been buoyant with enthusiasm, but once the doors were opened to the public the doubts crept in. Trade, however, proved to be slow but steady; a good number of people came into the shop – and a pleasing proportion of them even bought things! Ted and Mrs Dalton, who were so proud of the three of them, had done a good job with publicity by telling all their friends and neighbours about the shop.

'Right, Amy.' Ben slipped her coat around her shoulders as they locked up for the night. 'We've been too busy for driving lessons, but you must start now. Howard can go home with Ted and you can have a drive.'

'What?' Pushing her arms into the coat she blinked at him. 'I'm not old enough, Ben. Suppose a policeman catches us?'

'Don't worry, I know a quiet piece of spare ground.'

'Good luck,' Howard called out as he disappeared into Ted's shop.

Amy was relieved to see that the place Ben took her to wasn't a road. The ground was rough and uneven but it was a large enough space to drive around. The first problem was the seat. Ben was so tall he had it pushed back as far as it would go. Quite the reverse was needed for Amy, and even with it right forward she could only just reach the pedals.

Ben studied her driving position, frowning. 'We'll have to put a cushion behind you. That should solve the problem, but for the moment sit well forward in the seat.'

She wriggled until she was comfortable. 'Now what do I do?'

Following his instructions carefully they started to move. Her steering wasn't too good so Ben kept one hand on the wheel to guide her. The gears were tricky, but she quickly learned that you had to push the clutch down twice to get into first gear. Double-declutch, Ben explained.

It came as a surprise but she discovered she loved it and was sorry when he took over again and drove them home.

When the engine had been turned off, Ben gave her a playful tap on the chin with his large fist, looking highly delighted. 'You're a natural, Amy, and will be driving on your own in no time at all.'

'Do you think so? I really enjoyed it. When can I try again? I've got to steer better, haven't I?'

'You'll soon get the feel of that. We'll have another go after work tomorrow.' He got out, came round and held open the door for her. 'Come on, that's enough excitement for one day. I'm starving.'

Mrs Dalton called them into her dining room as soon as they walked in the door. Howard and Ted were already there. 'You've all been working very hard this week, so I've cooked you a dinner tonight.'

Ben kissed her cheek. 'You spoil us, Mrs Dalton.'

'Get away with your flattery, Benjamin.' She pushed him towards a chair, flushed with pleasure. 'I'm proud of my family and I like to give you a decent meal now and again. I'm sure you're all too busy to eat properly.'

'How did you get on with the driving, Amy?'

Before she could answer Howard, Ben said, 'She took to it as if she's always been behind a wheel of a car. By the time she's ready to take her test she'll be an excellent driver.'

Howard nodded. 'That'll be handy, because although I'm making progress, we need the three of us to be able to drive.

We're being asked more and more often to deliver some of the larger pieces.'

Over an excellent meal they discussed the business and sorted out a schedule for one of them to man the shop while the other two worked to keep it well stocked. Mrs Dalton said she was happy to help out serving customers if they liked, and was clearly very pleased when her offer was accepted with much gratitude.

The rate at which items were being sold meant they were all working like mad to have enough to fill the shelves and walls. They wondered if trade would disappear after Christmas but, although it did slacken off, they went on selling steadily after the New Year of 1936 arrived. And by the spring Amy was driving confidently: she couldn't wait until she was old enough to go out on the roads.

# 18

August had been quite hot, but the last few days had been stifling. Amy paused as she arranged a new window display, studying the street outside. The heat was shimmering on the road, giving the illusion that it was wet in places, but the people walking by didn't appear to be bothered about it and trade was brisk. That was why she was doing the window in such heat; so many things had been sold.

Humming to herself as she decided where to put Howard's beautiful sculpture of a horse and her foal, she was completely lost in her task. This was something she had discovered she loved doing. Howard was getting better and better, as was Ben, and even her decorating was earning high praise, giving her confidence in her ability. But more than anything she was delighted to see Ben and Howard's talent recognized. That was more important to her than all the personal praise in the world. She loved her 'brothers' and did everything she could to help them.

A sudden flash made her look up quickly. She saw two men outside watching her. One had a camera up to his eye and was taking picture after picture. Frowning, she moved out of the window. Had Ben asked someone to photograph the shop without telling her? And if so, why were they taking pictures of her? And they must have been, because the window was nowhere near finished. They'd had a lot of publicity lately, but she always kept in the background. She considered that Ben and Howard were the artists and should have all the attention.

When Ben came down from the gallery, Amy told him about the men.

'I haven't asked anyone to take pictures of the shop.' He looked outside. 'There's no one there now. I expect it was just a keen photographer wanting a picture of a lovely girl at work.'

She pulled a face at him. He was always saying daft things like that. 'Well, I wish they wouldn't. I don't like it.'

'You'll have to get used to this.' His smile was teasing. 'We're getting famous, and you're part of the team.'

'You're the clever ones.' She shook her head in denial, and ducked laughing as he tried to ruffle her hair. 'Don't do that. It took me ages this morning to make it behave.'

'Ah, you didn't manage it then?'

She launched herself at him, her little fists pummelling his chest. 'Cheek! I've a good mind to have it cut short.'

'Don't you dare! It's a dream to paint.' With that, he disappeared up the stairs, taking them three at a time.

Still laughing, she resumed her job of dressing the window. The irritation she'd felt about the photographer was forgotten.

'Ben.' Howard burst into his bedroom the next morning waving a newspaper at him. 'Get up. Have you seen this?'

Yawning, Ben took the paper from his friend, glanced at the section being pointed out, then shot to his feet, the bedclothes tumbling on to the floor in a heap. 'Oh, hell! Get Ted, but whatever you do don't wake Amy.'

Five minutes later Ted arrived. He was bleary-eyed from sleep, but he had managed to pull on some clothes. 'What the blazes is the matter? It's only six-thirty.'

'Amy said someone was taking photographs of her yesterday while she was in the window. I dismissed it as unimportant.' Ben held out the paper for Ted to see. 'I was wrong, and now we know why they were there.'

Ted read in silence, and then groaned in dismay. 'Oh, dear God! This is going to crucify her.'

Ben took it from him again and read out loud.

'MURDERER'S DAUGHTER IN CHELSEA
'Amy Carter, daughter of notorious murderer Gregory Carter, is part of a prestigious art gallery in the King's Road. She has prospered since her father was hanged at Pentonville Jail nearly two years ago.

'She has forsaken her humble roots and now lives a life of luxury, even though she has never been able to read or write. Her former neighbours told this newspaper that she has turned her back on all her friends in Wapping, and now considers herself too good even to visit.'

Howard paced the room. 'Can we keep this from her?'

'No, that wouldn't be fair.' Ted sighed deeply. 'She's bound to find out. Her reading is good enough now for her to be able to make out the gist of the story, and you know how she scans the papers to see how much she can read.'

The three of them stood there in various states of undress, their expressions ranging from grim to furious.

'How did this happen?' Howard, terribly agitated, continued to stride up and down.

'God knows.' Ben's large hands clenched into fists. 'But if I find the person responsible I'm going to beat him to a pulp.'

'Violence isn't going to help,' Ted pointed out firmly. 'There will be reporters waiting outside the shop this morning, so we're all going to have to protect her as much as we can.'

'Of course we'll do that,' Ben growled, 'but we've got to stop this right now!'

Howard sat on the bed, picked up the paper and read it again. 'It's all lies!' He surged to his feet and threw the paper down in fury. 'We saw how her neighbours treated her, didn't we, Ted? They never lifted a finger to help her.'

Ted retrieved the paper. 'Yes we did, so let's turn this against them, shall we?'

'How?' The boys spoke in unison.

'I know a reporter on a reputable paper and I'll have a word with him to see if we can get the truth printed.'

'That's a good idea.' Ben still looked ready to hit someone. 'But Amy must agree.'

'I wouldn't do anything without her permission.'

'Oh, God!' Howard groaned. 'How are we going to tell her?'

'I'll do it.' Ben straightened to his full height. He had met the little waif and brought her home when she had nowhere to go. Up to that time her young life had been unbelievably hard, but since she had been with them she had grown and blossomed, learnt to laugh and be happy. And now her past was about to rear its nasty head. The thought of what this was going to do to her was like a physical pain to him. But at least this time she wouldn't be alone!

'Mrs Dalton must be a part of this.' Ted opened the door, turned his head and said grimly, 'Wake Amy and meet us in the kitchen.'

Ben and Howard followed him out.


A firm rap on her door made Amy jump as she was struggling to tame her hair with a brush.

'Amy, you up?'

'Come in, Ben.' She peered at the clock and her mouth turned up in amusement. What was he doing up so early?

He must be extra hungry and didn't want to cook his own breakfast.

As the door opened she turned to smile at him and was astonished to see Howard there as well. Her smile died before it had time to form when she noted their grim expressions. She leapt to her feet. 'What's the matter? Are Ted and Mrs Dalton all right?'

'They're fine.' Ben reached out and gently pushed a strand of hair away from her eyes. 'We want you to come to the kitchen. There's something we have to tell you.'

Amy allowed them to guide her along the passage, really worried now. She had never seen them look like this.

When she saw Mrs Dalton and Ted waiting for them the breath caught in her throat. 'What on earth has happened?'

Mrs Dalton already had the kettle boiling to make tea. 'Sit down, all of you. I'll make a large pot of tea while we decide what to do about this.'

'Do about what?' Amy let Howard ease her into a chair. 'I wish someone would tell me what's going on. You're frightening me!'

It was Ben who spoke. 'Do you remember you said someone had been taking photographs of you while you were arranging the shop window?'

She nodded, her heart missing a couple of beats.

'Well, there's an article in today's newspaper about you. You're going to have to be brave, Amy, because it isn't nice.'

It took a couple of goes before she could draw in enough breath to talk. 'Show me.'

Ted slid the newspaper in front of her, open at the right page.

Dipping her head she began to read, her finger slowly tracing each word on the headline and then moving further down the article.

'I'll read it for you, Amy.'

Ben's hand came into her view as he tried to take the paper from her. She pushed him away. 'I'll read it myself!'

They left her alone then to struggle, not only with the words, but also with the horror of what she was gleaning from her laborious efforts. Her finger began to shake. She had been feeling so safe and happy. How could this have happened? Her stomach churned as dismay and anger warred inside her.

'What's this word?' She stabbed at a place on the page.

Ben leant over. '"Prestigious". Amy . . .'

They were crowding her; she needed space. Scrambling to her feet she went and leant against the back door, sinking down until she was sitting on the doormat. The silence stretched as every word was examined and deciphered where possible, until there was no doubt in her mind what was being said about her. Vicious pain ripped through her, the paper falling from her hands as she wrapped her arms around her middle. She was dry-eyed, unable to shed the tears fighting for release, as she recognized what this could do to the people she loved.

'I'm so sorry,' she moaned.

Ben immediately knelt in front of her. 'You haven't anything to be sorry about.'

'I have!' She looked up wildly, searching his face and Howard's as he sat next to her as well. 'I've ruined everything for you. The shop was doing so well, now no one will come there.'

'You're thinking about us?' Ben took her face in his hands. 'This isn't going to hurt our business.'

'It will. It will,' she wailed. 'I'm a murderer's daughter. It says so in the paper, and now everyone will know.'

Scooping her into his arms, Ben rose to his feet. 'We can deal with that. Ted's got a plan.'

Tucking her head in his shoulder the dam she had been holding back broke. She howled like a baby. 'I . . . I've ruined every . . . everything for you.'

'No you haven't, my lovely girl.' Ben walked up and down with her, waiting for the storm of tears to subside. 'Knowing the public, they'll be queuing up to buy something. But that isn't what's important here. We've got to do something about the lies. How much of it were you able to read?'

'Enough,' she mumbled, feeling comforted and protected. He was carrying her like a distressed child. 'What are we going to do? I'll have to leave here, and I don't want to!'

'You'll do no such thing, Amy.' Mrs Dalton spoke firmly. 'You belong here with us and we won't let anyone drive you away. And as Ben said, Ted has a plan.'

Ben leant back until he could look into her face. 'Want to hear what it is?'

She nodded, the tears dried now. 'Why did they write those things about me?

'Money!' Ted said as Ben sat her in a chair again. 'I'll bet one of your ex-neighbours sold that information to the newspaper.'

Her eyes blazed with anger now. 'Can we find out who?'

'We'll find them.' Howard's mouth was set in a determined line. 'And when we do they are going to receive a visit from us!'

'We'll all go and give them a piece of our minds.' Mrs Dalton pushed a cup of tea in front of Amy. 'No one goes about upsetting my girl and gets away with it.'

Amy gazed at each one in wonder at their vehemence.

Then she turned to Ben and Howard, still concerned about them. 'You said this wouldn't ruin your careers?'

'Absolutely not!' Howard smiled then. 'And it won't hurt yours as a ceramic decorator, either.'

That made her eyes open wide. 'Is that what I am?'

'Of course you are.' Howard turned to Ben with a look of mock disgust. 'Doesn't this girl of ours take any credit for her talent?'

'Doesn't look like it.'

'Amy, Amy.' Howard's sigh echoed around the kitchen. 'You're as much an artist as we are. Without you we wouldn't have our successful shop.'

The tears gathered again. 'But what about this?'

Ted picked up the paper and tossed it on to the draining board in disgust. 'That can go where it belongs, in the dustbin. But there's something I'd like to do, with your permission, Amy.'

'What's that?' They were all acting as if this was of no importance, but she still felt sick with worry. Suppose they were wrong and it did ruin their business? She would never be able to forgive herself.

Ted then explained about the reporter he knew, and how he was going to see if he could get him to print her side of the story. 'It will prolong the publicity, I'm afraid, but we can't let this go unchallenged.'

Casting Ben an anxious glance she chewed her lip until it was sore. Always she turned to Ben, her friend, brother and saviour.

'I believe it would be right to do this,' he said gently, 'but it must be your decision.'

'Trust us, Amy,' Ted urged. 'None of us would ever do anything to hurt you.'

'I know,' she whispered, facing Mrs Dalton. 'This has

to be your decision as well, because I'm living in your house.'

'I don't give a toss what people say about me, my dear. Many already view me with suspicion because I took three men into my home.' She laughed. 'They can think what they like. I've got nothing to be ashamed of – and neither have you. What your father did he's paid for with his life, but you are innocent of any crime. I say go ahead, Ted, and let's get the buggers.'

As they all laughed, Amy gaped at her. She had *never* heard Mrs Dalton swear before. 'What will you say, Ted?' Surrounded by people who cared, she was suddenly buoyant with hope that everything would be all right in the end.

'I'll tell the truth, of how your neighbours turned their backs on you while you tried to cope with the tragedies of losing both parents, never offering help or support for a girl hardly old enough to care for herself. And I want you to write a letter to go with the report.'

She was horrified. 'I can't do that!'

'Yes you can. I'll help.'

'But, Ted, what about the mistakes?'

'A couple of spelling mistakes won't matter, but it must be in your own handwriting, and words.' Ted squeezed her clenched hand in encouragement. 'You can do it.'

'All right, I'll try.' She blew out a pent-up breath and shook her head at Ted as if he were mad.

Her agreement brought forth a round of applause.

'Right, everyone.' Ben rubbed his hands together in anticipation. 'Let's get ready for the battle.'

Flanked by Ben on one side, Howard on the other, Mrs Dalton marching in front and Ted behind them, Amy groaned in dismay when she saw a crowd with cameras

183

waiting outside the shop. Her step faltered and immediately two arms came round her shoulders and held her firmly.

Ben ducked his head and whispered, 'It's all right, we've got you surrounded, and Mrs Dalton will soon clear that lot out of the way. Do you know she comes from a family of tough dockers?'

She shook her head mutely, hardly able to believe that of the refined Mrs Dalton.

'A fight's nothing new to her and I think she's enjoying herself.' Ben grinned down at Amy. 'She married well but has never been ashamed of her roots.'

'Well I never!'

Howard chuckled. 'And Ted's an effective rearguard.'

Amy's laugh held a touch of hysteria. They might all be making light of this disaster, but she was frightened. Her family's past had reared its ugly head just when she had believed it was gone and forgotten.

'Clear off!' Mrs Dalton was waving her umbrella at the reporters. 'Haven't you got anything better to do than hound my little girl?'

'You ain't her mother. She's dead, isn't she?' One of the reporters held a pen and pad in his hand.

'She is, but I'm her mother now, and I'm not going to let any of you slander her. *So clear off!*'

As the umbrella waved dangerously close to his face, Amy gasped. 'She's going to attack them!'

'Go to it, Mrs Dalton!' Ben stepped forward to stand by his landlady.

Ted took his place beside Amy, shaking with laughter. 'They don't stand a chance now.'

Amy couldn't believe her eyes when Ben lifted one short man away from the shop doorway and plonked him down several yards away.

'Oi! That's assault,' the man protested.

'You were causing an obstruction.' Ben eyed the man from his six feet four inches of height. 'Do you want to make something of it?'

The man visibly blanched. 'There's no need for that attitude. We're only doing our job.'

'Then I suggest you go and do it somewhere else.' Ben's tone was deceptively mild.

With the shop entrance now cleared, Mrs Dalton unlocked the door and let Howard, Ted and Amy inside.

Once Mrs Dalton was also in, Ben stood in the open doorway, pretended to spit on his hands and rubbed them together. 'Anyone who tries to come in will be thrown straight into the gutter.' He lifted his eyebrows in query. 'Who wants to be the first to try?'

Amy shot Howard a glance of alarm. 'He doesn't mean that, surely?'

'Oh, yes he does.' He grinned at her in delight and called to his friend. 'What some help?'

'No thanks, I can handle this puny lot.'

Amy looked from one to the other in disbelief. 'You're all enjoying yourselves.'

'Haven't had this much fun since we left university. Ben doesn't often use his size as a weapon, but when he does anyone in his way would be wise to scatter. He doesn't make idle threats.'

The men outside obviously decided that discretion was called for and began to leave. Ben rested his hands on the top of the doorframe, dipped his head and watched. 'Don't bother to come back. I'll be here all day, and I'm not in a very good mood after the way you've slandered my sister.'

'Sister?' One man was brave enough to hesitate for a moment. 'She's an only child.'

'Not any more, she isn't.' The tone in Ben's voice made the man walk quickly away up the street.

Ted turned to Mrs Dalton. 'That skinny kid you took in after he'd skipped university has grown into his height, hasn't he?'

She nodded, looking at the two boys with real affection in her eyes. 'They both have.'

Howard slapped his friend hard on the back when the door was closed at last. 'That was brilliant, Ben. Now they're thoroughly confused.'

'Oh dear.' Amy was trembling. 'I'm not sure you should have done that. They will write awful things about you tomorrow.'

'Let them try.' Ben was totally unconcerned as he winked at her. 'You watch our sales increase.'

'Especially when we gain public sympathy after they read the truth.' Ted was enjoying himself as well. 'Come on, Amy, let's get our letters written.'

'Go to your shop and do that,' Ben suggested. 'And don't forget to give your business a plug as well, Ted. We might as well get something out of this while we clear Amy's name.'

It took Amy five attempts to write the short note to show that she could indeed read and write. Ted helped when her spelling needed correcting – which was often, much to her dismay. It took a great deal of effort on her part, but when it was finally done she realized how much she had progressed.

'That's great,' Ted praised her.

'You sure?' She was very doubtful. 'Have I said the right things?'

Reading it through again, Ted nodded. 'You've said how hurt you've been by the lies told about you by neighbours who turned their backs on you when you needed help. And how grateful you are to the kind people who took you in and gave you love and understanding. You've done this very well and hit just the right note.'

She was still very uncertain about it. 'What about the spelling? Is it good enough?'

'It's good enough.' Ted nodded. 'You couldn't have done this a year ago, could you?'

'I couldn't have done it now without your help.' She grimaced. 'It's taken me over an hour to write a few sentences.'

'No one's going to know that.' Ted put it with the letter he'd finished a long time ago, and headed for the door. 'Look after the shop for me and I'll see if I can get this in tomorrow's paper. And that will be an end of it.'

As he left the shop she placed her head in her hands, hoping he was right.

# 19

The next morning, the paper Ted had contacted carried both letters and a short piece by the reporter. Amy allowed Ben to read it to her this time, sighing with relief when he had finished.

'Will they leave me alone now?'

'I expect so.' Ted nodded. 'This has been unpleasant for you, Amy, but you can put it behind you now.'

'That's what I thought before, but is anyone ever going to forget that my father was hanged for murder?'

'Time heals everything, my dear,' Mrs Dalton said kindly, then stood up with a determined air about her. 'But I'm going to make sure this sort of thing doesn't happen again.'

Ben watched her with suspicion. 'What are you going to do?'

'I'm just going to have a little talk with Amy's old neighbours, that's all.'

Amy leapt to her feet in alarm. 'No, please don't do that!'

'Now, don't you worry. I only want to see why they did this.'

'Not on your own, you don't.' Ben also stood up, quickly followed by Howard.

'We're coming with you, Mrs Dalton.' Howard was frowning.

'There's no need for that.' She waved away their concern. 'If I turn up with the two of you, they'll slam the doors in my face.'

'At least take Ben with you.'

'I'm quite able to take care of myself, Howard. Besides,

he's too big and threatening.' Mrs Dalton eyed the pair of them and pursed her lips. 'Come to think of it, you both are. When did you change from boys to men? I never noticed it happening.'

'Time has a habit of doing that.' Ted grinned. 'Couple of monsters now, aren't they?'

'I beg your pardon?' Ben struggled to keep his expression severe. 'We're still the same lovable boys we used to be, aren't we, Howard?'

'Of course.' He backed away from Ben before speaking again. 'You can call him a monster, if you like, but I'm not as big as him.'

When his friend lunged for him, he ducked behind Amy for safety.

'Will you two stop playing around?' Ted shook his head. 'But they're right, Mrs Dalton, you mustn't go there on your own. Take Ben with you.'

'If I do you mustn't say a word or interfere in any way, Benjamin.'

'I'll be so quiet you won't know I'm there.'

Mrs Dalton actually snorted. 'Impossible.'

'I'm coming too.' Amy didn't like this at all. She would be much happier if the whole thing were left alone, then perhaps it would just fade away.

'No you're not!' Everyone in the room spoke in unison.

'I am. If you're going to cause trouble then I'm coming with you.'

Ben lowered his head until he was eye to eye with her. 'Are you looking for a fight, little one?'

Pushing him away, she laughed, unable to help herself.

'Amy, I would much rather you didn't come.' Mrs Dalton was serious. 'I'm hoping to get them to talk freely to me, but I don't think they will if you are with me.'

'You sure?'

'Yes I am, my dear.' Then she turned her attention to Ted. 'Did your reporter friend find out who was behind this?'

'A Mr Preston, from number thirty-two Farthing Street.'

'Mrs Preston was my mother's friend.' Amy was staggered. She had never liked Mr Preston much, but these were the last people she would have thought nasty enough to do this to her. 'At least she was her friend until my dad's trial.'

'We'll go and see them.' Mrs Dalton sailed towards the door. 'Come on, Benjamin.'

'And we must open the shops.' Ted hauled himself out of the chair. 'I'll take you both in my van.'

Farthing Street looked even drabber than Ben had remembered, and there were a lot of men hanging around in groups looking bored and dejected. He was glad he hadn't allowed Mrs Dalton to come on her own.

He pulled up outside the house and before he could warn his landlady to be careful, she was marching up to the front door.

'What you want?' A man was leaning by the open door, a cigarette hanging from his mouth.

'I've come to see Mr and Mrs Preston.'

A woman came out then, looking worried and harassed. 'Oh, Bob, you haven't been gambling again, have you?'

'Course not!' He eyed Mrs Dalton, his gaze flicking to Ben as he stood close by. 'Brought your muscle with you?'

'This is my son; he gave me a lift.' Her gaze didn't waver from the couple in front of her. 'I'm here about Amy Carter.'

That caught their attention.

'I am reliably informed that it was you, Mr Preston, who is responsible for that scurrilous piece in the newspaper.'

He gaped at her, then turned to snarl at his wife, 'What's she on about?'

'She's asking if you told the newspaper those things about Amy.'

'Well, why don't she talk plain English? What if I did?'

'I would like to know why you would hurt an innocent girl with your lies?'

'They wasn't lies!'

At the belligerent tone of the man's voice, Ben took a step forward, making the man stuff his hands in his pockets. 'She ain't been near us, and when the landlord of the pub said his missus saw her in that posh shop, I decided to make a bit of money out of the story. We're all out of work here and the kids need feeding.'

'I'm sorry to hear that, Mr Preston.' Mrs Dalton's demeanour remained perfectly civil. 'And how much of that money went on beer?'

'None of your bleedin' business!'

Ben took another step forward.

'If you care to look in today's *Express* you will see a letter from Amy, pointing out how hurt she was by your accusations.'

Preston snorted. 'She can't read nor write. Always was a stupid kid.'

A deep rumble came from Ben as he took two steps forward this time, bringing him within three feet of the man. Mrs Dalton reached out and stopped him coming any closer.

'I assure you she is very intelligent and can read and write. If you contact the newspaper they will confirm that the letter they received was written in her own hand.' She fixed her attention on Mrs Preston. 'The truth of the matter is that you all abandoned her after the death of both her parents. It was despicable to leave a defenceless young girl on her own like that.'

Quite a crowd had gathered now and she spoke loud enough so all could hear. 'I'm sorry you are having a tough time, but you would be wise not to let anything like this happen again . . . or we shall be *very* angry.'

'That paper didn't pay enough anyway.' Mr Preston stomped past them to join his friends and walk up the road.

'I'm sorry about that.' Mrs Preston looked near to tears. 'Amy's mum was my friend and I wanted to help, but I was told not to go near them. He didn't mean no harm. He was just looking for a way to earn some money.'

'That's as maybe, but Amy was very upset.' Mrs Dalton fished in her handbag. 'How much of the money did he give you?'

'Not much, but he didn't say what they paid him.'

'I'll bet he didn't.' She took out two one-pound notes from her purse and handed them to Mrs Preston, who took them with trembling hands. 'Take this for food, and don't let your husband see it.'

'I won't.' The money was quickly shoved in the pocket of her pinny. 'Thank you, that's very kind of you. I'll try to see that he don't do nothing like this again.'

'That's all I ask. Amy has had enough sadness in her young life and I don't want to see her upset any more.'

Ben followed her back to the car, amazed by what he had just seen. Once they were on their way, he said, 'You gave her money!'

'That woman was not responsible. I suspect she has no control over her husband, and has to do as she is told. I grew up in places like this, and before I married my dear husband, I saw this sort of thing every day.'

'You're a marvel, do you know that, Mrs Dalton?' Ben cast her an admiring glance.

She gave a knowing smile. 'That's just what my husband used to say.'

When Ben walked into the shop Amy rushed up to him, very anxious. 'What happened?' Her hands clenched and unclenched as she listened to his explanation of their visit to the Prestons, breathing a gusty sigh of relief when she knew it hadn't turned into a fight. Ben was quite able to take care of himself, but she had been worried about Mrs Dalton confronting her former neighbours.

Ben studied her face. 'It's all right, Amy. Mrs Dalton handled them politely, but firmly, even slipping Mrs Preston a couple of pounds to buy food.'

'Mrs Dalton's such a kind woman.' Amy nodded, still looking worried. 'Will this be the end of it, Ben?'

'I think we can safely say that it is.' His smile was teasing. 'How's business?'

After huffing out a large breath to release the tension, she returned his smile. 'We've been *very* busy – and there's a pretty girl upstairs who's interested in one of your landscapes. Howard's keeping her company.'

Ben shot up to the gallery, as usual taking the steps three at a time, making Amy's grin as wide as it could get.

She began to put fresh items on the shelves, arranging them with her usual care to show to their best advantage. A surge of happiness ran through her. When she'd first seen those awful headlines she had been devastated, believing that the life she was building now had been tarnished – even destroyed. But she should have known better. Ben, Howard, Ted and Mrs Dalton had known about her father from the beginning and it hadn't bothered them. Neither had they changed towards her when they'd found out about her difficulty reading and writing. She had been silly to believe that a few nasty words in a newspaper would make them turn away from her. The thought that they might do that had been very frightening. But they had accepted her for what she was, without reservation. She would always be grateful to them for that . . .

The rest of the day was hectic. They sold three cats, two dogs, five vases, Howard's sculpture of the mare and foal, and Ben's pretty girl had bought one of his paintings.

By the time they closed the shop that evening, the three of them were in buoyant mood, and Amy's confidence had returned. None of the customers had made unkind remarks, in fact quite the opposite. They had all been very kind and chatted quite normally to her as they'd decided what to buy.

'Right!' Howard counted the takings – he had taken on the role of seeing to the financial side of the business. 'I think it's fish and chips all round this evening. Amy won't have to cook as she's got more painting to do. Tonight.'

'You're a slave-driver, do you know that?'

'I've got to be.' He did a little jig on the spot. 'I can't believe you sold my horse sculpture, Amy.'

'It was beautiful, and I didn't have any trouble at all. I hope you've got something to put in its place as that was the centrepiece of my window display.'

'There's always my naked lady.' Howard raised an eyebrow in query.

'That'll be perfect.' Amy couldn't hide her amusement as she remembered her first reaction to seeing him working on it. 'And what about you, Ben, have you got something to put on that empty space on the wall?'

'I'll see to it. Now, let's get those fish and chips. I'm starving!'

'You always are.' Amy and Howard burst into laughter as they spoke together.

When they'd finished the meal, Amy washed up as Mrs Dalton dried the dishes and put them away. Somehow, over the months Amy had become cook and washer-up for the boys as well as Ted. Although the kitchen was for Ted and Amy's use, Ben and Howard had abandoned their own cooking facilities and joined them for every meal. And it wasn't unusual for Mrs Dalton to join them quite regularly. They were becoming more of a family by taking meals together, and Amy loved it. It was so good to sit around the table listening to the talk and the joking. Any problems were dealt with by a joint effort, as had happened with the newspaper.

'Why do you keep looking at the clock, Benjamin?' Mrs Dalton put the last of the cups away. 'Are you going somewhere?'

'I'm going round to Miss Jackson's house.'

Ted looked up from the evening newspaper he had bought on the way home. 'Who's that?'

'The girl who bought my painting today. I said I'd hang it for her.'

Amy spun round, her eyes glinting with amusement. 'I told you she was pretty. What's her first name?'

Ben shrugged. 'No idea.'

'It's Sally,' Howard told them. 'When I was talking to her she seemed a very self-assured, capable girl, but as soon as she set eyes on Ben she became quite helpless.'

Mrs Dalton chuckled. 'I expect girls go like that all the time when they see him. You'd better go and put up her picture. She might buy another one.'

He smirked. 'That's what I'm hoping. See you later.'

After he'd left, Amy sat beside Howard, all eager. 'Do you think he really liked her? He ought to have a nice girlfriend.'

'Oh, he's taken out lots of girls, but nothing has ever lasted. It's the same with me. We've always been too broke and too involved in our art.'

'Things are changing now.' Amy nudged Howard's arm and grinned. 'You can both afford to take girls to the pictures or something.'

'Are you trying to marry us off?' Howard sat back in his chair, a suspicious expression on his face. 'What about you? You're getting old enough to have a boyfriend.'

'No one's going to be interested in me! I'm not pretty, and . . . and . . .'

'Amy.' Howard took hold of her hand as it clenched into a fist. 'You mustn't have such a low opinion of yourself. I agree that you're not conventionally pretty, but you are more than that. You have a fascinating, unusual face, and it makes everyone look twice. You're growing into a stunning girl. Why do you think Ben is always painting you? You're different. Be proud of that difference, and remember, your past is over and done with. No man worth a damn is going to let that bother him.' He traced her generous mouth with his finger. 'Just you smile and he'll be lost.'

She blushed at the compliments, but she found it hard to believe. 'You and Ben do say the daftest things.'

Howard sighed and shook his head. 'What would you do with her, Ted?'

'Just leave her to grow up and find out for herself. When the men are falling over themselves to be with her, perhaps she'll believe you.'

*

196

The next day Mrs Dalton came to help out at the shop because Howard was busy in his workshop and Ben was only stopping in for half an hour to hang two new paintings.

While there was a quiet moment, Amy nipped upstairs to see what Ben had brought in. She liked to know something about the pictures in case a customer asked questions.

He was standing in front of one, head on one side, as he made sure it was hanging correctly. When he stepped back, Amy couldn't believe her eyes.

'You can't sell that!'

'Why not?' He slipped a hand around her shoulder as she stood beside him.

'Because . . . because it's me,' she spluttered. 'No one's going to buy that.'

'We know it's you, but to anyone else it's just a picture of a young girl sitting with her knees up and gazing across the river. It's only a side view of your face, and you've changed a lot since I painted this.'

She stepped back to give the picture a critical examination. 'Well, I suppose . . .'

'It's a good painting, Amy, and I like it.'

'It is nice.' She had seen this many times in his studio, but it looked different somehow in the gallery. He had painted her quite a few times now, but had never attempted to sell any of the canvases before. He was right though; it was doubtful if anyone would recognize her.

'Good.' He ruffled her hair as he walked past her. 'I've put the price on it, so don't take a penny less. I'm not having my favourite girl being sold for a pittance.'

Running her hand through her hair to try and put it back in order, she looked at the ticket, and then spun round just as he headed for the stairs. 'Does this say twenty-five pounds?'

'That's right, and worth every penny. You'll sell that today.' With a confident wave he disappeared down the stairs.

'Well I never!' she muttered to herself after he'd gone. 'If anyone's interested then Mrs Dalton will have to deal with them, because I'll be too embarrassed.' But it wasn't likely to sell at that price.

It was late afternoon when a smart young man came in and went straight up to the gallery. Mrs Dalton was busy serving so Amy went up to see if she could help.

She stood back and watched him walk round studying the paintings. Much to her discomfort he stopped in front of her picture. And stayed there.

After a couple of minutes he turned his head and looked directly at her. She felt a jolt as his gaze fixed on her. His eyes were so blue they reminded her of a summer sky.

'Do you work here?'

Nodding, she walked over to him. 'Can I help you, sir?'

'Hmm.' He turned his attention back to the painting. 'This is good and might be just what I'm looking for. The flat I'm renting is very bare and I'm tired of seeing blank walls.'

It was hard not to blush as she thought of this good-looking man having her picture in his home. Still, she was here to sell. 'Benjamin Scott is an excellent artist, and this is a particular favourite of his.' She had picked up the sales patter quite quickly.

'I can see that.' Stepping back he gazed at it again, then turned, his startling eyes amused. 'That's you, isn't it?'

So much for the belief that no one would recognize her!

'It is.' There was little point in denying it.

198

'Are you a friend of the artist?'

'He's my brother.' She always referred to Ben and Howard in this way now.

'Ah.' He studied her carefully. 'Are you artistic as well?'

'I decorate the vases and dishes we have on sale downstairs.'

'Really? I saw a rather nice vase in the window, and thought my mother might like that.'

'You can have a close look at it when we go downstairs.' For some reason he was making her feel shy and uncomfortable. 'Would you like the painting, sir?'

'Probably.' He rubbed his chin thoughtfully. 'Why don't you come and have a cup of coffee with me while I decide? There's a café a few doors down from here.'

'I couldn't leave the shop, sir.' She was torn between wanting to go, and wanting to get away from him.

'Don't keep calling me "sir".' He smiled and held out his hand. 'I'm John Sterling.'

'Amy.' She shook his hand politely.

'Nice to meet you, Amy. Now, I'm sure you can leave your post for half an hour, can't you?'

Drawing in a silent breath, she nodded. He was thinking about spending rather a lot of money with them. 'I'll see if it's all right.'

Turning, she hurried downstairs and saw Mrs Dalton talking to a customer who was trying to decide between two vases. She beckoned her over. 'The customer upstairs is interested in the river painting,' she whispered, 'but he wants me to go and have coffee with him while he makes up his mind. If there's a chance of a sale I can't turn him down. I won't be more than half an hour.'

'That's all right, my dear. I can cope on my own for a

short time.' She winked at Amy. 'If he does buy then you must ask Ben for commission on the sale.'

Returning to the gallery, Amy said, 'Half an hour is all I can spare.'

'That's fine.' He ushered her out of the shop and along to the café, where he found a table by the window for them.

She waited while he ordered, and wondered what she was going to talk to him about. If it were Ben or Howard sitting opposite her, she would be chatting away quite happily.

When the coffee arrived, he smiled and handed her the sugar. 'Where do you live?'

'Chelsea. What about you?' She thought that was safe to ask seeing that he'd done the same.

'I've got a flat near St Bart's.'

'Sorry?'

'St Bartholomew's Hospital. I'm studying to be a doctor.'

She sat up, impressed. He must be very clever. 'Do you like it?'

'I've never wanted to do anything else.' He was serious now. 'It's hard work, but in another couple of years I'll be qualified. This is one of my rare days off and I decided to try and get something restful and soothing to look at when I do eventually get back to the flat. It's an exhausting schedule.'

'Do you have to do lots of exams and things like that?' She was relaxing in his company now.

He nodded. 'I'm often reading and studying half the night, but it's worth it. Becoming a doctor is the most important thing in my life.'

They talked for another ten minutes, and she found out that his parents lived in Hampshire somewhere, but she was careful not to say much about herself.

Keeping a sharp eye on the clock above the counter, Amy

stood up when it was time to go. 'Thank you for the coffee. Have you made up your mind about the painting?'

'Of course. I'll buy it and the vase for my mother.'

That evening over supper, Ben was smug. 'I told you it would sell, didn't I?'

'Yes, but I had to go to the café with him while he made up his mind.' She pulled a face at Ben. 'And he knew it was me!'

Mrs Dalton interrupted. 'He was a nice young man and couldn't take his eyes off Amy.'

'Ho, ho.' Ben and Howard both grinned.

'Sounds as if you've got an admirer.' Ted raised an eyebrow in amusement. 'We're going to have to start beating them away from the door soon.'

'Don't be daft!' She couldn't help laughing. They did say the silliest things. 'He's nearly a doctor.'

'What difference does that make?' Ted asked.

'Well, everything.' She began to clear the table to give herself something to do. 'He's clever, and I won't see him again.'

# 20

It was July of 1937 and Amy had almost forgotten John Sterling. Almost. But at times, when she was decorating a pot, she would find herself trying to mix the blue of his eyes, and then she would scold herself irritably. They had only met once and spent half an hour together, for heaven's sake! He had been an intelligent and dedicated man, and certainly wouldn't have been interested in her, even though he had bought the painting. However, she did hope it looked nice in his flat.

It had been an eventful few months and the time had just flown by. Ben was still seeing Sally now and again, but the only time they ever saw her was when she came to the shop. She was clearly in love with Ben, but none of them could quite work out how he felt about the pretty fair-haired girl with hazel eyes. The shop was still doing well. Trade fluctuated though: some weeks they sold quite a lot; others, almost nothing. Still, they were paying their way and they all had a little money in their pockets now. The amount in Amy's old teapot was mounting up, and she was very happy, loving the work she was doing. But best of all, she was helping Ben and Howard earn a reasonable living, and that gave her the greatest joy. Her only sadness was that although her reading had improved, it was still a laborious task. Over the last few months she had begun, reluctantly, to accept that, no matter how hard she tried, she would never read and write like the others. It caused her great frustration, but she knew now that it would always be like this. It was something she had to live with.

'This fruit bowl is such a beautiful blue.'

A customer claiming her attention brought her out of her musing. 'Yes, it is lovely.'

'It will look just right on my sideboard, so I'll have to buy it.'

Amy smiled and wrapped it for her, aware that someone else had come into the shop. After giving the customer her change, Amy looked up, her mouth opening in surprise.

'Mr Sterling.' He looked tired, but the easy smile and startling blue eyes were still the same. 'Do you want another painting?'

He shook his head. 'No. I wondered if you had half an hour to spare for a cup of coffee?'

'Oh, I don't think . . .'

'Please, Amy. I wanted to come sooner, but I've had exams and been working very hard. There's hardly been time to sleep, let alone come to see you.'

She didn't have the heart to turn him down and, if she was honest, she wasn't sure she wanted to. It was hard to believe how pleased she was to see him again after all these months. 'Ben's upstairs; I'll go and see if he can manage without me for a while.'

'Ah, he must be the artist who painted the picture I bought.' John headed for the stairs. 'I'll go and have a word with him.'

It was nearly an hour before they came down, talking and laughing like old friends.

Ben glanced at his watch. 'You might as well take an hour, Amy, and have lunch with John.'

A cup of coffee she didn't mind, but not lunch. She wasn't

being given a choice though, and that made her purse her lips in annoyance. 'Do you two know each other?'

'Only just met.' Ben leant against the banister, amusement glinting in his eyes. 'I'm quite capable of looking after the shop all by myself.'

If John Sterling hadn't been there watching with interest, she would have walloped Ben. It would only have made him laugh, of course, but she could tell by his expression that he was well aware that he was pushing her into something she wasn't keen on doing. Tipping her head to one side, she looked back at John. 'If I have lunch with you, are you going to buy another painting?'

'Ben said he's got another one of you I might like.'

'He's got dozens!' She glared at Ben, her eyes warning him not to do this to her. He was going too far with his teasing this time. John was a very attractive man, but she didn't want to get too friendly. Once he found out certain things about her, he would run like hell, and that would hurt. She wondered if this fear would ever leave her. But to have someone she liked and respected turn away from her in disgust would tear her apart. The only way was not to let some people get too close.

'I'll have plenty to choose from then.' John's lips twitched at her obvious disapproval. 'I might even buy that large bowl you've got in the window.'

'Oh, well, in that case . . .' She lifted her hands in surrender. She could never be angry with Ben for more than five minutes, and he knew it. 'I must warn you, Mr Sterling, that I'm *very* hungry.'

'So am I.' He shot Ben a sly wink before ushering her out of the door, giving her no chance to change her mind.

She thought they were going to the café again, but John had other ideas. He walked past it, turned left down a side road and stopped outside a smart restaurant. It was hard to control her groan. He didn't seem to be a struggling trainee doctor, and she would never be able to read a menu in a place like this! Simple meals were easy enough for her to decipher, but there wouldn't be anything simple here. She kept all this to herself, trying not to let the worry show on her face. It had been some time since she'd had to make up excuses to hide the fact that she couldn't read properly.

'The food's very good here.' He held the door open for her.

And expensive, she thought, walking into the dimly lit restaurant and wishing they were back at the humble café. Just wait till she got her hands on Ben later!

They were shown a table at once, and as soon as the menu was placed in front of her, she knew she had been right. Not only was it complicated, but it was in another language. The English was in brackets under each item, but she was far too tense to be able to read it.

'What are you going to have?'

No way was she going to struggle with that! Closing the menu and placing it back on the table, she managed a smile. 'You choose for me.'

'All right.' He looked quite pleased, then rattled off a few names. 'How does that sound?'

'Wonderful.' She had no idea that food could be so complicated. 'But don't forget I've only got an hour.'

He laughed. 'The service is fast.'

It would need to be if they were going to eat that much. She was sorry now that she had told him how hungry she was.

'Would you like wine with your meal?' John asked.

She shook her head in horror, remembering what the champagne had done to her. Never again! 'Just water, please.'

As the meal progressed, she began to relax in his company, just as she had the first time they had met. They talked about his studies and hopes for the future, the shop, and general things. He was easy, relaxing company.

They had thin soup first, then fish with a lovely sauce over it, followed by steak and various vegetables. When offered something from the array of gorgeous puddings and cakes, she reluctantly refused, knowing she couldn't eat another thing, and it was no good trying to force it down. The food had been a revelation to her, but she had enjoyed every mouthful.

When they arrived back at the shop, she rushed up to Ben and told him how sorry she was. Lunch had taken an hour and a half.

'Don't worry about it, Amy.' Ben waved away her apologies. 'Did you enjoy your meal?'

'It was lovely.'

'Good, that's all that matters.' Ben smiled at John. 'I'll take a break now. See you tonight, John.'

'About seven?'

'Fine.' Ben strode out.

'Now, Amy, show me that bowl, will you? My mother loved the vase.'

He bought it, and while she was wrapping it, she asked, 'Are you going out somewhere with Ben tonight?'

'No.' He handed over the money. 'I'm coming to your house to see the paintings he's got in his studio.'

The bowl nearly slipped out of her hands in surprise.

'He's very good and I'd like to see what else he paints. They are all landscapes and flowers on show upstairs.'

'That's because they sell quite well.' Amy finished the parcel and handed it to him. 'But he does paint other things.'

'I look forward to seeing them.' He studied her carefully

for a few moments. 'He told me he has a lovely portrait of you.'

'Oh, you don't want that!' She was glad she wasn't holding something delicate at that moment or it would surely have shattered on the floor. She didn't like the idea of someone having a big picture of her face on their wall, and Ben had assured her he would never sell that painting.

John merely smiled. 'I'll see you tonight, then.'

Just wait till you get back, Ben. I'm going to have a few words with you!

It was an hour before Ben returned to the shop and at the time Amy was too busy to talk to him, but as soon as there was a quiet time, she cornered him.

'You're not going to sell my portrait to John, are you? You told me you wouldn't part with it.' She gazed at him imploringly. 'I don't think I would like my picture on some-one else's wall. He doesn't know about me, and if he found out, he would hate the picture . . . and me.'

Ben's expression was sad. 'No he wouldn't, Amy. You were not responsible for what your father did.'

'I know, but I don't want him to have it. Please, Ben.'

'I won't part with it, Amy, I promise.' He ran his large hand over her hair. 'Don't worry. I would never do anything to upset you.'

She breathed a sigh of relief. 'I know.' Of course he wouldn't.

'I believe John Sterling is a good man, and he likes you very much. Give him a chance.'

Amy chewed her lip and frowned. 'I'm afraid to.'

'Then tell him everything about yourself. I'm sure it won't make any difference.'

'No, no I can't.'

*

Right on the dot of seven, John arrived, and Mrs Dalton brought him into the kitchen where they were all gathered. It was a favourite spot now.

'Let me introduce you to everyone, Mr Sterling.' Mrs Dalton made him sit down. 'The man at the end with his nose stuck in a book as usual, is Ted Andrews; Benjamin Scott you've met; next to him is Howard Palmer, the sculptor, and Amy Carter you also know.'

John looked confused. 'But you all have different surnames. Amy said Ben and Howard were her brothers.'

It took Mrs Dalton twenty minutes to explain the unusual set-up of the house. 'So you see, John – I may call you that?'

He nodded.

'We consider ourselves a family, and the boys are like brothers to my dear Amy.'

Amy was relieved when Mrs Dalton didn't go into details of how she came to be with them.

'Now you've met everyone, come up and have a look at the paintings.' Ben unfolded himself from the chair. 'Then I'll take you to see Howard's workshop and some of his special pieces.'


'That's beautiful.' John gazed at the portrait of Amy, mesmerized by the skill of the artist in depicting such an unusual and arresting face. 'How much do you want for it?'

Ben turned round from propping pictures up on the bench for John to see. 'That isn't for sale.'

Tearing his gaze away from the portrait, John frowned. 'Name your price.'

'Two hundred pounds.' Ben grinned and went back to his task.

'I'll take it.'

Ben spun back to face John. 'Whoa! I was only joking.'

'I'm not. I'll get you cash first thing in the morning, or you can have a cheque now.'

'That's tempting.' Ben ran a hand through his hair in astonishment. 'The one you bought was of a young girl sitting by the river, and unless you looked carefully, it could be anyone. But this is a full head and shoulders portrait. It's the first I ever did of her, and rather special. I don't know that I could part with it, and I promised Amy I wouldn't sell.' He gave a quiet chuckle. 'She thinks she's got a funny face and doesn't like the idea of it being on someone's wall.'

'And you won't break your word.' It wasn't a question.

'Never.' He leant against the bench, his expression serious. 'She'd had a tough life before she came here.'

John studied Ben intently. 'In what way?'

'It isn't my story to tell.'

'No, of course not.' John studied the painting again and sighed with regret. 'You've painted her with such love, and it shows.'

'I do love her.' He looked pointedly at John. 'But my feelings for her are as a brother.'

'And you'd do anything to protect her, even turn down two hundred pounds for a painting.'

'Yes, even that, and if you knew the courage she has shown, and is still showing, then you would understand.' Ben clenched his hands as he remembered how they had found her beside her mother's grave, forlorn and desperate. He didn't believe he would ever forget that day. It was imprinted on his mind like a bad nightmare that wouldn't go away.

'I like her, Ben, and I won't hurt her.'

'You'd better not, or you will have to face four very angry people.' He pushed away from the bench, relaxed and smiling again. 'Do you want to have a look at the other paintings?'

'Of course, that's what I came for.'

Ben raised a quizzical brow. 'Really? I thought you came to see Amy?'

'That too.'

After about an hour every picture had been examined carefully and John eventually chose a painting of the Thames from the Richmond Terraces. Ben had captured the panoramic view superbly.

'How much?'

'Twenty pounds.'

John gave him twenty-five. 'Could I commission you to do a painting for me? My parents live in a very nice Georgian house near East Meon in Hampshire. It's their twenty-fifth wedding anniversary in three months' time and I'd like to give them something special. Would you do a painting of the house for me?'

'I could do that.' Ben fished out a pad and pencil from the drawer and pushed it towards John. 'Give me the address and instructions how to find it. I'd have to go and have a look, make some sketches and maybe take a few photographs as well.'

He watched John as he wrote down the instructions, suddenly realizing that this was no struggling student doctor. Still, he didn't want to take advantage of that fact. He liked John Sterling. 'How long will it take to get there by car?'

'Well, I can make it in just under an hour and a half. Depends how fast you drive.'

'Too fast, according to Howard.' Ben nodded. 'Allowing for the time and travelling, it will cost you around thirty-five pounds.'

'That's fine.' John's smile was one of pleasure. 'My parents will be delighted to have a painting by you. They greatly admired the one in my flat when they visited; in fact my mother wanted to take it home with her. Will you be able to do this without them knowing?'

'I'll do my best.' Ben chuckled. 'Is there any shrubbery for me to hide in?'

'If you get down on your knees you might be able to hide.' John grinned as he eyed the tall man in front of him. 'If they do see you, for goodness' sake don't tell them your name or they'll guess I'm behind your visit.'

'I'll tell them I'm Howard Palmer, sculptor.'

'Good idea.' John picked up the painting he'd just bought. 'Let's go and see the sculptor and his assistant, shall we?'

Completely absorbed in painting a spotty dog, Amy didn't hear the door open. With the tip of her tongue peeping out of the corner of her mouth, she carefully daubed a brown patch around one eye.

'What do you think, Howard?' Looking up she found three pairs of eyes fixed on her face, and she immediately noticed the parcel under John's arm. 'You've bought one, then?'

He nodded. 'It will look lovely in my bedroom.'

'What did you choose?' She knew Ben had quite a lot of paintings upstairs. He was a prolific painter, always working on something. And she loved them all.

'Well . . .' John patted the parcel. 'There were so many to choose from, and I couldn't resist the lovely portrait—'

'Ben!' She was immediately on her feet. 'You didn't sell it, did you?'

'No, of course not, Amy.' His mouth twisted in a wry smile. 'I was sorely tempted, though, but I wouldn't break my promise to you. Not even for such a large price. John's got more money than sense to accept an amount I quoted in jest.'

John shrugged. 'It was worth every penny of that. If you ever decide to sell, please give me first refusal.'

'That's a promise.'

Howard couldn't contain himself. 'How much did he offer, Ben?'

'Two hundred pounds.'

The vase Amy had picked up to paint next crashed on to the floor, scattering in small pieces around her feet. She pushed them under the table with the toe of her shoe, muttering, 'Now look what you've made me do.' Her eyes were wide when she looked at Ben. She didn't like the idea of that painting being in anyone else's house – it was too personal – but she shouldn't have made him promise never to sell it. 'You can't turn down money like that.'

'I can, because it isn't something I can easily part with. John wanted the one I've got hanging in the studio. I did that painting immediately after sketching you by the river. I believe it's the best thing I've ever done.'

'But you've painted others.' She felt awful now.

'You didn't tell me you had more of Amy.' John put the painting down and shook his head. 'I thought I'd seen everything you had up there.'

'I've got more of her stacked in a cupboard.' Ben held up his hand to stop John returning to the studio. 'But they aren't full-face portraits like the one you saw, and I won't sell any of them. One day I shall have an exhibition showing Amy through the years.'

Amy's mouth dropped open. This was the first time he'd mentioned the idea. But it was ridiculous! He was always pulling her leg. He must be joking. She gave an inelegant snort. 'You're daft, Benjamin Scott, do you know that? No one would come to see paintings of me.'

Ben smiled knowingly. 'We'll see.'

'I'll do a couple of busts of her as well.' Howard winked at Ben. 'That should bring in the crowds.'

They were looking highly amused now. How they loved to tease her, and she found it hard to keep a stern expression.

'Just look at that face.' Ben leant on Howard. 'Is it any wonder I can't stop painting her?'

John joined in with the easy banter. 'Let me know when you're giving the exhibition and I'll be first through the door.'

'You're all as daft as each other.' Amy was laughing openly now. 'Why don't you go to the pub and have a drink? I've got work to do.'

'Good idea.' Howard brushed dust from his sleeve. 'Will you join us, John?'

'Love to.'

Wiping imaginary sweat from his brow, Ben said, 'We'll have a couple to steady our nerves for tomorrow.'

'What's happening tomorrow?' John picked up his painting again.

'Amy's taking her driving test.' Howard pretended his hands were shaking. 'I think we'd better make it three pints. My nerves are ragged already.'

When she made to lurch at them with a rather large bowl in her hands, they shot out of the door, calling, 'Bye, Amy.'

'They're potty.' She settled down again to paint, but there was a smile on her face. She loved the way they teased her.

## 21

'Stop shaking, Amy, there's nothing to it. You'll pass easily.'

'It's all right for you to look so smug, Howard; you took your driving test last week. But suppose I can't read the road signs, or I turn left instead of right?' She hadn't been worried about the test yesterday, but now it was almost here, she was terrified.

'Which hand have I put the ring on?' Mrs Dalton asked, pouring her another cup of tea.

Amy admired the lovely pearl and coral ring Mrs Dalton had loaned her for today. 'My right hand.'

'Remember that and you won't make a mistake.' Mrs Dalton smiled reassuringly.

Ben leant back in his chair, making the front legs leave the floor. 'We've been over and over the area they use for tests, and you know all the roads.'

She nodded. The last few weeks Ben had been making her drive all the time, and as soon as Howard had passed his test, they had both taken her over the route. 'Suppose they take me somewhere different – somewhere we haven't been?' She worried her bottom lip. 'And what about the Highway Code, suppose I can't remember that?'

Ted picked up the booklet, opened it and fired questions at her. She answered every one correctly. 'You're worrying over nothing.'

She stirred her tea. That was true; they had all taken turns in reading it out to her until she knew it off by heart, but if she panicked it would all disappear from her memory.

Things had a habit of doing that. Oh, she would be so relieved when this was over.

'Time to go.' Ben stood up. 'Come on, you're going to do just fine. I have every confidence in you.'

The teasing of last night had gone and they were giving her all the support she could want.

'I'm coming too.' Howard joined them. 'Mrs Dalton's minding the shop until we get back.'

Amy walked to the car with Ben and Howard on either side of her. She was old enough now to have learnt a bit about life, and Mrs Dalton had had a frank talk with her about what happened between a man and a woman, but there was nothing sexual between her and the boys. They had always treated her like a sister, and it was that kind of love they shared. She knew they went out with girls from time to time, and she prayed they would both find themselves good wives one day. She adored them so much, especially Ben, and she only wanted the best for them.

She looked from one to the other. 'I won't let you down.'

'You'll never let anyone down, Amy.' Ben spoke gently as he opened the car door for her. 'You drive.'

Before pulling away from the house she waved to Mrs Dalton and Ted, who were standing on the step. 'Good luck,' they called.

With another wave she drove up the road towards the dreaded test. She knew that if she failed she could take it again, but she wasn't going to fail!

The examiner was quite stern-looking; he said little, and Amy longed to have Ben or Howard with her to give her confidence. She concentrated hard, trying to remember everything she had been taught.

The test itself was just a blur; her nerves had jangled all

the way through, but she had done everything he'd asked her to. Was it good enough?

When they finally stopped she watched him writing, wishing she knew what it meant. Then he turned to her and actually smiled.

'I'm pleased to tell you that you have passed, Miss Carter.'

'Oh, thank you.' She could have hugged him, but controlled herself. Not the thing to do at all!

When the examiner got out and went back into his office, she erupted out of the car and rushed towards Ben and Howard who were standing only a few yards away, waving her certificate in triumph. 'I've passed. I've passed!'

She was swung off her feet and passed from one to the other. Neither of them had any trouble lifting her.

'This calls for a celebration.' Ben put her back on the ground. 'We're taking you somewhere special tonight.'

'Oh, where?' She was beside herself with excitement. She had done it, actually done something this difficult. She remembered her struggles at school; this would have seemed impossible to her then.

'Wait and see, nosey.'

'Let's go and tell Mrs Dalton and Ted.' She would never have got through this without their help and support.


'Where are we going? You can tell me now, can't you?' Amy was finding it difficult to stop chattering. All five of them were going out together. Mrs Dalton was wearing her best hat, and when Amy had tried to return the pretty ring, she had been told to keep it as a gift for passing her test first time. She had never owned anything so lovely.

'We're going to the cinema.' Mrs Dalton smiled as Amy helped her on the bus. They had decided to travel like this instead of taking two cars.

'Oh, lovely.' It was a long time since she'd been to the pictures. The last time had been with Gladys. Amy's expression sobered for a moment as the memories flooded in, but the sadness didn't linger. The past was over and done with, and she was too happy to dwell on that awful time. 'What are we going to see?'

Ben leant over from the seat behind. 'Charlie Chaplin in *Modern Times*.'

'I like Charlie Chaplin.' She looked across the aisle at Ted. 'Where's it showing?'

'In the West End. The boys know where.'

The scene when they arrived was enough to take Amy's breath away. Everything was bright with coloured signs and lights. There was an air of lively enjoyment among the people thronging the streets, all going to theatres, cinemas or restaurants, she guessed. And the clothes? Wow! Her head was turning this way and that way, determined not to miss a thing. She walked straight into John, who was standing outside the cinema.

'I'm so sorry,' she exclaimed, before realizing who it was.

'That's all right.' He smiled down at her, still holding her arms, steadying her after the collision. 'Congratulations on passing your test.'

'Thank you.' She took a little step back. 'Are you going to the pictures as well?'

'Ben invited me to join you for the celebration. Do you mind?'

'Er . . . no.' Catching sight of the huge picture of Charlie Chaplin twisting his cane, she couldn't help laughing. 'Are you all sure you want to see this?'

'It will be fun.' Ben took her arm and they went in to buy the tickets.

\*

John managed to sit beside Amy, and during the first half he spent more time watching her animated face than he did the screen. From the first moment he had set eyes on her in the gallery, he had felt a strong attraction towards her. She had an unusual beauty all her own, and he could understand the artist in Ben wanting to keep painting her. There was an innocence and vulnerability about her. Ben had hinted that she'd had a troubled past, and he was curious to know what it was. However, it was obvious that everyone in that house loved her and would protect her from any further hurt if they could. She was unique and if it hadn't been for his punishing schedule he would have made more time to see her; to get to know her. He knew how young she was – not eighteen until December – so he could bide his time, qualify as a doctor, and then try to take her out a few times.

In the interval he bought them all ice creams and, as they chatted, he again watched her enjoying the treat. Her pleasure in small things was infectious, almost childlike, and he couldn't help wondering again what kind of a life she'd had. Had someone hurt her? That thought angered him. He began to glimpse how the others felt and why they protected her so fiercely.

The lights dimmed as the main feature began and he sat back to see what the film was like.

It was incredible, and when it came to an end and the lights went up, Amy's face was glowing, her eyes appearing dark green in the soft lighting.

'Wasn't that wonderful?' She sighed blissfully. 'Thank you all so much for bringing me.'

'It was a pleasure, Amy.' Ben was in an aisle seat to give him enough room for his long legs. He uncurled himself and stood up. 'Let's get something to eat. I'm starving.'

As they all laughed, Ted muttered, 'Now there's a surprise.'

It was agreed that fish and chips would go down a treat, so they headed for a place John knew about ten minutes' walk away. The restaurant was modest compared to the one he had taken Amy to, but the food was very good, and they had a large pot of tea to wash it down. Amy enjoyed that much more than all the fancy drinks. John had them in fits of laughter about some of the pranks they got up to at the hospital, prompting Ben and Howard to relate some of their escapades at university. She loved to hear them talk like this – it was such a different world to the one she had grown up in – and she couldn't remember being so happy before. Passing the driving test had been a huge step forward for her, making her feel more confident and quite grown up. She'd have to remind the boys that she wasn't a kid any more. That thought made her smile to herself, as she imagined the teasing it would produce.

She watched John talking, totally relaxed and at ease with her 'family' – and that was what they were to her now. Ted and Mrs Dalton were the steadying influence in her life, offering affection and encouragement, and Ben and Howard were her friends, constantly urging her to try new things – making her grow.

'We must get going.' Mrs Dalton broke up the chatter. 'Otherwise we'll miss the last bus.'

Outside they said goodbye to John and made their way home. It had been an exciting day, and a really lovely evening, Amy thought, and she had adored the film. She hoped John had enjoyed it as well; he'd certainly seemed to. He was terribly nice, but he made her feel shy the way he looked at her.

As soon as they were home, Mrs Dalton urged them all

into her kitchen. 'We'll have a nice cup of cocoa to round off the evening, shall we?'

They readily agreed, knowing there would probably be a slice of homemade cake to go with it. Amy wasn't at all hungry, but none of them ever refused Mrs Dalton's cakes.

'What a nice young man John is.' Mrs Dalton smiled her approval. 'He's quite taken a shine to our Amy.'

'Oh, he hasn't!' She felt herself blush. 'He's made friends with Ben and Howard, that's all.'

'He doesn't keep popping up because of us.' Howard gave her a teasing grin. 'And a man doesn't take a girl to a fancy French restaurant unless he's interested in her.'

'That's true enough.' Mrs Dalton became serious. 'Amy isn't eighteen for a few months yet, so I shall expect you boys to keep an eye on her, and see that John behaves himself.'

'We will, Mrs Dalton,' they answered meekly.

Ben gave Amy a sly wink, making her laugh. She didn't know where they got such daft ideas from. John would *never* be interested in her. He was a nice-looking, intelligent man, with a good future ahead of him. He would need to find himself a pretty girl.

Feeling tired, she yawned, making Mrs Dalton pack them all off to bed.

Before putting out the light, Amy gazed at her certificate in wonder. She was finding out that she wasn't useless, after all. In the time she had been here, new talents had been unearthed. She was decorating pots, helping to run the shop, and now she could officially drive on her own.

Switching off the light, she settled down, a smile on her face. She was tired, but too excited to sleep. It had been a lovely day, and Ben had been proud of her – they all had. And she was quite proud of herself!

*

Two days later, on the Sunday, Amy went up to Ben's studio. She loved to watch him paint. His concentration was total, and he often didn't know she was there.

But today he did, and turned his head. 'Ah, I thought you'd brought me a cup of tea.'

'I'll make you one, if you like.' There was a small room just off the studio with a sink, a small gas stove and a cupboard on the wall. That was all there was room for. The ceiling was so sloping she knew Ben had to crouch to do anything in here. It was no wonder he always came to the kitchen she shared with Ted. But he had all the necessary things to make a simple meal in the cupboard.

She took the tea in to him and studied the picture he was working on. 'That's lovely.'

He sipped his tea. 'Hmm. I'm doing this for John. It's his family home and he wants to give it to his parents on their twenty-fifth wedding anniversary.'

'My goodness! Does he live in a place like that?' It looked very grand to her.

'He comes from a family with money, Amy.' Ben watched her carefully over the rim of his cup. 'Does that frighten you?'

'No, why should it?' She gave a little toss of her head. 'It's nothing to do with me how much money he's got.'

'But he likes you, and if he wasn't so busy studying, he'd be camping on our doorstep.'

She gave him a sceptical look. 'You do say the daftest things, Ben. Why on earth would he do a thing like that?'

'Come here, Amy.' He put the cup down and led her over to stand in front of the portrait on the wall. 'What do you see?'

With a puzzled frown she tipped her head on one side and gazed at the portrait she had seen so many times. Then she shrugged. 'Me.'

'And?'

'And what? It's just the picture you did of me when I first came to live here. A very good one,' she added hastily, making him chuckle.

'Thank you, I think. Just forget it's you for a moment. Now what do you see?'

Giving a deep sigh, she squinted at it through half-closed eyes. He was in a funny mood today; she had better humour him. He went like this sometimes when he'd been painting for hours on end. 'It's a picture of a girl with a funny face.'

'Amy!' He lifted his hands in despair. 'What are we going to do with you? You've got one of the most appealing faces I have ever seen, and John thinks so too. He said you were lovely.'

'Oh, Ben.' She laughed. He'd gone too far this time. 'My dad said it looked as if God had used all the leftover bits when he made me.' Her smile died.

'Now, don't look like that.' Ben framed her face with his hands. 'That was a long time ago. And your father was wrong. All the best bits were saved just for you. I'm an artist, so I know,' he teased gently.

She managed a smile. 'You see things differently, just as I see words differently.'

'That makes us both unique then, doesn't it?'

Remembering her father like that had brought the horror back. She tried hard not to think about what had happened to him, and most of the time now she was successful, but an unguarded remark made it come alive again.

'All right now?' Ben asked.

She nodded, her gloom disappearing as she looked at him. She could never stay unhappy for long when he was around. He seemed to understand her every mood, without it being explained.

'Good. Now what were we talking about? Ah, yes, John. Do you like him?'

She bit back a groan. They were back to that again! 'He's very nice.'

'Well, why don't you go out with him when he asks?'

'He won't ask.'

'Yes, he will. He told me he's going to as soon as he's passed his exams and qualified.'

That news sent alarm through her. 'I can't go out with him. Suppose I have to write to him . . . or something? He'll laugh himself silly.'

Ben leant against the bench again and folded his arms. 'We don't, and you often leave little notes for us in the shop.'

'No, well . . .' Her smile was amused. 'That's because you're all unique.'

'True, and we all love you just the way you are, funny face and all.'

'Aha!' She rounded on him, laughing. 'You've admitted it at last.'

'I said "lovely".'

'You didn't. I've got good hearing. And anyway, why are you trying to get me fixed up with John? What about you and Sally?'

He raised an eyebrow. 'Who?'

'Oh, Ben, you are the limit. You never seem to keep a girlfriend for more than a couple of weeks.'

They were both laughing now. It was how they nearly always ended up.

She headed for the door.

'Where are you going?'

'To play with Oscar. He thinks I'm lovely too.'

'Ah, and I was hoping you were going to spoil us and cook lunch.'

'It's in the oven and will be ready in an hour.' Then she left to search for the cat.

# 22

Over the ensuing months, John became an infrequent but welcome visitor to the Chelsea house. When he had time he took Amy out for a meal or to the cinema, or he'd pay a flying visit to the shop and drag her out for a coffee, before rushing back to his studies. Becoming a doctor was his burning ambition and she admired him for his dedication. But it was more than that. She went out with him because she wanted to be with him. It didn't matter how many times she told herself this would only end in pain when he found out about her, she always accepted his invitations. If she didn't see him for several weeks, she missed him very much. Step by step she had allowed herself to look forward to his company. If her feelings were turning into something deeper, then she refused to think about it.

Nineteen thirty-eight had arrived with troubled talk about Hitler, and much speculation on what he might do. Amy was confused and worried, but refused to accept that there was a real possibility of war. It was now the middle of October, and her main concern was waiting to hear if John had passed his final exams. She hadn't heard from him for a while, but she knew how much this meant to him. He was desperate to pass.

After their meal she made the usual large pot of tea and grimaced when the talk once again returned to what was happening across the sea. 'I think you're all making far too much of this. There won't be a war.'

'We hope you're right, Amy.' Ted sighed. 'But that's what we all thought last time.'

'And what a terrible business that was.' Mrs Dalton frowned. 'But Amy's right. No one will risk something like that again.'

'Perhaps not.' Ben stood up when someone knocked on the front door. 'I'll get it.'

When he returned he had John with him, then the frowns were replaced with smiles and cries of delight. He had a stethoscope hanging round his neck.

'You've passed!' Amy shot to her feet. 'Oh, congratulations.'

They all crowded round him. The men shook his hand and Amy and Mrs Dalton kissed his cheek.

'Sit down, doctor.' Mrs Dalton couldn't stop smiling. John Sterling had become a great favourite of hers over the months. 'We've just made a pot of tea.'

'Thanks.' John was still holding Amy's hand, but released it reluctantly when he was ushered to a chair. 'My parents are giving me a party tomorrow evening, and you are all invited. Ben knows where we live.'

'That's very kind of you, John.' Ted nodded towards Mrs Dalton and Amy. 'Look at their faces. I know just what they're thinking: what shall we wear?'

'Well, of course,' Mrs Dalton said. 'We must go shopping first thing in the morning, Amy.'

She nodded, feeling slightly flustered by such an invitation. Being friends with John was one thing, but going to his grand-looking home and meeting his family was quite another.

John only stayed for half an hour, as he was going home that evening. When Amy saw him out he kissed her gently and smiled. 'My parents can't wait to meet you.'

'Oh dear,' she couldn't help saying.

'Don't worry, they're very nice and I've told them all about you.'

He kissed her again, and she had to admit that she did like being held in his arms like this.

She stood in the doorway watching him drive away, not moving until he was out of sight. Then the worry began to gnaw at her. Suppose they asked about her life before she came here? What on earth was she going to say?

'Everything all right, Amy?'

Ben had come up behind her, making her jump at the sound of his voice. For a big man he moved so quietly. She poured out her anxiety. 'John said he'd told his parents all about me, but he doesn't know some things. I should never have become fond of him. What am I going to do, Ben? They'll find out!'

'It won't make any difference.'

'It will. It will!' A single tear trickled down her cheek. 'I don't want to go to the party.'

'Shush, don't upset yourself.' Ben handed her a clean handkerchief. 'John will be hurt if you don't go, and there's nothing to worry about. Everyone will be too busy enjoying themselves to ask questions, and we'll be with you.'

'Yes, of course.' She wiped her eyes. 'I'm being silly, aren't I?'

'John cares for you far too much to let what happened to your father worry him,' Ben said gently. 'In your mind it is still a terrible thing, and I can understand that because it was, but you weren't responsible. Get it out in the open and perhaps it won't haunt you quite so much. Tell John, Amy.'

'I can't.' She shook her head. 'And it isn't only that, is it? What about my reading? He's a clever man and he'll think I'm stupid.'

'He won't. It's clear to anyone who knows you that you're an intelligent girl, and you are doing much better now.'

Her bottom lip trembled as she gazed at him imploringly. 'Why can't I read easily like everyone else?'

'I don't know the answer to that, but I do know that John won't give a damn about it.'

'You're wrong. If I tell him I'll never see him again.'

'That's a chance you're going to have to take sooner or later.' He pushed an unruly strand of hair out of her eyes. 'You hide it very well, but you found the courage to tell us, and that was all right, wasn't it?'

Nodding, she sniffed. 'I thought Mrs Dalton would throw me out and the rest of you wouldn't want anything more to do with me.'

'Amy, Amy.' He sighed. 'What on earth did people do to you to make you have so little confidence in yourself?'

'They laughed at me and called me names, and said I wasn't right in the head.' She sniffed again. 'I pretended I didn't care, but I did. It hurt so much.'

'I'm sure it did, but they're the ones we need to feel sorry for.'

Her eyes opened wide in surprise. 'How do you make that out?'

'Because, my little Amy, they were too stupid to see what a very special girl you are. Not only are you intelligent, but you're talented as well.' He stooped down until his face was level with hers. 'So let's go to the party and help John celebrate. You can walk in there with confidence, because you are as good as anyone else, and don't you forget it!'

'No, sir.' Her mouth turned up slightly. Whenever her self-esteem was at a low ebb he always managed to make her feel better. 'Do you know something?'

He shook his head.

'You're unique.'

'Of course I am. And now I want to finish my tea.'

They laughed together, and she slipped her hand through his arm as they made their way back to the kitchen.

The Sterling house was even more impressive than in Ben's painting; that had been beautiful, but he hadn't been able to show the extensive grounds. It looked like a park to her as they walked round the side of the house towards the sound of laughter and music.

Amy was clutching a special gift for Mrs Sterling and staying close to Ben and Mrs Dalton, feeling more confident with them near her.

'My word, just look at that.' Mrs Dalton stopped and stared at the scene.

There was a marquee on the lawn with the front open to reveal tables laden with food and every imaginable drink, including a barrel of beer.

'No champagne for you, Amy,' Ben whispered in her ear. 'I don't want to have to carry you out of here.'

If she'd had a free hand she would have thumped him; instead she giggled. 'Are you ever going to let me forget that?'

'Never!'

'Wow, look at all that food.' Howard grinned at his friend. 'Do you remember when we used to accept any party invitation just so we could get something to eat?'

A deep rumble of amusement came from Ben. 'We endured some pretty dull evenings, but at least we came home full up.'

John spotted them and came over, all smiles. 'Good, you've made it. Come and meet my parents.' He took Amy's arm. 'What is that you're holding on to so tightly?'

'A present for your mother.' Now the moment she'd dreaded had arrived she tried to remind herself what Ben had said about her being as good as anyone else. It was hard to hold on to that in this gathering of smart people.

'If it's one of your pots she'll be thrilled.' He led them towards a very elegant woman with blonde hair, wearing the most exquisite black dress Amy had ever seen. It had black jet beads on the bodice and sparkled when she moved.

'Mother, I'd like you to meet Amy, Mrs Dalton, Ben, Howard and Ted.'

When Mrs Sterling smiled it was easy to see whom John took after. 'I'm so glad you could all come. John has told us so much about you.'

'It was kind of you to invite us.' Mrs Dalton gazed round in approval. 'You have done a marvellous job of the party.'

'Thank you. We wanted all John's friends to join us in our celebration.' Fixing her gaze on Amy, she studied her carefully for a moment, then smiled. 'I absolutely love the things John has bought me from your shop, Amy. You are very talented.'

'Oh, Howard's the clever one, I just paint the things.' Feeling shy she thrust the parcel at her. 'I did this for you.'

While Mrs Sterling opened the box, Amy edged closer to Ben, seeking protection from his towering form. Suppose Mrs Sterling didn't like the present?

'Oh, this is exquisite.' John's mother held up the biscuit barrel, which was decorated in dark blue with vibrant pansies on the body and lid. 'Look at this, Charles.'

The man who had just joined them smiled at his wife's pleasure. 'That's lovely, Mildred.'

'I must give this pride of place on the sideboard.' She kissed Amy on the cheek. 'This is very thoughtful of you. Thank you very much.'

Amy's relief was great as she watched John's mother go into the house, and she just stood there with a wide smile on her face, not saying a word.

'Now, let me see.' John's father gave them his full attention. 'Don't introduce yourselves. Let me see if I can get your names right.' He turned to Ben first. 'You must be Benjamin, the artist who painted that wonderful picture of our house.'

Ben inclined his head. 'I'm pleased you like it.'

'We most certainly do, and it has been much admired.' Mr Sterling eyed Ben with interest. 'You are a fine artist, young man. I would like to see more of your work, so we must have a talk before you leave.' He looked then at Howard. 'And you must be the sculptor. I'd like to come and see some of your work as well.'

'You'd be welcome any time, sir.'

'And you must be Mrs Dalton who has made our son so welcome in your home, and Ted who owns the bookshop.'

Ted nodded. 'You seem to know all about us.'

'We do. John has told us what a fascinating shop you have. He said he could spend hours in there browsing the shelves, if he only had the time.' He indicated where the food and drink was. 'We are delighted you could come. Please enjoy yourselves.'

Ben and Howard were the first at the food, as usual. Not being interested in anything to eat just yet, although it all looked delicious, Amy studied the other guests. They were all smart, dressed in the height of fashion, and she was glad Mrs Dalton had made her buy a new frock and shoes. Her frock was green, to bring out the colour of her eyes (Mrs Dalton had insisted), and the shoes were black suede with a silver buckle on the front. To finish things off she was wearing her first pair of silk stockings.

'Come and dance with me, Amy.'

'Oh, I can't dance.'

John held out his hand. 'It's easy. I'll show you.'

Casting a quick glance at the other couples moving to the music on a large paved area just in front of the house, she hesitated. 'I'll tread on your toes.'

'No you won't.' John smiled. 'And even if you do I won't feel it. You're not very heavy, are you?'

Deciding that if he was willing to risk it she might as well try, she placed her hand in his and allowed him to take her over to the dancers.

'Just relax,' he told her when she stood stiffly in his arms. 'I'll lead you.'

After a couple of minutes she began to feel rather pleased with herself: she was quite enjoying it, and only stepped on his feet about four times. The waltz was quite easy, but the quickstep was more than she could cope with.

As the evening wore on she felt more and more at ease. Everyone was happy, and she really liked John's parents. They were proud of their son, and rightly so. She even danced with his father, *twice*.

It was past midnight when they thanked Mr and Mrs Sterling and headed home. It was quite a long drive, but well worth it to have attended John's party.

A week later, on Sunday afternoon, John and his parents arrived. Amy was working with Howard amidst their usual mess when they walked into the workshop.

'No, don't stand up, Amy.' Mrs Sterling made her sit down again after she'd leapt to her feet. 'We don't want to disturb you.'

Amy felt she should shake hands with them, but after glancing at her paint-smeared palms, decided against it.

'My mother and father just want to have a look round.' John stood beside Amy. 'It's a lovely day out there; let's go for a ride. Though I bet you haven't even looked.'

'Well, we have been rather busy.' She saw Oscar decide that there were far too many people for his liking, and he shot out of the door. The cat followed her around all the time, and would sit for ages just watching her working.

'Wash the paint off and I'll take you to Richmond Park. The trees are glorious in their autumn colours.'

The chance to spend some time with him was too good to turn down, and she might get some ideas for new decorations. 'All right. Give me time to change.'

It only took her fifteen minutes and then they were on their way. Although there was a nip in the air, the sun still had a little warmth in it, and it seemed no time at all before they were turning in the park gates. The place was a glorious riot of gold, orange and brown. The leaves were falling in the slight breeze and settling in a multi-coloured carpet on the green grass.

Amy was busy picking up leaves to take home with her so she could copy them for her vases. 'This is lovely.' She straightened up, holding out a large leaf. John was standing and watching her with a slight smile on his face. His expression made her wonder what he was thinking. 'What?'

'Come and sit down, Amy, I want to talk to you.' He reached out for her and guided her over to a seat.

She waited patiently, still holding the leaves she had gathered.

'I've been so busy studying that I haven't had time to see you as much as I would have liked. But now I've qualified I want you to know how I feel. You know I've become very fond of you, don't you?'

'I like you too.'

'I want more than liking, Amy.'

'Sorry?' She traced the outline of a leaf with her finger, her heart racing. Then she looked up, trying to hide her worry at the way this conversation was going.

'I love you, Amy.' When she didn't say anything, he continued. 'I know you won't be nineteen until December, and you'll probably feel you are too young to commit yourself, but I need you to know that I'm serious about you.'

Her hands began to tremble and she had to be careful not to crush the leaves. Why that worried her was a mystery – there were plenty more on the ground – but it was hard to think straight. In one way she was overjoyed to hear him say these things, but she wasn't being fair to him. The last thing she wanted was to hurt him. Ben had said she should tell him . . .

'What's the matter, Amy, don't you care for me?'

'Oh, yes, I do, very much.' Her eyes fixed on his face, knowing she had to tell him. Being sure that he would not want to see her again was like a physical pain. He was too precious to her though, and she couldn't deceive him.

'Then what's the problem?' He placed his hand over hers. 'Talk to me, Amy.'

She gulped, trying to gather her courage, and then blurted it out. 'There are some things you don't know about me. My father was hanged for murder. He killed a man who was trying to rob him . . .' She tailed off, unable to continue.

He brought her hand to his lips, his eyes full of compassion. 'That must have been terrible for you, but I don't give a damn. It's you I love, and nothing will ever make me change my mind about that.'

'Don't be too sure, John.' She held on tight to him, dreading the next bit. 'There's something wrong with me and I can't read or write very well . . . I'm not stupid!' she added with some force.

When he didn't speak, she took a quick look at his face. He didn't look appalled, and that was what she had expected.

'And you think that would make any difference to me?'

She nodded.

Putting his hands on her shoulders, he turned her to face him. 'Now you listen to me, Amy Carter. I've fallen for a girl with large green eyes, unruly dark hair and a wide smile; a girl who paints beautiful pots and views the world with innocent enjoyment. I don't care about your family, where you come from or the fact that you have difficulty reading.' He gave her a gentle shake. 'It doesn't matter to me.'

She could hardly believe what she was hearing, but he spoke with such conviction it was impossible to doubt his sincerity. 'I was frightened to tell you,' she whispered, 'but Ben said I should.'

'And he was right.' He kissed her firmly, and then held her away so he could look at her. 'Thank you for telling me, I know it must have taken a lot of courage.'

'You're so clever I thought you'd laugh at me.'

'Not a chance, my beautiful girl.' Slipping his arm around her shoulders he pulled her close. 'Will you tell me when you realized you had trouble reading?'

'Is this the doctor talking?' She was feeling rather light-headed at the moment, and thought she could chance a little joke.

'Of course. This is a free consultation.'

Settling her head on his shoulder, she told him the whole story, surprising herself at just how easy it was to talk about now. Of course that was because of Mrs Dalton, Ted and the boys. Their kindness and understanding had made her more confident and not quite so ashamed as she used to be. She had been afraid to tell John because she hadn't wanted to lose him.

When she finished, he shook his head. 'It's been very hard for you, hasn't it? I don't know what has caused this in you, but I'll make some enquiries and see if anyone in the medical professions knows.'

'I don't suppose they do.' She smiled up at him. 'Mrs Dalton taking me in was the best thing that ever happened to me. They've all helped me very much.'

'And now you've got me as well.' He kissed the end of her nose playfully. 'So, do you love me?'

'Oh, yes, I think I do.' She sighed as all the worry and tension left her.

# 23

By the time April 1939 arrived, Amy could no longer ignore the talk of war. It was the only thing to mar her happiness. The threat was in all the newspapers, the cinema newsreels and on the wireless. Production of armaments was increasing, and it was clear that the country was preparing for the worst. Young children had even been fitted with gas masks.

They were listening to the wireless one evening when it was announced that conscription was to be brought in for twenty- to twenty-one-year-old men.

Amy gazed at Ben, Howard and John as they sat around the kitchen table, their expressions serious. Relief was her immediate reaction to the news. She knew Ben and Howard were twenty-five, and John a year younger.

'None of you will have to go.' She smiled rather shakily, terrified for the men she loved so much.

'Not yet.' Ben stood up and began to pace the floor. 'But this is just the start.'

'If we do go to war, then I shall join up straight away.' Howard looked his usual calm self, but his mouth was set in a determined line. 'There won't be any point waiting because they'll have us all in the end.'

'I'll do the same.' Ben stopped his pacing and leant against the sink. 'What about you, John? They're going to be crying out for doctors.'

'Oh, you won't have to go into the forces, will you?' Now Amy was really alarmed.

'I'll be needed at the hospital, I expect, so they might not call me up.' John squeezed her hand. 'But we'll have to wait and see what happens.'

Ted and Mrs Dalton came into the kitchen.

'I can see from your faces that you've heard the news.' Ted looked in the teapot and, finding it almost full, poured two cups as Mrs Dalton sat down as well.

'Ben and Howard say they will join up if war comes.' Amy chewed her lip with worry. 'What will we do about the shop?'

'We'll have to close it.' Ben gave her an apologetic pat on the shoulder. 'I'm sorry, but there won't be much call for luxury goods like ours.'

'I think you are all jumping ahead too far,' Mrs Dalton told them. 'It might not come to anything, and I'm a great believer in not crossing your bridges until you come to them.'

'The voice of reason.' Ted grinned. 'But she's quite right.'

'Of course she is.' Amy gave Mrs Dalton a grateful smile. 'One step at a time, eh?'

The tension broke as they all laughed at Amy's use of one of Mrs Dalton's favourite sayings.

Two weeks later John had some time off so he took Amy to Brighton for the day. The weather was perfect: blue skies, a soft breeze, with the sun giving enough warmth to hint at the summer to come. They walked hand in hand along the pier, silent, content in each other's company. It was often like this with them; they didn't need constant talk – a smile now and again was enough. Amy loved this quietness about John. In fact she loved everything about him. He never mentioned her difficulty with reading, or if he'd managed to find out anything from his medical studies, and she didn't ask. It obviously didn't bother him at all, and that made her happy.

At the end of the pier they stopped and she shaded her eyes with her hand to look out to sea. 'What a beautiful day. There's a ship out there and it looks so tiny.'

John draped his arm around her shoulder. 'Will you marry me, my darling?'

She spun round to face him, eyes wide with surprise. For some time now she had hoped he would ask her, but hadn't expected it yet. He was settling in at a new job at St Thomas' Hospital, working long hours. But she loved him so much . . .

'Oh, yes please!'

Laughing at her response, he hugged her tightly. 'You've made me very happy. Let's go and buy you a ring.'

They ran back along the pier, as joyous as a couple of children, and headed for the shops. They went from one jeweller to another, inspecting the window displays.

'What kind of ring would you like?'

'Er . . . I don't know really.' They all looked terribly expensive to her. 'You mustn't spend too much.'

'Don't you worry about that. You choose one and I'll tell you if I can afford it.'

That assurance made her relax and she set about the exciting job of finding something pretty.

'What about that one?' He was pointing to a large solitaire diamond.

She shook her head. 'I've only got small hands, and I'd like a coloured stone if possible.'

'An emerald to match your eyes.' He urged her through the door and up to the counter.

A man approached them, smiling. 'Can I be of assistance to you, sir?'

'We'd like to see a selection of emerald and diamond rings, please.'

'Certainly, sir.' The man pulled up two chairs for them to sit on.

Amy wasn't sure about this. None of the rings in the window had a price on them, and it all looked rather posh. While the man was busy, she whispered to John, 'They're going to cost too much in here.'

He merely squeezed her hand and smiled in his quiet way.

When a tray was put in front of her with at least a dozen rings sparkling in the overhead lights, she had to bite her tongue to stop herself from gasping out loud. They were all so beautiful.

'Take your time,' the man told her. 'You want to find something you love, don't you?'

She nodded, her eyes lingering for a moment on one particular ring, but she quickly dismissed it. That would cost the earth! She searched the tray for the smallest and, thinking it would be the least expensive, pointed towards it. 'That's nice.'

'It is, but I don't think it's the right one for you.' John reached out and picked up the one she had noticed first of all: a square-cut emerald with a diamond on either side. 'Try this.'

She held out her left hand and let him slip it on her finger. It fitted perfectly, but she wasn't daft; clearly it would cost a lot of money. She knew John and his family weren't poor, but he couldn't be earning much as a newly qualified doctor.

'That's perfect for the young lady, sir.' The assistant looked very pleased.

'I think so too.' John looked at Amy. 'Do you like it, darling?'

'It's beautiful, but—'

'We'll take it.'

Amy was horrified. John hadn't even asked the price.

He gave her a little shove. 'You go and look at all the other lovely things in the window while I see to this.'

She removed the ring and put it on the counter. By now her hands were trembling. How much is it? she wanted to ask, the words fighting to tumble out, but she didn't want to embarrass John. 'I liked the other one as well,' she murmured softly.

'No you didn't.' John made her stand up. 'This one caught your eye straight away, and I like it as well.'

She gave a helpless shrug. 'You don't miss much, do you?'

'Of course not. I'm a doctor, remember? Now, off you go.'

Knowing it was useless to argue, she went outside and waited for him to buy the ring. She couldn't believe this was happening; she felt numb with happiness.

He came out of the shop and stood beside her. 'See anything else you like?'

'Oh, no! I think you've spent quite enough on me today.'

He smiled and patted his pocket, looking very pleased with life. 'Now we've got the ring let's go back and tell your family.'

'I wonder what they'll say?' She fell in step beside him, holding tightly to his hand.

'They already know. You didn't think I'd ask you to marry me without their permission, did you?'

'You've talked to them about this? What did they say?'

'They gave me their blessing – every one of them. I was afraid Ben would object, thinking you were too young, but he didn't.'

'What about your family?'

'They know as well.' He smiled down at her. 'Don't look

241

so worried; they're delighted they're going to have you as a daughter-in-law.'

'Well I never!'

Back in Chelsea everyone gathered round to congratulate them and admire the ring as John put it on her finger in their presence. They were now officially engaged.

With a flourish, Ted produced a bottle of champagne he had bought – just on the off chance, he told them. Amy was cautious of the drink now, only sipping hers, and making Ben smirk.

'When's the wedding going to be?' Mrs Dalton was clearly very happy about the engagement.

'We haven't discussed it yet, but I'd like it to be this September.'

Amy gave John a surprised look. 'But that's less than five months away.'

'Why the rush, John?' Ted refilled all the glasses except Amy's as she hid it behind her back. 'Amy won't be twenty until December. You've got plenty of time.'

'I don't think we have.' John sighed. 'I honestly believe we shall be at war by the end of this year or early next, and who knows what will happen then? I would like us to have some time together before that happens.'

A cold chill ran through Amy and she sent up a silent prayer that the country would stay peaceful and they would not have to be parted. None of them.

'John could be right.' Ben gave Amy an encouraging smile. 'If that's what you want, I think you should get married this year. No point in waiting when the world is in such a state of tension.'

'I'm happy to get married as soon as John wants.' Amy didn't like this talk of war creeping in to spoil her happiness, but she was sensible enough to know that it had to be considered and faced, should it happen.

'I'm sure we can get everything arranged in time.' Mrs Dalton picked up a paper and pen from the dresser. 'What date did you have in mind?'

'I've got a week's holiday due me from the fifteenth of September.' John was still holding Amy's hand. 'Are you sure you don't mind us being married this year?'

'If that's what you want then I'm quite happy about it.'

'Good, that's one thing settled.' Mrs Dalton wrote down the date. 'Now, where are you going to live?'

'Live?' Amy glanced from one to the other, her eyes lingering on each person, and then settling on John. 'Can't we stay here? Mrs Dalton, can't John move in here?'

'Of course he can.' Mrs Dalton nodded to John. 'I don't know what you were planning, but Amy's room is big enough for a double bed, and there's the kitchen and sitting room you can use. We'd be happy to have you here, John, if that would suit you. You're almost one of the family already.'

'That is very kind of you, Mrs Dalton, and I think it would be the most sensible thing for the time being. I have to work long hours at the hospital and often at night, and it will be a comfort to know that Amy is here with you.'

Amy smiled in relief. In the excitement of John's proposal it hadn't entered her head that she might have to leave this house. Perhaps one day she would, but not yet – not when there was talk of war. It was unsettling. The house and the people in it had been her safe haven for almost five years. 'Are you sure you don't mind, John?'

'Not at all, darling. One day we'll buy a home of our own, but there's no rush.'

Mrs Dalton appeared to be in her element scribbling

down notes. 'Now, John, I consider Amy as my daughter, so I'll see to the wedding arrangements, but I would welcome your mother's help.'

'We'll tell her; she will be delighted.' He laughed quietly. 'In fact you'll have a job to keep her out of it.'

'Good, good.' Mrs Dalton sat back, turning her attention to Amy. 'We'll have a private discussion about your dress later, my dear.'

'I want to be a page boy.' Howard's expression was perfectly serious, only a slight twitch of his mouth giving away his amusement.

'Me too.' Ben joined in the fun.

'Oh no you don't!' Mrs Dalton was trying to keep a straight face. 'If you think we're putting you two great hulks in satin breeches, then you can think again.'

Amy giggled at the thought while everyone else roared so much they had to wipe their eyes.

When they'd calmed down, John said to Amy, 'Who will you ask to give you away?'

There was only one person to give that role to, as he had been a father figure to her from the moment she had arrived here. 'Would you do it, Ted?'

'I'd be honoured to, Amy.'

That was put on Mrs Dalton's notes. 'Ben and Howard can act as ushers in the church. Have you any pretty little girls in your family who could be bridesmaids, John?'

'Sorry, I'm an only child and we don't have a large family.'

'Then we won't have any,' Amy declared, 'and it will make things easier, because we don't have a lot of time.'

'I agree.' John stood up. 'I have to get back to the hospital now, but we'll go and see my parents tomorrow afternoon, darling. I'll collect you at two o'clock.'

'All right.' She went with him to the door, already nervous

about that meeting, even though he'd told her they already knew about his intentions. But his lingering goodnight kiss removed all the worries from her head.

'Congratulations!' John's parents greeted them as soon as they stopped outside the door.

There were kisses all round as Amy stood shyly at John's side. Mr and Mrs Sterling looked delighted, which was an immense relief. John had told her that he'd phoned them last night with the good news and they were pleased about the engagement, but she had still been on tenterhooks about seeing them. After all, she'd only met them once.

'Come in.' Mr Sterling took her arm, smiling down at her. 'Then you can show my wife your ring. She's dying to see it.'

Once inside the ring was examined and approved of.

'This is beautiful, John,' Mrs Sterling said to her son. 'And just perfect for Amy.'

'I thought so.' He gave Amy a loving glance. 'She was determined to choose something smaller and cheaper, but I didn't let her get away with that.'

Amy turned the ring round and round on her finger. 'I didn't want him to spend too much.'

'Don't you worry about that. John's a sensible boy and wouldn't have bought it if he couldn't afford it.' Mrs Sterling patted her hand and gave a cheeky wink. 'We have to let the men buy us pretty things. It gives them so much pleasure.'

John's father laughed out loud, picked up a bottle of champagne and opened it with a bang, the cork flying across the room. Then he poured four glasses and handed them round. 'We must drink to the happy couple. John, Amy, we wish you a long and happy marriage – as long and happy as ours has been.'

As they clinked glasses, Mrs Sterling said, 'We are so happy John has chosen a fine girl to be his wife, and we will be proud to have you as our daughter-in-law.'

'Thank you.' Amy, sipping her drink, was quite over-whelmed by their genuine pleasure. More champagne, she thought wryly, determined to have only one glass in case she disgraced herself. Alcohol seemed to go straight to her head.

'Tell us about your plans.' John's father grinned in amuse-ment as his wife sat forward eagerly.

'I hope you're going to let her help, Amy. She can't resist arranging an event.'

'Well . . .' Amy hesitated for a moment. 'Mrs Dalton did say that she would appreciate your help, Mrs Sterling.'

'Splendid. I'll get in touch with her, and between us we shall make this a memorable wedding.'

The rest of the afternoon was taken up with discussions about the wedding. Where it should take place, how many guests to invite, and many other things.

'We must see what plans Mrs Dalton has before making any decisions, my dear. She is, after all, acting as the bride's mother,' John's father pointed out.

'Of course.' Mrs Sterling gave a rueful smile. 'You must excuse me, my dear. I get carried away, but these are only ideas. I shall discuss everything with Mrs Dalton and work with her. Do you have any wishes of your own?'

Amy looked at John. There was only one thing that concerned her. Mrs Sterling's plans seemed rather grand, but understandable as it was her only son being married. A quiet wedding would have suited her, but she couldn't disappoint John's mother and Mrs Dalton. 'Could we keep it quite small?'

'I agree with Amy, Mother. Not too grand, eh?' John squeezed Amy's hand. 'All we want to do is get married, don't we, darling?'

'Yes.' She nodded firmly. That was all she wanted.

When John returned to the hospital that evening there was time for a cup of coffee before he went on duty. The day had gone well, and by the time they left his parents, Amy was quite at ease. They liked her and were thrilled he was going to marry her.

He sipped the scalding hot drink, a deep frown furrowing his brow. He was pushing Amy, but deep inside him there was a feeling of urgency. He wasn't usually one to indulge in what was called intuition, and he blamed the growing threat of war for making him so unsettled. The future was uncertain and, if war did come, all kinds of mayhem could burst upon their lives. He wanted a few months of peace with Amy before that happened. And if their fears were proved ungrounded then so much the better. He would be able to settle down to a happy life with the woman he loved.

The door of the rest room burst open and a colleague shot in. 'John, emergency!'

He was immediately on his feet and running.

# 24

Since the compulsory conscription of twenty- to twenty-one-year-old men in April, Ben and Howard had become increasingly restless. Amy watched them anxiously through the months of May, June and July. She just knew they were going to join up. Ted had been having serious talks with them, urging them to wait, and explaining what had happened in the last war, but all they said was that it would be very different this time. They all talked about it as if it were a foregone conclusion, and she prayed every night that it wasn't.

On the brighter side, the plans for the wedding were nearly in place. They were going to be married in a small village church – All Saints – near John's home, and the reception would be held in the Sterlings' lovely garden, weather permitting. When they had met the vicar, Amy had been enchanted with the church. It was small, had an intimate feel about it, and was reached down a leafy lane, enhancing the air of tranquillity about the whole area. Mrs Dalton had found a good dressmaker and Amy's simple dress was nearly finished.

John and Amy had watched the 'mothers' to see they didn't get carried away, but they needn't have worried; they worked together in harmony with Mrs Dalton's practical nature helping to curb Mrs Sterling's more ambitious ideas.

Amongst all the turmoil, Amy spent as much time as possible in John's calm company, and couldn't wait to become his wife. She often gazed at the beautiful ring, not being able to believe this was happening to her. They loved each other to distraction, as John was showing in his time alone with her. But his lovemaking always stopped before they went too far, often to her intense frustration. The wedding was only weeks away now and she knew it was right to wait, but when she was in his arms it was so difficult.

The moment she began to dish up the dinner, everyone appeared as if by magic, including Mrs Dalton, who joined them even more often now, as she said that Amy's cooking was better than hers.

'Smells good.' Ben ruffled her hair as he passed her to sit down. 'I want to do another portrait of you, Amy. Can you make some time to sit for me on Sunday?'

'John's working, so I'll be free.' She cut the steak and kidney pie into six slices, popping one piece back in the oven, just in case John arrived. He would turn up any time he had a couple of hours to spare, and Mrs Dalton had given him his own key.

After putting the vegetables on the table, she handed round the plates.

'Come up to my studio early.' Ben helped himself to potatoes. 'I want to spend all day on the painting.'

Normally she would have sighed jokingly and said, Not another picture of me, but she didn't this time, being only too pleased he was going to settle to his painting again. He had been spending more time at the shop, or out with Howard, only painting in short bursts. But for all his restlessness, his work was good, and getting better with each piece. Howard was the same.

She sat with them at the table, her expression troubled. 'Don't join up until after the wedding, please. We would be very unhappy if you weren't there.'

Howard reached across and squeezed her hand. 'We'll be

here, Amy. We wouldn't miss your wedding for the world.'

'Don't worry.' Ben's smile was gentle. 'We won't do anything until we see you safely married to John.'

Her sigh was one of pure relief. They never lied to her, so she could relax now they had promised.

August was turning out to be a glorious month and they were hoping the weather would last for another three weeks for the wedding. Amy had the last fitting for her dress and was thrilled with it. She was slim but not very tall and had insisted on an uncluttered style. They had decided on a pattern that suited her petite figure perfectly. It had a heart-shaped neckline and short puff sleeves; the material was a lightweight white satin and fell from her narrow waist perfectly, straight in the front and gathering into a small train at the back. Because of her abundant hair – she had been threatened with instant reprisals should she have it cut – the dressmaker had fashioned a circle of imitation roses and pearls. The veil was short and billowing. The effect was stunning, and Amy couldn't believe it was her when she looked in the mirror.

'Oh, my dear, that is beautiful.' Mrs Dalton gave the veil a little tweak before stepping back to view the completed creation.

The dress was carefully removed and packed in layers of tissue paper. Amy paid for it and they left with their huge parcels, heading for home.

'You can leave this in my wardrobe,' Mrs Dalton said, as they crept indoors. 'Then there won't be any danger of anyone seeing it before the wedding.'

'I want it to be a complete surprise to everyone.' If the boys saw them they would insist on seeing the dress, but they were going to have to wait like everyone else.

After hanging it up, Amy hurried back to the shop.

There was a subdued atmosphere when she walked in, and she was surprised to see Ted there with Ben and Howard, and not a customer in sight. The men were in deep discussion about something.

'You all look very serious,' she said, still feeling elated about the dress. 'Why the long faces, and where are the customers?'

'Britain has just signed an assistance pact with Poland,' Ben told her.

'And what does that mean?'

It was Ted who answered. 'It means that if Germany invades Poland we will have no choice but to fight.'

Her pleasure evaporated, but still she clung to hope. 'That might not happen.'

Howard shook his head. 'Hitler has his eyes on Poland. I believe we shall be at war in a matter of weeks.'

That was something she didn't want to accept, but her family were no fools, they kept up with the news. As the wedding approached, she had tried to shut out the speculation. Reading the newspapers was still a rather wearisome task for her, and she had used that excuse as a reason for not keeping up to date with what was happening in Europe. If they were right then she wasn't going to be able to do that for much longer. Wrapped in the comforting cocoon of her love for John and her family, she had pushed the talk aside. Now she knew she was going to have to face it just like everyone else.

Ted was sixty-eight, so he would stay at home, but there would be no chance of that for the boys. She gazed at them and her heart ached. They would go for sure. Thank God John was in a profession that would be needed here.

The shop door opened and the man filling her thoughts

at that moment strode in. Rushing over, she kissed him. 'Oh, John, have you heard the news? Is there really going to be a war, and will we have our wedding before it begins? I'll be so sad if our wonderful day is spoilt . . .'

He placed a finger on her lips to stop the worries pouring out. 'Shush, darling, nothing anyone does will spoil it for us. Whatever happens we shall be married, and we'll face the future together "for better or worse", as the ceremony says.'

'Of course.' She smiled then. 'I'm just being silly and selfish, aren't I?'

'No you're not. Everyone's worried.' He draped an arm around her shoulders. 'Ben, the vicar wants us to have a rehearsal for the ceremony, so can I take Amy away for the rest of the day? This is the only time I can get off to fit in with the vicar's plans.'

'We'll allow it, even though she's only just arrived.' Ben gave her a teasing smile. 'But don't think you can make a habit of this flitting in and out.'

'No, Ben.' Her laughter was back. They were all worrying about nothing.

She had such an expressive face, John thought. It was easy to gauge her emotions, and the rapid changes in them. When he'd walked into the shop, worry had been etched on her face for all to see, yet with just a few encouraging words she'd been back to her usual happy self. Matters on the political front were looking grim and he was glad he'd pushed her into an early marriage. The boys had told him that they were going to join up immediately after the wedding, and if he hadn't fallen in love with Amy, he would have been doing the same thing. The army was going to need all the doctors and nurses they could recruit, but he wasn't going to leave Amy. He had promised Ben he wouldn't. Both the boys loved her like brothers and felt responsible for her. Ben, in particular, was possessive, concerned with her happiness and wellbeing, and had taken him aside one evening to make sure his little girl was going to be looked after and not left alone. And he could understand Ben's concern after he had told him the full story of her father, and how they had found her, forlorn and rejected, beside her mother's grave. He could see what a deep impression that had made on the big man. It must have been heartrending.

John smiled to himself as he remembered how Ben had been acting like the stern father, but John had come away with a much better understanding of the depth of feeling Ben had for Amy. Their relationship had puzzled him in the beginning, but there wasn't anything sexual about it. Ben really did look upon her as a little sister who needed to be loved and protected. The rest of them in the Chelsea house also loved her, and he knew how easy that was. He had taken one look in her gorgeous eyes and fallen so hard it had literally taken his breath away.

In a little over two weeks she would be his wife, and he would make her happy. He loved to see her smile.

The rehearsal didn't take long, and when the vicar was satisfied they knew what they had to do, he let them go.

John helped Amy into the car as they left the church. 'Mother's expecting us for tea.'

'Oh, why didn't you tell me? I would have brought her a vase or something.'

'You don't have to give her something every time you come.' He started the car and headed for his house.

'But I like to give her things. She's nice.'

'She thinks you're nice too.' He cast her a quick sideways

glance, wondering how she had come out of her past so untainted by bitterness. She had a generous, loving nature, and he was the lucky man who had won her heart.

He would make damned sure she never regretted marrying him.

# 25

The pact with Poland had been signed on 25 August, and seven days later Germany invaded Poland. Britain called for an undertaking from Hitler to withdraw his troops. Everyone held their breath.

On Sunday 3 September the whole nation gathered around their wireless sets, waiting for the Prime Minister to speak.

Amy held tightly to John and Ben's hands, praying as she had never prayed before. Her prayers had been answered when she had been in danger of being homeless and unloved. Please God, she implored silently, stop this madness and I'll never ask you for another thing.

At eleven-fifteen they all leant towards the wireless as Chamberlain began to speak. Amy listened with mounting horror as he said: 'I have to tell you now that no such undertaking has been received and that consequently this country is at war with Germany.'

Ted turned the wireless off and there was utter silence in the room. Amy, stunned, watched the sun stream through the window and shine on all the people she loved. What did the future hold for them? Certainly hardship and danger; anything else she didn't dare contemplate. But she had faced grief and tough times before and, if necessary, she would do so again. Step by step they would get through this, and she mustn't be selfish, thinking only of herself.

Lifting her head she spoke huskily as emotion clogged

her throat. 'Ben, Howard, you must do what you feel is right, and if you miss our wedding, we'll understand.'

Ben stood up and gazed out of the window at the empty street, then turned back to face her. 'No, it's only twelve days away. We'll be there, won't we, Howard?'

'Nothing is going to make us miss it.' He smiled. 'We'll make it the best damned party we've ever had. We might even let Amy have *two* glasses of champagne!'

'Hold on a minute, that's taking things too far.' Ben joked, relieving the tension and making them all laugh; even if the mirth was a bit shaky.

With that settled she faced John. 'I desperately want you to stay here with me, but I know the forces will be looking to recruit all the doctors they can find, so if after the wedding you want to join up as well, I won't make a fuss.'

'No, my darling, I won't be doing that. The hospital has already asked me to stay with them. We are going to be needed here as well.'

Tears of relief gathered, but she doggedly refused to let them fall. This was not the time to show weakness. The thing they had feared was upon them and would have to be confronted. She wasn't going to act like a silly, selfish child and make things more difficult for her men. They must see that she could handle whatever was thrown at them. She said calmly, 'I'm so relieved. Thank you.'

Gas masks were being issued to everyone and Anderson shelters delivered to those who wanted them. The boys insisted that Mrs Dalton should have one and immediately set about digging a deep hole in the middle of the lawn.

The next day the shelter arrived as promised and Amy and Mrs Dalton watched them put it together.

'I'm not sure I want to sleep in a hole in the ground.' Amy grimaced at the thought.

Ben stopped what he was doing, swiping his arm across his face to wipe the sweat running down, and glared at her. 'The first sign of bombs dropping and you'll get in here, my girl.'

'Yes, Ben.' She yelped when he lunged for her, and darted behind the apple tree for safety.

'Are you attacking my future wife, Benjamin Scott?' a stern voice said.

'John!' Amy ran towards him, laughing. 'He was going to dump me in the hole because I said I didn't fancy sleeping in there.'

'Is that so?' John gave Ben a sly wink and she was lifted off her feet by both of them and lowered into the hole.

Standing with her hands on her hips, she gazed up at them. 'And how am I supposed to get out of here? Shouldn't there be steps, or something?'

'Give us a chance.' Howard did his best to look offended. 'Once we get this monstrosity fixed together we'll know where to put the steps.'

John reached down as Amy held up her arms and lifted her out. Then he said seriously, 'You'll use this if it's necessary, Amy.'

'I promise, darling, I was only joking.' Since war had been declared the atmosphere had been strange, as if everyone was determined to keep laughing. 'Are you staying for dinner?'

He made a show of considering this. 'What have you got?'

'Lancashire hot pot.'

'Then I'm definitely staying.'

'Oh, good.' Her face lit up with pleasure. 'I'll go and do extra potatoes.'

The day before the wedding, Amy went to stay with John's parents. Ted and Mrs Dalton were also given rooms in the house, but the boys and John were staying at a neighbour's place just along the road.

'Can't have you running into John,' Mrs Sterling declared. 'It's unlucky for the bride and groom to see each other before the ceremony.'

John laughed at his mother's superstition. 'I don't believe that. We're going to have a lovely, lucky marriage, aren't we, darling?'

'Absolutely.' She could only see happiness for both of them – war or no war!

The ceremony was to be at eleven and, after she'd dressed, Amy was suddenly overcome with nerves and reached for a chair.

'Don't sit down!' John's mother caught her arm. 'You might crease the dress. The car will be here in fifteen minutes.'

'Right.' Amy smiled at the mothers with pride. Mrs Sterling was elegant in cream, and Mrs Dalton resplendent in pale blue. 'You'd better go now or I shall beat you to the church.'

John's mother picked up her bag and slipped her arm through Mrs Dalton's. 'Come along, Jean, we'll just have time to see that the men are doing their jobs properly.'

'Jean?' Amy smothered a giggle. 'Gosh, I've never heard Mrs Dalton's Christian name before, Ted.'

'It's rarely used.' Ted picked up her bouquet of roses and handed it to her. 'They seem to be getting on well, don't they?'

'Yes, and that's nice. I think they've had a marvellous time making the arrangements together.'

'I'm sure they have. Ah, here's the car.'

John watched Amy walk towards him, his heart beating erratically. When he'd bribed her to go to the café with him, on the promise of buying a painting from the shop, he had decided then that she was going to be his. And soon she would be.

He heard his best man, a colleague from the hospital, whistle softly through his teeth.

'No wonder you were in a hurry, John. She's really something, isn't she?'

Without taking his eyes off Amy, John nodded. Harry Tenant was a paediatrician and a damned good one. He'd never seen Amy before, but had readily agreed to be his best man. John could have asked Ben or Howard, but it hadn't seemed right somehow.

He reached out for her hand as soon as she was close enough, and felt a thrill as her delicate fingers tightened around his. This petite girl always declared that she wasn't pretty, but in his eyes she was the most beautiful woman he had ever seen.

After smiling at him, she turned and gave her flowers to Mrs Dalton who was in an aisle seat, and the ceremony began.

Everything went as they had rehearsed it, but this time it was for real. They both spoke clearly, without hesitation, secure in their love for each other.

It had been necessary to restrict the amount of guests attending the church because it was so small, but everyone present sang the hymns with enthusiasm.

Soon the vicar was saying that they were now man and wife, and John wanted to swing Amy round and round in sheer joy, but he managed to restrain himself and kiss her briefly. He would rectify that when they were alone at last.

The signing of the register came next, and he watched her, his hand on her shoulder, knowing this was going to be the hardest part for her. Ben had told him that if she was nervous or flustered she found reading or writing became even more difficult.

She made a perfect job of it and he was so proud of her, but he didn't miss the quiet sigh of relief when she put down the pen.

'Well done, my darling.' He spoke softly. 'That was excellent.'

Her smile at the praise was radiant, and once again he blessed the day he had walked into their shop in the King's Road. He had bought a painting and a vase, but he'd found something far more precious: the girl he wanted to spend the rest of his life with.

Amy couldn't believe it was all over and she was now Mrs Sterling. The ceremony had gone in a flash, or so it seemed, and the part she had been worried about hadn't been a problem. She had been afraid that nerves would make her mess up signing the register, but she had managed it quite well by taking her time. How she had improved since her school days.

Taking John's arm, they walked out of the church and into the sunshine. There had been concern that the outbreak of war would have put a damper on this day, but it hadn't. Nothing could.

After the photographs had been taken they all went back to the house where more guests were waiting for them. A mouth-watering buffet was enjoyed, then the speeches, toasts and cutting of the cake. Amy had never seen so much food in her life, but was too excited to eat, and she only sipped her drink.

'This must have cost a fortune,' she whispered to John. 'I had no idea it was going to be so lavish. Mrs Dalton wouldn't tell me what they were planning.'

'Don't worry about it, sweetheart.'

'But I do. I paid for my dress, but Mrs Dalton wouldn't let me give her anything towards the other things.'

John led her away from everyone to a quieter place in the garden. 'I can see this is going to fret you, so I'll explain. This wedding has been a joint effort. My parents have supplied the drink and some of the food; Mrs Dalton the rest of the buffet. Ben bought the cake, Howard paid for the cars and Ted the flowers. They all insisted.'

'Oh.' Amy's eyes misted. 'They didn't tell me. Everyone's been so kind.'

'That's because they love you.' He kissed her firmly. 'I have paid for the church and the honeymoon.'

'Are we going away? You've been very secretive about what we're doing.' Now she was excited again. 'Where are we going? I've never been away for a holiday. Are we going to stay in a guest house or hotel?'

He waited for her questions to stop, highly amused. 'I was going to take you to Paris, but I changed my mind after war was declared.'

'Paris!' Her eyes opened wide. 'Have you been there?'

'Yes, several times. It's a fascinating and beautiful city. I'll take you there when the war's over.'

'I'll keep you to that.' Slipping her arms around his waist, she smiled up at him. 'So where are we going?'

'I'm not telling. It's a surprise, but' – he glanced at his watch – 'go and change and we can slip away, hopefully without too much fuss.'

'All right.' She went upstairs to the room she had used last night, being careful not to trip over her long dress. Mrs Dalton had laid out her going-away clothes, as she called them, on the bed.

Mrs Dalton followed her. 'Let me help you out of your dress. You looked so lovely today. John's a lucky man.' She chatted away happily as she removed the headdress and veil, then the dress.

Amy gave her a hug. 'Thank you for arranging such a lovely wedding, and the food was wonderful.'

'We all pitched in.' Mrs Dalton was flushed with pleasure. 'Had to see our little girl married in style, didn't we?'

She bustled about packing the dress carefully in a large box, and then left Amy to wash and put on her new outfit.

Everything was new, right down to the underwear, which was silky and delicate. Amy couldn't help comparing it to the garments they made in the factory all that time ago, but these were much better. Her dress was pale lemon with a narrow ribbon of white lace around the neck and short sleeves. She had also gone mad and bought a beige woollen jacket in case it turned chilly, and a hat to match. It all looked very smart, and she was glad she had saved her money so there had been enough in her old teapot to buy all this. Especially now they were going away! She couldn't resist a little jig of pleasure. She had thought he had something planned, but he had stubbornly refused to tell her anything.

With one last glance in the mirror, she made her way downstairs again, to find John waiting for her. 'How long are we going for?'

'Four days is all I can manage.'

'Oh, I'll need to take more clothes with me.'

'It's already done. Mrs Dalton packed a case for you and it's in the car.'

'Well I never! You have all been keeping secrets, haven't you?'

Hearing a chuckle behind her, she turned to see Ben and Howard waiting.

'I should slip away now, John,' Ben said. 'While everyone's still eating and drinking.'

Amy hugged both of them, then whispered imploringly, 'Don't leave until we're back, will you?'

'We won't,' Ben promised. 'You both enjoy yourselves, and don't give anything else a thought, will you?'

'We won't.' John took her arm and they crept out of the front door.

If they thought they were going to slip away unnoticed, then they were mistaken. The car, festooned with ribbons, had a large notice on the back – 'Just Married' – and a string of tin cans tied to the bumper.

John muttered under his breath as he caught hold of Amy's hand and made a dash for the car. 'Quick!'

Their effort to avoid the confetti was useless; the guests had formed a solid line all the way to the car. Running the gauntlet, they were smothered from head to toe in brightly coloured pieces of paper.

John bundled Amy in, shut the door firmly and rushed round to the driver's side. 'Don't open the window!' he shouted as he leapt in the car.

But it was too late. Amy, thoroughly enjoying the fun, had wound down her window to wave at everyone. Her mistake instantly became obvious as a hand shot in and filled the car with confetti.

Putting his foot down hard, John roared up the road, the

cans clattering behind, and the wedding party shouting at the tops of their voices.

Once out of sight of the house, John screeched to a halt, jumped out, a penknife already in his hand, and cut off the notice and the cans.

Amy joined him, almost helpless with laughter, and began removing the ribbons.

When the car looked respectable again, John grinned at her. 'Well, Mrs Sterling, everyone's going to know we're just married. You're covered in the stuff.'

'So are you.' She reached up and began to pick bits out of his hair. 'And I don't care who knows. It was a wonderful wedding, and I'm so very happy to be Mrs Sterling.'

'Oh, my lovely girl.' He gathered her into his arms. 'I must have done something really good in this life to have deserved you.'

'Me too,' she murmured, holding on tightly.

He held her away so he could look into her eyes. 'Let's forget about the confetti and go on honeymoon. I can't wait to make love with you.'

'Nor me.'

They scrambled back in the car, not caring about the mess, eager to get away so they could be alone at last.

'We're going to the Isle of Wight?' Amy couldn't contain her excitement as John drove on to the ferry. 'Have you been there? What's it like?'

'Small.' He helped her out of the car. 'Come on, let's go on deck.'

'I'm gasping for a cup of tea.' Her mouth was dry after the champagne, though in truth she hadn't drunk much. Seeing Ben with that gleam of devilment in his eyes had been enough to make her careful and not overdo it. But she hadn't eaten either, and now her stomach felt quite empty. 'And perhaps a sandwich?'

'I expect they've got something, but if not it's only a short journey. We can find a café in Shanklin.'

Amy had never been on a boat before and rushed to the rail, fascinated by the sea. No matter how desperate she was for a cup of tea, John couldn't persuade her inside.

Watching the different colours as the boat carved its way through the small waves, she couldn't help thinking of her father. Was this how he'd felt about the sea, longing to sail away again after only a couple of weeks at home? She closed her eyes for a moment, realizing that the horror of his hanging no longer caused her pain, only sadness that it should have happened to him. She had taken another step forward by letting go of the past.

'You're very quiet, darling.' John bent his head to look at her. 'What are you thinking about?'

'The sea is very beautiful and I was wondering if my father felt a love for it.'

'I expect he did.' He pulled her close. 'Does it still hurt?'

'No.' She smiled. 'No it doesn't. It was terrible, but I've moved on now.'

'Good.' John pointed ahead. 'Look, we're coming into dock.'

'Oh, so soon!' Everything else was pushed out of her mind in the excitement of seeing a new place. She sighed blissfully. So many new things to see and experience, and all with the man she adored. She had thought she might be apprehensive about their first night together, but she wasn't. There wouldn't be anything to worry about with John, and she couldn't wait to be his wife in every way.

As soon as the boat had docked, they drove off and made for a café right on the seafront. There they had a pot of tea and cakes. With her thirst quenched at last, they got back in the car. John headed a little way along the coast and stopped at a small whitewashed hotel.

She beamed at him. 'Are we staying here?'

He nodded. 'What do you think of it?'

'Oh, it's pretty, and right by the sea.'

'One of the doctors at the hospital recommended it. He said it was comfortable and the food was excellent.'

They tried to brush off most of the confetti before checking in, but there were still little pieces clinging to them. Amy decided that, as soon as she could, she would find an envelope and put some in as a souvenir of this special day.

The inside of the hotel was bright, homely and not too grand, she was pleased to see. It was all right for John, but this was new to her. While he was signing the register, she peered through a door at the dining room. The tables were beautifully set out for dinner with spotless white tablecloths and a small vase of flowers on each one.

A man came from behind the desk and picked up their cases, his lips twitching when a couple of small silver horseshoes fell off them. 'I'll show you to your room, Dr and Mrs Sterling.'

He led them up two flights of stairs and to the end of a short corridor. He opened a door and waited for them to enter. 'There you are, sir. A nice quiet room for you, and there's a bathroom next door.'

'Thank you.' John's gaze swept around the room. 'This will do very nicely.'

'I'm sure you will be very comfortable, and if there's anything you need, please ask.' He put the cases beside the bed.

Amy watched John give him a tip, and as soon as the door had closed and they were alone, John reached for her.

'Come and kiss me before I die of frustration.'

She rushed into his arms, just as eager, and in no time at all they were naked and on the bed, lost in the need and passion for each other.

Making love was even more wonderful than she had imagined. As this was her first time, John tried to take it slowly, but she felt only pleasure. When this became obvious, all restraint was abandoned.

Wrapped in his arms afterwards, she sighed and smiled up at him.

He kissed her nose, pulling a face. 'Oh, damn, I meant to take it easy and leave it until after dinner. I had it all planned. A nice relaxing meal, then a stroll along the seafront before returning to our room, where I was going to undress you slowly, then lay you on the bed and love you. Instead of that, as soon as we were alone, all my plans were forgotten, because I love you so much, my darling.'

'I'm glad you didn't wait. It was lovely.' She peered at his watch. 'What time is dinner? I'm starving.'

They stretched out on the bed, completely at ease with each other, and laughed as John told her he was ravenous as well.

It was a perfect start to the honeymoon, and their life together.

# 26

For four days they didn't give the war a thought, refusing to listen to the radio or buy newspapers, but as soon as they arrived back home, reality rushed in.

'They've joined up,' Mrs Dalton said when they were all sitting down with a cup of tea in front of them.

Howard stirred sugar into his tea. 'We told you that's what we were going to do.'

'I know.' Mrs Dalton looked sad. 'But I was hoping you would wait a bit longer.'

Ben shrugged. 'No point, they'll get us eventually, and this way we can go in together and, hopefully, stay in the same unit.'

Amy gazed at them, worry gnawing at her, and whispered, 'I'm going to miss you. When are you leaving?'

'In three weeks.' Ben frowned. 'Will you be letting our rooms, Mrs Dalton?'

'Certainly not!' She was scandalized. 'This is your home, and the rooms will be there for you whenever you want them. I know you'll be spending time with your parents when you're on leave, but everything will be just as you've left it.'

'That's good of you.' Howard leant over and kissed her cheek, making her glow with pleasure. 'It will be a comfort to know this is all still waiting for us.'

'It isn't a question of being good.' She tried to pretend she wasn't touched by the gesture of affection. 'You are all my family.'

'What are you going to join?' John asked.

'Army.' Ben smiled at Amy and then glanced back to John. 'You mind you take good care of our little girl while we're away.'

'You can be sure of that.'

'What are we going to do about the shop?' Amy couldn't imagine not having the boys around all the time. Why did there have to be a war when everything was so perfect? Emotion clogged the back of her throat.

'The lease runs out in a few weeks and it won't be worth renewing it.' Ben pushed his hair away from his eyes. 'I'm sorry, Amy, I know how you love the shop, but we've got to put our plans on hold for a while. And you've got a husband to look after you now.'

'And when the war's over we'll open a bigger and better shop.' Howard pursed his lips. 'This is only a temporary setback.'

'Of course it is.' Mrs Dalton turned to John. 'And you needn't worry about Amy being on her own in the shop, because I'll help to close it down.'

'Thank you, Mrs Dalton, that is a relief to know. And what about you, Ted?'

'I've already joined the ARP, and I'm going to try and keep my bookshop going.' Ted's expression was grim. 'Got to do something to help.'

'And I'm joining the WVS – Women's Voluntary Service.' Mrs Dalton had a determined air about her. 'They need drivers, Amy, so would you consider it as well? With John's permission, of course.'

'Well, I'd like to do something.' She curled her fingers around John's hand. 'What do you think, darling? I won't if you don't want me to.'

'I think it's a good idea. I shall be working shifts at the

hospital, and without the shop you'll want something to do, won't you?'

Amy nodded and smiled her thanks.

'Right, that's settled then.' Mrs Dalton bustled around clearing the table. 'Now we've all got something useful to do for the war effort. Let's hope it doesn't last too long.'

'Amen to that,' they all muttered.

When the time came to say goodbye to Ben and Howard, Amy hugged them, refusing to cry. There were families doing this all over the country at the moment. Children were being evacuated and sons and fathers were joining the forces. It had to be accepted as a way of life now, hard though it was.

'I'll keep everything clean and tidy for you to come back to.'

'Not too tidy.' Howard grinned. 'It won't look like home if you do.'

'Don't you take any chances, Amy.' Ben gave her a stern look. 'If things get rough at any time, you are to stay in the shelter.'

'I promise, and you be careful as well, both of you.'

Ben suddenly laughed. 'I don't know why we're making all this fuss. We've got basic training first and then we'll be home on leave. I'm leaving my car for you to use, if you can get petrol. That's bound to be one of the first things to become scarce.'

John managed to arrive before the train left, so they were all there to see them off. They waved until the train was out of sight.

The next two weeks flew by, but it was a sad time for Amy as she packed up the unsold items in the shop and took them back to the house. The pictures were stacked in Ben's studio, and she couldn't help wondering how long it would be before he was back, standing by the easel, brush in hand and a frown of concentration on his face. The sculptures and pots were carefully packed in boxes and piled in the corner of Howard's workshop. Gazing around the empty room, Amy sighed deeply. What happy times they had spent in here. She was going to miss them both dreadfully. How glad she was to have John, and know that he wouldn't be going into the forces.

That evening she sat down and wrote a letter to Ben and Howard. It was still difficult for her to do, but she knew they understood about the mistakes, which wouldn't worry them at all. John was working nights for the next week and she couldn't settle without him beside her, so it didn't matter how long it took her. Mrs Dalton would do the envelopes for her in the morning.

With the shop now closed, Amy and Mrs Dalton joined the WVS; as she was a driver, Amy was given a huge welcome.

'You're just what we need. Come with me.' Mrs Porter, a woman of imposing stature who was very expert at giving orders, sailed out of the hall they used as a meeting place and stopped by a battered old van. 'We're going to convert this into a tea wagon. Think you can drive it?'

'Erm . . .' Amy looked up at her face and didn't dare refuse. 'Yes, of course.'

'Splendid! Run it round the block and see how it feels.' After thrusting the keys in Amy's hand, she sailed off again on some other errand of importance.

'Shall I come with you?' Mrs Dalton had pinned her badge on to her coat and was wearing it with pride.

'Please.'

After pulling the seat as far forward as it would go, Amy just managed to reach the pedals. She then started the engine and edged her way, very cautiously, up the road. Much to her relief it wasn't as difficult as she'd feared, and she was grinning with confidence by the time they arrived back at the hall.

'Well done!' Mrs Dalton climbed out. 'Ben would be proud of you.'

'I hope they come and see us when they're on leave and don't spend all their time with their parents.'

'They will, my dear. Our house is home to them, and they're bound to want to spend a few days with us. They'll be eager to get at the paints and pots again after being away.'

'Of course they will.' Amy walked back into the hall with Mrs Dalton. 'I miss them so much.'

'We all do. Will John be home tonight?'

'Yes, thank goodness, and he will be on days for the next two weeks.'

'That's something to look forward to then.'

Amy nodded. It certainly was. During the day she could keep busy, but the nights dragged when John wasn't there. It was amazing how quickly she had become used to having him beside her, and the thrill of having him reach for her in the night to love, or just hold in his arms. She loved being married to him, and wished sometimes that he didn't have to work such long hours. But she was being selfish. Many women didn't know when they were going to see their husbands again. She was very aware of this and was careful to be grateful for every second they could spend together.

For the rest of the afternoon they had lessons on First Aid, how to make tea in the large urns, and all sorts of information deemed useful for when the fighting began.

On arriving home, they found Ted in the kitchen, reading

a newspaper and wearing a tin hat and an armband with 'ARP' on it. They both burst out laughing at the comical sight.

'What's so funny?' he asked, his lips twitching with amusement.

'Why are you wearing a tin hat indoors?' Amy spluttered again.

'I'm just trying it out for size, and I'm about to go out on fire-watching duty.'

'But there aren't any fires.'

'Not yet, Mrs Dalton, but we've got to be prepared.' He winked at them. 'We've got a dartboard though, and I'm getting quite good.'

John arrived then. 'Good Lord, is there a raid on?'

'He's got to be prepared.' Amy giggled and wrapped her arms around her husband. Nothing much seemed to be happening with this war, and it was easy to make light of it after the concern at first. 'Finished for the day?'

'Hmm.' He whispered in her ear: 'A whole night together, but first I must eat. I'm starving.'

'It won't take me long to get dinner. The casserole only needs warming through while I cook some potatoes.' Amy put the vegetables in a bowl and glanced at Ted and Mrs Dalton. 'Do I cook for four?'

'Not for me, Amy.' Ted picked up his gas mask. 'I'm off for the night.'

'I'm not stopping either. You two have some time on your own.' Mrs Dalton left with Ted.

When they'd eaten and washed up, they went into the sitting room to listen to the wireless for a while, and tell each other what they had been doing. John always wanted to know everything she had done and he told her about some of the funny things that happened at the hospital, leaving out all the distressing parts of his job.

Sitting comfortably on the settee, John pulled her towards him and gave a deep sigh of contentment.

'Tired?' she asked, looking up at him.

'No.'

'Oh, good.' She snuggled close and listened to the deep rumble in his chest as he chuckled.

'Christmas is only seven weeks away and I was wondering what this year will be like. Everything is so uncertain, isn't it?'

'It is, my darling.' John squeezed her shoulder. 'And it's most unlikely that Ben and Howard will be here, so we can spend Christmas with my parents, if you like? I should be able to get a couple of days off.'

'That would be nice, but I wouldn't like to leave Ted and Mrs Dalton on their own.'

'What about one day with my parents and one day here?'

'That would be perfect.' Amy hugged him. 'You're such a sensible man.'

'I know. That's why I married you.'

She nibbled his ear. 'Let's go to bed.'

# 27

The New Year came in quietly, and by March 1940 everyone was calling it the phoney war. Quite a few of the children who had been evacuated to the country were returning, homesick for their families and the familiar streets of London. City-born and -bred, many of them found the open countryside a strange place. But Amy didn't care how phoney the war was. All those she loved were safe, and that was the most important thing to her. Two weeks ago Ben and Howard had arrived home on embarkation leave, and they'd had the most riotous party to send them on their way. No one knew exactly where they were going, of course, as troop movements were kept secret, but it was almost certain they were joining the British Expeditionary Force in France. They looked wonderful in their uniforms, and Amy had disgraced herself by sniffling as she'd hugged them before they had boarded the train. She had told herself that she wasn't going to cry, but hadn't been able to help it. Mrs Dalton had been dabbing her eyes as well.

John was still working long hours and after a busy night would come home exhausted and collapse into bed to sleep, but he soon recovered. After a long shift like that though, they always had a couple of days together. They were bliss-fully happy and every day she counted her blessings for having such a wonderful husband – and in-laws. John's parents were frequent visitors to the Chelsea house now, and she and John went to them for lunch whenever John had the time off. Amy loved them; it was no wonder John was such a lovely person with parents like that. As soon as the war was over they were planning to have a large family, and John's mother and father didn't hide their wish to have grandchildren.

The war was the only cloud on Amy's horizon, but as the months went by without much happening, she began to relax. Some women in the WVS were saying that it would be over by Christmas, but when she had told Ted that, he'd just shaken his head, saying that was what everyone thought in the last war. As gently as possible he had urged her not to pin her hopes on that.

On 10 May, Winston Churchill replaced Neville Chamberlain as Prime Minister, and Germany invaded France. The phoney war was over.

The next couple of weeks were a worrying time as the Germans moved further and further into France, and Amy prayed that Ben and Howard were safe.

John was home on 26 May, and it was late in the afternoon when an ambulance screeched to a halt outside the house, and Harry Tenant, the doctor who had been their best man, ran in.

'All hell's been let loose, John. We're needed.'

'What's up? What's happened?' Amy called, but John had jumped aboard the ambulance and roared up the road without stopping for an explanation.

Mrs Dalton joined Amy on the step. 'They're in a hurry.'

Pursing her lips, heart thumping, Amy said nothing. She hadn't liked that air of extreme emergency.

While they were still standing there in stunned silence, Mrs Porter arrived in the van, rather out of breath. 'Just grab your hats and badges. We're needed.'

Amy and Mrs Dalton collided as they both tried to get

through the door at the same time, but it only took them a few minutes to join Mrs Porter. They had known the WVS would go wherever help was needed, but the war had been almost unreal until this moment. It was terrifying.

'Where are we going? And what the hell's happened?' Mrs Dalton straightened her hat, which had been knocked askew in their haste.

'We're needed at Dover!'

'Dover!' Amy and Mrs Dalton spoke together, looking at each other in alarm.

'Just got word. Our army is trapped on the beaches at Dunkirk and they're trying to bring them home by boat. It's a dreadful mess evidently.'

'Oh dear God!' Amy felt sick. Ben and Howard were over there.

'They need all the help they can get to deal with the troops as they come ashore, and we've been asked to do what we can. Our main task will be to supply them with a hot drink and sandwiches.'

'That's where John's gone then.' Mrs Dalton squeezed Amy's hand. 'There'll be wounded on those ships.'

Amy nodded. She was beyond speech.

The scene that greeted them at Dover was something Amy would remember for the rest of her life. It was chaos, but organized chaos as the ships docked and the weary, battered men came ashore. The majority managed under their own steam; others were helped by friends, and more arrived on stretchers.

Even Mrs Porter seemed stunned into inactivity for a moment. 'Oh dear Lord . . .'

'Come on, ladies.' A soldier with sergeant's stripes on his sleeve marched up to them. 'These poor buggers need tea

277

and something to eat. You'll find everything you need over there.' He pointed to three army lorries. 'And if some of them look like civilians, they are. They're taking any small boat across. If it floats it's going over to France.'

Mrs Dalton was the first to recover. 'Let's get on with it. Has everyone got cigarettes, because they're going to need them?'

Mrs Porter took several packets out of the van and handed them out together with boxes of matches.

Amy grabbed mugs of hot tea and sandwiches, moving among the men coming off a ship that had just docked with a gaping hole in its side and listing badly.

'Thanks, ducky.' A grime-smeared soldier of indistinguishable rank took a mug from her, gulped down the tea and grinned, his teeth appearing very white against his blackened face. 'You haven't got a fag, have you?'

She held out the packet and he took one, cupping his hands around the match she had struck. His hands were steadier than hers, she thought wryly.

After taking a long draw, he tipped his head back, blew out the smoke and sighed. 'Thanks, pet, you're an angel.'

'How . . . how bad is it over there?'

'Bloody awful.' He gave her a studied look. 'Got someone over there, have you?'

She nodded, her mouth in a tight line of worry.

'Well, they're doing their best to get everyone home, but there are thousands on those beaches and it's going to take time. The bastards are trying to sink the ships as they come in.'

That wasn't at all comforting, but she thanked him and carried on giving help where she could. She searched faces, constantly looking for Ben and Howard. And she worried all the time about where John might be, hoping with all her heart that he hadn't gone across to help on the beaches. That was just the kind of thing he would do.

After six hours she was nearly dropping with exhaustion. It was dark now, but the ships were still coming in loaded with troops. As she looked around, her eyes gritty with fatigue, she couldn't help wondering if this country was beaten? Had they lost the war?

Mrs Porter found her. 'Ah, there you are. Take a break. We're going to be here until dawn, and possibly longer than that. See that building over there?'

Amy's gaze followed where she was pointing.

'They've taken a lot of the wounded there before moving them to various hospitals, but there are a couple of rooms where we can rest.'

'Thanks.' Amy walked towards the building where there were army and civilian ambulances lined up, feeling numb, and her head ringing from the constant noise and bustle. A ship sounded its horn, making her jump, but she knew it meant one was on its way back to France. She couldn't rest, there was too much to do. Perhaps she could help with the wounded? She did know some First Aid, and a lot of the men just seemed to need someone to smile at them.

She had thought that it would be like a hospital in here, quiet and controlled, but it wasn't. There were men everywhere, some only needing dressings changed and others in a more serious state. She could see the doctors working to sort out those who needed immediate despatch to hospital from those who could wait a bit longer.

And then she saw John. Her relief was enormous. He was here! Making her way over to him, she waited until he had finished putting stitches in a nasty head wound, then she touched his arm gently. 'John.'

He turned. It seemed to take a moment before it registered that she was really standing beside him. 'Amy, how long have you been here?'

'Some hours; I've lost track of time. I'm here with Mrs Dalton and the WVS. Is there anything I can do to help you?' She wanted to stay as near to him as possible.

His expression was grim as he turned and called an army nurse over. 'This is my wife and she's been trained in First Aid, so could you find her something to do?'

'Yes, doctor, I would be grateful for help with dressings.'

'Good.' John didn't have time to say anything else as another ship had docked. It had been attacked on its way back from France and had quite a few badly injured men on board.

For three days, Amy and Mrs Dalton worked, helping in any way they could, with only snatched moments of sleep now and again. They were dirty, exhausted and worried sick about the boys. It was only when John sought them out and demanded they go home and rest that Amy realized it was impossible to go on any longer. Mrs Porter took them home, ordering that they both rest and be ready to go back in two days' time, if they were still needed.

Once clean and with a good meal inside her, Amy slept for twelve hours without waking up. When she surfaced, Mrs Dalton told her they were still bringing home the troops, so they decided to go back immediately.

It was on the sixth day of the evacuation that Amy saw a familiar figure.

'Mrs Dalton!' She ran over and dragged her towards the men coming ashore. 'I saw Howard. I'm sure it was him!'

But they searched the faces in vain.

'You must have been mistaken, Amy. It's almost impossible to recognize anyone amongst this crowd.'

She hadn't been wrong. She couldn't have been.

'You're right. There he is.' Mrs Dalton grabbed her arm and they fought their way over to the dishevelled and weary soldier.

'Howard!' Amy had tears running down her cheeks as she rushed towards him.

After only a moment's hesitation, he held out his arms, and she ran into them, crying with relief. He was filthy, smelt something awful, but he was the most wonderful sight in the world to her.

'Blimey, mate!' one soldier shouted. 'Wish I had a welcome like that.'

Mrs Dalton kissed him on the cheek, also overcome with relief.

'Where's Ben?' Amy looked up at his haggard face, and knew in that instant that the news was not good. 'Tell me, please. Tell me he's all right.'

'I don't know, Amy. He was one of those guarding our escape. They'll be the last to leave.'

'But he's still alive?' Mrs Dalton had gone very pale.

'I don't know,' was all he said, bowing his head. 'He doesn't stand much of a chance.'

Amy was sure her heart had just been torn to shreds.

'Howard!' John pushed his way through the mass of men. 'Are you hurt?'

'Don't think so. A few cuts and bruises, that's all.'

'I'll take care of him, doctor, and see he gets back to his unit.' An army nurse working with John had followed him.

'Thank you, nurse.'

Amy watched Howard walk away, the nurse with her hand on his arm, and she began to shake. 'Ben . . .'

John held her around the waist and caught a WVS woman

as she walked past. 'I want my wife taken home. Please see to it.'

Amy had become oblivious to her surroundings. He couldn't be dead! She wouldn't believe it. Howard didn't know for sure. He would survive and be picked up with the last group. He would. He would.

Mrs Porter bustled up. 'I've been told you're looking for me, doctor.'

'My wife's received some bad news. Would you see that she gets home, please? I'll come as soon as I can.' John tipped her head up with his fingers to make her look at him. 'You must rest, darling. I'll do what I can to find out where Ben is, but it's going to take time. Men are scattered all over the place and he might already have made it back. They aren't only coming ashore here, there are small boats landing further along the coast.'

'Are there?' Hope sprang to life in her again, and she nodded. 'He'll turn up somewhere.'

'Of course he will.' John smiled gently. 'Now go home. You've done all you can here.'

She clung to his arm. 'You come home soon as well. You're exhausted.'

'I'll be back tonight, I promise. And don't give up hope.'

'I won't.' Amy kissed him, and then allowed Mrs Porter and Mrs Dalton to lead her away from the chaos, but after only a few steps, she turned back to John. 'Where are they taking Howard? Can't he come home with us?'

'No, darling, the army have everything organized, and he'll be taken good care of.'

She nodded, dry-eyed with shock and worry for her two boys. They were such an important part of her life. Howard would be devastated if Ben didn't come back, and she couldn't imagine life without his teasing presence. Squaring her shoulders, she walked calmly through the crowds. They were very close: she would know if he had been killed – and he hadn't. She would not accept that unless there was irrefutable proof!

Watching intently as Amy walked away, John sighed with relief when he saw her head come up, her step sure. He knew she had courage and had faced terrible things in her past, but he hadn't known how she would take this blow. She adored both the boys, which was understandable, after what they had done for her, but the bond between her and Ben was something special. It had concerned him when he had first met them, but he had soon discovered that what they shared was not a physical love, more a meeting of minds. This disaster was going to hit her hard, but that lifting of her head showed him she was going to handle this with her usual fortitude. She might only be small, but that petite form held a strong person.

Still, he'd make sure he got home tonight. He was due a break after working almost non-stop for five days – or was it four? After casting a glance around, he shrugged. What did time matter? The only important thing was that the troops were being brought home. And what then? The Germans were now only just across the Channel, and if Hitler didn't invade at once then he was a fool. Britain was now on its own.

He watched, deep in troubled thought, as he saw a sergeant major gathering together the uninjured. He saw the lines snap to attention on command, then march smartly away. If it hadn't been for their dishevelled appearance and lack of weapons, you would never have guessed that they had spent days on the beach, being bombed as they tried to get on the ships coming in for them. From what some of the men had told him, it had been nothing short of hell on earth. And must still be for the poor devils over there – including Ben.

'Stay safe,' he murmured as he went back to work.

A faint sound of marching feet and singing reached his ears, making him nod grimly. All right, we're in a bloody mess, but the Germans will still have a fight on their hands if they try to invade. Time would be needed to recover from this disaster, but would the country get it?

It was nearly midnight when John finally arrived back in Chelsea, and Mrs Dalton met him as he came in the door.

'Is Amy all right?'

'Yes she is, and fast asleep at the moment.' She patted his arm. 'Why don't you have a bath and get some rest as well? You look exhausted, John. The water's hot.'

'Thanks, you're an angel.' He grimaced. 'They're still bringing them back. God knows how long it's going to take.'

'What's going to happen to us now? Can we survive a crushing defeat like this?'

'We've got to.' He ran a hand through his untidy hair. 'The alternative is unthinkable. But we must accept that the war is now coming to us, and we are going to have a tough fight on our hands.'

'No doubt.' Mrs Dalton's smile was wry. 'But we can be a stubborn race when our backs are to the wall, and not easy to beat when we get mad. And this Dunkirk business is going to make us mad. Hitler has still got to cross that strip of water and he won't stand a chance. We'll blow him out of the water. Now, you go and have your bath.'

John laughed at the determined glint in her eyes, but he wondered what they were going to use, as most of the armaments had been left behind in France.

After he ran the bath, he found he was so tired he hardly had the strength to remove his clothes. Many people would be hoping that the Channel would prove a difficult obstacle for the Germans, and it would, but Britain was now within easy reach of their bombers. He must try to persuade Amy to go and stay with his parents.

Feeling almost human again after scrubbing himself clean, he went to their room and stood beside the bed, drinking in the sight of his sleeping wife. She was curled up like a kitten and hugging his pillow. After gently prising it away from her, he slipped into bed and pulled her towards him, his tiredness disappearing. Without waking properly, she wrapped her arms around him and sighed.

He kissed her gently and she stirred. 'John.'

'Shush, go back to sleep. I didn't mean to wake you.'

'I'm glad you're home at last.'

'Me too.' He couldn't resist making love to her then. She was so warm and responsive in his arms. Their loving was slow, gentle, giving and receiving comfort.

The next morning, after John had gone to the hospital, Amy went to visit Ben's parents.

'Oh, Amy, we're so pleased to see you.' Mrs Scott clasped her hands tightly. 'Do you know what's going on? I expect John has been busy with the wounded. Has he been able to tell you anything?'

Both of Ben's parents had deep circles under their eyes; they had obviously not slept properly for some days.

'We can't find out a damned thing!' Mr Scott's voice was husky with worry.

'That's why I've come to see you.' She sat down, tense, knowing that what she had to say would bring little comfort, but at least it might give them hope. 'I've been with the

WVS helping at Dover. They are bringing the men home by the thousand. Howard is safe, we saw him—'

'Oh, thank God!' Both spoke at the same time, and then waited anxiously for her to continue.

'He said Ben was still at Dunkirk with the rearguard trying to protect the evacuation, and would be amongst the last to leave.'

'He's still alive then.' Mrs Scott's hands were shaking.

'Yes, as far as we know.'

'Tell us what it's like when the ships arrive.' There was a little more colour in Mr Scott's face now.

For the next hour she talked, explaining about the ships, big and small, and the help that was there to greet the returning men.

As she drove back to Chelsea she hoped her visit had been of some help, but no amount of optimistic talk could hide the fact that Ben was in grave danger.

All they could do now was wait.

# 28

The first week in June and Dunkirk fell. The manner of the evacuation was being hailed as a marvel, but Amy felt only a crushing sadness. There was no sign of Ben. He hadn't made it back, and France was now under German control.

She was clearing up the breakfast things when she heard a noise above her. Someone was moving around in Ben's studio. She knew it couldn't be Mrs Dalton or Ted because they were both out. Had Ben come back and they hadn't known? She ran upstairs, her heart in her mouth. The door was closed, so she opened it carefully. There was someone there in army uniform, standing utterly still, gazing at an unfinished painting. He wasn't quite tall enough to be Ben.

'Howard.' She spoke softly and went to stand beside him, slipping her hand through his arm, feeling the rough texture of khaki under her fingers and the tenseness of his muscles.

He covered her hand with his, squeezing it as he began to speak. 'We've known each other since we were three years old. We lived next door to each other until Ben's parents moved away five years ago. We went to the same schools, the same university, left together and came here . . .' He bowed his head, voice husky with emotion. 'He's always been around, solid and dependable. I can't imagine life without him.'

'He'll be back.' Amy had caught the tone of hopelessness in Howard's voice; he believed his friend was dead.

'You don't know what it was like over there. It was hell, Amy. Those left behind were on a suicide mission to protect the thousands of men on the beaches. They wouldn't have stood a chance . . .'

'He'll be back,' she repeated firmly. 'If he was dead I'd know it.'

Howard glanced down at her taking in the determination in her voice and stance. 'I do believe you would,' he said slowly.

'Now.' She was resolved not to let him brood. 'Are you on leave? Can you stay for a while?'

'No, sorry, I've only got a forty-eight-hour pass. I'm on my way to my parents, but I stopped off to see Ben's family before coming here.' His expression was tortured. 'They've received notice that he is reported missing.'

'Well, what else could they say? He obviously didn't get on one of the ships. He might be hiding in France or taken prisoner. It doesn't mean he's dead, Howard, so if you've come to say goodbye to Ben, then don't, because he'll walk through that door one day, pick up a brush and start painting as if he'd never been away.'

He turned to face her, giving her a hug. 'I hope you're right. You're a real tonic, Amy. Tell John, Ted and Mrs Dalton I'll see them next time I'm on leave.'

She saw him out and watched him stride up the road. She knew how he felt. A part of his life was now missing, and it was the same for her, but she hadn't given up hope, and neither must he. She must go and see Ben's parents at once.

August of 1940 came in hot and fine with clear skies, and the expected invasion hadn't materialized.

'Hitler's made an almighty blunder by not invading immediately after the fall of France.' Ted shook his head as if he couldn't understand it.

They were all sitting in their favourite place, around the

kitchen table. John was home for a couple of precious days, and Amy cherished these times together.

'He's got to knock out our air force first.' John stirred his tea, sighing. 'Those poor devils in the air are involved in the most desperate fight. Some of the injuries the pilots are suffering from burning planes are dreadful. When this lot's over I'm thinking of going into reconstructive surgery. Do you know they are rebuilding faces?'

'Oh, the poor souls.' Mrs Dalton was clearly upset. 'So many young men are fighting and dying over our heads.'

'They know the importance of what they're doing. By their courage and determination, they have given this country a chance to recover. A much needed few months to replace the armaments left in France, and strengthen our forces.' Ted poured himself another cup of tea.

'But what a terrible price.' Amy spoke for the first time. She was as aware as everyone else of what was happening. 'The Battle of Britain', Churchill had called it after Dunkirk.

'But I tell you what' – Ted leant forward – 'if our fighter pilots can defeat the might of the Luftwaffe, then we shall win. What is happening now is crucial to the outcome of the war.'

'It's a lot to ask of one small country though, isn't it?' Mrs Dalton's expression was grim. 'If we only had some help.'

'If you're looking to America, then don't bother.' John sat back. 'They're helping by sending food and ammunition, but they won't enter the war unless provoked.'

'No, of course not, and you can't blame the ordinary American people for wanting to stay out of the conflict.' Mrs Dalton poured the cat a saucer of milk. He seemed to be the only one untouched by the talk of war.

'Most of the world doesn't think we stand a chance.' Ted

slapped his hand on the table. 'But they're wrong! By God, they're wrong. It's going to be a grim fight, but I can't ever see this country surrendering.'

'I agree.' John stood up. 'Are you ready, Amy? I told Mum and Dad we'd be there for lunch.'

'Any news of Ben?' It was always the first question they were asked when they visited John's parents.

'No.' Amy shook her head. 'But in this case, no news is good news, as Mrs Dalton keeps reminding us.'

'His parents must be frantic with worry. Not knowing what's happened to him must be so hard to cope with.' Mr Sterling handed them both a small sherry to drink before lunch.

'They are dreadfully worried, of course, but' – Amy gave a bright smile – 'like me, they believe he could still be alive.'

John watched Amy, her chin tilted up at a determined angle, and marvelled at her strength of character. When they married he had thought he couldn't love her any more than he already did, but he had been wrong. He knew what Ben meant to her, and yet she never allowed her smile to dim when talking about him, or her conviction falter that he was alive somewhere. She spent her time visiting his parents, giving comfort and bolstering up their hopes, and writing letters to Howard, her tongue between her teeth with the effort. He couldn't imagine what it was like not to be able to read or write without a tremendous effort, but she never complained, and never stopped trying to improve. Ben had told him once that Amy was special, and he wholeheartedly agreed with that.

After lunch they took their tea into the garden and sat in the shade of an apple tree.

'Look at that.' John's father pointed to the trails in the sky. 'There's a dogfight going on up there.'

They all stared up, silent, until Mrs Sterling spoke.

'What's going to happen next, John? Will they start bombing civilians?'

'I expect so, if they can't break our air force. And London is bound to be the first on their list.'

'Amy, why don't you come and stay with us?' Mrs Sterling looked at her hopefully. 'We've got plenty of room and would love to have you live here with us.'

'That's kind of you, Mrs Sterling, but I wouldn't like to be away from John, or Ted and Mrs Dalton. We've got an Anderson shelter in the garden, so we'll be safe enough. I won't run away. If John stays, then I'm staying.'

John knew from the set of her mouth that she meant it. Nothing would make her leave those she loved, no matter how bad things became.

'Don't worry, Mum.' He laughed. 'If it gets too dangerous, I'll bring her to you, even if I have to shove her in the boot. She's small enough to fit in.' He ducked as she aimed a playful punch at him.

'Don't you dare try it. I am in the WVS, you know, and will be needed in a crisis. I've learnt to drive quite a large van loaded with tea urns and other necessities.'

'Can you reach the pedals?' he teased.

'Just about.' She giggled. 'One of the women's husbands said he could fit wooden blocks on the pedals to make it easier for me, but I told him I can manage.'

John raised his eyes to the heavens. 'I don't know what she gets up to when I'm not there. Can you imagine her driving a large van?'

'I'll have you know that I'm a very good driver. Ben

taught me.' A faint cloud crossed her expression for a fleeting moment, then it was gone, and her smile was firmly back in place.

God, how he loved her.

On the way home, Amy watched the passing scenery with a smile on her face. She always enjoyed their visits to John's parents. They were so nice . . .

'I think you should consider Mum and Dad's offer to stay with them, Amy.'

'Are you trying to get rid of me?' she teased.

'No, but I want you to be safe should the bombing start.'

'Darling.' She shuffled close and leant against his shoulder. 'Do you think I could stand it being safe and cosy, knowing you were in danger all the time?'

'I'd get down and see you every spare moment.'

'Where would you get the petrol from? You know this is the last time we can use the car for a while. And anyway, there's no point in discussing this because I must be where you are. I promise I'll go to the shelter if things get too close, but I want to be there and know you'll be able to come home and find me waiting for you. Day or night.'

He glanced at her briefly, then back at the road. 'I like the sound of the "night" bit.'

'Me too.' She sighed and nestled her cheek on his shoulder. 'Don't send me away, John. I couldn't bear to be parted from you.'

'All right, but let's just pray that our fears are groundless. I know this is a hell of a time to start our married life, but we'll get through this and grow old together, surrounded by our children and grandchildren.'

'That's a future I can really look forward to.' She grinned up at him. 'How many children shall we have?'

'Oh, at least six.'

'Sounds good to me. I always wanted to belong to a large family.' Her happiness faded. 'Do you think any of our children will be like me?'

'I hope so.'

'No, I mean, do you think they will have trouble with words like I do?'

'I really don't know, darling. A couple of doctors I've spoken to are aware that a condition like yours does exist in a very few people, but they haven't discovered the cause of it yet.'

'Let's hope they do, because I don't want our children to be called stupid. It hurts, John.'

'That won't happen because we'll have your experience to guide us. I've watched your frustration as you've struggled, and you have made a lot of progress. Our children will have both of us to help them.'

'I thought I was the only one in the world who couldn't read, and until I met Ted no one tried to help me, except my granny, of course.' She brightened. 'Our children won't have to try and deal with it on their own, and they'll have two wonderful godfathers who understand as well.'

John pulled the car over and stopped, turning to face her. 'You do realize that the longer we go without news of Ben, the fewer are the chances that he's still alive.'

'I know that, darling.' Her eyes swam with unshed tears. 'I'm not a fool. If I've got to bury him, then I'll grieve, but while there's a shred of hope, I'll cling to it.'

'I'm sorry to have pointed that out to you, but I needed to know you were prepared to face the worse, should it happen.'

'I'm prepared, and I'll face it.'

# 29

'What the hell's happening?' Mrs Dalton hurried into the kitchen, colliding with Ted, who was cramming his tin hat on his head and grabbing for his gas mask.

'Looks like they're bombing the docks! Get in the shelter, both of you!'

Oscar was cowering under the table as the sirens wailed out the warning, so Amy picked him up and hurried to the shelter with Mrs Dalton right behind her. Once safely inside they listened to the drone of planes and the crunch of bombs as they rained down.

'So, it's started.'

Amy nodded, trying to soothe the terrified cat. 'It's all right, Oscar, they're not near us.'

He didn't look as if he believed that and scrambled out of her arms to burrow under a blanket. It visibly shook as they watched.

'I wonder where John is?' Amy chewed her lips with worry.

'He'll be busy at the hospital tonight.' Mrs Dalton pulled a small bar of chocolate out of her pocket and handed Amy a piece.

'Where did you get this?'

'Been saving it for such an occasion.' Mrs Dalton sucked the sweet. 'As soon as the all clear sounds I'm going to see if there's anything I can do. People are going to be homeless after this night.'

'I'm coming with you.'

'Good, we might need you to drive the van. It looks like the East End is taking a pasting. September the seventh is a day we're all going to remember.'

When the all clear sounded, they scrambled out and faced in the direction of the London docks. The red glow in the sky told the story.

'Oh, dear God.' Mrs Dalton grabbed Amy's arm. 'Come on, we'll be needed.'

They ran to the hall used by the WVS and pushed aside the blackout curtain to find the room full of women.

'Ah, good, you've made it.' Mrs Porter sailed towards them. 'We've just received word that the homeless are being taken to schools and church halls. People will be in shock. Amy, will you drive the van?'

'Yes, Mrs Porter.'

She clapped her hands. 'Let's get going, ladies.'

They weren't allowed near the fires, but were directed to a nearby school. Amy knew the area well as it was where she had grown up, and couldn't help wondering if her old street was still standing. But there wasn't time to waste, for the school hall was crowded with people, ranging from the very young to the elderly. All were clearly shocked, but were sitting quietly, except for a couple of babies crying for their feed.

Mrs Porter marshalled her army of ladies into action. 'Get the tea urns boiling if there's any gas in the kitchens. They'll all need sweet, hot tea.'

Fortunately the gas was still on, as this school was far enough away from the bombing not to have had all the services turned off.

By the time dawn came up and they were relieved by a fresh group of workers, Amy was exhausted and ready to go home, and it didn't look as if Mrs Dalton would even be able to stand up for much longer. Amy drove them home in the van, dropping the ladies off at their various addresses.

John didn't arrive home until mid-afternoon and, after having something to eat, he sprawled on the bed and slept. Amy didn't disturb him, seeing that he needed rest before returning to the hospital. After last night's raid she knew that all the medical staff would be rushed off their feet caring for the injured. She couldn't help wondering, rather wistfully, what it would be like to live a normal life again. And have a normal married life with the man she loved. But that wasn't possible at the moment and was something that had to be accepted.

Ted and Mrs Dalton were out once again trying to help those who had lost homes and family, but for Amy, John came first. If the raids continued – and there was every reason to suppose they would – he was going to be much needed, and she would do all she could to help him.

'Hello, darling.' He came into the kitchen, unshaven but looking less exhausted, and wrapped his arms around her, resting his chin on her head. 'Any tea in the pot?'

'No, but I'll soon make some.' She held on tight for a moment, then turned away to put the kettle on to boil.

After drinking two cups, he sat back. 'Quite a night, wasn't it? They couldn't wipe out our air force, so now they're going to try and bomb us into submission.'

'It could get very bad, couldn't it?' There was a question in her voice.

'Yes, and I want you to go and stay with my parents, darling.'

She shook her head vigorously. 'Not unless you come too.'

'I can't do that.'

'I know you can't, and I won't leave you, John. I must be near you, and we'll face the danger together.'

His sigh was resigned. 'Promise me you'll stay in the shelter during the raids.'

'I promise, but as soon as they're over I'll be out there helping in any way I can.'

He squeezed her hand. 'You be careful.'

'I will, and you must be as well.'


That became the pattern of their lives. No one got much sleep as the bombers came over night after night. They got so used to it that they managed easily on a couple of hours' rest snatched when they could. People emerged from shelters or the underground stations and made their way to work as normal, picking their way through the rubble of the night's destruction. You could almost set your clocks by the arrival of the planes, and if they didn't turn up on time, Londoners said to each other in a matter-of-fact way: 'They're late tonight.'

Amy visited Ben and Howard's parents regularly, just to make sure they were all right. She helped with the WVS and tried always to be around when John was, to see that he rested and had proper meals.

When Christmas arrived, she was overjoyed to learn that John had three days off, and they all had an invitation to stay with his parents. So with Mrs Dalton and Ted, they set off on Christmas Eve in high spirits. It was a welcome respite from the constant tension of the Blitz.

During the blissfully peaceful nights, John and Amy made love, knowing they weren't going to be disturbed by the wailing of the sirens and the whistle of bombs hurtling down. Ted and Mrs Dalton thoroughly enjoyed themselves, and Mr and Mrs Sterling were happy to have lively company.

When they arrived back home, Howard was waiting for them.

'Howard!' Amy threw her arms around him; relieved he was looking so much better than the last time she had seen him in Ben's studio. 'Are you staying?'

He swung her round, laughing at her exuberant greeting. 'I've got seven days' leave, so I'm spending four days here and the rest with my parents and Chrissie.'

'Who's Chrissie?' they all asked at the same time.

'You remember the nurse who looked after me at Dover? Well, that's Chrissie, and we've been seeing each other whenever we could.'

Amy beamed at that piece of news. 'Is it serious? And why didn't you bring her here?'

'She won't be on leave for another four days. And to answer your question, we like each other, but until this blasted war's over, that's all it's going to be. Then we'll see.'

Amy gave a yelp of delight and launched herself at him again. This was just what he needed to help him recover from Dunkirk. 'That's wonderful!'

'Will you put my wife down?' John watched the scene with amusement as Howard lifted her off the ground and handed her back to him.

'Sorry about that, but she keeps throwing herself at me.'

They were all talking and laughing as Mrs Dalton made a large pot of tea, and then they sat round the table to catch up with all the news. No one mentioned the war; it was just so good to have at least one of the boys home for a while. The other one was still sorely missed.

'What are you going to do while you're here?' Ted asked.

'Sleep mostly, then I thought I'd throw a few pots, just to keep my hand in.' Howard looked round at the smiling faces. 'Then I'd like us to have one hell of a New Year's

Eve party. I've promised to go to my parents the next day, but I'd like to celebrate here, and include Ben, even though we don't know where he is.'

'Excellent idea.' Mrs Dalton patted his hand. 'This house is full of his presence, and it's right we should think of him at the start of a new year.'

Amy agreed. No more information had been received about Ben's whereabouts, and she was more than ever convinced that he was still alive, no matter what anyone else said. 'And pray that he'll be back for the next one.'

Ted lifted his cup in salute. 'Wherever you are, Benjamin Scott, your place at this table will be waiting for you.'

'Hear, hear.' Mrs Dalton smiled at Howard. 'I don't know where you've been lately, but it's lively here now, so be prepared to spend your nights in the shelter.'

It had been wonderful to have Howard home for a few days and to welcome in 1941 together. The time had gone far too quickly, but Amy sang to herself as she prepared breakfast. There was a feeling of snow in the air, and the people huddled in shelters or underground stations would have had a cold night. Only the firemen would have been warm as they'd fought the fierce fires.

Frowning at the clock, she turned out the gas under the kettle. John was late this morning. It was nearly ten o'clock and he usually arrived home around nine after a night at the hospital. Ted was still out as well, and Mrs Dalton was having a well-earned rest after being up half the night with the WVS, so she wouldn't disturb her.

Oscar rubbed around her legs. At least the cat wanted some breakfast, so she saw to him and then stood staring out of the window at the bleak January morning. How she wished this war was over, but no one believed it was going to end for a long time yet. Her singing stopped as she began to fret. Where was he?

At eleven o'clock there was a knock on the front door, and she hurried to open it, smiling. John must have forgotten his key.

But her smile faded when she saw a colleague of John, Dr Hayward, standing there in a dishevelled state.

'David, you look exhausted.' She stepped aside. 'Please come in. I'm afraid John isn't home yet.'

He followed her into the kitchen, not saying a word, and when she turned and looked at his face, it felt as if she had just walked into an icy river.

'What's happened?' The words came out in a whisper as cold dread gripped her.

'Sit down, Amy.' He helped her, holding her hand tightly. 'I've got some bad news . . .'

'John!' There was only one reason David would be here like this, and she surged to her feet. 'Has he been hurt?'

He took a deep breath. 'I'm so sorry, Amy, but there's no easy way to tell you this. John was killed last night.'

'Nooo . . .' Her anguished cry echoed throughout the house and had Mrs Dalton stumbling into the kitchen, struggling to put on her dressing gown. 'No! *No.*'

'What's going on?' Mrs Dalton demanded.

David, cradling Amy in his arms, lifted tortured eyes. 'John's been killed.'

'Oh, dear God!' Mrs Dalton's legs gave way just as she managed to grab a chair and sit beside Amy. 'Come here, sweetheart.' When Amy turned to her she enveloped her in her arms.

'It isn't true. It can't be,' Amy moaned. 'Not my John.' The cries of distress racked her body.

'How did it happen?' Mrs Dalton spoke quietly to David,

who was looking totally helpless in the face of such over-whelming grief.

'John went in an ambulance to help at a bomb site, and when they were getting the injured on to stretchers a gas main blew . . .' He dipped his head and shook it in disbelief. 'They were all killed. I was no more than twenty yards away and wasn't even scratched.'

Suddenly Amy sat up. 'Where is he? I want to see him.'

'I don't think that's a good idea—' David's protest stopped when he saw her expression.

'Where is he?' She struggled to her feet and spoke through clenched teeth. '*Where is he?*'

'He's in the hospital mortuary.'

'Wait!' Mrs Dalton caught hold of Amy's arm as she made to move. 'Let me get dressed and I'll come with you.'

Amy sat down again.

Within ten minutes they were in David's car. None of them spoke, but Mrs Dalton sat in the back with Amy, holding her trembling hands.

Once at the hospital, Amy was oblivious to her surround-ings, holding on tightly to David and Mrs Dalton for sup-port. It didn't feel as if her legs belonged to her, and every step was torture, but she had to do this. She would never be able to believe it if she didn't see him for herself. It couldn't be John. They must have made a mistake . . .

They stopped outside a door and David left her for a moment. The sound of raised voices could be heard through the door, and then he returned.

'Sit down, Amy.' David was beside her again. 'You'll be able to see him in a few minutes, but . . .' He stooped down in front of her. 'He was badly injured. Are you sure you want to do this?'

'Yes.' Her eyes were wide with pain. 'I *must* see him.'

A man opened the door. 'All right, you can come in now. You've explained, doctor?'

'She knows.'

Amy was led into a large room crowded with trolleys covered with sheets, so many dead. It wasn't going to be him. It wasn't!

The man stopped at one trolley and turned down the sheet to expose the face, and she could deny it no longer. John's face was cut and bloodied, but there was no doubt it was him. No matter how injured, she would know that precious face. With a deep moan of utter despair she reached out to touch, but the man pulled up the sheet quickly.

'Come on, my dear.' Mrs Dalton was shaking. 'Let's get out of here.'

But Amy couldn't move; all she could do was stare at the trolley as her mind tried to grasp that this was the last time she was ever going to see him; never again would she sleep in his arms after making love. He had been so vibrant, so alive, so loved . . . and now he was gone.

She was swept off her feet and carried out.

'His parents,' she managed to gasp.

'They are being told now.' David sat her on a chair in the corridor and barked out an order to a passing nurse. 'Get us some hot, sweet tea.'

It appeared very quickly but Mrs Dalton had to hold the cup to her lips as she was incapable of doing anything, or thinking, or knowing where she was.

The next thing she was aware of was being tucked up in her own bed at home.

'Try to sleep.' Mrs Dalton kissed her cheek, and allowed Oscar to slink on to the end of the bed before she left the room.

Alone at last the dam broke and she sobbed her heart

out, grabbing John's pillow to her. What was she going to do without him? It was too cruel to lose both the men she loved.

'Oh, darling John,' she cried out. 'I loved you so much. How do I live without you?'

# 30

The wind was cold enough to cut a man in half, but Ben shoved his hands in his pockets, hunched his shoulders, and stared before him. There was a strip of wire at his feet, then a gap of about three yards, and then a tall fence; beyond that was open country for some twenty yards, leading to a wooded area. His thoughts soared over the trees, across the sea and back to Chelsea. The pain was almost physical as he remembered his studio. How he missed the smell of paint, and seeing Howard covered in dust as he chipped away at a piece of stone.

His head bowed in worry. Did his parents believe he was dead, and had Howard made it back? If so, what was he doing now? Was he still alive? And what about Amy, John, Ted and Mrs Dalton? The POWs knew that London was being bombed because they had a small radio hidden in the roof of one of the huts, and the guards took great delight in passing on such news. Was Amy still in London, or had John made her leave for somewhere less dangerous? He hoped all those he loved were safe.

At Dunkirk they had managed to hold out until most of the troops were off the beaches, then they had been overrun and taken prisoner. He was now somewhere in Germany, but he wasn't quite sure where.

There were so many questions running through his head today. Questions he had no hope of finding answers to.

'Major wants to see you.' Another one of the prisoners stood beside him and looked up. 'Bloody freezing out here.'

'Won't be for long, Shorty. In another few weeks spring will be here. Wonder if there are bluebells under those trees?'

The man gave him a pitying glance. 'Couldn't give a toss, mate. All I know is that beyond those trees is freedom.'

Ben snorted. 'There's a lot of ground and water to cross before you would find that.' They all dreamt of escaping, and there were always schemes being planned, but nothing had come of it so far. But it gave everyone something to think about, and a feeling that they were doing something. 'What's the Major want with me?'

'No idea, but you'd better find out, and it's warmer in his hut.'

Well aware that their every move was watched, they began to walk towards the hut, seeming relaxed and unhurried.

Shorty peeled off before they reached hut seven and went in a different direction.

The Major was sitting at the table, and another prisoner by the name of Charlie was leaning against a bunk bed. He was a rather shifty-looking individual and Ben had the impression he might have been a crook before the war.

'Ah, Scott.' The officer indicated he should sit. 'I believe you are an artist?'

He nodded.

'Give him the pass, Charlie.'

Charlie pushed himself away from the bunks and tossed something in front of Ben.

He whistled in surprise when he saw what it was, picked it up and examined it carefully. 'Where did you get this?'

'I took it out of a guard's pocket.' Charlie smirked. 'I made my living as a pickpocket before this lot started.'

Ben glanced at him. So his first impression of the man had been correct. 'You must be good.'

'He is.' The Major gave a faint smile. 'And proving rather

useful to us in here. Now, do you think you could copy that?'

'If I had the right pens and paper.'

The officer opened a drawer and took out various pens, inks and good-quality paper. Ben almost drooled. What wouldn't he give to have some of that to draw on?

'As I've said, Charlie's skills are proving to be of great value. You need to work quickly because the pass must be returned to the guard before he misses it.'

'How long have I got?' This was going to be delicate work, but Ben was sure he could do it.

'An hour at the most.' Charlie propped himself against the bunks again and examined his fingers. 'Got to slip it back in his pocket before he goes off duty.'

'I'd better get a move on then. I'll do the best I can in the time.' Ben set to work at once. He hadn't done such fine work since he'd been at college, but he revelled in the challenge. It was wonderful to have something positive to do, instead of ambling around, longing for freedom and worrying about those at home.

Only five minutes over the hour he had a passable replica, and handed it to the Major. 'I could have done better with more time.'

'That's excellent. If it isn't scrutinized too closely it will get someone out of the gate.' Major Roberts smiled then. 'You're very good, Ben.'

'Thank you, sir.' Ben hid a smile when the officer called him by his first name. He didn't do that to many. 'I'd like to try and get out with it.'

'Sorry, you're too tall, and we need your forgery skills. We're lucky enough to have a tailor as well, and he's making a German uniform out of an old blanket. Quite a talented lot we have in here.' He tossed the pass back to Charlie. 'Better return that now.'

Charlie disappeared without making a sound.

'Can you make another two passes? If it's successful we might be able to get a couple of men out before they rumble what we did.'

'Of course.' Ben eyed the paper with longing. 'Any chance of having a sheet of that, sir?'

'Sorry.' He put it back in the drawer. 'It came from the commandant's office and will be recognized in this state, but' – he gave Ben a sympathetic glance – 'I'll see if we can get you something to use for yourself. Miss your art, do you?'

Ben nodded. 'It's one of the hardest things for me. There is so much crying out to be recorded here, and I haven't anything to do it with. I assume Charlie got that as well, but how the hell did he get into the office?'

'I don't ask.' The Major shook his head. 'Come here tomorrow morning and do the others for us.'

'Right.' Ben stood up and left, making his way back to his own hut, dipping his head to hide his amused smile. *What do you think of that, Amy? I'm a forger now!*

He hoped the Major could find him paper and pencils, but if not, perhaps he could bribe Charlie to find him something. The man might like a portrait of himself.

He had to find a way to pass the time, because he could be here for years. They were never going to let him take part in an escape plan, because his height made him too conspicuous.

The amusement faded as he contemplated the bleak future and wondered when, or if, he would see his family and friends again.

\*

Four weeks later two men walked out of the camp with the passes, and those left behind waited anxiously. But they were to be disappointed when after three days one of the men was caught, and the other was only free for five days. Still, it gave them all heart to know that it was possible to escape, even if the chances of reaching safety were very slim indeed. There was a scheme to dig a tunnel next.

# 31

It had been two months since John had been killed. The first daffodils were beginning to push through the ground in anticipation of spring, but Amy's grief had been all-consuming, and the passing of time had made no impression on her. The pain had been so intense that she hardly remembered the funeral.

She had flatly refused to leave London and stay with his parents, although they had pleaded with her to do so. The loss of their only child had devastated them. A son with so much promise had had his young life cut short, like so many in this dreadful war. Seeing their grief, Amy had wished she could comfort them, but she had nothing left to give. She was utterly bereft.

'I've got a nice egg for your breakfast.' Mrs Dalton came into the kitchen and searched for a pan to boil the egg.

'I can't take that. It's your ration.'

'You need it more than me. Doesn't she, Ted?'

He tossed his gas mask on the chair as he came in and studied Amy. 'You have it, my dear. You're far too thin.'

'I insist!' Mrs Dalton made her sit down. 'I'll get Ted something to eat as well, while I'm at it.'

Knowing it was useless to protest further, Amy spread margarine on a slice of bread. She knew everyone was worried about her, but she just couldn't seem to take an interest in anything. She wondered when, or if, the pain of losing John would ease to a bearable level.

When the egg was put in front of her, she sliced off the

top, but when she saw and smelt the runny yolk, her stomach heaved.

She made it to the bathroom just in time and was dreadfully sick. Mrs Dalton had followed her and held her shoulders until the nausea passed, then she filled a glass with water. Amy gulped gratefully.

'Now, what brought that on?'

'Must have been something I ate. My stomach's been upset for about a week, but that is the first time I've actually been sick.'

'Hmm.' Mrs Dalton studied her thoughtfully. 'You've only had the same as us, and we're feeling all right. You say your stomach's felt a bit uppity for the last week. How long does it last?'

Amy shrugged, already feeling better. 'An hour at the most. I expect it's delayed shock.'

'Maybe. Have you missed your monthly?'

Amy held out the empty glass, her hands shaking. 'I don't know, I haven't been taking much notice of anything.'

'Do you keep a note of the times?'

'Yes.' Her heart began to thud, and she rushed from the room, picked up her small pocket calendar and began to flick through the pages, once, twice, three times.

'Two,' she whispered. 'I've missed two.' Then she began to howl, tears flooding down her face.

Ted came charging in. 'What's the matter?'

'It must have been Christmas.'

'What, what?' Ted was looking worried. 'Tell me, Amy.'

'I might be pregnant!' Since John had been killed she had just been going through the motions of living. Her loss had been so great that it had drained all the life out of her; now it surged back. Did she still have a part of John – a small living part of him? Oh, please let it be true!

'We must get you to a doctor without delay.' Mrs Dalton was smiling now. 'And if it's confirmed you will have to start looking after yourself.'

Suddenly, Amy's hope faltered. The shock of losing John might have upset the normal cycle of her body. It might be no more than that. John always took precautions, didn't he, but had they been careless at Christmas? Oh, she wanted this so much, but mustn't raise her hopes. 'We're jumping to conclusions.'

'Perhaps, but we'll go and see my doctor right now and find out.' Mrs Dalton stood up with an air of confidence. 'But I'd say you're expecting. You've got the look about you. Don't know why I didn't notice it before. Wash your face and get your coat.'

'I'll drive you. I've still got a little petrol left.'

Amy was too stunned to object to Ted using his precious petrol ration like this. Instead she said, 'I didn't eat the egg; it will be cold by now.' What a silly thing to think about at a time like this, she thought, giving them a tremulous smile.

'Don't worry about that. It'll make a nice sandwich and you might enjoy it later.'

The very thought made Amy's stomach churn uncomfortably. 'No, I think you'd better eat it.'

It didn't take her long to wash and make herself presentable, and they were on their way.

When they arrived at the doctor's, Ted stayed in the van. Mrs Dalton came in with Amy, had a word with the nurse on duty, and after only a five-minute wait, Amy was called in.

Dr Grant was grey and middle-aged, with a gentle manner. His examination was thorough and while the nurse helped her to dress again, he waited at his desk for her.

Hands clasped tightly in her lap, Amy looked at him with

pleading eyes, almost afraid to hear him speak in case he told her it wasn't so.

'Well, Mrs Sterling, I'm pleased to be able to confirm that from my examination, and what you have told me, I judge that you are around three months pregnant.'

Her response to that was to burst into tears, making him frown in concern.

'Do I take it that you are not happy about the baby?'

'Oh, no,' she sobbed. 'I'm deliriously happy.'

He smiled then. 'You are obviously feeling very emotional at the moment.'

'With reason, doctor.' She then explained what had happened to John, and this was the first time she had been able to put the horror of it into words.

He listened, his expression sad. 'In that case I'm happy you are carrying his child. Now, I want you to come and see me every four weeks, and you must take care of yourself.'

'I will. I won't let anything happen to this precious baby!'

He wrote something on a form and handed it to her. 'This will mean you can get things like orange juice and a few extras to make sure you eat properly.'

'Thank you.' Amy put the paper in her bag, shook hands with him and went out to Mrs Dalton, who was waiting anxiously.

Amy sniffed and nodded. 'I am expecting John's baby.'

'That's wonderful!' Mrs Dalton kissed her in delight. 'Let's go and tell Ted the good news.'

Amy was so elated by this wonderful news that she could hardly think straight, and the excited talk in the van as they went home passed right over her head.

As soon as they arrived back, Mrs Dalton made a pot of tea and they sat at the table. Amy nibbled a biscuit, gazing at Mrs Dalton and Ted in wonder. 'I can hardly believe this is happening. John would have been so thrilled. We'd planned to have a large family . . .'

'Now, now,' Mrs Dalton said when she saw the tears gathering. 'You mustn't upset yourself.'

'But our child will never know its father . . .'

Ted gave her another biscuit. 'That's sad, but the little one will have a wonderful mother, grandparents, and all of us here.'

'John's parents will be pleased, won't they?'

'I should say so. Drink up your tea and then go and pack your case.'

Amy looked up quickly at Mrs Dalton. 'Why?'

'Because you're going to stay with Mr and Mrs Sterling until the baby's born.'

'I can't do —'

'Amy.' Ted stopped her protest. 'What would John have done if he'd been here?'

'Well . . . sent me away from the danger, I suppose.'

'There's no suppose about it, my dear. You've got the baby to think about now, and you mustn't take any chances.' Mrs Dalton had her 'won't take no for an answer' face on.

'Is there any petrol in Ben's car?' Ted looked equally determined to send her out of harm's way.

'Not much, but I don't want to leave you here on your own.'

'We'll come and see you regularly, won't we, Ted?'

'Of course we will. You won't be able to keep us away, and if the raids stop you can come home again.' Ted was on his feet. 'While you pack your things, I'll see if I can wangle you some petrol.'

'How are you going to do that?' This was all moving too fast for Amy to take in.

'Never you mind. There's ways when it's necessary.' Then he was gone.

Within an hour Ted had returned with enough petrol to get her to Hampshire. 'I'll drive you there and get the train back.'

'You'll do no such thing, Ted.' Amy decided it was time to take some kind of control. 'I'll drive myself and stay for a couple of weeks. But I'll be returning, because I have to see the doctor every month.'

'You can transfer to a doctor down there.'

'No, Mrs Dalton.' Amy's mouth set in a determined line. 'I'm not staying there until September. This is my home and it was John's for a while. I want our baby born in this house, if possible.'

'That would be lovely.' Mrs Dalton looked quite overcome at the thought. 'But there's plenty of time to decide things like that. John's parents are going to be over the moon about this.'

It didn't take Amy long to pack a few clothes, and then she was on her way, eager to tell John's parents the good news, but determined that she was not going to be persuaded to stay there all the time. She needed to be in the home she had shared with John, Howard, Ben and the rest of her family. Oh, darling, she thought, I wish I could hold you and tell you about the baby.

But she didn't allow herself to dwell on the sadness too long; there was so much else to think about. It was a bright day, and although it was only mid-March, there was enough warmth in the sun to give a hint that spring was not far away, and the months ahead did not seem so bleak. She was expecting John's child!

There was little traffic on the roads now petrol was

rationed, so she relaxed, glad to have this time alone to gather her thoughts.

The front door was opened as soon as she drove up, and Mrs Sterling came out to greet her.

'Amy, what a lovely surprise.' She gave her daughter-in-law a hug. 'Come in. How long can you stay?'

The grief of losing her son was etched on her face and she seemed to have aged ten years over the last few weeks. Amy hoped that news of the baby would help to ease the pain a little. She knew it had for her, although she would never get over the loss.

'I was wondering if you'd let me stay for a couple of weeks, Mrs Sterling?'

'We'd love that, and I think it's time you called us Charles and Mildred, don't you?'

Amy smiled her agreement.

'You can stay for as long as you like. Have you brought a case with you?'

'It's in the boot.' Amy went to the rear of the car, but before she could remove the case, Mildred had picked it up eagerly and they went into the house.

'I'll show you to your room after we've had a drink. Dinner will be an hour yet, so would you like a sherry?'

'Not for me, thank you.' She looked around, searching for any sign of her father-in-law. She wouldn't give her news until they were both here.

'Charles will be home any moment.' After pouring herself a small drink, Mildred sat opposite Amy. 'Oh, it's so good to see you, my dear. How have you been keeping?'

'It's a struggle, but Mrs Dalton and Ted have been a great support.'

'I'm sure they have.' Mildred listened for a moment. 'Ah, here he is.'

Amy heard the key in the front door, and remembered how she had waited eagerly for the same sound as John arrived home. She had been told that time would ease the pain, but it was still almost crippling, and she didn't believe it would ever go completely. She had loved him so much, and still did. Time could never change that.

'We have a guest, dear.' Mildred greeted her husband with a smile on her face. 'Amy's come to stay for a while.'

'That's wonderful.' He kissed her cheek. 'I hope it's going to be a long stay?'

'A couple of weeks.' She waited until he had settled. Like his wife, he looked drawn and tired. 'I've come unannounced because I have some news for you.'

'Is it Ben?' Mildred clasped her hands together tightly as if expecting bad news.

'No, we still haven't heard anything about him. But this is good news.'

Charles sighed. 'That will make a change, Amy. What is it?'

She pitched straight in. 'I'm pregnant. It must have happened at Christmas, while we were here . . .'

She tailed off. Her hurried explanation appeared to have had a stunning effect, for they were both on their feet, staring at her, as if they hadn't understood what she had just told them.

'I'm very happy about it.' Amy was concerned now. They weren't saying anything. They couldn't be unhappy about the baby, surely? This wasn't the response she had expected. 'I thought you'd be pleased.'

That remark snapped them back to life. Mildred began to cry and smile at the same time, and Charles dipped his head as if trying to control his emotions.

Then he looked up. 'Oh, my dear, you couldn't have given us better news.'

Mildred finally recovered, taking hold of Amy's hands. 'This is absolutely wonderful. We shall all have something of John in the child. What a gift!'

Amy breathed a huge sigh of relief. 'Gosh, for a moment I thought you weren't happy about it.'

'We were stunned, that's all.' Charles sat beside her, grinning broadly. 'You did the right thing leaving London. It will be safer here for you and the baby.'

'I won't be staying all the time,' she told them firmly, as she knew they would try to persuade her to remain with them. 'I won't do anything to put the baby at risk, it is far too precious, but I would like it to be born in Chelsea. We were so very happy there for the short time we had together.'

'We understand.' Mildred's eyes were shining with joy. 'For the next two weeks you can relax, sleep and eat. And whatever your decisions are, Amy, we will respect them and do all we can to help. How are you feeling?'

'All right at the moment, but I was sick this morning.'

'Well, you just tell me what you want to eat.' She looked at her husband with a smile of amusement. 'Do you remember that I had a craving for pickled gherkins?'

He chuckled. 'Don't remind me.'

Amy was delighted to see the change in them. They were such good people. Now the news had been accepted with joy, she was suddenly tired, yawning time and again. It would be good to take things easy for a while, away from the threat of air raids. A time of quiet to let this all sink in, and prepare herself for the birth of John's child – their child.

'Oh, I've brought my ration book with me. You can't feed me without it.' Amy pulled a face as she held it out. 'Better not try and give me an egg at the moment.'

'I understand.' Mildred's eyes filled with moisture again as she gazed at Amy. 'Do you know how much this means to us, Amy? You are carrying the grandchild we thought we would never have. This is a bittersweet day for all of us.'

Amy couldn't agree more.

That was the best night's sleep she'd had for some time. Amy stretched, looking round the pretty pink room, relieved Mildred had been thoughtful enough not to put her in the room she had shared with John over Christmas.

There was a knock on the door and Mildred came in with a cup of tea and a plate of plain biscuits. 'Good morning, my dear, did you sleep well?'

'Very soundly. I hardly remember getting into bed last night.' She propped herself up and took the cup. 'You mustn't wait on me. I'm usually the one who does all the cooking and clearing up in our house.'

'You must allow me a little indulgence.' Mildred smiled and sat on the edge of the bed. 'What would you like for breakfast? I've got some bacon —'

The cup crashed down on the bedside table as Amy scrambled out of bed and rushed for the bathroom.

When she came back Mildred was waiting for her. 'I shouldn't have said that, should I?'

Amy shook her head, picked up the cup and gulped her tea down.

'Ah, you're obviously all right with tea, so what about a fresh pot and some toast?'

Her stomach didn't rebel at that suggestion. 'That will do fine.'

'You just take your time and stay in bed as long as you like. It's only nine o'clock.'

'Good gracious! I've usually been up for a couple of hours by now.'

'There's no reason for you to get up early while you're

here.' Mildred walked to the door, and then looked back, amused. 'My sickness stopped when I reached four months.'

'That's something to look forward to then,' Amy muttered as she crawled back into bed, picked up a biscuit and nibbled cautiously.

# 32

Bowing to pressure from Charles and Mildred, Amy had stayed for three weeks, enjoying the peace of the country-side, and had returned to London feeling rested. But the raids had been bad, and after a particularly nasty one, she had willingly returned again, much to her in-laws' delight. They were naturally worried about her being in danger, and even more so now that she was pregnant. However, by the end of May the bombing had stopped and she had been able to come home. She loved John's parents dearly, but Chelsea was her home and she didn't like leaving it for too long. There were still raids in various cities and indus-trial areas, but the persistent night-after-night bombing of London had stopped, much to everyone's relief.

Now it was 26 September and the house was full, eagerly awaiting the birth of her baby. Charles and Mildred had arrived four days ago, quickly followed by Howard and his girl, Chrissie.

'Do sit down, Amy.' Howard placed a chair behind her as she stood in the kitchen door, hands in the small of her back. 'You're as round as you are tall, and top heavy.'

She grimaced at him, but sat down as he held on to her shoulders. Apart from about four weeks of morning sick-ness, she'd had a trouble-free pregnancy, and the months had gone quickly enough. Now she was fed up – the baby was a week overdue.

Howard crouched down in front of her. 'You'd better get a move on, Amy, as Chrissie and I have only two days left of our leave, and we want to see the baby before we go back.'

'I want to see it too.' She sighed and rubbed her back again. 'Why don't you marry Chrissie?'

'When the war's over.'

'But that could be years yet. We've survived Dunkirk, the Battle of Britain, as Churchill called it, and the Blitz, but we're still on our own in this fight. America is showing no sign of joining us.'

'Look on the bright side.' Howard grinned. 'Hitler didn't invade.'

'Not yet!' she glowered, making him roar with laughter.

'Oh dear, we are in a bad mood, aren't we?'

She cuffed him round the ear. 'So would you be if you had this.' She ran her hands over her very large bump.

'But it's John's baby,' he said gently.

The scowl disappeared and love filled her large eyes. 'I want to hold it.'

'Won't be long now.' Chrissie came in, looking extra pretty without her army nurse's uniform. 'Time you had a nice bath.'

'Bath?' Amy gave her a disapproving look. 'I had one this morning, and you know what a job I had getting in and out of the tub.'

'I'll help you again. I'm used to bathing bigger people than you. Come on, you'll feel better after it.'

With a resigned sigh, Amy hauled herself out of the chair, muttering, 'I bet she's a terror on the wards.' Then she grabbed hold of Howard. 'Ooooh!'

Mildred was immediately by her side. 'What is it? Have the contractions started?'

Amy nodded. 'I think so. I've never felt anything like that before.'

Chrissie checked her watch. 'Let's see when the next one comes. Walk around if you want, Amy.'

Howard put his arm around her and they walked slowly up and down the kitchen.

The next contraction had Chrissie springing into action. 'Ted, you go for the midwife. Tell her to hurry. The contractions are only eight minutes apart. This is going to be fast for a first baby. Oh, and let the doctor know as well.'

Amy smirked at Howard. 'Bossy, isn't she?'

'Into the bedroom with you.' Chrissie took over from Howard.

'Everything's ready.' Mildred came the other side of Amy and they led her into the other room.

In the end it was eight hours before her daughter decided to grace them with her presence, and came into the world yelling at the top of her voice. To Amy it was the most wonderful sound she had ever heard.

'Let me see her!' She struggled to sit up, but was pushed down again. 'Show me!'

The baby was put in her arms and she searched her little face, looking for John's likeness. It was hard to tell, but one thing was clear, their daughter didn't have Amy's wide mouth or up-tilted eyes, or at least not yet.

'Be like your daddy,' Amy whispered, her voice thick with tiredness and emotion.

The doctor was there as well, and after examining both mother and baby, declared himself satisfied. 'You have a fine strong daughter, Mrs Sterling, weighing in at six pounds, ten ounces. You have done well, but now you must rest.'

'Thank you.' Amy could hardly keep her eyes open.

'You are lucky to have a skilled army nurse staying with

you. She will look after you and the baby for the next two days.'

Amy smiled her thanks at Chrissie, hoping Howard did marry her soon. If she hadn't married John when he'd asked she wouldn't have this beautiful baby now. She liked Chrissie very much and they got on well together.

When she was washed and put in a clean nightdress, with the baby in the cot beside her, she fought to stay awake for a little longer, knowing how anxious Charles and Mildred would be to see their son's child.

'All right now?' Chrissie made sure the bed was tucked in properly. 'Shall we let everyone come in, then you can sleep?'

'John's parents first, Chrissie.'

They came in very quietly and gazed into the cot, where their granddaughter was now sleeping peacefully. There were tears, and that was quite understandable. Even Charles had to blow his nose.

Mildred bent over the bed and kissed Amy on the forehead. 'She's beautiful. Thank you, my dear.'

Charles did the same. 'What will you call her?'

'I'm going to call her Grace.'

'Excellent choice.' He glanced at his wife who was now mopping up fresh tears. 'Don't you think so, my dear?'

'Yes, that's a beautiful name; she's a gift of grace.'

'You must leave now.' Chrissie urged them out. 'Amy's very tired.'

Amy was vaguely aware of the others coming in, but she was exhausted mentally and physically. John's child had been born safely, she was perfect, and that was all that mattered . . .

Amy's recovery was quick, and by the time Howard and Chrissie's leave ended, she was already up. Charles also had to return to work, but Mildred stayed for another week, reluctant to let her grandchild out of her sight. The baby was a real blessing, and had given them all hope for the future after the crushing sorrow of John's death.

Baby Grace was a contented little girl and only cried when she was hungry. Over the next few weeks her hair began to grow and, although it was going to be light brown and not black like her mother's, it was fast turning into an unruly mop. It was the only thing she seemed to have inherited from Amy, which her mother was pleased about.

By the time she was two months old, the resemblance to her father was beginning to show. She had gentle blue eyes, and it hurt Amy sometimes when she saw those bright, intelligent eyes watching her, reminding her so much of the man she had lost, but there was also joy that she had been given the wonderful gift of his child.

As December arrived they began to plan for a special Christmas. Baby Grace was going to be the centre of attention, and spoilt on her first Christmas, Amy was sure.

Then on 7 December they received the astounding news that the Japanese had bombed the American fleet at Pearl Harbor.

There was an air of suppressed excitement around the camp. Ben could feel it, *see* it in the faces of the other prisoners. He swore under his breath. There was so much to sketch here and he couldn't get enough blasted paper. Charlie had pinched a pencil for him from somewhere – no one ever asked where Charlie got the things he turned up with – and he'd been given a small notebook, but that was now full.

Charlie sauntered up to him. 'The Japs have bombed Pearl Harbor and sunk most of the American ships. The Yanks are now in the war with us.'

Ben watched him walk away to pass on the news to the next group of men. So that was what had happened! He clenched his fists. Things were going to get interesting, and he was stuck in this bloody place! He would have to see the Major and ask if there was any way he could get out. He was going to go mad if he had to stay in here much longer.

'Heard the news?' The Major fell into step beside him as he prowled the fence, trying to take in the implications of America joining the war.

He nodded. 'I can't believe the Japanese would do such a crazy thing. You sure it's true?'

'Positive. Heard it myself on our illicit wireless set. This means Britain is no longer alone. The Germans have now lost the chance to invade. They should have done it immediately after Dunkirk.' Major Roberts grinned. 'That was Hitler's big mistake. He gave us a chance to recover and he'll live to regret it.'

Ben stopped and bowed his head. 'God, Major, I want to get out of here. Is there any chance?'

'Not at the moment. The tunnel we were digging collapsed, nearly killing the man down there. This soil is too sandy and we couldn't find enough wood to line it right to the trees.' He gave Ben a sympathetic shrug. 'We all want to get out.'

'Major!' Shorty hurried up to them. 'There's some people arrived and they're at the commandant's office. We think they might be Red Cross or something, because one of the blokes got close enough to hear them speak, and they ain't German.'

'They might be Swiss. I'll see what I can find out.' The Major marched towards the office.

Shorty looked up at Ben. 'Exciting day, ain't it? If it is the

Red Cross I wonder if we can get some fags? I'm desperate for a smoke. Don't suppose you've got any?'

'Sorry, I'd give them to you if I did. I'd rather have some decent food.'

'Ah, well, I expect you would.' Shorty's glance swept up and down Ben. 'There's a lot of you to fill up.'

Both stood, hands in pockets, staring through the barbed wire.

Shorty broke the silence. 'What do you think will happen to us when the guards see that they are going to lose the war? And by God, they will now. We'd have beaten them on our own, of course' – he gave a confident nod – 'but with the Yanks on our side they don't stand a chance. Do you think they'll abandon us or shoot us?'

'Just take off and leave us, I expect.' Ben smiled down at his companion, knowing how badly Shorty wanted to survive and see his wife and two kids again. 'If they start getting nasty you can hide behind me.'

'Too right!' Shorty roared, pounding Ben's arm, his gloom vanishing. 'Remind me to stick close to you.'

'What are you doing in the Christmas concert?' Ben changed the subject, keeping the conversation light. It was too painful for any of them to dwell on home, how long they might be here, or what might happen to them, although the questions were always with them.

'Don't tell anyone, but I'm dressing up as Vera Lynn to sing "The White Cliffs of Dover".'

'Oh, God!' Ben shook with amusement. 'You'll have everyone crying!'

'Not a chance.' Shorty smirked. 'They'll be too busy laughing at me in a frock. It ain't a pretty sight.'

'I can believe that.' Ben gazed down at the man who looked like a diminutive prize-fighter.

'What're you doing? You ought to be a chorus girl with your long legs.'

'No fear! I've been recruited to do something with the scenery.' Ben gave a wry smile. 'Little Amy would never let me live that down. A forger might be acceptable in the circumstances, but a chorus girl? I'd never hear the last of it.'

Shorty eyed him with renewed interest. 'Amy your girl?'

'She's like a sister to me, and is married to a doctor. But she's special and you'd like her. She's shorter than you.'

'Pretty, is she?'

'No, more fascinating, I'd say. She has a wide mouth, strange up-tilted green eyes, and an unruly mop of black hair. It's a face that's a joy to paint.'

Shorty gave him a beseeching look. 'I'd like to meet her one day.'

Ben straightened up. 'I'll make sure you do. When we get out of here you must tell me where you live and you and your family can come and meet my lot. You'll like everyone at the Chelsea house.'

'Thanks. I'll keep you to that, Ben.'

'It's a date. Now, let's go and see if the Major has found out anything of interest.'

The men all gathered round the officer as soon as he returned.

'I'm afraid I can't tell you much. The commandant wouldn't let me in, and by the time I had argued my way through the guards, the visitors had left, but one of the other guards did tell me they were from the Red Cross and they were gathering names of all prisoners.' The Major glanced around the crowd. 'That, at least, might mean we'll receive parcels, and maybe letters.'

There were mutters of satisfaction about that. After the chaos of Dunkirk, none of them knew if their loved ones

327

had been told whether they were dead or alive, or just missing, which was the most likely thing.

Ben stepped forward. 'My friend was with me at Dunkirk, and I'm desperate to know if he made it back.'

'I'll see if I can find out what this visit was all about, but don't hold out too much hope. The last thing the Germans want is for us to know what's going on.'

They all dispersed then, their frustration showing.

Somehow Charlie had come up with a large tin of white paint and a sheet big enough to cover the back of the stage they had erected. Ben was of the opinion that the man was more than a pickpocket: he was a skilled burglar.

'You're obviously good at getting in and out of places unseen,' Ben said, 'so why don't you escape from this blasted camp?'

'I will one day, when I'm ready.'

Ben believed him. The man was devious enough to have a plan and not tell anyone else. 'Take me with you when you go.'

'Sorry, mate, but I'll stand more chance on my own. Always worked alone, you see.' Charlie opened the tin with a penknife he kept hidden in his shoe. 'This stuff any good to you?'

'Not like that. We will have to divide it up and put in something to make green, blue and brown, keeping a little of the white, of course.'

'That's easy enough.' Charlie began to pour equal amounts into various tins he'd 'found'.

They worked together, trying various ways of colouring the paint. A little ink dealt with the blue, then they crushed some grass, which was added to another tin to make green.

Stirring vigorously, Ben grimaced. 'I don't think I want to know what you're going to suggest for the brown.'

'That's a tricky one, I must admit.' Charlie disappeared out of the door, chipped away at something, came back and opened his hand to let fine granules run into the paint. It turned an orange brown as he stirred.

'What have you put in it?'

'Rust.'

'Rust?' Ben gaped in astonishment. 'I bet Michelangelo never had to go to these lengths to get his colours.'

'Who's that?' Charlie looked completely blank.

'Never mind.' Ben surveyed the paints. The colours were awful, but it was better than nothing, and no one was going to worry about the artwork.

After a couple of hours, he had a snowy woodland scene painted as a backcloth to the makeshift stage. It was no work of art, but he had enjoyed the challenge.

'Hey, that's great.' Shorty stood with his hands on his hips. 'Real colourful. Reminds me of the New Forest.'

'Really?' Ben stepped back and mirrored Shorty's stance. 'Well, all I can say is that you must have poor eyesight. That's the worst painting I've ever done in my life, and the worst materials I've had to use.'

'Nah, you're wrong. You're a real clever bloke.' Shorty had a gleam in his eyes. 'I've thought of something you can do in the concert – something we can do together.'

Ben eyed him with suspicion. 'Such as?'

Shorty whispered so no one else could hear, and Ben snorted. 'You must be joking?'

'Come on, it'll cause a laugh, and that's what we need in this place. It's a hard time of year to be separated from our families. Let's find somewhere to practise.'

Ben couldn't argue with Shorty's views. Christmas away from home was hard on all of them.

With everyone busy preparing for the concert it was easy to find an empty hut. By the end of an hour, Ben was howling with laughter. 'You're half my size and we look ridiculous!'

'That's the whole idea.' Shorty rubbed his hands together, thoroughly enjoying himself. 'We need a couple of hats, so let's find the tailor and see what he can rustle up for us. There's still three days to Christmas Eve, and we'll have the routine off pat by then.'

The evening of the concert arrived and everyone was in high spirits, looking forward to the show. It was helping to take their minds off their families and home.

There was a varied programme of singers, tap dancers, comedians and impressionists. Shorty's rendition of 'The White Cliffs of Dover' was excruciating and much enjoyed by them all. He quickly changed out of his frock, grabbed Ben and dragged him on the stage when they were announced.

Their impersonation of Flanagan and Allen caused up-roar. A more ill-suited pair could not be imagined. When Shorty put his hand on Ben's shoulder, he had to stand on tiptoe to reach, and milked the joke for all he was worth. No one could hear how bad the singing was, because the entire audience was joining in at the tops of their voices.

The concert had been a great success, but the sadness would come tomorrow – Christmas Day – as each man silently yearned to be at home with his family, and worried what 1942 would bring.

# 33

Baby Grace kicked and waved her arms about, happy to have a clean nappy pinned in place.

'You've had a lovely Christmas and New Year, haven't you?' Amy picked up her daughter and settled her back in the pram, looking forward to the summer when she would be able to put her in the garden. She had to watch Oscar though, as he appeared to be fascinated by the new arrival. Amy had found a piece of net curtain to fix across the hood of the pram so he couldn't jump in.

There was a knock on the door and, seeing Grace was already asleep, she went to answer it, as Mrs Dalton was busy trying to tidy Howard's workroom after his brief visit home.

'Oh, how lovely to see you,' Amy exclaimed, seeing Ben's parents on the doorstep. 'Please come in.'

It wasn't until they were in the kitchen that she noticed Ben's mother had been crying. She felt a cold chill run through her. Was there news about Ben, and was it bad?

'We've had another telegram.' Mr Scott spoke gruffly. 'Show it to Amy, my dear.'

Her heart crashing against her ribs, Amy shook her head. She knew she wouldn't be able to read it in this state; the words would be an incomprehensible muddle. 'What does it say?'

'He's alive.' Mrs Scott's voice wavered. 'He was taken prisoner at Dunkirk.'

'Oh . . .' Amy had to sit down as relief swept through her. 'I always felt he was still alive, but it's wonderful to have it confirmed. Do you know where he is?'

'They haven't told us that, but somewhere in Germany, I expect.' Mr Scott smiled then. 'But thank God he's alive. The not knowing has been agony.'

Amy agreed with that. The uncertainty about Ben had been awful for all of them to deal with. 'Howard will need to be told at once.'

'We sent a message to him this morning, as soon as the telegram arrived.'

'He will be so relieved as well.' Amy looked at Mr Scott and smiled, then stood up, went to the door and called, 'Mrs Dalton, come quickly, we've had some wonderful news!'

Mrs Dalton arrived at once, out of breath from rushing up the stairs, and when Amy explained about the telegram, she raised her eyes to the ceiling as if giving thanks to a higher being.

'That's the best way to start nineteen forty-two. I'm so happy. Thank you for coming to tell us.'

'Being a prisoner of war won't be easy for him though. We must remember that.' Mr Scott dropped the note of caution into their joy. 'This conflict isn't going to end in a hurry, even though we've got help now. He could be there for a long time.'

'We know that, my dear.' Mrs Scott dabbed her eyes. 'But he's alive, and we can be thankful about that.'

'And he's out of the fighting.' Mrs Dalton put the kettle on to boil. 'We'll have a nice cup of tea.'

Amy picked up Grace, who had begun to grumble. 'What do you think about that, poppet? When the war's over your Uncle Ben will be coming home and we'll get him to paint your picture.'

The only response to that piece of news was for the baby to study these new people over her mother's shoulder.

'My goodness!' Mrs Scott was now on her feet. 'She's grown since we saw her just after she was born. May I hold her?'

Amy handed her over. 'She's looking more like her father every day.'

'She's a darling.' Mrs Scott walked around the kitchen telling Grace how beautiful she was.

'She'll stand any amount of that!' Amy watched for a moment, smiling, then laid out the cups and a plate of biscuits.

Ben's parents stayed for an hour and when they left, they promised to let Amy know if they received further news.

Ted arrived soon after they'd gone and was as relieved as everyone else to hear the news, but, like Mr Scott, he was cautious. 'He's going to hate being confined like that without his paints, but he should be safe unless he tries to escape.'

'He mustn't do that.' Mrs Dalton looked worried. 'He's got to sit tight until the war's over.'

'If he does anything silly I'll never forgive him, and neither will Grace. I've told her all about him, and he'd better come back. We'll be very cross with him if he does anything daft, won't we, sweetie?'

Grace's face began to pucker, working up to a cry. Amy kissed her. 'Now, don't you worry because we'll write a long letter telling him to be a good boy. And we'll write to Uncle Howard as well.'

Ted and Mrs Dalton watched Amy chatting to the baby as if she could understand, smiles of amusement on their faces.

Amy carried on. 'Your mummy has a job with writing, so I'm banking on you growing up bright like your dad. He

333

could read the most difficult books without any trouble at all. He was ever so clever. He was a doctor.'

She had talked to Grace about John from the moment she had been born. It hurt terribly, but she was determined to do it. Her father might not be here for her, but Amy wanted to make him a part of their daughter's life through her memories of him.

Ted chuckled. 'Have you told her the first Americans are arriving in this country?'

'My goodness, do you hear that, poppet, our new allies are coming to see us.'

Mrs Dalton tickled the baby under her chin. 'You're not going to have any trouble learning to talk, are you? Not the way your mum tells you everything.'

There was worrying news in the following months of 1942 when Singapore surrendered to the Japanese, Britain's shipping was being sunk in alarming numbers, and Howard was sent abroad again. They suspected that he was going out to face Rommel's crack army in North Africa for, according to the news, the fighting was fierce out there, but of course they didn't know for sure. Even the men didn't know where they were going until they were on the high seas heading for their destination. Wherever he was going they all prayed earnestly for his safety. His girlfriend Chrissie had also left the country.

It was even more worrying when Tobruk fell to Rommel's Afrika Korps in June, and thousands of British soldiers were taken prisoner. Amy, Ted and Mrs Dalton gathered around the wireless every evening, dreadfully worried about their two boys. Was Howard also a prisoner now?

Grace was one year old in September, and completely oblivious to the drama being played out around her. She was turning out to be fiercely independent, just as her father had been, according to John's parents. She was a handful and kept Amy on the run, giving her little time for herself, but she noted each step of progress with great joy.

Then in November El Alamein was taken and Rommel was said to be in full retreat. Everyone was ecstatic about this first real victory and Churchill ordered that all the church bells be rung in celebration. The unusual noise caused Grace some consternation, as she had never heard them before, and they frightened the life out of Oscar. He shot into the shelter for safety.

'I thought we were going to hear them pealing out just after Dunkirk to signal an invasion by the Germans.' Ted nodded in satisfaction. 'That won't happen now. We've been lucky.'

Six weeks later Howard walked in, tanned, thinner, but unharmed. Amy threw her arms around his neck in delight as he lifted her off the ground.

Grace was rather put out by this and crawled towards them, hitting Howard on the shin with a wooden toy brick.

'Ouch!' He put Amy down and scooped the little girl up in his arms, making her squeal at the top of her voice. 'What did you hit me for?'

'I expect she thought you were attacking me. And if you don't put her down, you could end up with a black eye. She's still holding the brick.' Amy took Grace from him and set her back on the floor.

Grace gazed up at the strange man.

'This is your Uncle Howard.'

Ted and Mrs Dalton arrived just then and made a great fuss of Howard, overjoyed to be having him back with them for a few days. He continued to spend part of his leave with them, and part with his parents, so everyone was happy.

Grace watched intently, jiggling up and down as she caught the mood of excitement. She tugged at Mrs Dalton's skirt. 'Tea?'

'Good idea.' Ted picked her up. 'You know that when visitors arrive we always make tea, don't you?'

Grace grinned at everyone.

Over tea, Howard told them he had been in North Africa, but was damned glad to be home again.

'Will you be going back?' Ted asked.

'Don't think so. I've been brought back for something else, but I don't know what it is. I'm here until the New Year, and who knows what nineteen forty-three will bring.'

'That's true.' Amy stirred her tea, her expression sad. 'Poor Ben, he's been a prisoner for over two years. He must be so fed up with it.'

Howard agreed. 'And it could be another two before this lot's over.'

Another Christmas stuck in this damned awful place. Ben stared gloomily out of the hut window. How much longer, for heaven's sake!

'Ah, there you are.' Shorty joined him. 'What're we going to do for this year's concert?'

'Break out of here?'

'Wrong time of year, and even if you get out it's bloody impossible to make it back to England. Look at Charlie: he got out, though no one knows how, and he was caught after only two days. It's dicey, Ben, you could get shot, and I want to see my wife and kids again.'

'Oh, hell!' Ben watched the guards marching towards the huts. 'They're going to do another search. What the devil are they looking for?' This had happened quite a lot just lately. Sometimes the searches were only brief, but enough to unsettle the prisoners. Perhaps that's what they did it for.

'They suspect someone's hatching an escape plot, I expect.'

The rest of the men who lived in the hut came in. 'Here we go again,' one of them muttered.

The guards stormed in and they all watched as beds were stripped, mattresses tossed on the floor, and every inch of the place searched.

'Thorough today,' Shorty whispered.

Ben had a pile of drawings tied to the underside of one of the slats on his bed. In past searches the guards hadn't bothered with them, seeing instantly that they were only drawings on old cigarette packets and any bits of paper Ben had been able to find. But one guard who they all knew was a nasty piece of work ripped them off and flicked through them, a sneer on his face. With great deliberation, he tore them into tiny pieces, then let them rain from his fingers to cover the floor.

It took all of Ben's self-control to stop himself from punching the man's face. His fists clenched and he felt Shorty grip his arm in a warning not to do anything silly. He uncurled his fingers with great effort, thankful to the man who had become a firm friend.

When the guards left they all set about putting their hut back to rights again, then Ben picked up every piece of torn drawing as the rage bubbled inside him. Without saying a word, he walked out of the hut, knowing he had to be on his own for a while. It was silly to get in such a stew over a few rough drawings, but some of them had been good. He had captured the expressions on the men's faces, and he knew every emotion they were experiencing. Boredom; anger; loneliness – yes, even in a camp packed with men – and the most noticeable was despair: kept hidden, but always

337

just under the surface. Ben knew when a man was about to crack, and he recognized that danger in himself. It wouldn't take much more for him to explode.

It was bitterly cold and trying to snow. He took in great gulps of freezing air to try and clear his head and mind. He had wanted to kill that guard . . .

Leaning against the hut he opened his hand and let the pieces of paper fall, watching as the wind caught them, making them fly through the air. He would do some more, and hide them so they couldn't be found. He knew that his time here would always be etched on his mind, but he wanted a record of the men who were enduring this captivity, many with greater fortitude than he seemed to have.

Shorty walked up to him. 'Come inside, mate. It's bloody cold out here. And hang in there, Ben, this war ain't going to last for ever. The sods are beginning to take a beating. The writing's on the wall for them.'

'It feels as if we've been here for a lifetime . . .' Ben stared into space. Shorty was a tough little devil and was known as the voice of reason around the camp. He seemed to be able to bolster any flagging spirit with just a few words. But Ben knew that he was suffering as much as the rest of them, because at lights out he had seen Shorty take out a tattered old photo of his wife and kids and kiss them before settling down to sleep.

'I know, but at least we're alive, and' – he pushed Ben through the hut door – 'we've got to decide what to do in the concert. We were a real riot last year.'

When they got back inside, Ben saw two sheets of paper and a pencil on his bunk, and could have wept in gratitude.

'Can't have our war artist without something to draw on,' Charlie said.

'Thanks.' No one said anything else, but he suspected that they knew drawing was the only thing that kept him sane.

# 34

It was raining again; Grace was sitting at the kitchen table scribbling in a colouring book as Amy watched the water running down the window, lost in thought. She could hardly believe it was June 1944, and neither could the weather by the look of it. Where had the time gone? The last eighteen months had just flown by, and this September Grace would be three years old.

Turning her head she saw that her daughter had abandoned the colouring book in favour of the sheets of letters and pictures Amy's grandmother had given her when she had been struggling to read and write. Much to Amy's relief, Grace was bright, picked things up quickly, and did not appear to have the same problem as her mother. She was already copying the letters with no trouble at all, and Amy did all she could to encourage this. Only time would tell if her daughter would be able to read and write normally, but the signs were hopeful.

Turning her attention back to the soggy garden, she sighed, feeling anxious. Something was going on. The country was filling up with troops, tanks and military equipment of all kinds. The rumour was that the invasion of France was imminent, and if that were true, how long would it be before Ben was home? And it was certain that Howard would take part in the attack. Her insides clenched in apprehension. Along with everyone else she wanted an end to this wretched war, but she also wanted her two special men to be safe. She had lost the love of her life in the Blitz, and the thought of anything happening to her friends filled her with dread.

'Wretched weather.' Mrs Dalton came and stood beside her. 'You'd never think it was summer, would you?'

Amy sighed. 'Is it ever going to stop raining?'

The door burst open and Ted rushed in. 'It's started!'

'What, what?'

'The invasion. I just heard. The first troops have landed and are already moving inland.' Ted's face was alight with excitement. 'Looks like we've taken the Germans by surprise. They never expected us in this weather.'

'Thank God!' Mrs Dalton reached for the kettle. 'Let's pray this will be the end of it, and it's over quick.'

'Mummy?' Grace slid off her chair and looked up questioningly.

'The invasion has begun, sweetie, and the Allies are going into France at last.'

'Why?' Grace was still puzzled by the air of excitement.

Amy had always explained things to her daughter. She didn't always understand, but she was an intelligent child with an enquiring mind. She stooped down to Grace's level. 'You know there's this man called Hitler who's been bombing us?'

Grace nodded.

'Well, he's taken over lots of countries that don't belong to him, and our soldiers are going to make him give them back.'

'Is Uncle Howard with the soldiers?'

'I expect so.'

'Will he get hurt?' Grace's lip trembled. 'Like my daddy did?'

'We must pray very hard that he doesn't, and that both your uncles come back safely.' The fact that her father had

341

been killed was another thing Amy had never kept from her daughter. She was going to grow up knowing what a fine man her father had been.

'What's my Uncle Ben like?'

Amy stood up and smiled. 'He's very tall, paints lovely pictures, and is fun.'

'Will he paint my picture?'

'I'm sure he will.' She watched her daughter get back on the chair, satisfied that her questions had been answered, and her heart squeezed in pain. How like her father she was. Amy's head dipped as the yearning, which wouldn't go away, ran through her. Oh, darling, I wish you were here to see this day and watch our daughter grow into such a lovely girl. How proud of her you would be . . .

Turning to look at her mother, Grace said, 'Shall we write to both of them today?'

'Good idea; we'll do it after tea.'

Giving a pleased nod, Grace went back to what she had been doing before Ted had burst in with the news.

The tea was made and they all sat round the table. Mrs Dalton poured them a cup each. 'Where have they landed, Ted?'

'Normandy.' He stirred in some sugar. 'And there won't be another Dunkirk this time. France will be liberated, and then nothing will stop us going all the way to Germany. They've got us coming at them from one direction, and the Russians from another.'

'It'll be a bitter battle, though.' Mrs Dalton gave Grace a biscuit. 'But I expect Hitler will be kept too busy to bomb us any more. I'll be glad to take that shelter down and have the lawn back.'

Ted nodded, his face now serious. 'I hope Ben's holding in there. A few more months and he could be free at last.'

342

'Poor Ben.' Amy sighed. 'He's been a prisoner for such a long time. He must be sick of it.'

Caught up in the excitement of the invasion, they were unprepared for the shock that came on 13 June. Hitler unleashed his secret weapons on London in the shape of flying bombs. This wasn't like the targeted bombing they had been used to. Once the engines cut out they could drop anywhere. The noise they made frightened Grace.

'You go to John's parents.' Mrs Dalton bustled around, urging Amy into action. 'They'll be frantic knowing you and Grace are in the middle of this.'

At that moment there was another explosion, far too close for comfort, making Grace cling to her mother, eyes wide with terror.

'It's all right, my darling, we're going to stay with Granny and Grandpa until this is over.' Amy was furious as she threw things into a bag. 'Doesn't the bloody man know when he's beaten?'

'Evidently not. Now, get out of here, Amy, and don't come back until these damned things have stopped coming over.'

Seeing her daughter's fear was enough to have Amy heading for the in-laws.

They were welcomed with joy and relief, and Grace soon settled down, happy once again. But Amy worried about Ted and Mrs Dalton. She would have left Grace with her grandparents and returned to London, but she couldn't do it. Grace had lost her father in the raids; she mustn't lose her mother as well. That would be too cruel for the little girl, and she owed it to John to stay alive for their daughter.

Although Amy longed to return to their home in Chelsea, she had to stay put because things got even worse. In early September, the first V2 rockets landed on London, killing and injuring many. The flying bombs could be heard and seen, and some had been destroyed before they could reach their targets, but there was no defence against the rockets. There was no sound until they exploded.

Sitting in the garden enjoying the September sunshine, Charles lifted his face to the warmth and sighed. 'These rockets are Hitler's last effort. Paris was liberated last month, so we're making progress.'

There had been great celebrations when that had happened, but there was sadness for Amy as she remembered how John had wanted to take her there for their honeymoon, and promised they would go there together after the war. Dreams that would now never come true.

'And do you know what tomorrow is?' Charles swept his granddaughter off the grass, making her giggle.

'Mummy said it's my birthday and we're going to have a party.'

'That's right, and lots of people are coming. There's Ted and Mrs Dalton coming for the day, and the neighbours' three children.'

'Oh, goody!' She beamed at her grandmother and struggled to get down. 'Can we have cakes?'

'I think I can manage that.'

Grace began to run excitedly around, chanting that they were going to have a lovely party. Then she stopped suddenly. 'Will Oscar be coming?'

'Cats don't like travelling,' Amy told her, 'but I expect he'll send you a card.'

'Oh.' The disappointment at not seeing her favourite animal was evident. 'Will he still be there when we go home?'

'Yes, he will.' Amy studied her daughter. She was happy living here. Her grandparents loved her, she had made friends with children her own age, but it was obvious she missed everyone in Chelsea, including the cat who followed her around all the time. He used to be Amy's companion, but as soon as Grace had arrived he had transferred his affections to the little girl. Cats were fickle creatures, she thought with amusement.

'Mummy?'

'Yes?'

'When will Uncle Howard and Uncle Ben be coming home?'

'We had hoped it would be by this Christmas, but it doesn't look like that will happen.' Amy gave Charles a questioning look. 'What do you think?'

'Well, there's the winter ahead of them now, so that might slow down the advance, but my guess is that it will be over by spring of next year.'

Grace puffed out her cheeks as she thought about it. 'That's a long time, isn't it?'

They all agreed that it was, each one yearning for the end of the awful conflict.

It had been a terrible blow when the wireless set had been discovered and taken away. They felt really cut off now without regular updates on the progress of the invasion forces. The landings at Normandy were the last they had heard before the guards had found the set. They had a couple of engineers working on another one, but parts were hard to come by, even with Charlie's thieving skills.

Since the invasion, the guards' attitude had changed. Some were going out of their way to be friendly, others had become even more hostile.

Ben prowled the fence, head down. There were a multitude of emotions snaking through him: frustration; anger; the awful feeling of being cut off from the real world. It felt as if he had been here for ever. The laughter and fun of the Chelsea house were like a dream now, but he could remember every inch of his studio, smell the paints and turpentine. The memory of holding a brush or palette knife in his hands was painful. Would he ever be able to paint again, after spending years in this damned terrible place? He missed his family and friends, like everyone else, but his greatest deprivation was not being able to paint. Until he had been put in this camp, he hadn't realized just how much it had meant to him. Being an artist was all he had dreamt of doing for as long as he could remember . . .

'Ben!' Shorty joined him, looking animated. 'There's news. The Major wants to see us all in hut nine.'

'Do you know what it is?'

'Nope, but he's pretty chuffed about something. Perhaps they've got the wireless going.'

'I hope so. Not knowing what's going on beyond that wire is enough to drive me mad.' Ben turned and strode towards the hut, with Shorty trotting to keep up with his long strides.

The hut was packed and they only managed to push in right at the back. Some hadn't been able to get in and were hanging in the open windows.

'I'll make this as short as possible, because the guards will soon come to see what we're up to.' The Major held up his hand for silence. 'We've managed to get a wireless working, and there are two important pieces of news. Paris was liberated last month.'

A loud cheer went up.

'Quiet! We've also heard reports of London being bombed again with unmanned flying bombs and rockets.'

'Oh my God!' Shorty went pale. 'Hope my wife and kids have had the sense to move to the country.'

'But the bastards must be about finished,' one of the

346

other prisoners growled in rage. 'If the Allies are in Paris, then they'll keep going until they reach Berlin.'

'They will, and that's why I'm going to order you to stop all attempts to escape.'

There was a disgruntled mutter.

'I know it's tough to ask that of you, but we don't want to antagonize the guards. Let's sit tight, keep our heads down, and see how things shape up. We could be free in a few months.'

At that moment the guards burst in, ordering everyone out to the yard for a roll call.

They were carefully counted, and when it was found that they were all present, they were dismissed.

Ben continued his prowl, hands clenched into tight fists as frustration raged through him. He knew every inch of the damned barbed wire, and he wasn't the only one who had made a habit of walking the perimeter over the years. *Are you in Paris, Howard?* A few letters had reached the camp, but nothing for him. And what about his parents, Amy, John, Ted and Mrs Dalton? Had they survived the Blitz, only to be in danger from these new weapons? Who was he going to find waiting for him when he did eventually arrive home? Not knowing what was happening out there was torture. He had never felt so helpless in his life.

Shorty walked with him, his expression equally concerned. 'Good news, and bad news, eh?'

Ben nodded, lifted his head and sighed, glancing down at his friend in sympathy. 'Your wife would have taken herself and the children out of London, Shorty. She wouldn't risk anything happening to them, would she?'

'Nah.' His usual cheery smile was back. 'Course not. My missus is a sensible girl, and loves the kids too much to see them frightened. Bloody worrying, though.'

347

Ben nodded in agreement. At least he knew that John wouldn't allow Amy to be in danger. She was probably spending the war with his parents in Hampshire. 'I wish I was out there fighting with the others.'

'I know you do, so do I, but we've got to put up with this for a bit longer.' He hunched his shoulders. 'All we've got to do is stay alive until the boys reach us, and the first thing I'm going to ask for is a packet of fags.'

That made Ben chuckle, and consider his friend with respect. If it hadn't been for Shorty, he would have gone mad long ago, and perhaps done something reckless and got himself killed. 'You and your cigarettes.'

'Addicted, that's what I am, but I tell you what, Ben, once we get back to London, I'll buy you a pint, and chain-smoke my way through a packet of twenty.'

'I'll keep you to that.'

The birthday party was a riotous success, with Amy and the grandparents having as much fun as the children. Three of the neighbours' children had come, each bearing a small gift for the birthday girl, making Grace beam with pleasure. For a few hours the war was forgotten.

Ted and Mrs Dalton caught the late afternoon train back to London. Amy knew her daughter missed them as much as she did, but hopefully the war would soon be over and they could all be together again.

Little Grace seemed to have boundless energy and wouldn't allow them to sleep in the next day. They were all laughing about the party, and Grace's excitement was still bubbling over. But when Amy saw Ted walking up the path around midday, her pleasure faded.

She rushed to meet him, knowing something must have happened to bring him back so quickly. He looked very serious, and that frightened the life out of her. 'What's happened?'

'Howard's been injured. He's in a military hospital in Aldershot.'

'Oh no! How bad is he?' Amy held on to Ted for support. 'I must go to him.'

'He's got shrapnel wounds to his back and one arm, and a broken leg. There's no need for you to go all that way.' Ted took hold of her hand. 'His parents are with him, and Chrissie is also working at the same hospital, so he's being taken good care of. The doctors have said that he will make a full recovery.'

'Oh, thank goodness.'

'Ted, can you get a message to Howard? We've got plenty of room, and he can convalesce here.' Charles glanced at his wife who was nodding approval. 'Mr and Mrs Palmer will be welcome to stay as well.'

'They'll appreciate that. I'll let them know.'

Amy desperately wanted to go and see Howard, but Ted was right, he was being well looked after. 'Send him my love as well, Ted, and tell him to hurry up and get better.'

# 35

Over the next few weeks, Howard gradually recovered, but it was the middle of December before he was strong enough to come and stay with John's parents. Much to everyone's relief it was clear that he would make a full recovery from his injuries.

His parents had managed to save enough petrol to bring him down in their car, and when they arrived he had to be helped out, and stood beside the car leaning heavily on a stick. But that didn't stop little Grace from rushing up, all excited, and dancing around waiting to be picked up. Amy watched the scene in wonder. Her daughter had seen so little of Howard, and yet, whenever he turned up, she greeted him like this. Would she do the same with Ben, she wondered, or would she be cautious with a man she had only heard them talk about? Everyone said that the war would be over next year, but the worry remained. Since being told that he was a prisoner, they'd received no further news. Had he seen any of the letters she had written to him over the years? She hoped he had, but they were probably all sitting in some army office, gathering dust. Stay safe, was her constant prayer. Howard had survived and, having been declared unfit for further duty, was now out of the army. That was something to be grateful for.

She saw Grace reaching up to Howard, chattering away, expecting to be swept up high, as Howard always did when he saw her, but not this time. 'Grace!'

She spun round to look at her mother, holding on to Howard's hand.

'Uncle Howard can't pick you up this time.' She hurried over and kissed him on the cheek. 'Oh, it's good to see you. We've all been so worried about you.'

'Why are you walking like that?' Grace asked as she trotted beside him as they made their way towards the house.

'Because I broke my leg,' he explained.

'Ow, did it hurt?'

'Very much, but it will be all right soon, and then I'll be able to pick you up again.'

That promise produced a huge smile, and she danced up to her grandmother, telling her what Howard had said.

He watched, his hand resting on Amy's shoulder, then he gave it a squeeze. 'She's growing into the image of John, except for her hair.' He grinned down at her. 'That's an unruly bush, just like yours.'

'I hope that's all she's inherited from me.' This was still a worry for Amy, but they would know for sure in another year or two.

'She'll be able to read and write, Amy,' Howard said gently. 'It's most unlikely that the problem you have will be passed on to her.'

'I hope you're right.' She smiled up at him, pleased he was going to stay with them until the New Year. 'Now, you go and sit by that lovely wood fire while I help Mildred get the tea.'

The house was packed for Christmas with Ted and Mrs Dalton also staying over. Amy and Grace gave up their room and slept on the settee in the lounge, which the little girl thought was great fun.

Howard was delighted when Chrissie was able to join them for two days, and they toasted in 1945 together. But the absence of John and Ben was sorely felt.

By early January, Howard was walking without the aid of a stick, and able to move his arm freely.

Amy watched him staring out of the window as the weather made a half-hearted attempt to snow. He was brooding about something. She stood beside him, and asked softly, 'What's the matter, Howard?'

He glanced down at her and pulled a face. 'I'm restless. I need to work, Amy, so I've decided to go back to Chelsea and try to get my life back in order.'

Ah, so that was it. She had been watching him for the last week; he had been quiet, distracted, and clearly bored with the inactivity. She wasn't surprised by his decision. In fact, she had been feeling much the same herself. 'Good idea. We'll come with you.' She slipped her hand through his arm. 'The war can't last much longer, and we must start planning for when we open our shop again.'

His face came to life with a slow grin of pleasure. 'I'll make some pots and you can decorate them, and there's a sculpture in my head that I'm eager to start.'

'You going to tell me what it is?' How wonderful it would be to get those old times back, she thought, though she knew they would never be quite the same again after all they had been through. But it was comforting to start planning for the future.

'Nope, you'll have to wait and see. What about Grace, will you leave her here?'

'I can't bear to be parted from her, and things seem to be quiet at the moment, so we'll both come home.'

'Don't forget Manchester was hit by V one bombs on Christmas Eve. The danger might not be over yet.'

'Oh, I don't know.' She looked up with a wide grin on her face. 'The Home Guard were decommissioned in early December, so the politicians must think the war's as good as over.'

'The poor old Home Guard,' he chided her, 'they had to put up with a lot of jokes, didn't they? But they could have found themselves in the front line if things had gone differently. You're right, though, things must soon come to an end, but Hitler doesn't seem to have got the message yet. Once the troops cross the Rhine, he'll have to accept that he's finished.'

'Do you wish you were still out there?'

'I would have liked to get to Germany and see if I could trace Ben, but, truthfully, I'm glad to be home for good.'

'We're glad you're back, as well.'

Grace burst in and stopped their quiet conversation. 'Mummy, it's trying to snow!'

'I know, darling, but I don't think it's going to be enough to settle. You won't be able to play snowballs yet.'

'Oh.' Her disappointment showed, and then disappeared at once. 'Granny's knitting my new dolly another dress. She's nearly finished it.' She tore out again.

'It was so good of her grandma to give her that lovely doll she'd had as a child. Grace is thrilled to bits with it, isn't she?'

Howard gave Amy a speculative glance. 'John's parents are going to be upset when you leave and take Grace with you.'

'I know.' Amy sighed. 'But we can't live here all the time, Howard, however much they would like us to. Our home is with all of you in Chelsea, and when Ben comes back we can open the shop again. I can't let Charles and Mildred keep us all the time, it wouldn't be right, not for any of us. John has left us well provided for, but I want to keep that money for Grace, if I can. I very much want us to go back into business again.'

'So do I.' Howard ran his hand over Amy's hair in a soothing gesture, his face serious. 'I know this is painful for us, but we must face the fact that Ben might not be coming back.'

'I like to include him in our plans, and until we know what has really happened to him, in my mind it will still be the three of us.'

Howard nodded. 'But if the worst happens, we can go ahead on our own, can't we? We must face that possibility, Amy,' he stressed again.

'Of course.' It hurt, but she knew he was right. Even if Ben had survived the years as a prisoner, what was going to happen when the Allies fought their way into Germany? It was a frightening thought.

'Come on.' Howard shrugged his shoulders as if trying to dislodge a heavy weight resting on them. 'Let's go and break the news that we're leaving.'

Amy pulled a face. 'I'm not looking forward to that, but I must move on with my life. John's parents can always come and stay with us in Chelsea. Mrs Dalton will put them up for a few days, I'm sure.'

Her in-laws were in the kitchen with Howard's parents, listening to Grace's never-ending chatter, and Amy took a deep breath. This was one step she had known would come, but she had kept putting it off. It was only natural that John's parents adored the daughter of the son they had lost, and she hated to hurt them by telling them that she was leaving, but it had to be done.

Howard draped a supporting arm around her shoulder. 'I want to thank all of you for looking after me so well. It has helped my recovery to stay in this lovely house, and I'm grateful, but I'm now well enough to go back to Chelsea and start work again.' He smiled down at Amy. 'We've been talking, and have decided that, as it's unlikely the war will last much longer, we should be making plans to reopen our shop.'

'I thought it wouldn't be long before you decided to do that.' His father looked pleased. 'It's time we went home, as well.'

'When are you leaving?'

'I thought tomorrow, Mum.' He glanced questioningly at Amy. 'Is that all right with you?'

'Yes, that's fine.' She watched her in-laws' faces pale and Mildred fight for control. She did a good job of it and managed to smile. 'You're taking Grace with you, of course.'

'Yes, we've loved being here, but it's time to return to our own home. You can come and visit whenever you want, and we'll come here for the weekend often. You'll see a lot of Grace, I promise.'

'Well, in that case, I'd better finish this dress.' She smiled at her granddaughter. 'We can't have your dolly getting cold on the train, can we, sweetheart?'

Grace shook her head, making her mass of hair swirl around her face. Then she swivelled round to face her mother. 'Are we going home, Mummy? Have the nasty bombs stopped?'

'We think so, darling, but if they start again we'll come straight back here. Oscar will be so happy to see you.' Amy added that because she could see that Grace was still worried about the flying bombs.

'Are you staying for good, Uncle Howard?'

'I am.' He swept her up, making her squeal with delight. 'And I'm going to teach you to paint pots like your mother.' He lifted her high and then put her back on the chair.

Amy knew he had done this to show everyone he was strong again.

Charles stood up. 'We can't have you going back to London on a freezing cold train. Ben's car is still here, and there's petrol in my car, so let's siphon it off and then you can drive back.'

'We can't take your precious petrol,' Amy protested.

'I insist. Come on, Howard, give me a hand to get Ben's car ready.'

Mildred held out her hand to little Grace. 'We'll start packing your things, shall we?'

# 36

'What the hell's going on, Major?' Ben shivered in the cold, trying to shield Shorty from the biting wind whistling across the yard.

'It looks like they're going to move us. God, I hope I'm wrong.'

'There aren't any trucks.' Ben caught hold of Shorty to support him as he had a coughing fit.

'I'll go and find out what they're up to.'

The Major was back in five minutes, and stood in front of the assembled men. 'The bastards are moving us. I want you to put on every bit of clothing you've got, bring blankets and anything that will keep you warm. We've got to walk to the next camp. You've got ten minutes only, then we must be ready to march.'

'Oh, God, Ben,' Shorty gasped. He trembled with fever. 'I ain't never going to survive a forced march.'

'Yes you bloody well are!' Ben growled in rage. 'You're going to make it if I have to carry you every step of the way.'

Charlie looked ready to commit murder when they got back to their hut. 'The sods must be panicking, and that means our troops can't be far away. Don't you worry, Shorty, me and Ben will see you make it.'

'Where we going, Major?' Shorty croaked.

'They won't tell me, or why we're being moved. Let's hope it isn't far. Quite a few of the men are in a poor state.'

'Why don't the buggers just leave us and run.' Ben and

Charlie wrapped Shorty in a blanket, pulling it over his head to protect him from the severe weather. Others who were sick were being helped in the same way. They had all been in this camp for a long time, and were determined that everyone was going to survive the march. With the Allies getting closer each day, they couldn't die now. They wouldn't!

With grim determination they lined up again, and marched out of the gates that had held them prisoner since 1940.

Ben lost all track of time, or where they were going. Day after day they walked with very little food; many stumbled and fell, but were quickly helped up by friends. Shorty was so ill, Ben carried him piggyback style until he was numb with fatigue. Charlie took a turn now and again to give him a rest, but he wasn't nearly as strong as Ben. He had guts, though, and a burning hatred for the enemy that kept him going.

'Here, Ben, drink this.' Charlie handed him a mug of watery soup.

'Give it to Shorty.' Ben was too damned tired to lift his hand and take it.

'He's had some. Come on, mate, you're exhausted. You've got to stay alive or the little man won't stand a chance.'

Propping himself up and leaning his head against a wall, Ben took the soup and gulped it down. 'Where the hell are we?'

'In a church, but I've no idea where it is. It looks as if we're staying here for the night, so we'd better try and get some sleep. There's no knowing how far they'll make us walk tomorrow.'

Fear gripped Ben's empty stomach, knowing he was all but finished unless he could summon up some strength from somewhere. He leant over Shorty, wrapped like a baby in a blanket, and grimaced as pain shot through his aching back. 'How're you doing?'

'I'm feeling better. You can't keep this up, mate. I'll walk tomorrow. The fever's going.'

Ben studied his friend, and then shook his head, knowing Shorty wasn't telling the truth. There was still a sheen of fever on his face and, more worryingly, his eyes had a rather wild look in them. 'You still look terrible.'

'Have you seen yourself lately?' That attempt at levity sent him off into another bout of coughing.

'None of us looks very pretty at the moment.' Ben supported his friend until the coughing passed, then glanced around at the men: dirty, dishevelled and exhausted. If this went on much longer some were going to die. If it had been summer they might have stood more of a chance.

'I mean it, Ben.' Shorty caught his attention. 'I'll try and walk for a bit tomorrow.'

'Shut up and go to sleep. You'll walk when I think you're fit enough.'

The Major came and crouched in front of them. 'I've been talking to the priest and he told me the Germans are retreating right along the eastern front, and it's rumoured that the Russians have crossed the German border. They're on the run. We've got to survive this. The end is in sight.'

'We will, Major,' Charlie growled in fury. 'Why didn't they just leave us where we were?'

'God knows.' The officer stood up. 'I asked one of the guards where they're taking us, and he said to another camp.'

'How far is it?' Shorty rasped out. 'This big man has been carrying me for days, and he's had it, but without him I'd be dead now.' He began to cough violently.

'Will you shut up?' Ben pulled the blanket around Shorty's

head. 'I don't give a damn how far we've still got to go, we're all going to make it. Go to sleep.'

Exhausted, Shorty closed his eyes.

'Can you get us a bit more food, Major?' Charlie spoke softly and nodded towards their desperately ill companion.

'I've asked the priest if he can help. He seems a reasonable man, and is going to try and get us some bread in the morning.'

'Thanks. Anything will help.' Ben pulled Shorty towards him, and with Charlie on the other side in an effort to keep each other warm, his mind and body let go, surrendering to sleep.

Morning came, then night, then morning again, and Ben needed all his concentration just to put one foot in front of the other. Once he fell to his knees and was helped up by Charlie and one of the other men. He didn't know who it was, or care. He was aware that many of them were in a very bad way now, and those a little stronger were doing all they could to help the weaker ones. Shorty was now delirious and shouting for his wife and kids. That made Ben grit his teeth and keep walking. If this man died then he was going to kill someone, even if it meant his own life was forfeit.

Suddenly, the column stopped and Charlie gasped, 'A camp, Ben. We've reached a camp!'

With his head reeling and black spots dancing before his eyes, it was impossible for Ben to focus on anything. He felt Charlie grab hold of him and urge him on. They had become a team in their effort to save Shorty, and he was content to let Charlie take the lead and see they were all right.

'There's a lot of blokes already here, and they don't look too bad.' Charlie had a tight grip on him, moving him forward all the time.

As Ben walked through the gate he felt his face grow wet with tears of relief, aware that he wouldn't have been able to keep going much longer. He had always been strong, but this had taken every ounce of strength he had. Now he was utterly drained. Orders were being barked out in English, and men rushing round them . . .

'Here, mate, let's take him from you.'

As the burden was lifted from him he staggered. 'He's sick.'

'We'll look after him. We've got a medic here, and you look done in.'

'Thank God!' And Ben meant it. He had never been much of a churchgoer, but somehow, against all the odds, they were still alive. That was enough for the moment. Now his friend might stand a chance. The activity and conversations faded into the background, as if they were coming from a long way off.

'Where we going to put them all, Captain?'

'We'll sort that out later. Get them inside at once! These poor buggers have had a rough time by the look of them.

'Commandant!' the officer yelled at the top of his voice, fury very clear. 'We need hot food here, now! Or I'll see you all shot when the Allies get here.'

Ben and Charlie followed the men carrying Shorty. They'd brought him this far, and no one was going to part them from him now.

The hut was warm after the icy wind blowing outside, but only when Shorty was tucked up in a bunk and being tended by the medic did Ben and Charlie allow themselves to be pushed into chairs.

'Drink this.' A young corporal gave them a mug of tea. 'How long have you been on the road?'

They gulped the hot liquid down, both shaking their heads.

'Didn't keep count.' Charlie drained his mug. 'It seemed like a hell of a time, though.'

A kind of stew was also put in front of them; it wasn't much, but a whole lot better than anything they'd had for some time, and there was also a small piece of bread each.

They made short work of it and, after checking that Shorty had also been fed, Ben leant his head on the table. If anyone tried to move him now, he would refuse. He was staying in this camp, wherever it was, until the war ended. If the Germans didn't like it, then they would have to shoot him. He didn't care. There was no way he was going through something like that again.

His muscles screamed in pain when he moved the next morning. He was on the floor, as were many others in the crowded hut, but he'd slept right through the night in total exhaustion.

Dragging himself up he went over to check on Shorty, relieved when his friend looked back at him, clear-eyed and rational.

'Thanks, Ben, that's another couple of pints I owe you when we get back home. In fact I owe you more than that. I'll get my missus to make you a huge steak and kidney pudding.' He licked his lips. 'It's her speciality.'

'You'd better invite Charlie as well, because I wouldn't have been able to carry on without his help.'

'Done!'

Just then the Major came up to them. 'This place is packed and, now everyone's rested, we'll have to reorganize the living quarters. It's going to be damned uncomfortable, but it won't be for long. If the news I'm receiving is correct, then we'll soon be liberated.'

'Hope you're right, Major.' Charlie staggered over to the window. 'What's all the commotion outside?'

'The Red Cross have arrived with parcels.'

The strain left Charlie's face as he made for the door.

'There's no need to rush.' The Major caught his arm. 'I've put men in charge of seeing that they are distributed fairly.'

'You should have given me that job,' Charlie protested, looking a picture of innocence.

The officer gave him a disbelieving glance. 'You must be joking?'

'I've reformed, sir. No more thieving for me.'

Ben laughed, and was shocked at the sound. How long was it since he had found anything amusing?

'Sir.' Shorty raised his hand. 'Is there any chance we could get some letters through to those at home? My missus must be worried sick about me, and I know she'd be writing.' His hand dropped weakly. 'I'd love to know if she and the kids are all right.'

'We're doing what we can.' The Major patted Shorty's arm. 'Hang on in there. This isn't going to last much longer.'

As he walked out of the hut, Charlie muttered, 'They keep saying that, but I won't believe it until I see our blokes opening the gates to let us out.'

'Me neither.' Ben felt exactly the same. They kept receiving news that raised their hopes, only to have them dashed again. They had nearly died on that march, and now they'd been dumped in an overcrowded camp. He wasn't a fool, and knew that the next few weeks, or however long it might be, were going to be difficult. And there would always be the fear that the Germans would try to move them again.

He had been a prisoner for years without canvas or paints.

If he lived to return home, how would he ever be able to paint again? At that moment the separation from the people he loved, and art, which had been the focus of his life, was unbearable.

No, he wasn't going to raise his hopes just yet.

Over the next few weeks Shorty made a good recovery and, although much thinner and drawn-looking, his bright banter returned as he, once again, tried to cheer everyone up. But all his efforts were wasted on Ben who had become quiet and withdrawn. It was as if the march had drained something vital out of him. They were all aware that they would never be the same after their experiences and long captivity, but some had been changed beyond all recognition. One of them was Ben. The need to get away from the constant press of men was beginning to fill his every waking thought. Even when it was snowing he would stand outside drawing in deep breaths of icy air, oblivious to the flakes falling and settling on his hair. He'd seen men crack during his time in the prison camps, and he fought a silent, lonely battle for control.

It was now the beginning of March and spring couldn't be far away. How he longed to see the sun and the wild flowers shooting into bloom the other side of the fence. Beauty was in short supply in the camp. The sound of engines caught his attention, and he looked up to see trucks rumbling up to the gates with the Red Cross painted on them. Haven't seen those since we arrived at this place, he mused, but he didn't bother to move as the camp sprang into life.

'Ben!' Shorty tore up to him a while later. 'The Major's got some letters. Come on, there might be something for us.'

Pushing himself away from the wall of the hut, he ambled

after Shorty to where the officer was standing surrounded by men, all eager for news of home.

'Carlisle.'

'That's me.' Shorty leapt forward eagerly and took the envelope being held out to him. He looked up at Ben, unashamed tears in his eyes. 'It's from the missus.'

Ben watched him go into the hut to read it in private. He was glad his friend had received a letter from his wife. They had been few and far between over the years. The little man never made any secret of his love for her and his children. The names were being called in alphabetical order, but he hardly listened, not daring to hope. There were hundreds of men in this camp and only a few letters, so many were going to be disappointed – again.

'Scott.'

His head jerked up, and he stepped forward. There were three letters in all, and he recognized Howard's writing immediately, then his mother's and finally the last one was from . . . who? It looked like Mrs Dalton's writing. If it was, then that would be news of everyone in the Chelsea house. He was ripping open the one from his parents as he walked into the hut to join Shorty.

There were quite a few men in there now, so he leant against a bunk and started to read. The one from his parents was little more than a note, and all it said was that they were all right, and hoped the war would soon be over so he could come home again. The one from Howard was also only a few lines telling him how he had survived Dunkirk, and adding a few little snippets of information about his life since then.

Ben was sorry it was so brief and out of date, because he had a desperate thirst for information about home. He grunted in satisfaction when he found the third letter much longer. It wasn't from Mrs Dalton as he had first thought, but from Amy. Mrs Dalton had just addressed the envelope for her. Amy's writing was still peppered with mistakes and crossings out, but she had obviously made yet further progress over the last few years. He felt himself coming back to life as he pictured her sitting at the table with her tongue protruding in concentration. He could almost hear her chatter in his head, a smile touching the corners of his mouth. But the first piece of news had him gasping in horror. 'Oh, dear God, no. No!'

'Bad news?' Shorty was immediately at his side, his hand resting on Ben's arm.

'Amy's husband was killed in an air raid.' His voice was harsh with distress. He continued reading until he got to the part about Grace being born. That was good news, but pain ripped through him when he thought of what Amy had been through. As if her early life hadn't been bad enough!

Spinning round he crashed his hand against the wall in blind fury. 'I should have been there, not stuck in a POW camp. I should have been there!'

'Easy, mate.' Charlie joined them. 'My old dad was hurt in the bombing as well, but we couldn't have done anything about it, even if we had been there.'

'Is your old man all right?' Shorty asked.

'Yes, he's staying with my sister in Surrey.'

'That's good, then.' Shorty picked up the letter, which had dropped from Ben's hand, glanced at it and frowned when he saw the mistakes. 'How old did you say your Amy was?'

'She must be twenty-five now.' Ben gazed into space, his mind going back over the years since they had found Amy. 'She'll be twenty-six this December, I think. She's always had a job reading and writing.' He took the letter back. 'It must have taken her ages to write this, but she's never been short on guts.'

'She'll be all right, then,' Shorty pointed out, 'and from what you've told me, she has others at the house to look after her, hasn't she?'

'Yes.' Ben closed his eyes, and then opened them again. Of course. Mrs Dalton and Ted would have made sure she was all right. For the first time in a long while a genuine smile crossed his face. 'She's got a little daughter by the name of Grace.'

'That's a nice name.' Shorty was still watching his friend with concern, never having seen him erupt in fury like that before.

'What about your family, Shorty? Are they all right?'

Shorty's face lit up with a huge smile. 'They're fine. My nippers will have grown while I've been stuck in here, so we'll have to get to know each other again.'

'That's something we'll all have to do.' Charlie gazed out of the window. 'How much longer is this bloody war going to last?'

It was the beginning of April and Ben was woken at dawn by the sound of gunfire. It was very close. The hut was suddenly alive with men moving, rushing to look out of the windows and dragging on clothes.

Charlie was scrambling into his trousers. 'What's that?'

The door burst open, and a man from the next hut tumbled in. 'The guards have gone! That must be our troops. The gate's open!'

That set up a stampede to see for themselves.

The Major and the Captain were outside, yelling orders and trying to gain some kind of control. 'Everyone stay inside until the fighting's over!'

They were completely ignored as tanks began to rumble into view, and the cry went up, 'It's the bloody Yanks!'

The men surged forward to meet their liberators, but Ben stayed where he was, bowing his head.

It was over. At last, it was over.

# 37

'Mummy.' Grace ran in from the garden, giggling. 'Oscar's rolling over in the dirt. He let me tickle his tummy.'

Amy smiled at her daughter's animated face. 'That's because he's enjoying the sunshine. He's getting old now and doesn't like the cold.'

'What you doing, Mummy? Can I help?' Grace danced around, full of energy.

'You can pop downstairs and see if Uncle Howard's workshop is in a mess. If it is, we'll clean it up for him, and you can help me with that.'

'Ooh, Uncle Howard doesn't like it cleaned.'

'I know.' She crouched down in front of Grace. 'But he's out at the moment, so we can do it before he comes back. You'd better have a look at Uncle Ben's, as well, and see that you haven't left any of your toys up there.'

Still laughing, Grace ran out of the kitchen and down the stairs.

Leaning on the sink to look out of the window, Amy worried her bottom lip. It was the first of May now, and the war was almost over. The general opinion was that it would be only a matter of days before the end came, and the closer it got, the more she fretted. The Allies were in Germany, knocking on the door of Berlin, and still no word from Ben. Her hands clenched on the smooth sink. Where the devil are you, Ben? Prisoners were being released all across Germany; the Allies must have reached him by now, surely?

She had been gazing into space for some time when she felt a tug at her skirt.

'Mummy,' Grace whispered. 'There's a strange man upstairs, but he didn't see me.'

Amy was alarmed that her little girl might have walked in on a burglar. 'What's he doing?'

'Painting.'

It felt as if her heart had stopped beating as she fought for breath. Painting! Turning, she ran for the stairs, pausing at the top for a moment before opening the door to the studio. Grace had followed her and Amy put her hand on her shoulder to stop her running into the room. There was a tall man daubing bright splashes of colour on a canvas. The height was right, but he was much too thin, and whatever he was doing, it was nothing like the beautiful work Ben had always done. This was almost grotesque, as if the painter had no idea how to blend, or use colour . . .

Grace tugged her skirt, so she put her finger to her lips, telling the curious little girl to stay quiet.

He seemed completely oblivious to their presence as he wielded the brush almost as if he were angry. He was wearing civilian clothes, but an army kit bag had been thrown on to the old settee in the corner.

She tried to speak, but no sound came out. After taking a deep, steadying breath, she tried again. 'Ben.'

His hand stilled, but he didn't move. After what seemed ages, he threw the brush down, and turned.

When she saw his face, she nearly groaned in anguish. It was Ben, but not the same one who had laughed and joked with her before the war. Standing in front of her was an exhausted, troubled man.

He said nothing. Just opened his arms and she rushed

into them, holding on tightly. Neither of them spoke until Grace began to hit his leg.

'Are you my Uncle Ben?'

He released Amy and bent down to the little girl, running his hand over her unruly hair.

What he did next took Amy completely by surprise. He stood up, walked out of the studio, down the stairs, and out of the house. He hadn't said a word.

Grace's bottom lip trembled with disappointment and her eyes filled with tears. 'He doesn't like me.'

'That isn't true, darling.' Amy was having a job to stop her own tears from falling. 'He's been a prisoner of war for a long time, and he doesn't look well. We have to be very kind to him, until he gets used to being home again.'

Finding himself outside the front door, Ben stopped and, holding on to the wall for support, took deep, rasping breaths. He was shaking with the range of emotions surging through him, emotions he had tried to block out in order to survive the years as a prisoner of war. If you didn't feel, then you could get through the days, weeks, years. But he had been completely overwhelmed when he'd seen Amy, no longer the little girl he had kept in his mind's eye, but a grown woman. As he had held her in his arms he had been very aware of that change, and hadn't wanted to let her go. Then he'd seen her daughter staring at him with eyes of the same blue as John's had been, and Amy's tousled mop of hair. It had all been too much and, completely overcome, he had fled.

Making his way along the side of the house, he staggered into the garden, sinking down on the top of the shelter. He bowed his head. God, he was in a mess, and it would be best if he stayed out of everyone's way until he pulled himself together.

Amy didn't know how long she had been standing there, trying to take in the fact that Ben was home, and obviously a very disturbed man. He was going to need their help to readjust. Hearing the front door open, she rushed to the top of the stairs, just in time to see Howard come in. 'Howard! Come up here, quick.'

He still limped slightly, but it didn't take him long to reach them.

'Ben's back.'

'What?' Howard rushed into the studio, spinning round. 'Where is he? I've just been with his parents, and they don't know where he is.'

The tears would no longer be denied, and they flowed down her cheeks. It hurt so much to see Ben in that state. She had known he would be changed by his experiences – they all were – but not like this.

'Oh, God, Amy, what's the matter with him? Where is he?' Howard was very agitated now, after seeing Amy's distress.

'He's left, Uncle Howard,' Grace told him, her little face serious. 'He wouldn't talk to us.'

'I hardly recognized him.' Amy wiped her eyes and sniffed. 'He's had a bad time, by the look of him. He shouldn't be alone. We must find him. Where do you think he's gone?'

Howard ran a hand through his hair. 'He must have come straight here, so perhaps he's gone to his parents now.'

That didn't make sense. 'But he wouldn't leave here without seeing you first, surely? And why didn't you see him in the road when you came in?'

He didn't speak; he was staring at the canvas on the easel. 'Who did that?'

'Uncle Ben.' Grace screwed up her face as she looked at it. 'I can paint like that.'

'Sweetheart, you can paint better than that.' He looked at Amy with something akin to fear in his eyes. 'Even when he was five years old he could paint a beautiful picture. That's terrible, and it frightens me to think what state of mind he's in. Where the hell would he go?'

'Mummy.' Grace had gone to look out of the window. 'He's in the garden.'

They both rushed over. He was sitting on top of the Anderson shelter, staring into space.

Howard sucked in a deep breath as he gazed at the man who had been his lifelong friend. He was a shadow of the man they had all known. 'I'll go and talk to him on my own.'

'He'll be pleased to see you.' Amy straightened up and lifted her chin. 'I'll see about cooking lunch. He doesn't look as if he's had a decent meal in years.'

An hour passed and there was no sign of the men coming in, but at least Ben was talking to Howard as they both sat on the grass covering the shelter. There was a stew in the oven; it could just stay there until needed, it wouldn't spoil, and the dumplings could be added at the last minute.

Ted and Mrs Dalton arrived almost at the same time.

'Something smells good,' Ted said appreciatively, then caught sight of the man outside. 'Who's that with Howard?'

'It's Ben.' Amy's voice wavered.

'Benjamin!' Mrs Dalton was at the door before Amy could catch her arm. 'I didn't recognize him.'

'Leave it for a while. We mustn't crowd him. Something is terribly wrong, and we must let Howard see him alone. Even his parents don't know he's back.'

373

'That isn't right.' Mrs Dalton sat down heavily, distressed. 'They must be told at once!'

'I'll go and get them, but first, Amy, you must tell me exactly what happened when you saw him.'

It didn't take long to tell Ted the story; afterwards, he nodded grimly. 'He's going to need time and plenty of personal space in order to readjust. Those years as a POW have obviously taken their toll. I'll explain to his parents, and bring them back with me.'

'Thanks, Ted.'

He was back within the hour, with Ben's parents, who looked sick with worry.

'Why didn't he let us know he was home?' Mr Scott asked gruffly, never taking his eyes off his son in the garden with Howard.

Mrs Scott was fighting back tears, and saying nothing. Amy touched her arm in sympathy. 'He's been deprived of paints for such a long time, so he probably wanted to see that his studio was still as he left it,' she said gently. The Scotts were so distressed that she certainly wasn't going to tell them about the strange painting he had been doing when she had found him. 'He would have come to you later today, I'm sure.'

'Yes, of course.' His mother spoke for the first time. 'We desperately want him to come and stay with us to recuperate, but seeing the state he's in, it might be better for him to remain here.'

'Why don't you go and suggest that to him?' Amy was relieved to hear Mrs Scott's sensible suggestion. From what she had seen of Ben in the studio, and his frantic efforts there, it was clear that he should be here, breathing in the smell of paint. He could have solitude, if he wanted it. She would see to that.

Her thoughts went back to the time he had found her beside her mother's grave. She had needed help then; now the role was reversed, and it was her chance to repay that act of kindness. He had changed her life that day, giving her hope, love and a sense of belonging. They were clearly all the things Ben now needed.

'Mummy, is Uncle Ben going to stay with us?'

Grace had been unusually quiet, as if sensing that they were facing a crisis, and Amy smiled down at her. 'We hope so, darling, but we must let him decide that for himself.'

She nodded and climbed on to her chair. 'Is our dinner nearly ready? I'm hungry.'

'It won't be long, Grace, we must wait for Uncle Ben.' She glanced out of the window, watching Ben talk to his parents.

Howard came in, leaving them alone with their son.

'How is he?' Mrs Dalton asked as soon as he came in the back door.

'He's all right, but a bit disorientated after so long shut away in camps. It's all a bit hard to adjust to, and he doesn't want to talk about the last few years.'

'That's understandable,' Ted murmured.

'Uncle Howard?' Grace snagged his attention. 'Doesn't Uncle Ben like me? He wouldn't talk to me.' This was still troubling the little girl.

'He thinks you're beautiful. He told me so just now.'

Kicking her legs at that piece of news, Grace beamed at everyone in the room.

The Scotts came into the kitchen with Ben right behind them. He looked better; not quite so tense. Talking to Howard and his parents had obviously helped.

Ted shook his hand. 'Welcome home, Ben, you've been sorely missed.'

It was Mrs Dalton's turn then, and she reached up to kiss his cheek, then she stood back and gave him a stern look. 'Well, Benjamin, you've given us a lot of worry.'

A slow smile spread across his face at her chiding tone and, at that moment, Amy caught a glimpse of the old Ben. Relief spread through her. The next few weeks were going to be hard for him, but he'd always been a strong man, physically and mentally. Whatever demons he had running around in his head, they would soon be dealt with, she was sure.

'Sit down everyone.' Fortunately, Amy had made a very large stew, and with extra dumplings there was enough to go round.

As they enjoyed the meal the conversation was general, never touching on the war. Ben said very little, seeming happy enough to listen to Howard explain their plans for opening a shop again as soon as they could.

Grace hardly took her eyes off Ben, smiling when he looked at her, and giggling when he winked and popped one of his dumplings on her plate. Leaning towards him, she whispered, 'I'm full. Can I give it to Oscar?'

'Do cats like dumplings?' he whispered back.

She nodded. 'He eats anything.'

'In that case he can have it.'

Watching the gentle interplay between them, Amy saw that her outgoing daughter could help Ben adjust to normal life again.

As soon as the meal was over, Mr and Mrs Scott made to leave.

'Ben, you'll come and see us soon?' his mother asked, hopefully.

'Of course.' He stood up as well. 'I'll see you to the door.'

When they were out of earshot, Mrs Dalton's concern

showed. 'Did he say what has happened to him, Howard? I could hardly believe that's our Benjamin.'

'As I've said, he won't talk about it. We must leave him in peace. I'm sure he'll tell us when he's ready.'

'But you were with him for over an hour.' She couldn't let the subject drop. 'What did you talk about?'

'How Amy coped with losing John – that has upset him very much – and bringing up a baby on her own. He wanted to know how I got back from Dunkirk, and what I've been doing since. How bad my injuries were. What everyone's been doing while he's been away.' Howard shrugged. 'He wanted to know about everyone, but never once mentioned where he's been, or what conditions were like in the camps.'

'Terrible, by the look of him.' Ted frowned. 'We've got to leave him to come to terms with what has happened to him.'

'I agree with Ted.' Amy began to clear the table. 'He knows we're here for him if he needs us. I think that's why he came straight here, instead of going to his parents' first.'

'You're right,' Mrs Dalton agreed as she helped stack the dishes.

Ben didn't come back to the kitchen. They heard the front door close and his footsteps going upstairs.

They always had a cup of tea after a meal, so Amy made a pot, laid out the cups and cut a slice of the cake Mrs Dalton had made the day before. With rationing as it was this was a treat now. Putting the plate on a tray with a cup of tea, she picked it up and headed for the stairs. If he didn't want to talk, she would just leave it and come straight down again.

When she walked into the studio, Ben was sitting on the settee, looking absolutely spent. Smiling brightly, she put the tray beside him. 'You didn't come back for your tea. There's a piece of cake for you, as well.'

'Thanks, Amy.'

As she turned to walk away, he caught hold of her arm. 'I'm desperately sorry about John, and upset that I wasn't here for you. It must have been terrible.'

She knelt in front of him, holding his large hand in both of hers. He was so troubled, but she was determined to treat him as she had always done, and be honest. 'I'm sorry you weren't here, as well. I felt lost, just like I was when you found me after my mother had died. Only this time it was much worse. The pain was unbearable, and I didn't know how I could carry on, but then I found out that I was pregnant. It helped me and John's parents to realize we would have a part of John in our lives again.'

He squeezed her hand. 'You have a beautiful child, and she's so like John.'

'Except for her hair!' Her laugh was infectious, and when Ben joined in, it gave her hope that his recovery would be quick.

'I had noticed.' His sigh was deep and ragged. 'Give me time, Amy. I've got things to deal with.'

'We understand that you need space, but' – she shook his hand to make her point – 'we are here to help you. You mustn't keep everything to yourself. Do you remember how I tried to hide that I couldn't read or write properly?'

He nodded.

'Well, it was only when I admitted it and brought the problem out into the open that the shame and confusion no longer troubled me. When you're ready, you can talk to me about anything. You know that, don't you?'

'I do, but at the moment all I need is peace and quiet.' His grin was wry. 'You have no idea what it was like living with several hundred men, never being able to get away to be on your own, or walk through the gates to the open countryside.' He yawned and closed his eyes for a moment.

'You're exhausted, Ben. Why don't you go and have a sleep?' She stood up, sensing that he had had enough company for one day. 'I made up your bed last week, in the hope that you would soon be home.'

'I'll just rest here. The settee's a lot more comfortable than a lot of the places I've slept in.'

'I'll get a pillow and blanket for you.'

'That's all right, I can do it myself.' He spoke quite sharply.

Bending down she kissed his forehead. 'Get some rest. You know where I am if you need me.'

She walked out of the studio and down the stairs. All they could do was be there for him when he needed them.

Listening to her light footsteps on the stairs, Ben ran a hand over his eyes, glad to be alone again. He drank the tea and managed half the cake. It was going to take him a while to get used to such luxuries.

Hauling himself to his feet, he walked over to the easel, shaking his head in horror at the mess he'd made. Tossing the canvas aside he placed another on there, and just stared at the blankness, not knowing how to start. All of his life he had been able to picture a finished painting, and start work on it without hesitation, but now his mind was blank. He picked up a brush and covered the canvas in a pale coloured wash to get rid of the stark white, then he thought about the river where he had met Amy that first time, and began to paint.

Two hours later he stopped, gazed at his past work hanging on the studio walls and threw the brush down in disgust. That was terrible! No one would ever believe that the same man had painted this. Why couldn't he paint? Why?

Scraping the wet paint off the canvas, he started again, trying this time to copy the portrait he'd done of Amy.

It was nothing like the original, and quickly abandoned. He would just have to keep trying. He was unable to imagine his life without creating pictures. The thought appalled him.

Hardly able to stand up by now, he threw himself on the settee. Rest. He must rest, and then the next painting would be better.

# 38

For three days Ben hardly came out of his studio, and he wouldn't let anyone in. He took his meals up there, slept there, and all efforts by Howard and Ted to make him go to the pub with them, or get involved with plans for the shop, came to nothing. Everyone was worried sick, and Grace was upset with him. She had been looking forward to her Uncle Ben coming home, and she never saw him. Amy had tried to explain, but the little girl just didn't understand why he wouldn't come and talk to her like her Uncle Howard did.

'This can't go on, Amy.' Mrs Dalton frowned. 'We've kept out of his way, giving him the time and space he said he needed, but he's shut himself away in that studio of his, and I don't like it. Whatever demons he's dealing with, he ought to let us help. If only he would come down here, eat with us, and try to get back to a normal life. I know it's hard for him, but our Benjamin has always been a strong person. This just isn't like him.'

'I think it's time we intervened. Dinner will be ready in an hour, so I'll see if I can get him to eat with us instead of taking it upstairs.' With a determined set to her mouth, Amy headed upstairs.

Pushing open the door she took two steps into the studio . . . and stopped dead in astonishment. There were discarded pictures on the floor, the settee, the bench and every available space. He had used everything he could find to paint on: hardboard, paper and even cardboard, but most of them were on canvas.

'Where did you get all these?' she gasped.

He didn't stop what he was doing. 'I've painted over old pictures and on anything else I could find.'

'You've done all this in three days?' She still couldn't believe what she was seeing. It looked as if he'd been in a frenzy of painting. She began to sort through them.

'Don't bother looking at them,' he snapped, 'they're all rubbish.'

Some were terribly dark and gloomy, she had to admit, but one or two . . . Moving to stand beside him, she sucked in a deep breath when she studied what he was working on. 'Good heavens, Ben—'

'I know, it's terrible!'

She grabbed his hand when he made a move to slash a brush loaded with paint across the surface. 'No, no! It's fantastic.'

The look he gave her was one of absolute disbelief. 'Oh, come on, Amy, I can't paint any more. It's nothing like the work I used to do.'

'No, it isn't.' She stepped back slightly to view the painting of a group of men leaning against an old wooden hut. 'This is better.'

'Don't try to humour me.' He tossed down the brush. 'I was afraid when I finally got home I would have forgotten how to paint. Well, now I know I have.'

'That's nonsense!' She rounded on him, hands on her hips. 'Is that what this is all about? Is this why you've shut yourself away, trying to recapture the style you had before you went away? You can't lose your talent, Ben, it's part of you; it's what you are.'

'I don't know what I am any more.'

Her heart ached for him; for the inner torment he had been keeping to himself. Placing her hand through his arm, they stood side by side, gazing at the picture. 'It's better than good,' she said softly.

Ben ran his fingers through his hair, leaving it streaked with paint as he narrowed his eyes, studying the work in front of him. 'All right, tell me what you see. And I want the truth.'

She tipped her head on one side, quietly considering the painting for a few moments before speaking, then said, 'I see strength, despair, anger, frustration; each face showing a different emotion. I see that an artist with not only skill but also a stunning depth of feeling has painted this. I see a picture that takes away my breath.'

'But look at this!' Ben spun away and jabbed at some paintings he'd done before the war. 'It's nothing like them.'

He was very agitated, so she went over to him, looking up into his face. 'Of course it isn't. You've changed, grown, experienced goodness knows what. You're not the same person – none of us is – and that shows in your work. You are now painting with more freedom, more power, and much more feeling.' She gestured to the older paintings littering the room. 'In many of those I can see anger, hurt and darkness of thought, but not what you are now doing. Ben, you're a better painter.'

Hunching his shoulders, he stared down at her, varied emotions showing in his face. 'God, Amy, I want to believe you.'

'I'm telling you the truth. I wouldn't lie to you, or try to make you believe something that isn't true. Let Howard see this and he'll confirm it. What you have gone through over the last few years is reflected in your work. Stop trying to be what you were. That was the boy honing his talent. This is the mature you. You *must* accept that. We need you, Ben, and want you to join us for meals, just like the old

383

times. Dinner will be ready in about another half an hour.'

Without another word, she walked out, leaving him to think over what she had said. She had told him the truth, but he needed to see it for himself. She had done all she could for the time being. In the days he had spent shut away painting, he had found himself again; all he had to do was recognize that.

For quite a while after Amy had gone, Ben stared at the closed door, trying to assimilate what she had said. One thing was clear, though: that wasn't the little girl he had left behind. All she had suffered, lost and gained had changed her into a woman. A very wise one. And one who made him strangely edgy to be near.

Walking back to the painting on the easel, he tried to see it through her eyes. Was she right? Had he been trying to re-capture the talent of the boy who no longer existed? Had he been expecting to pick up a brush and paint in exactly the same way? Was this more mature artist as good as she said?

Out of the corner of his eye he saw the door opening again, and a little head with a mop of unruly hair peering in. He pretended not to see her.

She edged in quietly, a doll dangling from her hand. She was wearing a pretty pink dress with a frill round the hem and sleeves, and pink slippers with a white rabbit on them.

When she reached him, he looked down. 'Hello.'

Her face was serious as she swung up the doll and clutched it to her, then declared in a hurt tone, 'You don't like me, do you?'

'I do like you. I think you're very nice.' The corners of his mouth twitched. Her head was tipped right back in order to look at him. Another inch or two and she would topple over.

'Then why won't you play with me? Uncle Howard plays with me, and' – she looked smug – 'he lets me paint pots, like Mummy.'

'Well, he's a nice man.'

She nodded, her hair falling into her eyes. 'You're not nice.'

'Oh, dear, I'm sorry you think that.'

Pushing the errant strand of hair away, she huffed out a breath, turning her attention to the picture on the easel. 'What are those men doing?'

'They're waiting for the war to end.' He could see she wasn't impressed; she had a very expressive face.

'My mummy said you'd come back and paint my picture.'

'I will.'

'My mummy said that you'd play with me, but you don't. I haven't got a daddy, but Mummy said I had two uncles who would love me, because they were nice.'

The little girl's words tore through Ben, hurting dreadfully. He'd been thinking only of himself, but this little scrap had been deprived of her father. She would never know him. He crouched down in front of her. 'I'm sorry I haven't been nice to you. I didn't mean to hurt you, but I've been away for a long time, and wasn't well when I came back.'

'Mummy said you were a prisoner.'

'That's right.'

'What did you do?'

'I was fighting the enemy, and they caught me.'

She reached out a finger to touch a blob of paint on his shirt, giving a hesitant smile. 'Are you better now?'

'Much better.' Catching her round the waist, he surged to his feet. 'I'll start painting your picture tomorrow. Now, your mummy said dinner was nearly ready, so shall we go down for it?'

She nodded and slipped a little arm around his neck, and whispered, 'Mummy said I wasn't to come up here and be a pest.'

'I don't think you're a pest.'

'Are you going to be nice now you're better?'

'Very, very nice.'

Seeing her daughter in Ben's arms, and smiling happily, Amy thought her heart would burst. They had been so worried about him since his return but, as he settled Grace in her chair, he looked more at ease. He was still too thin for his height, but regular meals would take care of that.

Grace was still clutching her doll and giving her mother rather worried glances. Amy knew it was because she had gone upstairs when she had been told not to. But it had brought Ben down to join them, so she wouldn't be reprimanded this time. Amy smiled at her daughter to let her know it was all right.

As Ben settled in his usual chair, no one mentioned that it had taken him so long to begin to eat with them.

'Won't it be lovely when we can have a large roast again?' Mrs Dalton helped Amy to cut up the pie. It had more vegetables than meat in it, but it smelt good and looked appetizing.

'It certainly will.' Amy put a small portion of carrots on Grace's plate, along with mashed potato and pie. The rest of the vegetables were placed in the middle of the table for everyone to help themselves.

It was lovely to be eating together again, and the conversation flowed, with Ben joining in and laughing at the light-hearted banter that was a feature of their mealtimes. But Amy could see that, sometimes, his smiles were forced. Although this was a step forward, he was by no means back to normal. It was still going to take time and patience. She had been told that some of the men handled captivity better than others, but Ben's problems were the result of more than years of captivity. Something else had happened to him, she was sure.

Hardly taking her eyes off Ben, Grace dutifully ate her carrots, which was a sure sign she was feeling guilty, because she hated them.

'My goodness,' Mrs Dalton exclaimed as she cleared away Grace's empty plate. 'There's a good girl. You finished all your carrots.'

Grace pulled a face, but said nothing.

'How about coming for a drink?' Ted asked Ben. 'Howard's got some money. I sold one of his sculptures in my shop yesterday.'

'Have you still got your shop, Ted?' Ben looked surprised.

'Yes, I've managed to keep it going, just about. I've been putting some of Howard's and Amy's work in the window, and we've sold a few pieces.'

Ben stood up. 'We'd better help Howard spend his money, then.'

His friend grinned. 'All right, the first two are on me, and then it's up to the pair of you.'

As they left the kitchen, Ted turned his head and winked at Amy, and then they were gone.

Mrs Dalton wiped a hand over her eyes. 'He's coming out of whatever was troubling him, isn't he, Amy?'

'He's making an effort, but he's having a hard job to readjust. I had a talk with him while I was upstairs, and one of the problems he's been struggling with is that he believed he couldn't paint any more. He's obviously been trying to find his talent again after so long away from it, because the studio is littered with work he's done since he came back.

387

The one he's working on now is nothing like anything he's ever done, but it is full of feeling, and I think it's fantastic. I've told him so.'

Sitting next to her daughter, she turned her chair to face her. 'Tell me what you said to Uncle Ben.'

Grace straightened the dolly's dress. 'I wasn't a pest. I just wanted to see him. I wasn't going to speak to him,' she explained hastily, 'but he said hello, and we talked about things . . .'

'Such as?'

'I asked him if he was going to paint my picture, like yours. He said he'd been caught and shut up for a long time and he hadn't been well and he was going to be nice now.'

The explanation had tumbled out in one breath, and Amy watched Grace gulp in a lungful of air. She ran a hand gently over her hair. 'I know you weren't being naughty, darling. You've been a good girl, because you made him come downstairs and have dinner with us.'

'And now he's gone to the pub with Howard and Ted.' Mrs Dalton smiled at Grace. 'That's a step in the right direction, isn't it?'

Nodding as if she understood what Mrs Dalton was saying, Grace got off the chair to stroke the cat. 'Oscar's hungry, Mummy.'

After feeding the animal, Grace was put to bed. She liked to hear a story before going to sleep, and as Amy found it difficult to read without long pauses, she made up tales in her head. She had a long-running story about a very kind dragon, and she had to think up some adventure for him every night. Grace loved it, and often made suggestions as to what he could get up to. They both enjoyed it.

'Asleep, is she?' Mrs Dalton asked when Amy returned to the kitchen.

'Yes.' Amy laughed softly. 'We've had the dragon exploring a castle on top of a mountain, and finding another one being kept prisoner. We've had to free him so he could fly away with our dragon. Now I've got two to make up stories for.'

'You ought to write down that story.'

Amy gave Mrs Dalton an amused glance. 'And how long do you think that would take me?'

'Oh, darn it. I keep forgetting you still have trouble with words. You'll have to get one of us to do it for you.'

'I don't suppose anyone would be interested in it except Grace. It's partly her creation, anyway. Now, I think I'll wait up for the men to come back.'

'Me too.'

Not used to being idle, they busied themselves with sewing and ironing while they waited.

It was gone eleven when they heard the sound of muffled laughter. Amy went into the hall and watched the three men, shoes in hands, trying to creep in unnoticed.

'Put the kettle on,' she called to Mrs Dalton. 'They're plastered!'

After receiving three sheepish grins, she ushered them towards the kitchen and guided them to the nearest chairs.

'You've spent all of Howard's money, by the look of you.' Mrs Dalton tried to sound disapproving, without success.

Ted smirked, Ben looked completely out of it, and Howard ... Amy lunged forward as he began to topple sideways. Another couple of seconds and he would have ended up on the floor. And he wouldn't have felt a thing, the state he was in, she decided.

'What's wrong with them, Mummy?' Grace appeared in the doorway, having been woken up by the noise. 'Is Uncle Ben sick again?'

Amy swept her up in her arms. 'They're all going to be very sick in the morning, darling. They've had too much to drink.'

'Hello, little Gracie,' Howard slurred, holding out his arms.

It was Mrs Dalton who caught him this time. He was having a job to sit in a chair, but appeared to be the only one capable of speech.

'Whoops!'

'Oooh!' Grace's eyes were wide as she looked at her mother. 'Is Uncle Howard sick as well?'

'They're all right, Grace. They just need to go to bed.' She kissed her daughter. 'And so do you.'

Grace was almost asleep before she tucked her up in bed again. And when she returned to the kitchen, they were all drinking tea.

It then took her and Mrs Dalton almost an hour to guide each one to his bed, removing only their jackets and leaving them to sleep in the rest of their clothes. After that struggle, they both needed a cup of cocoa.

'I think they've had a good time.' Mrs Dalton shook her head. 'And it wasn't surprising that Ben couldn't speak. I expect that's the most he's had to drink since his student days.'

'A night out like that was probably what he needed.' Amy's grin was wide. 'But he won't think that in the morning. None of them will.'

They both dissolved into helpless laughter.

Ben squinted at Howard. 'How much did we drink last night?'

'Don't ask me. I lost count after six.'

Ben shuddered. 'How's Ted?'

'Still fast asleep when I looked in.' Howard pulled a face of disgust. 'How did we end up in our own beds? The last thing I remember was trying to get the key in the front door.'

'Ah, that was a tricky operation.' Ben was peering under his bed. 'Where are my shoes?'

'By the front door.'

'What are they doing down there?'

'Don't ask me. Mine and Ted's are there as well.'

'Ah, then we were probably trying not to wake anyone.'

'I don't think we were successful.' Howard sat on the floor by Ben's bed, watching his friend try to stand up without swaying all over the place.

Ben examined his crumpled shirt. 'God, I must have been in a state if I couldn't even undress.'

'We all slept in our clothes. Go and get washed and changed, and we'll go down for some breakfast. While you're doing that I'll try to drag Ted out of bed.'

'Breakfast!' Ben went quite pale at the thought of food and had to hold on to the wardrobe for support. 'You're joking. But I wouldn't mind a gallon of tea. When you have a chance and can see properly, I want you to have a look at the painting on my easel. Tell me what you think, and I want an honest opinion.'

'Have you ever known me to be anything else about your work?'

'No.' Ben wandered off to the bathroom to clean himself up.

After half an hour he felt almost human again, and joined Howard in the studio. 'Did you get Ted out of bed?'

'Yep, he's in the kitchen. I'm not sure if he knows how he got there, though.' Howard chuckled. 'I don't think he'll be doing that again in a hurry.'

'Nor me.' Ben turned his attention to the painting. 'Well, what do you think?'

Rubbing his chin, Howard stepped back a little. 'The style is different, but I'd say it's the best thing you've ever done.'

'Really?' That was still hard for Ben to believe. 'That's what Amy told me, but I thought she was just being kind.'

'Ben.' Howard looked at his friend. 'You know she never flatters us unless she really likes what we're doing. She's got a good eye, and if she says it's good, then it is. Are they actual men from the camp?'

Ben nodded. 'I was having such a job to paint again, I thought that if I did this it might clear my mind.'

'It's certainly done that. You haven't lost it, Ben, in fact you're better.' Howard's eyes gleamed with excitement. 'Do some more like it.'

'OK.' For the first time in years, Ben felt a stirring of hope and confidence in his ability as an artist.

The sound of little feet climbing the stairs reached them, and then the door burst open.

'Mummy said if you want breakfast, you'd better come now. And when are you going to paint my picture?'

Both men flinched at the sound of the high-pitched childish voice.

Ben scooped her up, making her giggle. 'As soon as I've had a dozen cups of tea.'

# 39

Three days later, it was unusually quiet in the kitchen.

'Where's Grace?' Mrs Dalton looked out of the window. 'I can't see, or hear her.'

'She's still having her portrait painted. Ben started *ages* ago, according to her, and she keeps reminding him to get on with it.'

'Ah, well, that will keep them both busy. That night out did our Benjamin good, didn't it? But he hasn't been out since, has he?'

'No, he's still rather withdrawn, but at least he's eating with us, talking more, and leaving his studio now and again. We're going to give him a few more days, and then get him involved in plans for the new shop. The sooner all three of us can get back to normal, the better.'

'Mummy!' Grace burst into the room. 'Uncle Ben won't let me see the picture until it's done. It's taking a long time.'

'He'll let you see it as soon as he's happy with it,' Amy replied, pouring her a glass of milk.

Grace took it and guzzled thirstily, but made sure she left a little drop to put in Oscar's saucer.

There was a knock on the front door, and Grace was already running. 'I'll go, Mummy.'

By moving very fast, Amy just beat her daughter to the door. Grace could reach the latch now, and had to be watched in case she ran out into the road.

Standing on the doorstep were a man, a woman and two children.

'Hello, you must be Amy.' The man smiled broadly, but he had the same strained look as Ben, and he was just as thin. 'Ben told me all about you. My name's Stan Carlisle, and this is my missus, Helen. The kids are Daisy, she's six, and Len, who's eight. We've come to see the big man, if that's all right. He said we could call any time.'

'Yes, of course.' She stepped aside. 'This is my daughter, Grace. Come in and I'll take you up to Ben.'

They came inside and Stan slipped an arm around his wife. 'I would have come sooner, but it's taken me longer to recover than I thought it would.'

Ah, that accounted for his appearance. 'Were you in the same camp?'

Stan nodded, and his expression sobered. 'How is he?'

'He's been having a difficult time. Come into the kitchen first and meet Mrs Dalton.'

'Would you like a cup of tea?' Mrs Dalton asked when she had been introduced.

'The missus will, and perhaps the kids can go in the garden for a while. I'd better see Ben alone first.'

'Of course.' Amy was a bit apprehensive about Ben seeing someone from the camp, but he was here, and they couldn't be rude. 'Er . . . he hasn't said a word to us about the camp. He doesn't seem to want to talk about it.'

'We all feel like that.' Stan gave her arm a gentle pat. 'Don't you worry none; he's a fine, brave man, and will soon get back into the run of things. It's going to take all of us time, but we'll make it.'

Grace had already taken the children out to the garden, so Amy showed Stan up to the studio.

The door was wide open, and Ben was engrossed in painting. 'Ben, Stan and his family have come to see you.'

'Hmm?' He turned his head. 'Shorty! What did Amy call you?'

'Stan.' They greeted each other with obvious pleasure.

'I never knew your real name. It's good to see you. How are you?'

Seeing that they were quite happy, Amy went downstairs again.

Helen was talking to Mrs Dalton and drinking tea. She looked up anxiously. 'Is everything all right? Stan's been fretting these last few days, wanting to see how Ben was, but he hasn't been too well. He's been very ill and had a bit of a relapse when he was repatriated. It sapped all his strength. I've never met the man upstairs, but I'd give him my last penny if he needed it, after what he did for my Stan.'

'What was that?' Amy and Mrs Dalton spoke at the same time.

'Stan would have died if it hadn't been for Ben. Hasn't he told you anything about the camps?'

'No, he's been very quiet,' Amy admitted, pouring Helen another cup of tea.

'My Stan was like that at first, then one night he had a terrible nightmare. Frightened the life out of me, I can tell you, but after that he told me all about it.'

They listened in horror as Helen told them about the march in the freezing weather, and how Stan had been too ill to walk, so Ben had carried him all the way.

Helen blew her nose. 'Nearly killed himself, Stan said. There was another man as well, Charlie, and the three of them stuck together. They all made it to the next camp, but Stan was delirious by then and doesn't remember much. But Ben saved his life, that's for sure.'

At that moment, Stan came into the kitchen carrying a painting, with Ben right behind him. 'Look at this, Helen!'

She smiled gently at his excited face. 'Introduce me to your friend first, Stan.'

'Oops, sorry, forgetting my manners. Ben, this is my missus, Helen. Helen, this is the big man himself.'

He stood back, beaming as they greeted each other, and then rested the painting on the table. 'Just look at this, pet. That's me, the bloke by the door looking furtive is Charlie, then there's a few of the others from our hut, and' – he pointed to a lone figure in the background – 'that's Ben. Always trying to find a bit of peace and quiet, he was.'

'Oh, it's beautiful, even though it's of the POW camp.' Helen was clearly impressed, smiling at Ben. 'Stan said you were clever, and he's right.'

'If you like it that much, it's yours.' Ben smiled back. 'I'll wrap it for you.'

'You can't do that, mate,' Stan said quickly. 'The painting's worth a lot of money; you can't give it away.'

Tipping his head to one side, Ben studied the painting. 'It's too personal to sell. You know what it's all about, so I'd like you to have it.'

'Well . . .' Stan was obviously struggling with his desire to own the picture and the belief that Ben shouldn't be parting with it for nothing. 'Let us give you something for it.'

'No way, Stan. If it hadn't been for you, I'd have gone barmy in that camp. Please take it. I can always do others.'

Amy watched Stan accept it with the hint of a tear in his eyes, and she knew Ben had done the right thing. It would give enormous pleasure to the family, and that's what every artist wanted for their work. This was the first time Ben had mentioned the camp, and she could see there was a deep bond between the two men, brought about by their shared experiences. From the little Helen had told them, things must have been desperate while Stan had been ill, and Ben would have cared, just as he had cared for the little girl he had met only once. She had always loved the boy; now she loved the man – in a much deeper way.

That realization came as a shock, and she struggled not to feel disloyal to John. But it was four years since he had been cruelly taken from her. No amount of time would ever dim the love they had shared, but she had moved on and rebuilt her life. The steps had been terribly painful, but she had made it. John had been her first, special love, and always would be.

Needing a moment to compose herself, she walked into the garden on the pretence of checking on the children. She didn't know when her feelings for Ben had changed from fondness and friendship to love, but it had happened. Her heart and body now desired him, but she must not let him know. He had enough problems trying to readjust and pull his life together, just like Stan, and goodness knows how many others. What he needed was uncomplicated support and affection, and that was what she would give him.

'Mummy.' Grace ran towards her. 'Oscar doesn't want to play with us, so I showed Daisy and Len where Uncle Howard bakes his pots.'

Amy smiled as the other two children rushed up to her, asking excitedly, 'Do you think we could see the things he makes?'

'Of course. I'll take you to his workroom later. Now, would you like a drink? Tea or milk?'

'Tea, please,' they both said politely.

Just as they walked in from the garden, Howard appeared from the hallway, covered in dust, as usual.

'Ah, the man we were just talking about.' Amy urged the

children forward. 'This is the sculptor in the family, and he'll show you where he works.'

He studied the two children, who were gazing at him expectantly, and then turned to their mother. 'They are very clean and tidy. My workroom's covered in dust.'

'Please, Mum!'

Helen nodded. 'A little dust won't hurt them.'

'Right, kids, your mum says it's all right, so let's go.'

Daisy and Len rushed after Howard, eager to see this fascinating place.

Grace didn't bother to follow. She was standing on tiptoe trying to look at the picture on the table. Seeing she was having a job with this, Stan swept her up and sat her on his knees.

'That's me.' He pointed to the shortest figure in the painting.

'Hmm.' Grace gave him a smug look. 'Uncle Ben's painting my picture too, but he won't let me see it yet. I don't like waiting.'

'I know that's hard, but it will be worth waiting for. Everything good is.'

She cast a sideways glance at Ben, then leant towards Stan's ear and whispered, 'Have you seen it?'

'I have,' he whispered back, 'and you look very beautiful.'

'My mummy's beautiful, but she thinks she isn't.'

'Ah, well' – Stan winked at Amy, who was listening with a faint smile on her face – 'beauty is in the eye of the beholder. My missus thinks I'm tall, dark and handsome.'

Grace didn't understand what he meant, but joined in with the laughter anyway.

Ben was the most relaxed Amy had seen him since his return. He looked highly amused as he watched Stan with Grace.

'Helen would change her mind if she'd seen you dressed

up as Vera Lynn and singing "The White Cliffs of Dover".'

'What!' Helen nearly fell off her chair. 'But you can't sing, Stan. You're tone deaf.'

'Neither can Ben.' He smirked. 'When we did a take-off of Flanagan and Allen, we brought the house down.'

Howard reappeared with the children, only splattered with a little dust. 'What's all this about?'

Ben sat back and folded his arms, a wry smile on his face. 'I was only supposed to paint the scenery, but Stan forced me into the show. He made a very unconvincing woman, by the way.'

Grace clambered down from Stan and disappeared in the garden with the other children.

'I tried to get Ben into stockings. Those long legs would have caused a riot, but he flatly refused.'

'You bet I did! I wasn't taking any chances with a camp full of deprived men.'

Tipping his head back, Stan laughed, a deep throaty sound. 'No one would have touched you, mate. You made the rest of us look like half-pints.'

Amy glanced across at Helen, but Stan's wife just shrugged her shoulders. It was obvious that this was the first she'd heard about it, as well.

She shook her husband's arm. 'Stan, you never told me about this.'

'Sorry, pet, I would have got around to it, eventually. Boredom was a great danger in the camp, and Christmas was a bad time for all of us, being away from our families. So, we always put on a concert on Christmas Eve to take the men's minds off home. You can't have a show without women in it, so we used to dress up. One or two looked quite good, didn't they, Ben?'

He nodded and rolled his eyes. 'And some looked

399

grotesque. But it kept a lot of us busy rehearsing and setting up the stage, and gave everyone a much-needed laugh. The guards thought we were a lot of crazy Englishmen, and they might have been right. When we weren't planning ways to escape, we were prancing around on a stage making fools of ourselves.'

There was a warm, comforting glow inside Amy as she listened. This was the first time Ben had talked freely about his time as a POW; even on their boozy night out, Howard couldn't recall him mentioning it at all. All right, he and Stan were only recounting the lighter moments, and she guessed they must have been precious few, but the tight knot he had inside him was loosening a little. This was an important step forward for him.

'Yeah, but it helped, didn't it? The Major in our camp was a good bloke; he understood the importance of something to occupy our minds. The International Red Cross sent us a few books, and a football, and these were a blessing, along with the occasional letters.' Stan squeezed his wife's hand. 'I only received three of your letters in all that time, but I treasured them, and read them over and over again.'

'How many of ours did you get, Ben?' Howard asked. 'As soon as we knew you had been taken prisoner, we all wrote regularly.'

'I received nothing from you until a few weeks before the Yanks liberated us.' His eyes became bleak. 'It wasn't until then that I found out what had happened to John.'

'Not knowing what was going on at home was a great worry.' Stan grimaced, changing the subject. 'Another way we used to occupy ourselves was with regular lectures. They were a mixed bunch in the camp, and you could learn about anything from fishing or keeping pigs to the ancient philosophers. Ben gave a few on the art of forgery.'

'Forgery!' Mrs Dalton exclaimed.

'Oh yes, he was our official forger, and damned good he was. Charlie pinched a German pass and Ben made such a brilliant copy that a couple of men just walked out of the gate. Unfortunately, they were soon caught again, but it gave us all a lift at the time.'

'Who was Charlie?'

'He was a pickpocket, Howard,' Ben explained. 'A real villain, but he was a good friend to Stan and me.'

'Yes, he was. He even gave some lectures on how to relieve people of their possessions without them feeling a thing. Very well attended, they were.'

'He gave me his address, Stan, and we must look him up sometime.'

'I'd like that. It will be interesting to see if he's kept his promise and gone straight . . . or straight for someone's pocket.'

They were laughing just as the front door closed with a crash, and Ted erupted into the kitchen. Amy and Mrs Dalton were on their feet in an instant when they saw his face and Howard rushed to his side. 'What's happened, Ted?'

'The Germans have surrendered. It's over! By God, it's over!'

Pandemonium broke out with everyone on their feet and milling about so they could hug each other.

Hearing the commotion, the children rushed in from the garden, joining in the celebrations. It was bedlam as each little voice yelled that the war was over.

Ben swung Amy off her feet, spinning her round and round. And she cried, great tears running down her cheeks.

The long years of war had been a mixture of loss and gain. She had tragically lost her darling John, and that loss was sorely felt in this moment of euphoria, but she had gained a daughter. And Ben and Howard had survived. That was something to be very, very grateful for.

# 40

The next day, 8 May, was the official VE day, and celebrations were in full swing. There were street parties going on all over the country, and their street was no exception. Grace was so excited to see the row of trestle tables stretching right down the road, laden with sandwiches and cakes. Every household had contributed something, making it quite a feast, in spite of the severe rationing. Many of the children were in fancy dress, and Mrs Dalton had taken the skirt off one of her silk evening dresses, sewing nearly all night to make Grace a dress and pair of wings. With her unruly mop of hair, Grace was an appealing-looking angel. John's parents had arrived last night, determined not to miss their granddaughter having fun, and also to spend this special time with their daughter-in-law. It was a bittersweet time for them all, and Amy was glad to have them with her. Grace was growing more like John every day, and he should have been here to enjoy this, but he wasn't, and no amount of longing and wishing could make it so. The little girl was happy, though, and had her two uncles. After what they had been through, that was not simply a blessing, but a miracle.

Ben's parents and Howard's had also arrived, filling the house to capacity, but no one seemed bothered about sleeping. Howard was disappointed that Chrissie hadn't been able to get away and join them as well. Amy couldn't help wondering just how serious their relationship was, and if there would be a wedding in the near future.

A neighbour had a wind-up gramophone outside their

house, so they had music as well. The children yelled and shouted as they enjoyed the food, and the grown-ups drank beer and danced to the sound of the Glenn Miller orchestra.

By the time it was dark, they were all tired out. Grace had already been asleep when her grandpa had carried her to bed and tucked her up; he and his wife had gazed at her with tears in their eyes, remembering their son who was no longer with them. Amy knew that many would be experiencing great sadness while the country went wild with joy.

That night everyone slept where they could – in chairs, on the floor – but nobody cared, and in the morning, the house gradually emptied as they all returned to their own homes.

Mrs Dalton sighed and put the kettle on. 'Now let's try and get back to normal, and the first thing to do is have a nice cup of tea.'

With nods of agreement, they all sat down in their usual places around the large kitchen table.

'I think this would be a good time to decide about the future.' Howard looked at Ben. 'We've got to get back in business. Amy and I have been working for some time, and now have a good stock of items to sell. We should open another shop without delay. After the austere years of the war, people will be looking for a way to brighten up their homes and lives.'

'Agreed.' Ben nodded, then gazed around the table. 'I know I've been difficult since I came back, and I still want to shut myself away, but I'm fighting it. You've all been understanding, and that has helped a lot. I've been grateful for your support.' His smile was wry. 'But the one who brought me back to my senses the most was Grace. She stood in front of me, little face showing her hurt, and told me I wasn't nice.'

'Ah well, she would,' Mrs Dalton said with more than a touch of pride. 'That little one speaks her mind, and too bad if you don't like it.'

That summing-up of her daughter brought a smile to Amy's face, and made everyone grin. Her little girl was next door at the moment, playing with their neighbours' two children.

'Getting involved in starting up our business again might help me adjust a bit more quickly.' Ben leant his elbows on the table. 'So what do you suggest, Howard?'

'Well, I've got two pieces of news. First, I think I've found suitable premises in the King's Road. A bit further up this time, and larger, but it will need a lot of work done on the inside before we can open. I only saw it last week and haven't done anything about it until you all see it.'

'Sounds good; we'll have a look at it today.' Ben nodded to his friend. 'And what was the second piece of news?'

'Chrissie is back at Aldershot again, and I managed to phone her yesterday. I asked her to marry me . . . and she agreed.'

Amy squealed in delight, throwing her arms around Howard's neck and hugging him. 'That's wonderful! Have you told your parents? When's the wedding?'

Laughing, he stood up, as everyone wanted to congratulate him. 'One question at a time. Yes, I've told my parents, and we haven't had time to make any plans. She will be in the army for another three months, so we will probably get married after she's demobbed.'

'I haven't met her yet,' Ben complained, but he was clearly delighted for his friend. 'So, when am I going to see her?'

'She's hoping to get a few days' leave soon.'

'This is so exciting.' Amy beamed with happiness. 'You'll like her, Ben. She's a lovely girl, and helped to deliver Grace.'

'I'll look forward to that. How did you manage a romance in wartime, Howard?'

'It wasn't easy, and I'll be damned glad when she's out of the services. We didn't make any decisions while things were uncertain, and we could only see each other occasionally, but we kept in touch as much as we could.'

Mrs Dalton looked thoughtful. 'Where are you going to live? You could have the whole of the basement, if that would be enough for you.'

Howard sighed with relief. 'I was hoping you would say that. We'd love to live here.'

'Oh, well, that's settled then.'

Amy felt their landlady's relief. In her excitement about Howard marrying, it hadn't occurred to her that he would move. This was such a happy house, and it would have been awful if one of them left, but it was large and had plenty of room for all of them.

They settled down again, getting back to the business of the shop.

'Paintings, Ben.' Howard did a rough sketch of the upstairs they would use as a gallery. 'You're going to have twice the wall space in this shop, so can you repeat that one you gave to Stan, and a few more like it?'

'I expect I could. I did a lot of drawings in the camp, but one sadistic guard found them and tore them to shreds.'

Amy bit back a gasp of dismay, knowing just how badly that would have hurt his artistic heart.

'I did more after that, but when they shifted us to another camp, I lost track of them. All I could concentrate on was staying alive. Still, I've got the pictures in my head, so I should be able to reproduce them.'

'Good. Start tomorrow. The more paintings we have, the better.'

Ben grimaced. 'I know you all liked the painting, and Stan loved it, but do you think the public would buy something like that?'

'I don't see why not,' Amy assured him. 'It was a study of men and emotions, and I thought it was a compelling subject, and beautifully painted.'

The glance he sent her was one of pure affection, making her heart trip.

'I finished Grace's portrait last night, so would you like to see it?'

'Why didn't you tell me?' Amy was already on her feet. 'Have you shown it to Grace?'

'I want to frame it before I do that.'

They followed each other up to the studio, gathering round in anticipation as Ben removed the sheet covering the picture.

There was a stunned silence, and Amy was speechless as she gazed at her daughter. Grace was sitting on the rough floorboards with her doll beside her, and her head tilted up, looking straight at the man who had been painting her. There was an impish little smile on her face, showing clearly that she had been enjoying herself. The light was coming in from the window behind her, filtering through her mass of unruly hair and casting a shadow on the floor. It was breathtaking, and the eyes looking out from the picture were John's.

'Oh, Ben, when did you learn to paint like that?' Howard was quite overcome, just like the rest of them.

Amy smiled up at Ben. She would have loved to show her gratitude by hugging him, as she had always done. But there was still a reserve about him that made her cautious. He was inclined to make a slight move away if she got too close. He was still having trouble adjusting to freedom. So instead, she just said, 'Thank you, that is the most beautiful picture I have ever seen.'

'Glad you like it.'

'Like it!' Mrs Dalton sighed. 'That's no way to talk about a painting of such exquisite artistry, Benjamin.'

Ted nodded. 'I agree. You have excelled yourself. When are you going to show Grace?'

'I'll frame it tonight and we'll have a proper unveiling in the morning.' He gave a wry smile at Amy. 'She will be my harshest critic, and tell me exactly what she thinks of her portrait.'

The next morning, they made a great production of the unveiling. Howard stood Grace on a chair in front of the easel, holding her firmly in place, and Ted bowed, giving her a little bunch of daisies to hold. She laughed, bouncing up and down in Howard's restraining hands.

'Are you ready?' Ben twitched the sheet.

'Let me see. Let me see!'

With a theatrical flourish, he whipped away the sheet.

She stopped moving, staring at the picture, open-mouthed and silent. Then she glanced from one person to the next, then back to the picture. 'I'm on the floor. I wasn't sitting on the floor, Uncle Ben. I was on that chair . . . And you've painted my dolly.'

Amy smothered a laugh at her daughter's puzzled expression. 'Uncle Ben only needed to sketch you first, then he painted you like that because it made a better picture.'

'It's called artistic licence,' Howard explained. 'He didn't want to make you sit on the floor for ages and ages. It would have been uncomfortable for you, and you wouldn't have been able to keep still.'

'He did make me sit for a long time.' She sniggered. 'Do I look like that?'

Putting a hand over her mouth, Amy had to turn away when she saw the look of mock dismay on Ben's face. She knew he was pleased with the painting, because she had seen it in his eyes the night before, but he was now going to tease Grace.

'Oh, she doesn't like it,' he moaned, mopping his eyes with a paint rag. 'My career is finished!'

Mrs Dalton and Ted were having as much trouble as Amy, but, somehow, Howard was managing to keep a straight face.

'I do like it, Uncle Ben.' Grace gave him a hesitant smile, tipping her head to one side. 'My dolly's pretty.'

That was too much for all of them, and they collapsed in helpless laughter. Grace's face was so expressive.

Ben swung Grace off the chair and into his arms, facing the picture. 'Don't you think you look pretty?'

She giggled, squirming round to see her mother. 'Is that really me, Mummy?'

'Yes, darling, that's exactly how you look. Thank Uncle Ben for doing such a lovely picture for you.' It warmed her heart to see him with her daughter, because around her, he was more like the Ben they had known before the war.

'Thank you.' Grace kissed his cheek, looking happier now her mother had told her the picture was like her. 'Can I have it in my room?'

'You tell me where you want it and I'll hang it for you right away.' He put her back on the floor.

'Please. Please.'

They all trooped downstairs, and, after making Ben hold it in place all around the room, it was finally put on the wall next to her bed. Every time she looked at the picture, she giggled.

'I'll get Oscar and let him see it.' Grace tore off to the garden to find the cat.

Ben was shaking his head and chuckling. 'I'm not sure if she likes it or not.'

'She loves it,' Amy said. 'We'll be having all the neighbours and children from the street in to see it.'

'Oh, Lord, yes.' Mrs Dalton looked at the clock. 'A couple of them are coming this afternoon, so I'd better make a cake.'

Because the celebrations were still going on, Ted hadn't bothered to open his shop, so they all decided to have a look at the place Howard had found, except Mrs Dalton, who was already busy with her baking.

'Off you go,' she ordered Amy. 'I'll look after Grace.'

The shop was the other end of the King's Road from their previous one, and even from the outside it was obvious that it had been neglected for a long time, and was in a dreadful state.

Ben slanted Howard an incredulous glance. 'You're joking, right?'

'Don't judge it yet.' He took a key out of his pocket. 'The owner said if we were willing to spruce the place up, we could have it rent free for the first three months, and cheap for the first year of opening. Wait till you see the space inside. It's perfect.'

It was a struggle to open the door and, even though Ben was getting his strength back, it took all three men to shift it enough for them to be able to get inside.

'How on earth did you ever get in to have a look round, Howard?' Ted was puffing after the effort.

'I got it open enough to squeeze through.' Howard began

to pace around, his slight limp hardly noticeable now, pointing out the finer points with enthusiasm.

Ted was scratching the bald patch on top of his head and muttering under his breath. Ben was silent, and Amy wide-eyed with disbelief.

'The place needs pulling down.'

'Amy, where's your vision?' Howard grinned with excitement. 'Can't you just picture shelves all along here, and look at the amount of window space. Ben, you go upstairs. There's huge scope for putting on a special exhibition, if you wanted to.'

Giving the banister a shake, Ben examined it doubtfully. 'I admit that the sweep of the staircase is impressive, but is it safe?'

'Of course it is!' Howard bounded up the stairs and back again to prove the point. 'Come on, show a bit of enthusiasm. The low rent will give us a breathing space until we get established.'

'Being in love has turned his brain,' Ted murmured. 'The four of us will never be able to lick this wreck into shape.'

'I heard that, Ted!' Undaunted, Howard laughed, giving Ben a shove up the stairs.

As he made his way up, they creaked and groaned under his weight, but they felt secure enough. Once at the top, he could see what Howard was on about. He paced the floor, kicking aside the rubbish as he went, imagining what it would look like freshly painted and lined with pictures. He stopped in the middle of the room and felt a stirring of pleasure. Yes, he could do this. Taking a deep breath, he tipped his head back; it was almost as if he were coming to life again. As the months and years in that prison camp had passed, he had withdrawn into himself utterly. It had been the only way to survive. When he had finally arrived home, he had thought the safe familiarity of his old home would rekindle his zest for life. But the people he knew and loved had changed, just as he had, and he knew that nothing was ever going to be the same. He had to start afresh – and he would. He was still having trouble handling the transformation in Amy. She had grown into a stunning woman, as he had always known she would. The young girl he'd met sitting beside the river no longer existed. In her place there was a mature woman with a young child, and already a widow. She'd loved John completely, and in one cruel night of the Blitz, she had had to face the future without him. Dear God, he wished he had her courage. One look at a blank canvas and he had panicked, terrified he wouldn't be able to paint again – convinced he couldn't. It was Amy who had made him realize that he had to accept the changes his experiences had made in him, and in the way he worked. A slight smile touched his mouth. And then there was Grace. He could see her now, standing beside him, accusing, and telling him that he *wasn't nice*. What a combination mother and daughter made . . .

'Ben!' Howard yelled. 'What're you doing up there?'

Realizing he had been standing there for some time, he made his way down again.

'Well, what do you think?'

Sitting on the stairs and stretching his long legs in front of him, Ben noted his friend's animated expression, and nodded. 'It's a perfect space.'

'Told you. We—'

'But' – Ben held up his hand to stop Howard – 'Ted is right. This is too big a job for us to tackle on our own. We'll need help.'

'How much help, Ben? We can't afford to employ builders.'

Amy sat down beside Ben. 'I can help.'

'So can I.' Ted gazed around again. 'It could look wonderful, if the job's done properly.'

Howard was shaking his head. 'We can't take your money, Ted, nor yours, Amy; you've got Grace to support.'

'You could make me a partner,' Ted suggested.

'And I'm going to be in this with you, so I must contribute.' Amy gave Ben and Howard a 'don't you dare argue' look.

'OK.' Ben unwound himself from the stairs. 'Let's do as much of it as we can ourselves, and see how it goes financially. We'll use your money only if it becomes necessary. Do you agree?'

Ted and Amy nodded.

'Good, now that's agreed, I'll go and have a word with Stan and see if he's found a job yet. If he hasn't, he might be willing to give us a hand. We must pay him a fair wage, though, as he's got a family to look after.'

'That's a wonderful idea.' Amy had taken a liking to Stan and his family. 'Do you think he'll do it?'

'I can but ask.'

'I knew you'd all agree, after you'd thought about it.' Howard was rubbing his hands together and grinning. 'I can't wait for us to get back into business again. I'll go with Ted and see about the lease.'

'And I must get back to help Mrs Dalton with our afternoon visitors.' Amy waved as they all went their separate ways.

As Ben made his way to Stan's, there was a spring in his step. Oh, it felt good to be doing something about a new shop. It was going to be a challenge, and that was just what he needed. He would be working hard and planning for the future – a future many poor devils wouldn't have.

# 41

They had hoped to have the shop ready within two weeks, but it was turning out to be a much bigger job than antici- pated. In addition to the amount of work needed, there were other delays. Grace had caught chickenpox from the neighbours' children. She was miserable, itchy and fretful, taking up a lot of Amy's time. Then Chrissie and Howard had decided to marry as soon as she was demobbed at the beginning of August. As Chrissie had little time to help with arrangements, Howard was always tearing off somewhere or other. Amy hadn't known that Chrissie didn't have any family of her own, so with Mrs Dalton's help they had taken on the role of Chrissie's parents. Ted was helping at the new shop whenever he could, but Ben and Stan were tackling the bulk of the work.

They would be lucky if they could open in another two weeks, Amy thought as she hurried to the bedroom.

The sight of her darling Grace, sitting up in bed, covered in nasty blister-like spots and looking a picture of misery, brought tears to her eyes.

'Mummy,' she wailed. 'I can't scratch with these on.' Her little hands waved around, showing the pink woollen gloves tied securely to her wrists.

'I know, darling, but you mustn't scratch; it will only make things worse.' Sitting on the edge of the bed, she pulled out a handkerchief and wiped the tears from Grace's face. 'You'll soon be better now.'

Her bottom lip trembled. 'I don't like staying in bed. Can I get up, please?'

'How's my favourite girl?' Chrissie arrived, looking smart and efficient in her uniform.

'Auntie Chrissie,' Grace sobbed, 'make me better.'

'Let me have a look at you.' Winking at Amy, she took hold of Grace's wrist, pretending to take her pulse, then she examined the spots. 'Hmm, if you stay in bed for one more day, you'll be feeling much better by tomorrow.'

'But I itch.' Grace's eyes swam with miserable tears.

'I have something to ease that.' She took a bottle out of her bag. 'We'll dab this on those nasty spots to make them keep quiet, shall we?'

Grace nodded as Chrissie undressed her, and began smoothing the white liquid over the affected areas.

Amy was having a job to stop her own tears from overflowing; she hated to see her normally happy daughter so unwell. It hurt, but all they could do was let it run its course. There were already signs of the spots drying up.

'There.' Chrissie put the stopper back in the bottle and left it on the bedside table. After slipping Grace's nightdress back on, she said, 'Does that feel better?'

'It feels all cold.' Grace gave a watery smile. 'And it doesn't itch quite so much.'

'Good girl.' Chrissie stood up. 'Put some more of that on at bedtime, Amy, and that should help her sleep.'

'Thanks.' She smoothed her hand over Grace's tousled hair. 'You're being a very brave girl, so I think a treat is in order. Would you like some jelly?'

'Yes please, Mummy.'

Collecting a dish of red jelly from the kitchen, Amy returned to Grace and fed her until it was all gone. As her eyes began to close, Amy kissed her gently. 'You have a nice sleep now.'

'Ah, she finished it all, then.' Mrs Dalton gave a satisfied nod at the empty dish.

'Yes, and she's asleep at last. The poor little darling had an awful night.'

'And that means you did, as well.' Chrissie tapped the chair beside her. 'Sit down for a while, Amy, you look tired out.'

'Thanks.' She sighed with relief. It seemed as if she hadn't stopped for days. 'It's lovely to see you. How much leave did you manage to get?'

'I've only wangled three days.'

'Have you seen Howard?' Mrs Dalton asked.

'Yes, I popped into the shop on my way here.' Her smile spread. 'You should have seen the state of them. But through the dust and frantic sawing, the shop is taking shape.'

'I should be helping, but I can't leave Grace while she's so poorly.' This had fretted Amy. She hated leaving them to do all the work, but Grace came first in her life. Her grandparents hadn't been able to come and help because Mildred had never had chickenpox, but as soon as Grace was no longer contagious, they would be here on the first train.

'Why don't you go there now for a couple of hours? It'll do you good to get out of the house for a while. I'll look after Grace for you.'

'Oh, would you, Chrissie? I would like to see how they're getting on.'

'Off you go, and tell them all to pack up by seven and come home for dinner.' Mrs Dalton tried to look stern. 'I don't want them creeping in at midnight too tired to eat.'

'I will, but I doubt they'll take any notice of me.' Without further delay, Amy grabbed her purse and headed for the bus stop.

The repaired door opened easily now, and they'd even fixed a bell so that it tinkled every time someone came in.

Ben looked up at the sound, rushing forward to shake hands with the man standing just inside the door. 'Charlie! It's good to see you.'

'Stan's wife told me where I could find you.'

Stan clattered down from upstairs, a wide smile on his face. 'How are you, mate?'

'Not too bad, thanks.'

'Come and meet Howard and Ted.' After Ben had made the introductions, he said, 'We've got some beer out the back, so let's take a break. We deserve one.'

They sat round on boxes with bottles in their hands.

'You two look better than the last time I saw you.' Charlie's smile was amused as he looked around at the mess.

'Regular meals make a difference.' Stan took a swig of beer. 'You don't look too bad yourself. What have you been up to since we got back?'

'I've been staying with my sister. I would have come a bit sooner, but my old dad's not been too good.'

'I'm sorry to hear that.' Charlie looked slightly ill at ease, and Ben had never seen him like that before. He hadn't even put down the packet he'd had in his hands ever since he arrived. Even in the camp he'd been sure of himself, brash even. 'I hope he's better now?'

'Yes, thanks, he's back to his old cantankerous self.' Charlie took a long swig of beer, and then held out the package to Ben. 'Er . . . these are yours. When they moved us out of the camp, you left these behind. I took care of them, hiding them when the march was over, intending to give them back to you. But when we were liberated, things got so chaotic . . . I grabbed them, but you were nowhere in sight, so I stuffed them in my jacket pocket, and forgot about them in the excitement of getting home . . .' He tailed off, taking another quick drink. 'I'm sorry, Ben, I never intended to keep them, honest.'

'If I remember rightly you had special pockets on that jacket of yours.' Stan grinned. 'All part of your trade, eh?'

'That's my past life. I'm going straight now.' Charlie watched Ben open the packet.

When the rough drawings spilt out, Ben gasped. His throat was tight with emotion when he saw the pictures he'd done during his time as a POW, and he had to swallow twice before he could speak. 'Thanks for taking care of them, Charlie. I thought they were lost.'

'I couldn't let that happen. That's a record of the men who were with us, and they're bloody good pictures.'

Stan found another bottle and thrust it at Charlie. 'It was good of you to save these, mate. I was too ill to think of it, and Ben was half dead when we arrived at that other camp.'

'Yeah, well, I know how much they meant to Ben. I thought he was going to kill that guard who destroyed the first lot of drawings.'

'Let's have a look.' Howard sat on the floor. 'These are fantastic,' he muttered, and then looked up at Charlie. 'This one's of you. What are you doing with that guard?'

'Picking his pocket.' He laughed, at ease now he'd returned the pictures to their rightful owner. 'Good, isn't it?'

Taking it out of Howard's hand, Ben searched in his pocket until he found a pencil, then he signed his name at the bottom, and gave it to Charlie. 'You keep this one. I'm very grateful to you.'

'Thanks, Ben. I'll have it framed and stick it over my bed

to remind me not to go back to my old ways.' He smirked and began rolling up his sleeves. 'Now, what the hell are you trying to do here? You look as if you could do with some more help.'

The door opened again at that moment, and Ben looked up to see Amy watching them, a smile on her face. For some reason, just lately he had felt uncomfortable when she was near him. He couldn't fathom out why, because he'd always enjoyed being with her.

'Well!' Her startling green eyes had an amused glint to them. 'You all look very busy.'

Howard laughed. 'We're just taking a well-earned break. Come and meet Charlie, a friend of Ben and Stan's.'

'Hello, Charlie.' She shook his hand.

'What the devil are you doing here?'

She spun round, startled by the sharp tone of Ben's voice. 'I've come to see if I can help for a couple of hours.'

He glowered at her. 'You should be at home with Grace.'

'She's asleep, and Chrissie is with her.' Amy frowned, hurt that Ben should think she would leave her daughter without proper care. 'She is a nurse, Ben.'

'That's all right, then.' He turned away, but didn't apologize for speaking so sharply to her.

Howard stepped in. 'We'd be glad of your help, Amy. You can start painting that wall, if you like. It's coming along, isn't it?'

'Yes. It's going to look really lovely when it's finished.' Picking up a brush and tin of paint, she smiled at Stan. 'How are Helen and the children?'

'Wonderful, thanks, but I'm sorry to hear your little Grace has caught fowl pest.'

'Fowl pest?' It took a moment for that to sink in. 'Oh, you mean chickenpox.'

They all laughed, irritating Ben even more. She was very friendly with all the men, and he didn't like the way Charlie was eyeing her. 'Have you come to work, or not?'

Her smile faded, but she said nothing. Turning her back on him, she began painting the wall. She worked for about half an hour, humming to herself, happy to be helping for a little while.

'It isn't necessary for you to do that, Amy.' Ben was across the room watching her with a frown of irritation on his face. 'I'll finish it later . . . and make a better job of it.'

After putting down the brush, she headed across to him, ready to give him a playful punch, as she'd always done when he was teasing. 'Come on then, let's see you do better.' It was only when he stepped back that she realized he wasn't joking. He meant it. Hurt, she said, 'What do you suggest I do, then?'

'I don't know. Make some tea or something.'

Wiping paint from her hands with a rag, she looked down to hide the hurt in her eyes. He was belittling her, and he'd never done that before. She was relieved Charlie and Stan were upstairs and couldn't hear him. 'I can see I'm not wanted here. I'm sorry I bothered you.' Then she walked out of the door.

'Wait, Amy!' Howard called. But she was already running for a bus just pulling up at the stop. He turned to his friend, keeping his voice low. 'Just what the hell are you doing treating our Amy like that? She doesn't deserve to be spoken to so rudely.'

Ben shrugged, feeling uncomfortable. He didn't understand why he'd done that either. Giving a ragged sigh, he said, 'I'm in a rotten mood. I'll apologize when I see her.'

'You'd damned well better.' Howard was furious. 'She's part of our lives, and she's a part of us. For years she's cooked our meals, helped us, and loved us. Don't you ever speak to her like that again. Now *you* can paint that damned wall!'

Ben didn't demur at the rebuke, knowing it was well justified. He was as angry with himself as Howard was. She had never done anything to deserve that rudeness from him, and he was at a complete loss to understand what had come over him just lately.

Amy caught the bus, paid her fare, and sat looking out of the window, stunned. What had she done to make him treat her like that? He had always been kind to her, laughing and teasing in his gentle way, but the man confronting her just now was someone she didn't know. Had he guessed that her feelings for him had changed, and she was now looking at the mature man with a deeper affection? She wasn't going to admit it was anything more than that – not after the way he had treated her. And anyway, he couldn't have, because she was treating him the same as always. She had been very, very careful not to let her feelings show.

She stared out at the people walking along, fighting to keep her tears at bay. He couldn't have any idea how much he had hurt her. Something was troubling him, but what? She'd believed he was well on the way to recovery, but he obviously wasn't, and seemed to be getting worse. It was very worrying.

Amy let herself into the house quietly and went straight to her room. The curtains had been drawn, and in the half-light she could see her daughter was still asleep. Without disturbing her, she sat in the chair beside the bed, leant back her head and closed her eyes, taking this chance to have a moment of peace and quiet.

Her thoughts turned to John, as they often did when she

was troubled. He had been such a solid, sensible, dependable man; how she had adored him. The fact that they'd had so little time together still hurt, even after all these years. It had taken ages, but she had eventually come to terms with the loss, but she knew she would never forget him. He would always be a part of her and their lovely daughter. After the birth of Grace, she had moved on, as she'd had to, determined to make a good life for the two of them, but it had been a mighty struggle. The next most important man in her life was Ben, and she had always believed he would be her friend, someone she could turn to for help and comfort. But after the open hostility he had shown her today, she was no longer sure of that. He had *never* looked at her, or spoken to her, like that before. There had been anger in his eyes, as if he couldn't stand the sight of her. Something had changed between them, and not for the better. It made her desperately sad, and she didn't know how to deal with it.

'Mummy?'

'I'm here, darling.' She was immediately bending over the bed, smiling. 'You've had a nice sleep. How do you feel?'

'A bit better, but I don't like this.'

'No one likes being ill, but once you're better, you'll forget all about it.' She sat on the bed and gathered Grace into her arms. 'Would you like us to go and stay with Granny and Grandpa when the spots have all gone?'

'Yes please.' This produced a faint smile. 'Would you put some more stuff on me? I itch again.'

After pulling the curtains back to let in the light, Amy used the lotion Chrissie had brought with her. It did seem to be helping.

'Can I have these off now, please?' Grace held up her hands. 'I promise not to scratch. I'll be a good girl.'

Amy swallowed hard. 'You're always a good girl, darling,'

she said, giving her a teasing smile as she removed the little gloves. 'Well, nearly always. Are you hungry?'

'A bit. Is there any jelly left?'

'Yes, we made one just for you. Would you like a glass of milk as well?'

'Please.'

'I won't be a minute.' Amy left the room and went to the kitchen, where Chrissie was helping Mrs Dalton to prepare dinner.

'Amy!' Chrissie looked surprised. 'We didn't hear you come back. You weren't at the shop long.'

Smiling brightly she opened the larder. 'They had everything under control and didn't need me, so I came back rather than get in their way. Grace wants more jelly, and a glass of milk.'

'I can't imagine the men turning down an offer of help.' Mrs Dalton frowned as she poured milk into a glass. 'They must have been in a generous mood.'

'They must have been,' was all Amy said before she hurried back to Grace. She didn't want to be cross-examined about why she had come straight back. It hurt too much at the moment. If it had been anyone else who had spoken sharply to her, she would have either ignored it, or laughed it off, but she couldn't do that with Ben. He meant too much to her.

Grace was sitting up in bed when she returned, much brighter. She finished the jelly with obvious enjoyment and guzzled the milk until the glass was empty. It was a good sign, and Amy was hopeful she would eat something more substantial soon.

'Will you tell me a story about fairies?'

'Not the dragons today?'

'No, let's make up a different story this time.'

'Hmm, let me see.' Amy gazed into space, then began. 'Once upon a time there was a little girl who lived in a wooden hut on the edge of a forest by a beautiful babbling brook. Everyone said she was a fairy, but she didn't believe that, because she didn't have any wings . . .'

# 42

Mother and daughter were too engrossed in the story to notice Ben standing in the doorway. The breath left his lungs at the picture they made. There were two unruly mops of hair close together, Amy's soft voice telling a tale, and Grace enthusiastically adding her own ideas as they went along. Ben didn't think he had ever seen, or heard, anything so beautiful.

In that instant he acknowledged that which he had been trying to block out ever since his return. That first meeting with her had shaken him, and there was no use denying it any longer. He loved her, deeply and irrevocably.

Stifling a groan of dismay, he stepped back and closed the door quietly, leaning against the wall with head back and eyes closed. What a damnable thing to have happened. Their relationship had always been a close friendship, without a hint of sexual desire, but that was no longer the case, as far as he was concerned. He wanted to hold her, kiss her and run his hands over her lovely petite body. He ground his teeth. He wanted her in his bed. He wanted her and Grace to be his to love and look after. But Amy would never accept him in that way, so he must keep his distance, and his desires in check. He had been snapping at her in self-defence. That was another thing he must control.

What a tangle! That prisoner-of-war camp had really messed up his emotions. Pushing away from the wall, he returned to the kitchen.

'There you are, Benjamin.' Mrs Dalton pursed her lips. 'Ted tells me you are in a bad mood.'

'Sorry.' He shrugged. 'I've been snapping at everyone. It must be the long hours we've been putting in at the shop.'

'All work and no play makes Jack a dull boy.' She waved a serving spoon at him as she quoted one of her famous sayings. 'It's time you went out and started enjoying yourself again.'

'Come dancing with us tonight,' Chrissie suggested.

'Not unless you can find me a pretty nurse as a partner.'

'I might be able to manage that. I'll nip along to the phone box and see if I can catch Paula. Luckily, she's on the phone at home.' Taking coins from her purse, she hurried off.

She was back within ten minutes. 'She'll meet us at Hammersmith at half past eight.'

'I was only joking, Chrissie.'

'Too bad, Ben, you've got to come now.'

Howard was grinning at his friend. 'Looks like you've got yourself a blind date.'

'Yeah.'

'Don't look so worried,' Chrissie chided. 'She's a nice girl, and quite tall, so she should suit you as a dance partner.'

Knowing he was cornered, he tried to look happy about it, but in truth he hadn't expected her to be able to do anything about it at such short notice. He couldn't seem to do anything right at the moment. And he didn't want some tall, unknown girl in his arms. He wanted the small woman in the other room, and her delightful child.

'Benjamin, go and tell Amy we're about to dish up the dinner.'

Hauling himself out of the chair, he walked out of the kitchen and along the hall, stopping at Amy's door. This time, he knocked softly before turning the handle.

They were still in the same position, and it felt as if something was squeezing his heart as he gazed at them. Amy was considering him warily; Grace was smiling at him, her little face covered in dabs of white lotion. He only just stopped himself from striding over and gathering them both to him to tell them how much he loved them. Instead, drawing in a deep, silent breath, he walked towards the bed, his movements unhurried.

'Uncle Ben.' Grace held up her hands. 'Mummy's taken off my gloves now.'

'Oh, that's better then, isn't it?' As Grace nodded, he reached out to touch Amy's arm, but let his hand drop to his side before touching her. 'Dinner's ready.'

'Thank you,' she said politely, looking back at her daughter. 'Would you like something to eat?'

Grace thought about this for a moment. 'Hmm, could I have mashed potatoes and gravy? And perhaps I could manage a sausage, as well.'

Ben didn't miss the relief that flooded across Amy's face, knowing the child had eaten very little over the last three days.

He spoke to Grace. 'I want to paint a picture of you and Mummy together, for the gallery when we open. I'll start on it tomorrow.'

'Ooh, but I've got spots, Uncle Ben.'

'I won't paint them.' He smoothed her untidy hair away from her face, smiling down at her earnest little face. 'There won't be a spot in sight.'

Grace sighed. 'I'll be glad when they've gone.'

'It won't be long, darling.' Amy swung her legs off the bed and stood up. 'Once you start eating properly again, they'll soon disappear. So, one plate of sausage and mash coming right up.'

427

Ben caught Amy before she reached the kitchen. 'I'm sorry about this afternoon. Please forgive me. I had no reason or right to talk to you like that.' Her expression changed from wary to a bright smile, making his heart thud.

'It hurt, Ben, but of course I forgive you.' She tipped her head to one side, questioning. 'I realize just how difficult it is for you to adjust to being home again, but if there is something bothering you still, you can talk to me about it. You know that, don't you? Don't keep it all to yourself, letting it fester.'

Shoving his hands in his pockets to stop himself reaching out for her, he said gently, 'How did you ever get to be so wise while my back was turned?'

With an amused shake of her head at his teasing tone, she disappeared into the kitchen to share the good news with everyone: 'Grace wants sausage and mash.'

'Ah, she's on the mend, then.' Mrs Dalton beamed. 'There's sausages in the larder, bought fresh this morning, and plenty of mash already made. I'll put your dinner in the oven till you're ready.'

'How long before the shop will be finished?' Amy asked, turning over the sizzling sausage.

'We're aiming for Saturday.'

'What?' She turned in astonishment at Howard's prediction. 'But that's only four days away, and from what I saw today, you'll never be ready that soon.'

'Yes, we will.' Ben was positive. 'We've also got Charlie helping us for the rest of the week.'

'We'll make it.' Howard sat down at the table. 'All the hard graft is done, and it's only a matter of decorating.'

'And shelving.' Amy put the sausage on a plate with the potatoes.

'Charlie's a marvel with that.' A deep chuckle came from

Ben. 'It seems he took an apprenticeship in carpentry after leaving school. Says he's always been good with his hands.'

'You should have seen the marvellous drawing Ben did of him in the camp, Amy,' Howard said.

'You've got drawings you haven't shown us?'

'I lost track of them, but Charlie saved them and brought them back today.'

'Where are they? Can I see them, Ben?'

'They're upstairs. I'll bring them down for you before we go out.'

'Oh, thanks, I'd love to see them. Are you going back to the shop?'

'No, I'm going dancing with Chrissie and Howard.'

Howard smirked. 'Chrissie's fixed him up with a pretty nurse.'

'That's nice. I hope you all have a good time.' After pouring lots of steaming gravy over the small meal, Amy took it to Grace.

His appetite gone, Ben tried to finish the braised steak and vegetables on his plate. Amy should be going out, dancing with the husband she loved, and sharing with him the trials and joys of watching their delightful daughter grow, but she had been denied that. Because of her reading difficulties, she had been a lonely child; now she must be lonely again. Oh, they were all here to support her when she needed it, but they couldn't possibly replace what she had lost. Nothing could, not even him.

He felt wretched, and in no mood for dancing with a stranger.

Pleased with Grace's nearly empty plate, Amy went back to eat her own meal. Grace had improved even since this morning, and that was an enormous relief. In another day or two she would be running around again and getting in everyone's way. It was a comforting prospect. And if they did manage to open the shop on Saturday, that would be perfect timing, because she would stay and help with that, then take Grace away for a week. A break would do both of them the world of good.

The kitchen was unusually quiet. Chrissie, Howard and Ben had gone dancing; Mrs Dalton was playing bridge with neighbours, and Ted was having a night out at the pub with some of his old ARP friends.

Removing the dish from the oven, she sat down to eat alone, wondering how Ben was enjoying his night out with the nurse. The fact that he was with another woman was pushed ruthlessly aside. He had a right to a life of his own, especially after being shut away for so long, and it might help to cheer him up. Although he had apologized and teased Grace, she knew him too well not to be aware that something wasn't right with him. If only he would talk about it, instead of bottling things up.

It didn't seem right eating at the large table on her own, and it was even more unsettling to know the house was empty, apart from Grace and herself. She couldn't remember that ever happening before, but things change. If John had still been alive they would probably have had a home of their own by now, and maybe a brother or sister for Grace. She sighed deeply. They'd had such plans.

'Mummy.' Grace trotted in and looked around the empty room. 'Where is everyone?'

'They've all gone out, sweetie. Do you want a drink or something?'

Shaking her head, she climbed on the chair next to Amy. 'I'm fed up with being in bed. Where've they all gone?'

Amy explained what each one was doing, causing Grace to think hard.

'Will Uncle Ben bring a girl home, like Uncle Howard has?'

'I expect so. He'll want to marry and have children of his own, probably.' Amy was realistic enough to know that would happen, but it would be so hard to see him in love with someone else. One day, the family they had built up in this house would no longer be. Ted had aged dreadfully in the last couple of years, and must be around seventy-five. Mrs Dalton was in her sixties. Chrissie and Howard would be bound to move away, and so would Ben. That would leave her and Grace. She could live with her in-laws, as she knew there would always be a welcome there for them, but it wouldn't be right.

A knot of fear gripped her. How would she manage on her own? Since coming to live here, she had been protected and loved, and the thought of living somewhere else held no appeal. Giving herself a mental shake, she sat up straight, her mouth set in a determined line. She was imagining a gloomy future without the people she loved, which was ridiculous. Even if they all went their separate ways, they would still remain friends, and there was the business to share. She had Grace, and that would be happiness enough. Anyway, she mustn't cross her bridges before she came to them! Smiling as one of Mrs Dalton's favourite sayings ran through her mind, she banished the gloom. Being alone in this usually bustling kitchen was making her imagination run riot. She was just being silly. The future would take care of itself, and there was no point worrying about it.

'What's that?' Grace was reaching across the table to pull a packet towards her.

'Oh, that must be Uncle Ben's drawings that he did during the war. He said he'd leave them for me to see.'

Tipping them out, she studied the pictures, fascinated. They were drawn on any piece of paper or cardboard he had been able to find. Some were caricatures, bringing a smile to her face. She hadn't known he could do anything like that. Others were more serious, showing the huts, the barbed wire and the expressions on the faces of the men as they coped with captivity. It was a wonderful study of camp life, and she caught a glimpse of what it must have been like. And it also helped her to understand a little better the struggle he was now having in adjusting to normal living again.

Spreading the drawings over the table in front of her, she breathed in awe. 'These are excellent. They must be displayed in the gallery.'

'They're not very pretty, are they, Mummy?'

'No, not pretty – but pretty special.' She put them back in the packet. 'Your Uncle Ben is a special man, too.'

Grace yawned, resting her head on her mother's shoulder.

'Would you like some milk?' But her daughter was almost asleep. 'Come on, darling, back to bed. We'll both have an early night, shall we?'

After a visit to the bathroom, they went to bed, and Grace was asleep almost immediately. Her short time up had tired her out, but it was a step towards recovery. Amy, however, was wide awake, staring into space, listening to the patter of gentle rain on the window and the creaking of the empty house. Without her noticing, Oscar had crept in with them, settling on the bottom of her bed, his contented purr rumbling in the quiet room.

Feeling soothed by the sound, her mind drifted to all that had happened to her since she had taken that first step into this beautiful house, and been welcomed by the warm, loving people who lived in it.

The next morning the kitchen was buzzing again, just the way Amy liked it.

'Chrissie, would you have a look at Grace for me? The doctor's coming this afternoon, but she's asking to get up.'

Popping a piece of toast in her mouth, Chrissie nodded and went to check on the little girl.

'Getting restless, is she? That's a good sign.' Ted gulped his tea, edging towards the door. 'I can't help you today, Howard. I've bought a load of books and they need sorting.'

'That's OK, Ted. Chrissie's going to pitch in today.'

'Right.' Then he was gone, eager to get at his beloved books.

Chrissie came back with Grace holding her hand. 'I can get up, Mummy, as long as I'm back in bed when the doctor comes.' She sat in her usual chair, a pleased smile on her face as she looked at everyone. 'I'm nearly better.'

'Well, that's a blessing.' Mrs Dalton picked up a bottle of milk. 'Would you like porridge?'

'Yes please, with treacle on it.' Her smile was even brighter at that thought.

'Definitely on the mend.' Howard nodded to Amy. 'Looks like you'll be able to bring her to the opening.'

'I hope so. It's amazing what a difference there is in her over twenty-four hours.'

'Children are resilient and often recover quickly from these kind of infections.' Chrissie sat down. 'And she's a healthy little girl.'

Nothing had been said about the dance last night, and Amy was curious. She sat opposite Ben. 'Did you have a good time at the dance?'

'Yes. Paula was a very nice girl, and an excellent dancer.'

'Good.' She noticed the packet of drawings was no longer on the table, and guessed Ben had taken them back upstairs. 'Thank you for letting me see your pictures of the camp. They are really wonderful, and would make an interesting display for the gallery.'

He merely shook his head, so Amy pressed the point. They ought to be shown, not tucked away upstairs. 'Ben, they would make a marvellous focal point. You could put them all in a large frame . . .'

'No!' He surged to his feet, glancing irritably at his watch. 'I'll see you at the shop, Howard.' Then he strode out.

'Oh, dear.' Amy sighed. 'I seem to have upset him again.'

'There's something terribly wrong with Benjamin.' Mrs Dalton pursed her lips. 'Do you know what's the matter, Howard? Was he all right last night?'

'He seemed fine, didn't he, Chrissie?'

'I'd say he enjoyed himself. He was laughing and joking with Paula, and she thought he was wonderful.'

'Then it must be me he's angry with.' Amy spoke quietly, not wanting Grace to hear.

'I can't imagine you've done anything to upset him, Amy.' Mrs Dalton began clearing the table. 'You've done your best to support him since he returned home, and you've always been the best of friends.'

'Not any more, it seems.'

# 43

It was only due to the sheer hard work and determination of the men that the shop would be ready for a grand opening on Saturday. Grace's spots had almost disappeared, and, although she was still rather listless, Amy had been able to take her to the shop on Friday, when everyone was needed to stock the shelves, hang pictures and do a window display. Chrissie's leave was over and she had returned to Aldershot. Amy was downstairs with Mrs Dalton and Howard, and Ben upstairs with Stan and Charlie. Grace also wanted to help, and Howard encouraged her to put things on the lower shelves. As Amy watched Howard with her daughter, she was pleased he was getting married. Chrissie was a lovely girl, and she hoped they would soon have a family of their own, because they were both very good with children.

Everything was ready by the time Ted closed his own shop and joined them for a celebratory drink.

'Well, I must say, this looks a real treat.' Mrs Dalton sipped her glass of wine, gazing round in appreciation.

'I think we ought to give Stan and Charlie a vote of thanks.' Ben raised his glass. 'Without them we still wouldn't be finished.'

'Hear, hear.' They all drank to the two men.

'It's been a pleasure.' Charlie downed his drink. 'I must be on my way, but I'll be here for the opening tomorrow. On Monday I'm starting work. I've found myself a job in a garage.'

'Well done, mate.' Stan finished his drink. 'I'll walk to the bus stop with you. See you all tomorrow.'

When they'd gone, Ben said, 'I've offered Stan a permanent job with us.'

'But we can't afford to employ anyone yet.' Howard was astonished. 'And you shouldn't have done that without asking the rest of us. We're all in this together, Ben.'

'Don't worry. He's going to work for me in the gallery. I'll pay his wages until we start making money.'

When it looked as if Howard was going to protest, Amy touched his arm gently. He realized what she was saying without words, and clamped his mouth shut. There was obviously an extraordinarily close bond between Stan, Charlie and Ben, because of the camp, and if Ben wanted to do this, then they shouldn't try to stop him. He had always cared about other people – that was why Amy was here now – and even the harsh years of war hadn't destroyed that quality in him. He was, and always had been, a kind man.

'OK, Ben.' Howard nodded. 'But you don't have to pay him out of your own money. This shop is going to be a great success. We'll manage.'

'Mummy.' Grace was tugging at Amy's skirt. 'Are we going home now? I'm tired and hungry.'

'All right, darling, you can have your dinner in bed, and on Sunday we'll go and stay with Granny and Grandpa for a week to make you all strong again. That will be lovely, won't it?' She pushed the hair away from her daughter's little face, to look carefully for signs of illness, but apart from being tired, she seemed all right. It had been a long day, but Amy had made up a bed for her in the corner of the shop, so she could have a nap during the afternoon.

Grace nodded and picked up her picture books, ready to leave at once.

'You mean you're going away the moment we open the shop?' Ben didn't look pleased.

'I know it's a bad time, Ben, and I was going to discuss it with you and Howard tonight—'

'Bad time is right. Can't you leave it for a while? How is Howard going to manage downstairs without you?'

'He won't have to, Benjamin,' Mrs Dalton said quite sharply. 'I'll stand in for Amy while she's away.'

'We'll manage fine.' Howard smiled at Amy. 'Of course you must take Grace away to recover fully. Don't be such a misery, Ben.'

But he was still irritated. 'She couldn't have chosen a more awkward time to disappear.'

Angered now by his continued sharpness towards her, Amy glared at him. 'Grace has been ill. I didn't choose the time. She is my child and I'll do whatever is best for her. I have always known you as a sympathetic, kind person, Ben. That person is still inside you somewhere, but you've buried him, and until you find him again, I suggest you keep your opinions to yourself. I will work long and hard for our business, as I did before, and I don't need you to remind me how important it is. But in this instance, Grace comes first.'

Amy was relieved to see that Mrs Dalton had left the shop with Grace, so she ran out to catch them up.

'I'll take her,' she said when she reached them. 'She's heavy.'

'She weighs hardly anything at all. I heard that little spat back there, and I hope you gave Benjamin a piece of your mind?'

'I did. What's wrong with him, Mrs Dalton? Just lately he seems so unhappy.'

'He's got a bee in his bonnet about something, and it's making him snarl like a bear with a sore head.'

Amy couldn't help laughing. Mrs Dalton was full of sayings like this. 'Perhaps I'm getting too defensive, but Ben
can hurt me more than anyone else I know.'

'That's because you care for him so much. Take Grace
to her grandparents, and stay there with her. That will keep
you out of Benjamin's way. We can only hope he'll have
sorted himself out by the time you get back.'

'I know it's not a good time to go away, but I must put
Grace first, and she needs a rest and some country air.'

'Of course she does; you both do.'


It was a glorious day. The sun was shining, the war in
Europe was over, and they were about to open their new
shop. It was the kind of day that brought people out of their
houses and, with a bit of luck, the King's Road would be
crowded with shoppers. The opening had been set for ten
o'clock, and they had decided to make a big show of the
event, in order to attract the public. Ted wasn't opening his
shop until the afternoon so he could be there. The shop
they'd had before the war had been a success, so they were
confident that this one would be as well.

Everyone was milling around in the kitchen, dressed in
their best clothes. The men were wearing suits; Mrs Dalton
was resplendent in a blue and white dress, complete with hat
in the same sky blue. Amy had a simple short-sleeved dress in
lemon, and Grace was wearing pink, with a pink ribbon in her
hair. She looked very pretty, but still rather pale.

'Are you all right, darling?' Amy stooped down in front
of her chair. 'It's going to be a long day again.'

'Don't you worry, Amy. I'll bring her back with me after
the opening, and she can have a nice rest this afternoon.'

'Oh, that's very kind of you, Mrs Dalton.' Amy was
relieved.

'Not kind at all.' She smiled at Grace. 'I love looking after the little mite.'

'Will you do that, darling? Mummy will have to stay at the shop all day.'

Grace nodded, seeming quite happy about the arrangement.

Howard frowned. 'She's still looking a bit peaky.'

'I know.' Amy worried her bottom lip. 'I'm hoping the country air will put that right.'

'I hope you're going to wipe that scowl off your face for the opening, Benjamin.' Mrs Dalton spoke sharply when he still didn't look pleased about Amy going away at this time. 'You've worked very hard to get it ready, and you should be proud of yourself, and everyone here, not looking bad-tempered enough to spoil everyone's day.'

Grace was listening, wide-eyed, and Amy could understand her surprise. No one had ever heard Mrs Dalton lecture Ben like that. He looked as shocked as the rest of them.

'Sorry.' He held up his hands. 'Of course Amy must take Grace away.' Standing up he lifted the little girl out of her chair, swinging her high until she squealed in delight. 'We're going to put a ribbon across the door of the shop, and we'd like you to cut it for us.'

'Why?' She slipped her arms around his neck, settling in his arms.

'So the customers can get in. Will you do it for us?'

Grace nodded enthusiastically, the long bow bouncing in her hair.

Seeing her daughter in Ben's arms like that brought a lump to Amy's throat, and, just for a brief flash, she saw John there. The pain ripping through her was too much to bear and, running from the kitchen, she stumbled into her

439

bedroom, shaking. Dear God! Would the hurt never go? She had loved two men in her life. One was lost for ever; the other she couldn't have because he only saw her as a sister. The tears tumbled from her eyes, and had to be quickly scrubbed away when there was a knock on the door.

Mrs Dalton came in. 'Are you all right, my dear?'

With a helpless shake of her head, Amy mopped up the rest of the tears. Before she could stop herself, the truth came spilling out. 'I'm getting John and Ben muddled up. When Ben picked up Grace just now, I saw him as her father. They looked so right together, and I could picture us as a complete family. I've always loved Ben, you know that, but now it's a different kind of love. I've tried not to show it, but he must have guessed, and that's why he's snapping at me.'

Mrs Dalton sat next to her and took hold of her hand. 'I don't think he has any idea that your feelings have changed towards him. Now, you dry your eyes, then we'll open the shop, and you can go away. A bit of peace and quiet in the country will help you sort out your feelings.'

'Yes, you're right.' Amy blew her nose, and then smiled. 'When I come back I'll be able to laugh at this silly notion. I've been so worried about him since he came home, and I'm feeling tired after Grace's illness. My imagination is running riot.'

'I'm sure that's all it is.' After patting her hand again, Mrs Dalton stood up and looked down at Amy, speaking gently. 'Don't be upset, my dear. You can love twice, but each one will be different. And each one will be special. You don't have to feel disloyal to John; he would be happy for you, and approve of Ben as a father for his daughter.'

Amy looked up in astonishment. 'You're talking as if this could be one day, but that's impossible. It's as if he doesn't like me any more. Haven't you noticed how he does his best to keep his distance from me?'

'I've noticed.' Mrs Dalton headed for the door, and then paused, looking round. 'You must ask him about that sometime.'

Amy watched the door close, and huffed out a ragged sigh. She had no intention of doing that. With the tension there was between them, it was better if she kept out of his way.

They were causing quite a stir in the road, and had gathered a sizeable crowd to watch the cutting of the ribbon. Charlie, Stan, Helen and the children were there; so were Ben and Howard's parents. Everyone had come to support the occasion.

'OK, Grace.' Ben took her hand. 'Let's cut the tape together, shall we? And when it's done, I'd like you to say in a loud voice, "I declare this shop open." Do you think you can do that for us?'

'Yes, Uncle Ben.'

Amy watched as her daughter held the small pair of scissors and, with Ben's help, managed to cut the ribbon.

Turning her to face the crowd, he whispered, 'Now say that it's open.'

She came over all shy when she saw everyone looking at her. She muttered the words, looking at her feet.

Ben stooped down beside her. 'Keep your head up, Grace, and say it again.'

'It's open!' she blurted out, and then made for Amy as fast as she could.

'That was wonderful, darling. Look at all the people streaming in to see what we're selling.'

\*

The day surpassed all their expectations, with a steady flow of customers and quite a few sales. It augured well for the future, and they were all in high spirits when they closed at six o'clock. Ben, Howard, Ted and Stan decided to go somewhere for a meal and then to the pub for a drink. They invited Amy as well, but she was anxious to get home to Grace, so she refused. She hadn't missed the brief flash of relief in Ben's eyes at her decision to go straight home. It was becoming clear to her that he didn't want to be around her any more than he could help, and that hurt dreadfully.

'Mummy!' Grace rushed to her as soon as she arrived back. 'Did you have lots of people?'

'Lots and lots.' She bent down and kissed her daughter, happy to see her more rested. 'We're going to Granny and Grandpa's tomorrow, so we must pack our things this evening.'

'Ooh, I must take my dolly. Granny said she'd make her a new dress.'

Mrs Dalton cast the little girl a fond glance. 'She's looking forward to going away.'

'Yes, and her grandparents can't wait to have her there for a whole week.' Amy set about peeling the potatoes. 'We only need to cook for us, because the men are eating out.'

They'd had their meal and cleared up by the time the men returned in quite a happy mood. Mrs Dalton tutted when she saw their expressions, glazed from a pint too many, and put the kettle on to make a large pot of tea.

There was a great deal of laughter and talk about their first day back in business, and even Ben's gloom appeared to have lifted, but Amy didn't linger round the table with them. It was Grace's bedtime, and she wanted to be ready for an early start in the morning.

'Say goodnight to everyone, Grace.'

She trotted round to each person in turn, a broad smile on her face. 'We've got to pack our bags,' she told them excitedly. 'We're going on a train tomorrow.'

Amy was surprised to see Ted and Howard already in the kitchen when she got up at six-thirty the next morning. 'My goodness, what are you doing up at this hour?'

'We're coming with you. You can't manage Grace and your cases on your own.'

'That's very kind of you, Ted, but I'm only taking one small bag. I'll be all right.' They were so thoughtful, but she didn't want to spoil the only day they had to relax.

'We're taking you.' Howard put bread under the grill to toast. 'Get Grace and I'll see to your breakfast. You're always looking after us, but you've had a worrying time with Grace, and we're going to spoil you today. Off you go and get your little girl ready.'

By the time Grace was washed and dressed, Ben and Mrs Dalton were also up.

'Are you coming on the train with us as well, Uncle Ben? Mummy said Ted and Uncle Howard are coming.'

'It doesn't need three of us to carry your cases, and I've got too much to do.' He softened the sharp tone of his voice with a smile.

'Oh.' The disappointment showed. 'You didn't paint our picture like you said.'

'No, but I'll do it while you're away.'

Grace drank her warm milk, watching Ben over the rim of the cup. Her expressive eyes said quite clearly that she couldn't quite fathom out this big man, but she liked him. Putting down the cup, she stood up. 'I'm ready, Mummy. Can we go now?'

'Have a nice rest, my dear.' Mrs Dalton kissed Amy's cheek. 'And don't worry about a thing.'

'Bye, bye, Uncle Ben.' Grace was lifted up for a kiss. When she was on the ground again, she reached for Ted's hand, her smile wide with excitement.

'I'll be back in a week, Ben.' Amy stepped forward to hug him in the way she had always done. When he stepped back, putting distance between them, she stopped, her hands falling to her sides. He was stepping away from her mentally and physically now, and it wounded her.

'Mummy! We're going.'

Sighing deeply, she turned away from him and walked out to the front door, where her daughter was waiting impatiently.

# 44

Two days later, Ben was pacing the studio, unable to sleep or work. That step back he'd taken had been involuntary, done in self-preservation. Having her close to him was torture. His hands itched to run through her unruly hair; to draw her close and breathe in the fresh clean smell of soap and something else that was intrinsically her.

He had hurt her. It had shown in her lovely eyes and, like a fool, he had stood there and let her walk away without an explanation. In the past he would never have acted in such a cruel way. Coming back to civilization had been, and still was, difficult to adjust to. Seeing the change in Amy had knocked him for six, as Mrs Dalton would say.

Howard wandered into the studio, and stood in front of the canvas on the easel, a deep rumble of amusement running through him as he studied the painting. 'You've captured mother and daughter to perfection, but what made you paint them curled up on the bed like that?'

'I saw them in that position. Amy was telling Grace a story.' Ben shoved his hands in his pockets, not looking happy.

'Aren't you pleased with it?'

'Hmm, it's coming along quite well.'

'Then why the long face?' Howard cast his friend a curious glance. 'What's the matter, Ben? And don't try to deny it; we're all aware that you've got a problem of some kind. Why don't you tell me?'

'I've hurt Amy by snapping at her.'

'We know that too. Why you're doing it is a mystery. What has she done to you?'

'She's grown up.' Ben gave a dry laugh. 'All the time I was in the POW camp, I kept a picture in my head of a young, immature girl. And when I saw a woman with a small child, I was knocked completely off balance. She's changed so much.'

'Of course she has. We all have.' Howard frowned. 'What's your point? Are you saying you don't like her now she's all grown up?'

'Like her!' Ben propped himself against the bench, shaking his head. 'Of course I like her. The problem is I like her too much.'

The frown disappeared from Howard's face, and he tipped back his head and laughed with pleasure. 'You've fallen in love with her. That's wonderful. You're made for each other. But you certainly hid it well. I've known you all my life and I never guessed.'

Ben scowled. 'I'm glad you think it's so funny. How do you think she would react if the man she's only ever considered as a friend suddenly grabbed her and made passionate love to her?'

'Why don't you try it?'

'Amy would be horrified, and I'd get a terrible telling-off from Grace.'

There was silence as each man pictured the scene, then they both roared with laughter.

'Yeah.' Howard pulled himself together. 'She does speak her mind, doesn't she?'

Ben nodded, feeling the tension ease at last. 'God, Howard, I'm damned confused.'

'Well, there's only one way to sort this out, and that's to tell Amy how you feel.'

446

'Oh, I don't think—'

'Ben, those years in that camp have addled your brain. Amy loves you; she always has. She isn't going to throw up her hands in horror if you tell her you love her in a different way now she's a woman.'

'But she loved John so much.' Ben ran a hand through his hair, confusion etched on his features.

'John's gone,' Howard said quietly. 'He was killed a long time ago. It tore Amy apart, but having Grace helped, and she's had the courage to move on. I think she's ready to fall in love again, and, in my opinion, you're the prime candidate. Get your feelings out in the open. She's a wonderful woman, and I believe you would be happy together.'

'I hope you're right.' Ben stared at the painting, feeling his heart rate accelerate. He needed these two more than he could ever remember wanting anything in his life. Even the yearning for freedom couldn't compare with this. If she couldn't think of him as a husband, then he'd damned well have to convince her!

It was late afternoon when Ben reached East Meon. After his talk with Howard, he'd left immediately for the station, cursing the lack of petrol. He could have made it in half the time by car.

Grace spotted him first, hurtling down the path, arms out wide. After only two days in the country, she was back to full health.

'Uncle Ben!'

He swept her up, spinning round and round with her, making her giggle. 'Hello, sweetheart, you look better.'

'My spots are all gone.'

'Ben!' Mildred and Charles greeted him. 'What a lovely surprise. Come in.'

'Thank you. I hope you don't mind me calling uninvited?'

'Not at all.' Charles smiled. 'You're always welcome here. Are you staying the night with us?'

'I don't want to put you to any trouble. I thought I might be able to stay in the village somewhere.'

'We won't hear of it, Ben,' Mildred Sterling said. 'There's plenty of room for you here.'

'Thank you.'

Amy came in from the kitchen, and couldn't hide her surprise at seeing him, but she didn't seem upset, he noted with relief. Still holding Grace, he bent and kissed her cheek. 'You're looking well; the rest is doing you good.'

'Hello, Ben, what brings you down here? Is everyone all right back home?'

'They're fine. I've come to see you.' He put Grace down and draped his arm around Amy's shoulder. 'We need to talk.'

But there was no chance at that moment, because tea was ready, and Grace had to tell him about all the lovely things they had been doing, like walking in the woods and visiting a farm and seeing all the animals.

'I sat on a horse!' Her eyes were wide when she told him this piece of stupendous news. 'He was ever so big, and Grandpa had to hold me in case I fell off.' Grace couldn't sit still. 'It walked along, didn't it, Grandpa?'

'It certainly did. You haven't shown your mummy the drawing you did this afternoon, have you?'

Grace shook her head. 'I copied out of one of my books.'

'Go and get it, my sweetie.' Mildred watched her granddaughter with love. 'I'm sure Uncle Ben would like to see it as well.'

Sliding off her chair, Grace ran into the front room,

returning almost at once, proudly holding out a sheet of paper.

When Amy saw it, the breath caught in her throat. There was certainly a horse there, but also other things.

'You've helped her with this?' Amy asked her mother-in-law.

'No, she copied all of it from the books she brought down with her. She's a very bright child, and picks up things quickly. John was just the same. You've done the right thing by giving her lots of books at an early age.'

'Ben.' Amy thrust the paper at him, too agitated to be able to read it herself. She'd seen Grace drawing letters of the alphabet, but never complete words. 'Is it right?'

Ben held Amy's hand tightly, feeling it tremble. 'The letters are all correct, even the D and B you have trouble with are round the right way.'

'How long have you been doing words, darling?'

'I do them in my colouring book.'

'Yes, I know, but the letters are already drawn, you only have to fill them in with coloured pencil.' Amy didn't know whether to laugh or cry; so she gripped Ben's hand as hard as she could.

'Well, I've done them all, so I've drawn my own. What's the matter, Mummy? Don't you like it?'

Letting go of Ben, she hugged Grace. 'It's absolutely beautiful, darling. Now you can help me with my writing.'

'Shall I show you how I can do it?'

'Please, darling.' Amy fought for control as she watched her daughter write A, B, C, copying from her book of letters. It had been Amy's greatest fear that Grace might have inherited whatever was wrong with her, so she had given her these simple books from the moment she could toddle.

She hadn't intended to start her on reading until she was four in September, but Grace had beaten her to it.

'She's going to be all right, Amy,' Ben murmured in her ear.

Leaning against him, she bit her lip in relief. 'I couldn't do anything like that when I was her age, and when I couldn't keep up with the others in school, they said I was stupid and lazy.'

Ben squeezed her shoulder. 'We know you're not stupid or lazy.'

She smiled. 'When we get back home perhaps we can ask Ted to help her with reading and writing, then when she starts school, she'll have a head start.'

'He'll love that.'

'Is my drawing of the horse all right, Uncle Ben?'

'It's perfect. He must have been a very handsome horse.'

Grace nodded and ran to her grandmother. 'Can I put it by my bed, Granny?'

'Of course you can. We'll go and do it now, and then you can get ready for bed.'

Grace went with her quite happily, chattering about the picture Uncle Ben had done of her and put beside her bed at home.

Ben stood up, pulling Amy with him. 'Do you mind if I take Amy for a walk?' he asked Charles.

'Not at all; off you go, and we'll put Grace to bed. Have a drink at the pub.'

They walked along in silence. Ben pulled Amy's hand through his arm and held it there. The relief at seeing that Grace might not have trouble with words was immense, and she was content to walk without talking. But: 'Er . . . We've passed the pub. Don't you want a drink?' Amy was still puzzled why Ben had turned up like this, but she was glad he was here. This was more like the man she loved and had always leant on for help and support.

'No, I just want to talk.'

Her smile was amused. 'You're not doing much of that.'

They turned down a quiet lane, stopping by a large oak tree. Ben leant against it, holding both of Amy's hands. He took a deep breath. 'After so long stuck in a POW camp, I was afraid I wouldn't be able to paint again.'

'You wouldn't have lost your talent, no matter how long you'd been away. It's a part of you, Ben.'

'I thought I had.' He smiled down at her. 'You made me see it was still there, only the technique had changed. I had changed.'

He fell silent again, and she said nothing, allowing him time to gather his thoughts.

After a while he continued. 'But the greatest shock was seeing the difference in you. That first time I met you by the river, I knew you were special, and that has proved to be very true. But I was not prepared for the way I felt when I saw you as a woman with a young child.'

Her heart was hammering in her chest, robbing her of breath. She wondered what was coming next. 'And how did you feel?'

'I fell in love with you.' He leant his head back and closed his eyes. 'It's been driving me crazy, until I was afraid to be near you. I'm sorry, Amy, but that's how it is, and I can't change it. I thought you ought to know. You loved John, and we've always been friends —'

'Will you stop talking for a minute?' She punched him in the chest, making his eyes snap open. 'You're confusing me. What are you trying to say?'

'I'm saying that I want more than friendship from you.'

She wanted to laugh, cry, throw her arms around him in

joy, but she resisted the urge – for the moment. 'And this is what's been making you grumpy?'

Pushing himself away from the tree, he shoved his hands in his pockets, frowning down at her. 'I was mad at myself for not being able to control my feelings. And mad at you for changing into such a desirable woman when I knew the whole thing was impossible.'

As he began to walk away, she grabbed his arm, holding on tightly. 'Just a minute! You're not going to tell me you love me and then walk away, surely? I loved John with all my heart—'

'Exactly!'

'Shut up, Ben, and let me have my say. When I lost John I thought my world had come to an end, but then Grace came along and, step by step, I recovered. I'll always love him, and I still have a part of him in Grace. But he's been gone for years, and I've moved on. When we met, I adored you with a young girl's gratitude, but you're right, things have changed.' She paused for a heartbeat. 'Now I love you like a woman should.'

He didn't look as if he could believe what he was hearing. 'Are you saying . . . ?'

Her smile spread. 'I love you, so will you take your damned hands out of your pockets and kiss me?'

She was lifted off her feet and kissed until they were both breathless and her head spinning. His hands tangled in her hair; the teasing smile she knew so well was back again.

'We could make it a double wedding with Howard and Chrissie in August.'

'Are you asking me to marry you?'

'Of course I am.'

'Then I accept. Oh, I'm so happy. I thought you would only ever see me as a sister, and it was going to be difficult not to let my true feelings show.' She hugged him as tight as she could, and then looked up, a teasing smile on her face. 'You know you won't only be getting a wife, you'll be getting a daughter as well. Are you sure you're ready for that?'

'Positive.' He kissed her again, gently this time. 'What do you think she's going to say about me becoming her father?'

'Hmm.' Amy tipped her head on one side, as if giving it careful thought. 'As long as you treat her mother right, she'll probably accept you.'

When he laughed this time, Amy knew he was really back to his old self again.

'Come on.' He slipped his arm around her, holding her close. 'Let's go and say goodnight to our lovely little girl.'

Happy, they stepped into the future together.

# Epilogue

*Chelsea, London, December 1989*

All the family had gathered for Amy's seventieth birthday. She laughed down at her great-grandson as he wriggled in her arms, knowing that if he had trouble reading and writing, there would be help for him. It had, at last, been discovered that the condition she suffered from was called dyslexia, and had nothing to do with a person's intelligence. She remembered the immense relief she had felt when her daughter began to read at an early age without difficulty.

Her thoughts went back over the years. In 1950 Mrs Dalton had died suddenly of a stroke, which had shocked them all. Her will provided another shock: she had left the house to Amy, Ben and Howard, on the condition that Ted be allowed to stay for as long as he wanted. Sadly, he died only a few years after Mrs Dalton. They had both been greatly missed.

Howard had married his Chrissie and now they had grand-children of their own. She had married Ben on the same day, and their marriage had been, and still was, a very happy one. She looked across at her husband, smiling as he gave his usual teasing wink.

Gazing round the crowded room, she considered that her life had really begun when Ben and Howard had brought her to this lovely house. Mrs Dalton had always urged her to take one step at a time, and she could see that her life had been a series of steps.

The first was Wapping, with all its frustration and grief.

Next, here, where she had blossomed in the atmosphere of love and gentle teasing, finding new talents and new ways of expressing herself.

Then, marrying John. The hurt was still there when she thought of how little time they'd had together, and sadness that a young life had been cut so short. The war had been another step along the road. It had been a rocky path, with many highs and lows: grief at losing John; joy when Grace had been born; and relief when Ben had finally returned home at the end of the war.

They had taken another step together and started up the shop again. Then she had married Ben and they had had two fine sons of their own. James was an artist like his father, and Luke a teacher. James had shown signs of having trouble with words, but it had only been slight, and they'd been able to help him from an early age.

They now had three shops being run by the children of both families. Ben and Howard had eventually received the acclaim their talents deserved.

And here she was at seventy . . .

'Cut your cake, Mum.'

She stopped reminiscing and smiled, seeing John in her daughter's face. Grace had been deprived of a father, but Ben had more than filled that void.

Standing up, Amy stepped towards the table.